"*Shing. Tap. Tap. Tap. Shing.* Its cl
paving the sheets . . . *Shing* . . . slamming its dark
hydra heads (*tap tap tap*) on its sable wall . . . *Shing*
. . . singing its own mechanical songs . . . breaking
nails, breaking hearts, the typewriter is not an
instrument of love . . ."

—Death (dangling her unlit cigarette)

"Cherry-picking, we remember the way we want. In
a daydream trance, the artificial baby is the warm
peaceful baby with its creators hovering over its
crib. They open their eyes, humming the end of *The
Owl and the Pussy-Cat*—'the moon, the moon, they
danced by the light of the moon.' The real baby is the
dead baby."

—Time, knocking back all of it
(the rocks *and* the olive)

"How could we've ever understand *them*—smoking
and drinking—when they can't even understand
us? 'Those poor *things*. They pay taxes . . . and then
beget more *things* . . .'"

—Great Scott's ghost

What Light Was

(a dialogue novel)

Shawn C. Hays | Stephen C. Hays

What Light Was
(a dialogue novel)

Copyright © Shawn Callaway Hays, Stephen Callaway Hays, 2025
First Edition (on the centennial of the first publication of *The Great Gatsby*)
Published by Rilke Hopkins Press, Nashville, Tennessee, U.S.A.

h.walton@riordanwalton.com

speaklowpoetry.com

What Light Was (Full Novel) ISBN: 978-0-9983504-4-8
What Light Was (Part 1: Mutability) ISBN: 978-0-9983504-5-5
What Light Was (Part 2: Necessity) ISBN: 978-0-9983504-6-2

Cover and interior design: Rilke Hopkins Press

Cover art: S. C. Hays (based on both C. D. Friedrich's 1818 painting "Wanderer above the Sea of Fog" and F. Cugat's 1924 painting "Celestial Eyes")

Authors page art: Ivy S. C. Hays

This novel is adapted from the works of Mary W. Shelley, Percy B. Shelley, Mary Wollstonecraft, William Godwin, John Keats, Lord Byron, F. Scott Fitzgerald, Zelda S. Fitzgerald, *The Great Gatsby* by F. Scott Fitzgerald, *Frankenstein* by Mary W. Shelly, Sir H. Davy, and the memoirs of E. Trelawny and T. Medwin. These writings, characters, and incidents are used fictitiously.

All rights reserved. No part of this adapted novel may be reproduced or transmitted in any form or by any means, electronic or mechanical, including photocopying, recording, or by any information retrieval or storage system, without the prior written consent of the publisher.

The events in this novel are works of artistic fiction used in a fictitious manner.

– for Ivy
– for Ava
– for Callaway

Part 1: Mutability

Prospero: "Hast thou, spirit, performed to point the tempest that I bade thee?"

Ariel: "To every article."

(1.) *ghost-green sunshine*

SCOTT
The disaster starts—Scott's *big crisis*—and the color of my lips deteriorates pleasantly. I am in the depths of an unholy depression—generally bored and feeling bad. At a dinner in an uncontrollable fit of grimacing, I chewed up and then spit out *a wad* of hundred-franc notes—like a scoop of war-ration green beans—and smiled.

A mania of bliss and rage now alternates in me like a jazz-mad shaking himself insane. If I'd spent this time reading or traveling or doing anything—even staying healthy—it'd be different, but I spent it uselessly, neither in study nor in contemplation but only, *generally*, in drinking and raising hell.

I got in trouble and was less welcome after a few of the garden parties turned too tame. I brought a little life to things with smashing some wineglasses and flinging food and tossing ashtrays at more *disciplined* guests. There was a tad more trouble after I poured a can of garbage over a patio of suspicious whisperings. Trouble is transitory. People forget the way they think they will remember. We'll bark like dogs until they let us back in—and it will be the best bourgeoise time when we collect all the purses, boil them, and serve them as high-class soup.

Well, it's Villa Marie on the lush, verdant, French coast.

Autumn is falling on your great author—F. Scott—on his diaphanous Zelda, and on the youngest *Pie*—their warbler, Scottie girl—and we've tried to simmer our whirlwind of foolish cares and shameless personas on the rear eye of our quiet *Euromantic* stove. Through our easy stretch of pines and cicadas to our pleasant shore of our Riviera, these old villas rot like water lilies, and the Mediterranean yields its mesmerizing pigments—moment by moment—to the brutal sunshine filtering through umbrellas, murmurs of merchantmen, and fresh fading mirages.

Through the evenings, the mercury-red, gas-blue, ghost-green signs shine smokily through tranquil rain in the translucent movement of the streets and in the gleam of bistros. From the seaside promenade and open-air cafes comes a sweet pungent odor of flowers and chartreuse and fresh black coffee in the luxuries of music, low voices, and cigarettes. Yet, the perfume is not faint—it is not illusive. There is too much *love* here—enough to sometimes want to return home.

Imagination must run honest and must seize on its intuitions of semblance and doubt, of fealty and mystery. Zelda was a sun—radiant and glowing, gathering light and storing it, pouring it forth in a glance to that part of me that cherished all beauty and all illusion. Her kisses were flowers. I would baby her whims, indulge her unreason, and wear her as she wished to be worn. Even so, this summer villa of impervious silence was then my veracity once my

April—my *Keatzian* songs of spring—had vanished blank and vacant.

~LIQUEFYING

"The trees and clouds were carved in classical severity. It was a gray day—that least fleshly of all weathers—a day of dreams and far hopes and clear visions. It was a day easily associated with those abstract truths and purities that dissolve in the sunshine or fadeout in mocking laughter by the light of the moon."

SCOTT

Disenchanted, my muse is shifting, and there is now a kindliness to intoxication—an indescribable gloss that it gives like memories of ephemeral and faded evenings. Here, idle, an outrageous betrayal has taken possession, supplanting my powerless foreign dream. It is finally now—sleepless at sunrise in my room full of such *morning*—that I am really alone amongst my patch of cold sun crisscrossed with shadows.

Presume, dare I deem what I might of myself—or that my marriage was mine—mercilessly, there is no delay to the deaf deadlines that destiny assigns. I didn't understand that there is not a way. I knew something had happened that could never be repaired.

"What mad pursuit?" This year—me and these

to Americans—their hotels, bars, and nightclubs. Well, now, it's Saint-Raphael for us in Villa Marie—out of the fire and into the sea.

Spirited in a clean, casual essence, it's a stone house with eclectic gardens on a high, suburban hill with an open tiled terrace overlooking the moonlight on the dark oceanic coast—with a bright casino at the beach below. I'm growing a noble-minded mustache and trying to not singe it with my trench lighter. *Flick. Flick.* From my study—wrapped in an air of repressed carnival—I see Fréjus with its amphitheatre and other ruins of the Romans. On the balcony in the evenings, these ancient clouds of skeeters seem to want more blood and liquor than the scourges at Great Neck.

Although some think of America as the vast upstairs to a butcher shop, this Riviera villa—from its marble fountain to its cordial glasses—is paid and paid with reproachless, middle-class, Americana *gold*. Yet, in the sudden problem of keeping my body and mind together, I have to think of something new that people want. Here, though, everything that people want has been thought of long ago.

~CONVERSION
Many had learned too much of painful and even exotic *ways to die* so that life presented itself—by contrast—in less agonizing, if more immutable, terms than before the trouble in Europe. When nobody could think up any more mathematical formulas

for destruction and no further ways for forwarding the plot, the war was declared to be a political inconvenience—and ended. People that had been spared active participation in the *gala debacle* converted themselves into a grand pleasure-chorus as effectively as possible.

SCOTT
I was twenty-one when the American Dream took possession of me and took to hatching my desperate stories. Occupied by my new *ethos*, we would stir up mistakable collegians, wanderlust, and poor immigrants from our debut of egoistic epigrams. I was madly in love with all our heroines, and my haunted mantra had emerged amidst this last year as a Catholic. "I will love this one beauty—her debutante body, her gypsy spirit, her elitist mind." Though warring aviators flew their impressive stunts over her lovely head, my living dream had become honey enough for its two young avatars. I could forever live full of handsome promise—for her—as long as I died a young Romantic. I was twenty-two when I wired Zelda Sayre from NYC, "Darling, Heart—ambition, enthusiasm, confidence—everything is a game, *everything* is possible!"

There is no freedom from hysteria. I was twenty-three when Temperance and Suffrage were enacted—and I was an instant celebrity. At twenty-four—in the sweet prime of Keats—I *had* achieved all my aspirations. I'm twenty-seven, and this spring and summer have been the worst year since the tortures of nineteen.

I'm in the dissonant snare of the twenties, and we've moved to the Old World to find a new rhythm to our lives from the growing *lack* of azure in our days, our defection that needs to maintain a Mesozoic structure before we dissipate—like after another bender—back into shapeless, spineless jelly.

~AU REVOIR, ARRIVEDERCI

"'At the end of the page it mentions 'orgies.'

'Even the word makes me feel like a butterfly. Flap! Flap!'

'Butterflies don't make a noise.'

'You've probably never seen a *tight* butterfly before—in all your life!'"

(3.) *it's an English thing*

~SEA-CHANGE

"They—*Mama* and *Papa*—were all saying 'yes' to the gramophone owners of France. 'Ariel' now passed from the title of a book to three record wires on the house-top. What did it matter? It had already gone from a god to a myth to Shakespeare—and nobody seemed to mind. People still recognized the word. So, 'Ariel' it was! They hardly noticed the change."

SCOTT

We're a handsome crowd dancing in the same room, but we don't all start the same. A sense of the fundamental decencies is parceled out unequally at birth. Reserving judgments is a habit I have from some advice in my younger and more vulnerable years. It's like light. It's two mysteries at the same time. My habit of *reserving* is a matter of infinite hope and it's opened up many curious natures to me.

Click. I think back when I drink. All of us were always talking, but I wrote things down. *Tap. Tap. Tap.* In the margins of my textbooks, I was writing the words that I wanted to read. I found theatre early, and it was the only school I wanted. My mother narrated ambition into me, and my boyhood was cradled in her reading me books. She had traveled Europe four times, and there was plenty "Mary"—my mother—before she married her Eddie Fitzgerald.

Typing is writing with two hands at once and it's put me in both the worlds—of both halves of my head. I'm trying to tell her. I'm wearing around an Anglo-Saxon tragedy I started before we migrated our farce from Long Island. Draped on a hanger, it could market as a soothing bio of youthful love letters, but—as I move around in it—it's become a pack of street sermons.

~MAD BAD BOOKCLUB

"I'm glad you're deep in Shelley and Bryon. I was a great Shelley fan and I never fully got over it. But anyway, the book is the thing, and all the rest is inconsiderable beside it."

"Shelley was a god to me once. Haven't you read *Ariel* yet? For heaven's sake, read it if you like Shelley. Still, who thinks 'badly' of Shelley now?"

— *To* and *From* Scott at Saint-Raphael

SCOTT

Ariel was great, but Shelley's not an Italian thing. An English thing in Italy is still an English thing. Shelley's an aristocrat who wants—more than people—to not be an aristocrat, but can't. It's an English thing. It's our language—and so is love—with all the words that have to have their own sort of money to work. "His creed was to become as pure as he thought his conduct was. Though he had many generous and exalted qualities, he yearned to cut out the canker of aristocracy." *Click.*

I'm trying to tell her and I'm trying to tell my old-sport dream. "One for us, and one for them." I must try some love stories with more action this time. We won't bicker *less*, so we'll just have to bicker better. Thank *Love* for letters—love letters. We can write her the storybook girl, and then she'll have the adamant boy—Romantics we can't escape. Engraving these lovers, we'll transcribe my *ella*—Zelda—and my typing-self into another story that's us again. Our letters will be love-triangles—*tap tap tap*—shaped in our brutal angles of being lovers, authors, and parents in one sporting math problem about time.

Time made us with a little more stardust. Mutating us through our determining adolescent deformities, we were marked for greatness. Like eccentric rotten children when we didn't get all that we wanted with our glittering gifts, everyone around us would have to pay and pay—and keep paying for all our brilliance. Besides, what would we do with freedom if we really ever found some of it? We seemed primed to find new chains—and vultures seemed primed to find us in them.

~BLOOD ALWAYS REMINDS ME

"'Maybe something will happen.'

Alabama wished nothing ever would again, but it was her turn to agree. They had evolved a tacit arrangement about waiting on each other's emotions, almost mathematical like the trick combination of a safe, which worked by the mutual assumption that it would.

'I mean if somebody would come along to remind us about how we felt about things when we felt the way they reminded us of, maybe it would refresh us.'

'I see what you mean. Life has begun to appear as torturous as the sentimental writhing of a rhythmic dance.'

'Exactly. I want to make some protestations since I'm largely too busy to work very well.'"

SCOTT

Like a fresh silk square tucked in a breast pocket, this ink sheet is set for lively spatters of typing. *Tap. Tap. Click*. Well, I've got my parallel—a backstory transition as inexplicable as Shelley's—a "one-year Oxford man." Okay, now let's get this prologue-kid out into the fairgrounds and to his first gun. *Tap. Tap. Tap.* She'll like this one—"The Blood Spangled Handkerchief." There we go—and then back to the States. Let's see, yes, Kentucky—where Keats's brother deteriorated—back with killing on his hands, wistful. *Tap. Tap. Tap.* Just got to connect the tragic dots—and keep it where the blood's at and where the gossips whisper. *Tap. Tap. Tap.* Things start in England, and there was plenty *Mary* before she married her Shelley. "Child of love and light, lovely from thy birth, of glorious parents—still their fame shines" from Saint-Raphael—from my mirroring villa of Mary.

(4.) . . . *of Woman*

~PROMISSORY

"I am well and tranquil, excepting the disturbance produced by *Master* William's joy—or is it *Mistress* Mary's?—who took it into its head to frisk a little at being informed of your remembrance. I begin to love this little creature and to anticipate its birth as a fresh twist to a knot, which I do not wish to untie. Men are spoilt by frankness, I believe, yet I must tell you that I love you better than I supposed I did when I promised to love you forever. Thus, I will add what will gratify your benevolence, if not your heart—that, on the whole, I may be termed *happy*. You are a tender, affectionate creature—and I feel it thrilling through my frame, giving and promising pleasure."

– Wollstonecraft to Godwin

SCOTT

Tap. Tap. Click. The beloved infamous author of controversy—the bold, bright, and scandalous mother of Mary Godwin—has died. For four years on his own, widower William Godwin—a more legendary author—raises Mary and her older sister, Fanny. Though, once he remarries, young Mary remains in argumentative discord with Godwin's wife, the mother of three other children. Mary is raised in her busy, blended home until she is fifteen.

When Mary is eight, her father and stepmother establish the M. J. Godwin and Company Juvenile Library—near the stenches of the slaughterhouse and sewer—in the heart of London. Headquartered from their pungent home, Godwin runs his popular bookshop and publishing business, heavily influencing the education of Mary and Fanny's generation. Their picture-book series of rhymes, tales, and educational fables spark young imaginations with their originality, producing a handful of influential volumes that will endure. His "juvenile radical propaganda" is famous for former fables being rewritten with some form of compassion for all the characters in each tale—giving a proud fly a convicted conscience and having the ants spare some food for the ignorant grasshopper.

In his book of collected poems for the rising generation, Godwin argues, "Prose in its purest acceptation is the vehicle of truth, is geometry, is logic, is chronicle, but it is poetry that represents to us the passions and feelings of the soul. It lays before us the sentiment and heart of the writer, or for the personages he introduces to our knowledge. Thus, we are acquainted with the world in our early years and before we are called upon to take an active part upon its theatre. Poetry is, in this sense, a school of morality."

Mary and Fanny are given advanced educations, steeped in history, mythology, literature, and languages from the schoolroom and library of their publishing firm. Coleridge's son plays games with Mary and Fanny, and they take drawing lessons from a friend of William Blake. Although Godwin's second wife is a translator and skilled editor, Godwin is the direct educator of Fanny and Mary, guiding them to prize their intellectual pursuits and the principle of practicing introspective scrutiny. For Mary, her dearest pleasure—writing stories—is conveying her curious sets of images into poignant and vibrant life. When Mary is eleven, her father prints Mary's clever contributions to a comical poem about an Englishman's misunderstood trip to Paris in a booklet under Godwin's promising imprint.

Academically, Mary's formative understanding of her society is from the intellectual milieu of both of her parents. Mary's outlook is shaped as she nurses on the refuge of her mother's name—whose enterprise was to displace the "pernicious effects which arise from the unnatural distinctions established by society" with "virtuous equality." The consummate approach of Wollstonecraft's cultivating text is that *mind* has no sex—no gender—and that *woman* should become socially emancipated as rational, moral, and independent, rather than remain disreputable through indolent, passive, and limiting roles, defending the needed redirection of the *artificiality* of early impressions and upbringings that "currently" form young women.

Godwin views rising intellectual and moral opportunities as links in the progressive chain of "Necessity," which, he endorses, will lead to the eventual dismantling of institutions. "Rotten institutions encourage hypocrisy, and the misuse of moral intelligence seeks control." In his millenarian vision for the future, Godwin argues that all institutions which seek to limit the power of the human mind and its acquisition of knowledge—such as government, punishment, religion, and marriage—are evils *in need* of eradication. Simultaneously, from her antimonarchist father, *the* architect of anarchism, Mary solidifies that the basis of his system—Godwin's controversial belief that "no vice can exist with perfect freedom"—is "the very keystone of the arch of justice" and foundation of the moral-truth-oracles of London's own philosopher king.

For Godwin, "cogent reasoning" is a "power" of intuitive perception, resembling Coleridge's theory of "Reason" and Blake's concept of "Imagination." Godwin, the rational Romantic, looks to the improvement of reason as the means of improving social conditions—toward "universal benevolence." Furthermore, Godwin stresses the practical and moral "culture of the heart," asserting that Necessity without love undermines the assumptions of "actual life." Under these authorial causes, Mary hopes to enjoin others as *rational* enough to live out the optimistic social theories of her parents.

Synthesizing her primal touchstones—child of love and light—Mary aspires to authorship under her two muses. The original British Romantics, both Wordsworth and Coleridge, were directly inspired

by the independent writings and personalities of
Wollstonecraft and Godwin. Academically, Coleridge
defended Godwin and—admiringly—offered to
write works for Godwin's press. Blake was also
fascinated by Wollstonecraft and fashioned a series of
his famous copperplate engravings as the illustrations
for a collection of Wollstonecraft's tales.

Books are Mary's childhood companions. Feeling
socially isolated, her youth culminates in a stint at
a shabby boarding school. Experiencing life via
reading, Mary lives in her ideas, in paper worlds made
from ideal words. Her parentage is her books, and her
first faith is that *those* from her father's library are the
ample provisions needed for life.

Suffering backlashes from her mood swings and
stubborn temperament, Mary discovers her lack of
worldly readiness. Yet, to further encourage Mary's
academic depths and to sharpen her perceptions,
Godwin sends Mary to better weather. Voyaging up
the east coast of England, Mary finds stability with
the family of one of his philosophical devotees in
Scotland. Godwin's wish is for her to become more
self-sufficient and to be brought up with more of an
independent mind—"like a cynic"—honoring the
convictions of Mary's mother "to resist feminine
subjection" and "to effect the growth of *woman* as
more affectionate, more rational, and more moral."

Tap. Tap. Click. Mary is blossoming. Like autumnal
foliage when played upon by the rays of the setting

sun, her strawberry blonde hair has a natural aura of sunny and burnished brightness. Mary recollects that while in Scotland her "true compositions," the airy flights of her imagination, are born and fostered. The tinder of the creative imperative is primed for kindling. *Tap. Tap. Click.* Here, Mary envisions this whaling port as the framework for her fictive explorer to embark on a quest through the northern pack ice. "Alone, alone, all all alone," agonizing to claim discovery of the nautical passage to India, Mary imagines the downfall of her early protagonist to be a semblance of Coleridge's tormented mariner. While she is still fifteen, Godwin records, "My own daughter is, I believe, very pretty" and describes his Mary as "singularly bold, somewhat imperious, and active of mind." He boasts that, through "her perseverance in everything she undertakes," his Mary "is almost invincible."

As exuded from Godwin's frequent guests, Mary is well aware of the conflicted social repressions that have altered London society after continual decades of war. Mindful of the active censures from reactionary political instabilities and the continual miseries that impel "the meager" toward revolution, Mary is youthfully ready to take part in the reformational aspects of her social order. Under her spring cloud of red-gold hair, Mary's homecoming from two formative years abroad rashly shifts to her flirting with a young radical scholar—an aspiring disciple of her father who begins to frequent the Godwin residence. Conquering Mary's earlier social sense of "incapacity and timidity" that had surfaced from her father's overly academic parenting, this vitalizing young poet has pledged his philanthropic assurance to relieve her family's debts in accordance with Godwin's economic, socialist values.

~COLD INKWELL

"Writers, poets—*authors*—suffer from the early prerequisite to not only need to fall in love with another's body and emotions, but also with the *mind* of this other. This extra criterion of *thought*, a tacky romantic requirement, further shrinks the pool of the admiring author for Cupid's archery—a diminished collective already horrified by the other dirty absolute that one of these two lovers must also seem to have a bottomless purse."

SCOTT

Concluding her curious childhood, Mary returns from those wild green heathers of Scotland as a young lady, having beautifully transformed into the mesmerizing image of her daring mother—fair, gloomy, piercing, and magnificent. During this energetic summer, her father's promising protégé then announces his ardent passion for Mary—transfixed in the grey-hazel-eyed daughter of Wollstonecraft and Godwin. Her agile scholar is tall, attractive, and youthful. With wavy, winning, dark hair and deep blue stag-eyes, her philosopher is restless, brooding, and untamed. Under his alluring, intelligent spell, Mary pens her poignant reply to her vibrant suitor—to her Percy Bysshe Shelley.

(5.) *Captain Wentworth*

~ROMANTIC PHOTONICS

"Light is produced during the collision of different bodies, but this phenomenon is probably, in general, either dependent on combustion, or on the excitation of electricity."

SCOTT

Well, here I am—a new Shelley staring down Death's best: old number twenty-eight—bases loaded. *Tap. Tap. Tap.* Now—mightily—here *we* are. *Tap. Tap. Click.* Write the thing, Scott-boy, write hard. Edit and test it—*thank Keats*—edit and soldier our rows of redressing prose to arrived, poetical cadence.

Tap. Tap. Click. "There is no light"—these husks of stars—there is no light . . . but what is light?

ZELDA

What are you over there *diddling* like jellybeans on those dreadful keys?

SCOTT

Mon belle de jour, it's the type of pulp that one *jellybeans* when one files a complaint with their handsome stenographer rather than first bidding him "good morning."

ZELDA

You're thinking so loud I can hear your commie abacus in my dreaming. It's too *good-morning* early for plagiarizing nature poets and socialists.

SCOTT

Alright—*since we're under oath*—it's this fascist theme called, "Plagued by the Nightingale Not Here." I'm hatching a lubricated letter to a charismatic of this fine Republic of affairs. It's emerged a haunting medley of old bathtubs and new saxophones. This masher busies himself with papercuts and fretting about aquatic feathers for his blue tunic.

~TOY F-PLANE BETWEEN THEM

"Love, jealous grown of so complete a pair, / Hovered and buzzed his wings, with fearful roar, / Above the lintel of their chamber door, / And down the passage cast a glow upon the floor."

SCOTT

I'm advocating for his conduct to not buzzsaw like a housefly about my brain—via your infectious brain. As you stirred from your gypsy daydream, a corked title for this *aviating* correspondence has formed at my fingers—"The Moral Outcasts, or Every Day the Vulture."

ZELDA

Fiery dust—regurgitating Johnnie K. or *lordly* Georgie B.? Such a loud sound and a *stench*—what a swinging service in our little coastal *Lauds* chapel. What do you want, Scott, really?

SCOTT

Oh, just something lasting—like the metal smell of blood—something that perseveres the vacations of the spoiled. To take a drink and take and take and not have the drink take me. So, I take to this typing, and then—*alakazam, damn!*—I'm the Dapper who says. Though this compulsion to write—jellybean jellybean jellybean—is concomitant with my compulsion to bicker and drink, Sigmund has it that writers write for the terrors of fame, money, and love of beautiful women.

ZELDA

Freud meant boys—beginners. You bean to obliterate your guilt, to type type type your way to the shelf. Here, I'll bet it's all the verses of wet wood you drank out of your glass art sculpture—your emptied Scotch bottles in that drawer under your book stack. Those books are as obese as *ego*. That yellowing mound of rhymes distracts you more than I can. Put away that heap of dead petals—busted daydreams bunched up. Any lovely way, I see papers *can* last—and hide in old drawers until they're supplanted by enough libation bottles to force them out. Lounging about, Scott's own fresh sheets can make a fine morning bed, but *house-band*, this little pillow of a white pile right here needs the ground pepper of lasting words to adorn it.

SCOTT

Reporting the extreme things as if they were the average things will start you on the art of fiction. So, let's sunrise wager, then. Let's see. On a page that *he* can fold into a paper airplane, have "Icarus" in his cockpit scratch out all the declarations of affections that his heart of wax can hold onto after he climbs six-thousand winged wondrous feet and passionately shuts off the motor so that he can *fly* at last. Then, we can verify if whether the sea or *a wreckage fire* covets and treasures paper more.

ZELDA

We'll start with your paperboy route first and see where things land. Do you need me to put more in the typewriter for you to control? Letters—and prep-school spelling with them—lasts too. Be my good letter-letter-letter speller, Dapper. I'll *bet* you really can control that little alphabet of jellybean clatter there—and bind us a real *rainbow* of lasting lowercase paragraphs.

SCOTT

That blended *ring* of a line, the tinkling of it—your fresh French pleasantness is boundless, a morning marvel. While beholden, *lover*, I have as much control over this ink machine menace as a convict over the cut of his clothes or of his American cuisine served him in an animal's tin. Also, it is out of my control that I feel less and less grandeur in each issue of that last batch of my short runs. Although I'm now heir to the hat of being the highest paid, my swarming mass of shorts back Stateside became a spirit-diminishing imperative. Still, we did get two-thousand per publish—for some, the thrill of three heavy. No. The love's lost. The gold's dross. Writers write books. Simple as it is, it's haunting.

So, our new-well is a novel. There's no other Riviera way—unless we rob someone else as much as we're robbed here. Well, I've shelved my own Gothic Revival of Byronic witches, wars, gargoyles, and spires—*The Count of Darkness*. Yet, as necessary as I now assume, there's this trying gauntlet of affliction in piecing and pacing this forming thing. In an ironic servitude to brevity, I obey what seems to be its own possessive *control* that it asserts over me here.

ZELDA

Mustn't mess *masterless*. Well, once again, I ascend. I *arise* to aid your hiatus from your roaring insights smothered in magazine advertisements.

Well, here's the iron of the real irony. You've severed things with that old Harvard-operative Ober, and loving Perkins isn't extending the martyrdom of his sainted advance. It's months, and we're about bust—*sans le sou*. The rich get richer riches, and the bouncing poor get their poor bouncing babies. We got fun and, so, we'll have this third revelation of a god's own fun.

~SURE SOUTHERN SPIRITUAL

"There's nought, no doubt, so much the spirit calms as rum and true religion."

ZELDA

So, be enjoined, Scott-o. Rattle those jellybeans and be a great man then—a great American expat. Write us a new anthem to march our undergrad lives to our jaundiced pyres—your third persevering Princeton-miracle, boy-o. Now, *hike*! *Mush*!

SCOTT

He's off! Since he's certainly not going to rewrite *The Demon Lover*, he has now found his new vein. *The crowd is on their feet*! *A photo finish*! Scott's *novel for the ages* is more *The Demon of Switzerland* for the tomato heart of his southern belle, a song—the Duck's Quack—that will not die. That's what he does, my delicate Zelda—chastiser of wonder. And what is most miracle is most true—true, at least, where our parents were born, before us flaps and flops.

ZELDA

Then do, my great believer. Now, let's recall. We've already played "The Tender Times" and "The Blooms Just Fall." Then, well then, we played "Faithful

Deteriorations" and "Fruitless Freedoms." What's next? Yes—"What's Flown and What Must Fly." I might like *that one*—like the first one. We could've called that first set your "Poor Boys Shouldn't Think of Marrying Rich Girls." Or, "Way Which *Seemeth* Right unto a Man." Or, let's meet in the merchant-middle and just settle for playing the "Yes! We Have No Bananas" record.

SCOTT

Whatever your pleasure—and we'll party in the ruinous disappearance of grace, in the abyss of celebrating Zelda's glitz and glamor that I get to straddle. Moonstruck, I'll wire Cole Porter and I'll herd in again our Frenchest orchestra to play for you all night here in our runaway villa, then I'll get to work in the corner over there with cotton in one ear and your sweet nothings in my other, and I'll ask you—from the dark circles of the bottle of my heart—ask you each Scotched morning—rattling you awake—if you still think I'm your tepid man of a lemon.

ZELDA

Well, my, *my* . . . the Midwestern Rooster does have his own pair of eggs. But, my Scott-cock-a-doodle—because there were no Keatzians before Keats and no Lincolnians before Lincoln—"biography" is the falsest art. Their ghosts might haunt our larking-about and might drink our liquor. "Did I solicit *thee* from darkness to promote me?" Life is obstinate, and they could receive a lesson of patience, of charity, and of self-control—to be guided by a silken cord that all could seem but one train of enjoyment.

Their best years of youth can be spent under gentle and feminine fosterage, which can refine the groundwork of young character so much that it might not overcome intense distaste to the usual brutality exercised elsewhere. Must the ardent adventurer be divorced from the domestic? Even where the affections are not strongly moved by any superior excellence, the companions of childhood always possess a certain power over our minds—which hardly any later friend can obtain. They know our infantine dispositions, which, however they may be afterward modified, are never eradicated. Additionally, they can judge of our actions—with more *certain* conclusions—as to the integrity of our motives.

During my youthful days, discontents visited my mind, but I was not overcome by ennui. The sight of what is beautiful in nature and the study of what is excellent and sublime in the productions of man could always interest my heart and communicate elasticity to my spirits. I knew I was formed from peaceful happiness. My heart overflowed with kindness and the love of virtue. I had begun life with benevolent intentions, thirsting for the moment when I would put them in practice and make myself useful to my fellow beings.

Yet, I was a listener unformed in mind, dependent on none, related to none. "The path of my departure was free," and there was none to lament my annihilation. Who was I? A life of any worth is a continual allegory and figurative mystery. I ardently desired acquisition and longed to enter the world, to open a field for the plan of such life marked out in unyielding excitement of new passion that must enslave me.

My legislator, let me see that I excite the sympathy of some existing thing. I shall feel the affections of a sensitive being and become linked to the chain of existence and events—from which I now refuse exclusion. My Shelley, I break the seal and drink the cup. Overwhelm me and extinguish—in horror and despair—all fear of ignominy or death! Bard of the birds, two larks when joined in the animation of flight—is the pair not named "an exaltation"? Let it begin. I shall need no other happiness.

(7.) *The Parvenue*

SCOTT

It was some worldly witched night a few back, and I was entranced—*lost*, remember?—in those inspired recitations of those Shelley poems that I wanted to seduce you with when we had quarreled? We were fit to forget it. Well, I—endearingly drunk—turned and humored instead one of Dancing Duncan's Romanticism rants. I finished two of her lines and chanted an expectant verse myself. Then, I had her unready and I told her. As I did, I found *us* in it.

Somehow though, it had started two years back when our *likes* were published on the cover of our second-born novel. I was to go over the blurbs with Maxwell at the office. With curiosity—on an old holding desk at Scribner's—I looked through the sharp stacks of the UK books that had been published that year. I saw Shelley's name and felt a jolt that some lost spicy poems had probably been found and finally put out.

Instead, it was old Shelley's shadow—little Miss Mary, the great doll behind the great dastard. Before I left Chaz's that day, I read her posthumous little drama. Like discovering a wall of diamond bigger than a hotel, in what tale is gold *not* monstrous to man's mind? In her "Midas," she had the old beautiful love of classical moral symbolism—that flowers and grapes are better than gold.

While we were still sauntering profligate in Long Island, Max wired me for the proof of our comedy. In that cable, he confided that I'd enjoy Mrs. Shelley's own tragic short "The Parvenue," questioning—in a mind made wild—the divided loves that are embedded in being raised to "a superior station." Was he nudging me with this little societal contrast of the proofs? Well, as they do, things have coalesced since I've sentenced myself to roost in Villa *Marie*.

ZELDA

"The flapper" was also conscious that the things she did were the things she had always wanted to do. Well, my merry, merry ears are all yours—till they're not. I'll listen in my new fun of the flapper—her skillful cigarette science of "In-Out." You'll like it even more than old grapes and ancient flowers.

The flapper visualized the transfer of what she heard that she didn't *like* as the burning cheer at the end of her long cigarette. Then, the grinning flapper—on a good strong disciplinary drag—took it *in* and exhaled it *out* into its new punitive shape. Her sublimations of "In-Out" became a clandestine pastime of the resolute flapper.

SCOTT

Humor *this* and then you may—are allowed to—make my morning more dismal. Enamored—*seeing us*—with an irradiated view of this "lesser" Shelley—I saw our living, parabolic forecast. I can hardly think

of much else this week since our loving *lover's row*—
this new story for my always you—my beginning,
my heart, my fire, my all, my high-bouncing joy that
makes me such a youthful bastard of a fool.

My luminous Zelda, I—your Great Fitzgerald—"the
lesser and greater" *like the lights of the world!*, God's
own moon and sun—I was so cocksure that you
were so fittingly fireproof until you *stung* me with
that fairyland term after I had *feigned* that flirt with
Old Wild Isadora, now hopelessly, wondrously lost
in eternal empathy at your response to all this, these
third-rate ways we've been, our goading each
other . . .

ZELDA

To have your way, take your life-of-words by
the horns and guide it around the bottles of flat
champagne and around the "if I could only have
peace and my wife" *hooey*—instead of needing to play
"there's got to be around this next little corner some
little idea that'll just fix every little thing." Tut, tut,
tut.

—Big boys and little boys, alike, were disapproved
of taking the flapper to dances, to teas, to swim, and
most of all—to heart. The words thrilled her. They
had come into her mind during a fresh golden April
afternoon. She kept repeating them to herself over
and over, "love in the night, love in the night." She
tried them in three languages—Russian, French, and

English. Russian was *third*, and she decided that they were best in English during the cruelest month.

SCOTT

It was her own offer—*me!*—she had pushed the charm of her pages at me—just then and just there—for the glory of the grimy fame of her dirty biography. Like some sand from an ashtray, you'd have me throw it back in her face in front of everyone and miss making a major mark in the East. You'd have me spill myself through those stone stairs *first* as if I knew she was going to show up at our socialite dinner and propose it that very damned day.

ZELDA

You'd have made a darling next little puppet-stringed Isadorable—smiling in my own blood on the ground—for her guilt-crowds to throw their loose red coins at your snazzy fast vodka feet. Yet, I rather recline on the warmth that you had enough soaked brains to trade those prized pages for that muse of a sketch I made you—that *looker*, that dandy handsome of a racketeer with that Able Gable mustache staring hungrily at his brownette with a peony pinned in her hair—truly grasping the truer lady of truer talent. I'd even outdone the stripped nymph in a martini from the last one. *Damn*, we liked her. Since there's no side effects—like cysts or foot-infection curses of old dancers—I've struck some new techniques with my Riviera parvenue paints too.

SCOTT

See! We cross. We find the stones in the mire. We've made a swamp of things—squelching through—yet we *can* mend what matters, washing away some of the slop from our curd hearts while we *still* know—to the other side—that we're irresistibly idiots, lovesick. Look—really look—at us, what we've tabloid become, how we avoid all of what will be our next dismal shocking-headline. Search us. Let's on to the hope of Rome from here and really share the best of what's us—our Scottie *daughter*—and drink our new life real slow. We'll play and picnic. You'll let me work, and, *then*, I'll let you quip about this new angle about *repurposing*—your "plagiarism is born at home."

(8.) *fire and music*

~INTO THE HEARTH

"He came in for his paper.

'Alabama, you are too big to sprawl on young men's laps.'

'But he's not my beau, Daddy!'

The Judge spat contemplatively into the hearth, disciplining his disapproval.

'It makes no difference. You are too old.'

'Will I always be too old?'

The beau rose to his feet, spilling her to the floor."

GODWIN

Well, he returns here to his favorite trio. Since our poet has been at our table these past evenings, I detect his shifting themes. Though he reads to us tonight of high craft, I am anxious of his recent contrasts. Nonetheless, it is this previous letter—that I keep most in mind—that affirmed Shelley's future endeavors for our publishing house. I filter what will be in our *heir* by what's established. It's this portion *here*.

"I was haunted with a passion for wild and extravagant romances—ancient books of chemistry and magic. From an enchanted reader, I converted to a writer of romanticisms myself, untangling my sentiments and testing my creative drives—which revealed many hatreds. Then, influenced by a veteran to me in my years of persecution, I discovered that in this universe, I must employ *reason* into the excited interests of my heart. From your inestimable book, I arose a wiser and better man.

I have duties to perform amongst history. Rather than a bleak record of crimes and miseries, history is better the selection of events that we *chose* to make and dwell on as the best. My new art will persuade and educate others to adopt the just principles of a cooperative society, aspiring as the arduous enemy against oppression and other mental tyrannies."
In this lucidity, he has enlisted with us as liberty's trumpet—and not its avenging sword. Mythopoetic, our noble bard will play his role—and by it, we shall find our lives promoted via his rescue of our home.

~PHILOSOPHICAL NEGLIGENCE

"'The constructive possibilities of evil have been greatly neglected, sir.'

'Experience is what he needs.'

'The young people don't seem to know how to misbehave anymore—except by accident.'

'We must all have some possibilities for evil—if we can just look on the wrong side of things.'

'Don't you think, sir, that life will *correct* the good in him?'"

PERCY

Tonight is about thought. There are two ways to think. We must imagine and we must reason. Imagination is synthesis, and reason is analysis. Yet, reason is the cold, uncertain, and borrowed light of the moon, and imagination is the sun of life.

In thought, reason is to imagination as the instrument to the agent, as the body to the spirit, as the shadow to the substance. The expression of the imagination is poetry. Poetry is not the mental rattle of an infant civilization. Poetry is the ordering principle at work in human creativity, the most unfailing herald, the companion of a great people to work a beneficial change in opinion or institution. With sacred rage for the insulted Muses, the poet is the vessel of craft and diviner of care for praise and sign and fire and music and romantic readiness.

The great instrument of moral good is the imagination, and poetry administers to the effect by acting upon the cause. The great secret of morals is love, a going out of our own nature and an identification of ourselves with the beautiful—which exists in thought, action, or person not our own. Poetry enlarges the circumference of the imagination by replenishing it—the power of attracting and assimilating multitudinous thoughts to one's own nature, forming new intervals and interstices whose void forever craves the strengthened faculty of our moral nature.

Poetry is the love that creates amongst the abyss of hidden, veiled beauty, awakening the mind and rendering it a receptacle for unapprehended combinations of familiar objects clothed in Elysian light. Pleasure accompanies poetry to all spirits who open themselves to receive the wisdom—mingled with its delight—a divine reception beyond and above consciousness.

A poet is a nightingale who sits in darkness and sings to cheer its own solitude with sweet sounds. His auditors are as men entranced by the melody of an unseen musician, feeling that they are moved and softened, yet know not whence or why. Poetry is a mirror which makes beautiful that which is distorted, the very image of life expressed in its infinity of unchangeable forms. The poet participates in the eternal and—like Janus—the poet has a double face, beholding the future in the present. The poet is the true prophet and true legislator whose mental conduct is a golden augury of a *world*—I reason—more golden.

Like ivy overtaking a woodland, there is a line of greed and dominance in things. In inconstant emanations of grace, indifference, and malevolence, poetry is excavation for truth through the inner sanctuaries and horror of things—through the beautiful and cruel. It is veracity from higher forces, awaking melodies in the silent chords of human hearts.

~DECEIVED AVIAN

"'And to have that bird singing as if everything were alright.'

'There's no sense of decency left!'

'The trouble with birds is they imitate the vaudeville acts, and the vaudeville acts imitate the birds till we can't tell a real deception from a misconception any longer.'

'I think it's nonsense—birds.'"

(9.) *thespians*

SCOTT

All authoring is connected. There are no isolations. Stories within stories—framing memory—the connections keep connecting. Only us rustic authors—rich in heartache and Bushmill—certainly recognize these autobio necessities—these subconscious conflicts, these elemental alienations to be exteriorized, not like these progressives—green critics unmown in gunfire—these unshaken straw-people marauding under hay-stuffed fedoras.

ZELDA

She whispers at his earlobe that every cheap Job needs his cheap comforter. What is needed in those scrunches of his grooves and twists of his brain—imbedded in a genius boy of infinite possibilities—is *not* discipline. All he needs is the whispering, rooted fear that he cannot be both great *and* good.

So, here you are—the great author trying out for *their* expat stage. You're teetering. In a little panic of a few straws, Scott's brainiac diseased liver sets up the next Romantic School of moralizers and rebels—from the old Lake Men and Cockney Boys to your soft self-exiled aristocrats—the Scotch School for expatriates and *all* Momma's money. Is that what they sell the best of the boys under all that serpentine ivy?

~SNAKEY P.

"Flourishing vine, whose kindling clusters glow / Beneath the autumnal sun, none taste of thee; / For thou dost shroud a ruin, and below, / The rotting bones of dead antiquity."

ZELDA

And after they bobble through your starchy syllabus rubric, nobody will need to go to kaleidoscope school ever again cause they'll know every damn Scott thing to get along in this liquefied Scotch world.

SCOTT

The ivory boys under the ivy, well, although *they* possess and enjoy too early in life and are then made too spineless and too cynical—*and* that they hate us when we discover this about them—they do preach a few helpful hidden hints under their invasive ivies. It was paid for me to remember three *golden* Tiger nuggets hammered in me from Princeton.

One, never be poor—never. Two, be gracefully idle and don't go downtown ten hours for the best twenty years of your life. Then, it's this third one that's the hardest to remember from the skipped lectures. Deceptive ivy serpentine or no binding vines—it's that *happiness*, in one's meaningless life, is merely a little form of *time*, the little first hour after an alleviation of an intense misery.

ZELDA

Well, *enroll* me—the Scotch School for Idlers. For a moment, *I* am quite sold, but will your academic betters and benefactors at Chaz and Sons—dear and dearest—exteriorize publishing your new romantic humor of the *lesser* Fitzgerald—her great endurance and her third-rate transgressions?

SCOTT

For serious consideration, you'll need to register your *full* application with attractive letters of reference to Professor Fitzgerald. *Also*, you'll need to attend his newly accredited class about himself, his wife, and their second blossoming.

ZELDA

Read me *all* the springtime about it, Scotter Brain, but they want *Americans*, not easy, lazy strolling things humming time.

~RUN ON, NOW

"'Mamma, I don't want to go to *school* anymore.'

'Why not?'

'I seem to know everything.'

Her mother stared at her in faintly hostile surprise. The child, thinking better of her intended expositions, reverted to her sister to save face.

'What do you think Daddy will *do* to Dixie?'

'Oh, pshaw! Don't worry your pretty head about things like that till you have to—if that's what's bothering you.'

'If I was Dixie, I wouldn't let him stop me. I like her beau.'

'It is not easy to get everything we want in this world. Run on, now. You'll be late to school.'"

ZELDA

Take the shortcut to being one of their worthy ones—molding into a surefire bust for their careerist writer-idol pantheon of hero-worship. Just pick your prize and write right for the badges of the schoolmasters of ever afterward to award you their profound and enduring insignia emblems every few years. You won't feel too sick about it. Just butter some parts with tads of mystique. Write some old for the old-timers and some new for the newcomers. They'll have to both ask each other, and that'll sell the start of it—and right through the rest.

SCOTT

Well, speak of. Here's what's telekinetic *yours*, my own clairvoyant homemaker. "Although the seasonal magic is no longer for me, it goes on and somehow makes me glad." This is the theme. I know I've hit it. It smacks right in the soul as fact. It's when the freshness and warmth and trust are traded for the rough strengths needed to repel despair. "The Vanished Spring"—this is the new rotten apple of my eye, the pang to recapture the lost opening April hours.

Well, wake up my saints—my suffering Blue Stocking muse—and suffer a reading of *the great us* and endure. O, Raphael, archangel of the mind, mayday—*mayday* on the Mediterranean. Our sainted intercession, surfing on your fish, our patron saint himself of happy meetings for restoring blindness and places defiled—of lowbrow tourists, of beach drinks, and free love. Render us double sight to perceive doubled halves. Impart us your centennial renewal, your impressionistic recapitulation *fantastique*!

ZELDA

Pausing all the fun of "In-Out" for new smoke, a lazier lady sees easy that Scott's pulpy supply of Mary Godwin so much wanted the love of her marriage to be more than just mutual affections exchanged, expecting rather that it would grow—in a grand ideal of virtue—into something even healing for others—mushy Scott's magnanimous Romantic. However, shortly into it, convinced—dismally—that it couldn't, when even just *having it* was all of life to her, falling so far from any real hope, tragically settling for something less—that even it—their basic civil love—was almost out of grasp. They were convinced that their voyage through the seas of each other would triumph in their discovering more than just ephemeral home comforts or more than mere "wonder in the familiar" together. Yet, they would find less.

SCOTT

Good show. Nevertheless, Mary's resolute psyche could bear being a famous author's wife. Percy Shelley had become the It-boy to all he met—magnetic, gifted, pagan, restless, destructive, and selfish. What else could *she* have done except write it that way—to him—for the world to court him back to her?

ZELDA

Clap, clap, but these little *Quija* tricks of transference are just the same path to poverty—and the rest is delusion. These parallels are some French grift to try to pay your way out of your rupture with a pocket full of peppermints. Stringing along these pirated *similarities* is just like fluttering moths to their holocaust of night candles on the front porch.

Here's how it hits us. Scott sits here and tells himself to Zelda. "Zelda, I am left sitting here with all this indeterminacy, more vanities of more vanities, lost in the vanity fair at the world's fair of faeries, lost in this open-ended opaqueness—while yet dwelling in absolute possibility—is the old heritage of liberty, the soldiering spirit to persevere, which we must, in all our provocative searches to nowhere. It seems all here. Zelda—remember?—you confided that your secret fascination in me was my resolve in myself, an indestructible hope and faith in my own efforts. Good God, how Mary must've been filled in her resolve in Shelley's efforts, his creativities, heroics, and his undefeatable charms."

SCOTT

He sees it—sees it good—all the jelly being made into beans. After Mary's second work is published, our young Romantics—disappointed and miserably hopeful with their cherished two-year-old boy and baby girl—craft their secret departure plans to Italy and the eternal city, as if to be their permanent convalescence as their fourth adventurous spring arrives. Is this not *us* stepping out of the sun? Although their ominous omega was near, it must've felt to be a spacious outset of innumerable open mornings to come.

ZELDA

They couldn't feel how ominous your College-of-One would be. In Fitz-carol's student reader booklet of prattle, "Crossing Mont Blanc"—open form, free of course—would be his great poem if he, the *greater* Fitzgerald, were greatly in verse. So, here's my last teaser. Arriving in Italy, there the Shelleys were—on "the other side" of mysterious Mont Blanc, the fulfillment of their hopes that was to be all their sirenical doom and tragic arc, sentencing their passions to disquieting silence and sickening grief, stripping Mary of all her *loves*—bereft—like characters from her own novel, debilitatingly realizing her own worst fears.

SCOTT

Yes, she wasn't his coy mistress. Being light and beyond all hope, knowing the terrors that can come from giving birth, still, Mary—lovingly lost—was confident beyond her heaven that Shelley would again be hers. Mary must've written her entirety into preparing herself and her husband for Italy, with all the expectation that time could be redeemed, that all of her tragedies with her Bysshe Shelley could be transmuted into a beautiful future through a fresh start on the continent, like had been their full happiness for six young weeks when they had eloped. This hopeful reprising of their relationship was buttressed with shocking wisdom—the end of the fall of a hand of years. Leaving their imperial homeland through the east side, they had become a field where nothing could grow.

ZELDA

The impression spread through the room that things would germinate and manifest just by being here. Well, my classical Confessor, the Riviera drift doesn't seem to be the proper *field* for your family's income to ripen prosperous. So, Scott Street-Smarts is just going to lift these withered entries like some grifter from these Brit books laying around here—to make it fit *this junior* and the *senior Itsgerald*—and Scribner's is going to swoon over your lazy new French brilliance? Married for four years just like us? Bravo, Scott-o, the Triangle Club of drama will have a full house with big write-ups in the *Tiger*—page-turners. Reserve all your Holder Hall boys their crabs-in-a-barrel section. Then, after everyone walks out, we'll all go play "Hop the Tombstones" in New England cemeteries till somebody breaks a nail or steals the flowers.

SCOTT

Staring out into these assigning waters, our patron Saint-Raph of the Med has *called me* to jellybean his vision for his masses of half-hearts. Instead of ale, Milton sent Raphael and his rod to heal Daddy-o-Adam's mind after his wife returned from the forbidden bushes. His vessel—in his trance—I shall champion his message. I shall type its all-seeing title as "Five Years Next November." So, then, *then what*? Maybe another November, or two? . . . Are we as stagnant, or worse? Never taking off, never advancing, starting over, just starting again every day? Who's more blind? From our first hypocritical missteps from our priggish virtues, our tragedies are inevitable, but they must run their thespian, staged course.

ZELDA

So, *she* got the wicked serpent demon, and *he* got the angelic sage? Well, after all that frolicking, who could resist some "apples red"? I like to rather imagine it was lush strawberries, but berries only grow on vines—like all the Ivy Boys that won't grow into durable trees, the *Berry* Boys. Still, we didn't get to play "Pure Maiden" and we haven't played "Earth Mother" yet, but I think we're maneuvering through "Harlot with a Halo" with strong aplomb through our Marie tomb.

SCOTT

Dab my brow. Yep, it all went down right here—right

down there at the casino so the Berry Boys would have a chance in this life. Good wife, I find *only* gratitude in your powders and perfumes of moral losses. They're the rude clouds that shore my best romantic vignettes and have me beside myself in the thrill of preparing to die for *five* years.

ZELDA

If all I am is the football from your playbook—the thing you're running around this practice field—then I believe I'll just have to sprout wings when you kick me through the posts so I can fly my sporting self into the next tomboyish city for the other team's "Pass the Pigskin." Sidelined, sitting there typing in your coach's chair, you think you've found a path that jets out days—but all you've landed on is a sharp, little bend that you'll turn to find yourself circling back from through a little cul-de-sac of distractions.

SCOTT

Onward—yes, my Raphael of the Riviera! I envisage this crest as it breaks in the drinks of tourists. From their imperial imprisonment, Mary would seek Italy with her Shelley to improve his wellbeing, and instead, reversing their hopes to improve their post-Britisher tomorrows, the pitiless foreign climate would erase their progenies.

During her last pregnancy, Mary would almost hemorrhage to death. Percy—the amateur man of science—would boldly cease these seven hours of blood loss and fainting, saving the life of his Mary during this ruthless miscarriage. Shelley makes a resolution of brandy, vinegar, and ice. Losing her last baby in an ice filled bath, Mary is convinced that she is also going to die. How could anybody not—seeing Death standing there, smoking, reading a love letter?

"I was about to die. I hardly wished that I had. My own Shelley could never had lived without me. The sense of eternal misfortune would have pressed too heavily upon him—and what would have become of my poor babe?"

Still, during the next month, Percy, Signore Shelley himself—the amateur seaman, at the anticlimax of twenty-nine years old—would be drowned in the downing of his yacht off immortal Italy while Mary was still twenty-four primed years old and would've completed her third book. Nearly, here sits your author on the same doubled heart's pace, the *same*—

—My barefaced Zelda, what is bearable? What's all our young wrath stacked against this list of punishing longsuffering? Her perseverance of love must've made Mary feel invincible, like you make me swell to ten feet as well, like you make me victory-march valiant—invincible—till I'm not, and I sit down, vulnerable, in this cold coach's chair, to write love alive again.

ZELDA

So, it's set in my master's marble then? Under the dreamy spell of our Riviera, we're the enchanted Shelley-Fitzgeralds? *Great.* Love doesn't sit and wait, loitering *till it's great.* No—*I see*—they wrote and loved and were in the great fallout of the miserable revolution, and a century later, we write and love and are here—in the dismal fallout of all our *Great War*—and . . . *look* . . . in France as well? So what? And a century from us, there'll be loving writers who survive war and wealth and elitists and . . . And *so?* We're all just people who argue in hotels—not some myth to exploit in some other world overseas.

Rather, I find myself more partial to Guinevere with her other knight, or to Helen with her Trojan—but listen like a good old sport that can learn his night-school lesson. The first poison? This theme all over again? It's not us—*my Jesus*, Scott. You want too much. You know *first* you're *their* hardy chronicler of boozers and disenchants. So, make the money and make it about somebody else—and with a little more jazz.

(10.) <u>*a "snake" of independence*</u>

~A ROOK'S CASTLE

"He was a living fortress, fabricating philosophical drawbridges, entrenching himself in his integrity. His superiority absolved his children from the early social efforts necessary in life to construct strongholds for themselves."

SCOTT

Crossed early in love, his mind filled his heart's reservoir of melancholy with New World eccentricities. As tea started to be shipped across the pond, Bysshe's father emigrated from Jolly Old England. His father was a self-determined merchant of Newark and inherited the colonial lands and wealth of his wife. He enterprised a lumbermill, pursued litigation, and sent Bysshe home to advance in England. By birth a colonist of New Jersey, Bysshe is raised as a promising boy in Sussex into to a handsome top hat of a man—through many useful marriages—of fortune. *There's the spirit.*

On the death of his British grandparents, young Bysshe has inherited their "ready money, mortgages, bonds, bills, notes, Plate, diamonds, rings, pearl necklaces, best linens, and their freehold land." Bysshe elopes with his first wife of alliance—and her wealth—to Paris. He is clever, tall, witty, friendly, and warm. Bysshe attends Oxford and receives legal training—and a brief flair for literature, quoting lines in an epistle from *The Tempest*.

Under the Shelley coat of arms, Bysshe begins to build his eminent domain. William Blake lives near Bysshe as he forms the illustrations for Wollstonecraft's *Tales*. The Duke of Norfolk secures Bysshe's baronetcy and ushers his oldest son into Parliament. At his favorite estate—with a mammoth Tudor style fireplace—Bysshe plants two American Sequoias as emblems of his youthful ambitions. Gifting this estate to his heir, Bysshe expects further Shelley alliances and more Shelley lands. Bysshe's son attends Oxford during the War for American Independence and serves as a recruiting officer. As Cornwallis is surrendering at Yorktown, Bysshe's son attains his Master's and enters his prude RMS career in litigation and politics.

Bysshe's grandson is a pretty fledgling with curly ringlets. During the year of his birth, the opera is mourning the death of Mozart, the animus of the guillotine is claimed, Paine is banished from England, the anti-slave trade bill is presented, and the shocking works of Wollstonecraft and Godwin are circulating. Percy Bysshe Shelley is called "Bysshe" throughout his childhood, resembling his grandfather, Sir Bysshe, more than his stuffed-shirt father, Mister Shelley. Nevertheless, both Percy's grandfather and father expect the same life script for their future heir—Oxford, expedient marriage, and Parliament. Conversely, at eighteen rebellious years old, Percy is addressing the cruel double standard that sons *must* always succeed while daughters do as they wish.

Discord escalates between Percy Bysshe and his anxious father. After successive inner family *rifts* and resultant social disgraces, Mister Shelley will disown his "prodigal son," preventing him from his previous advantages and from visiting his mother and siblings. Mister Shelley believes the purpose of academics is for worldly advancement into political power and conveys his secular strategy to Percy's younger brother. "You young rascal, don't be like your brother. Take care you don't learn too much. Never read a book, Johnnie, and you'll be a rich man."

Defiant and furthering this *smite*, Percy forswears to be a knight "for nothing"—feigning to disinherit his title, denouncing his parentage. He wishes to be an heir of something he's earned. Although he continues his privileged access to being *lent* credit, Percy berates the exploitation he was born into— that forced labor had built his family's lands. In the pretense of the forgoing of his birthright and driven by firm self-determination, Shelley pursues becoming an autonomous, socially purposeful author. Adversely, *charitable* Percy commences his great scattered decade of brilliance, mirroring *these islands'* diametrical Regency era.

~IAGO'S OCULAR PROOF

"If you can prove that it is by me, produce your evidence. I refuse to reply."

SCOTT

Percy Bysshe will evade his pursuing creditors through four years after his own obstinate expulsion from Oxford, having refused to acknowledge his mutineer authorship of an anonymous tract—rationalizing his *conjectural* academic views. Both of Shelley's occultic gothic novels and early poems are also published before his despotic dismissal.

Rather than dealings amongst free men in a country of liberty, the proceedings of his Oxford dons—afflicted of unsure fire—are a court of inquisitors. Of his erudite facility and faculty, Percy stresses a proper intellectual inquiry into this *matter*—demanding the full application of logical principles about "the nature of belief." This urgent spirit of Shelley's stubbornness is his antiauthoritarian *god* of skepticism—his pioneering quest for the limits of understanding—that *reason* must not prostrate before absurdity.

Percy's attitude at Oxford was bent in engaging others to intellectual discourse and arguments—to get to the bottom of things. From Shelley's youth, it was "the senses" that are the source of all knowledge to the mind—not mandatory subscription to statutes and articles of *the C of E*. Although Oxford was the headquarters for the standard debates of fair disputants, Shelley is expelled for his *contumacy* in refusing the convenient untruth of disowning the essay, which also deprives him of acceptance from all other universities.

~CALIBAN BECOMES ARIEL

"Glowing with ardor to attain wisdom, resolved at every personal sacrifice to do right, burning with a desire for affection and sympathy—he was treated as a reprobate and cast forth as a criminal. Youth is rash. It cannot imagine—while asserting what it believes to be true and doing what it believes to be right—that it should be denounced as vicious and pursued as criminal."

SCOTT

Before he is expelled, Shelley has tastes for chemicals, eerie magic, and impulsive madness. Shelley is born into the fearful symmetries of Blake's *Songs* and into the fearful red, white, and blue stirrings of murderous freedom in France. Rather than hunting quarry as a boy, Shelley wants to read blue "flutter" thrillers, wandering through the woods and staring into the stars at night. Playful and imaginative—in his high-pitched hypnotic voice—he speaks of volcanoes, fighting, and fairies.

~PRETEND AUTOPSY AT NAPTIME

"And did I cry at night and raise hell so you and Daddy wished I was dead?"

SCOTT

"Happy P. is as well as he can be," his mother writes. "You never saw a fellow enjoy more than he"—being raised on his estate with the pastoral beauty of ponds, meadows, a farm, forests, and gardens. Although Percy's favorite youthful pastimes are horseback riding and boating, he is expected to prefer the field sport pastimes. While he ensures that he does become a good marksman, he arranges for others to perform his killings—letting the gamekeeper bag all of the wild birds as Percy reads from books. In his family's drawing room, Shelley consumes his towers of stacked books and considers his scholastic lessons to be child's play. Discerning the social antagonisms of the aristocracy, Percy begins to feel that he is an outsider and internalizes a separating shadow-self.

As a boy, Percy wants to imitate American Ben Franklin in drawing electrical fire from heaven. When he discerns the ability to generate static electricity from rubbing *electrics*—amber gemstones—he plays mischievous pranks and fabricates fire balloons. Wandering, Shelley creates his fantasy world of the Great Tortoise of wisdom, of the wizard in the cave playing with fire—found from lifting a magical floorboard in a deserted room—and of the slithering, fearful Forest Dragon.

Further desiring to touch the invisible world, he waits a gothic night on coffins in a charnel house, wishing to find spirits. Shelley recollects, "While yet a boy I sought for ghosts, and sped / Hopes of high talk with the departed dead. / I called on poisonous names with which our youth is fed; / All vital things that wake to bring / News of birds and blossoming, —

/ Sudden, thy shadow fell on me; / I shrieked, and clasped my hands in ecstasy!"

On inspired nights of other necromancies, he searches for genii. "Oh! there are spirits of the air, / And genii of the evening breeze, / And gentle ghosts, with eyes as fair / As star-beams among twilight trees: — / Such lovely ministers to meet / Oft hast thou turned from men thy lonely feet. / The voice of these inexplicable things, / thou didst hold commune, and rejoice / when they did answer thee; but they / Cast, like a worthless boon, thy love away."

~NECROMANCER'S WAND

"Many advantages attended his birth, but he spurned them all when balanced with the impetuous pursuit of his duties. His pride was spiritual. When attacked, he neither fled, nor stood at bay, nor altered his course, but calmly *went on* with heart and mind intent of elevating his species. Whilst men tried to force him down to their level, he toiled to draw their minds upwards."

SCOTT

Preparing his son for the imitation of his own career, Mister Shelley teaches Percy how to speak to crowds with hand gestures and with the proper pitch and volume for producing charismatic intensity. Shelley is cheeky and pokes fun at his father's privilege, ending a boyhood letter, "not your obedient servant." Inclining toward medicine and surgery, Shelley shuns his father's hopes of him rising through the army. Among the affluent community at his lavish estate, Shelley is dismayed by his family's guests that perpetually speak about the social turmoil in England and France while snubbing participation in progressive solutions. In refusing to see how the turmoil is already at their own entrance halls, Percy considers the contradictory alliances of his family to be part of the very tyranny that his family ought to be decrying.

At fifteen, Shelley attends court hearings with his father, disagreeing with and debating the court decisions that his family celebrates. Percy is stunned at injustices that his father and others don't seem to mind—particularly, a sentence that was passed on a starving man who had stolen a sheep. Percy is frantic about the political corruption that he witnesses during his father's Parliament seating. The stiffening of several laws during the political turbulence of this period causes many people to depart England for America.

Percy's budding hatred begins for the hypocrisies of institutional power. As he enters Oxford, he purchases Godwin's text, affirming that the world's ills can be explained by the misuse of monopoly and the chains of false values. Two dire ideals that Shelley desires to promptly implement are the necessities of generosity and early education for the poor. As he grows rather odd, tall, and slim, Percy's social passions have just begun. Yet, his life is half over.

As a teen, Percy remains obsessed with magnetism, tinkers, telescopes, gunpowder, and transferring thunder into jars. He strolls through the quads of Oxford reading chemistry, poetry, and political science. Scattered throughout his rooms at Oxford are boots, papers, pistols, money, letters, prints, crucibles, a Japanese inkstand, and volumes of open books. Just as his fun starts, his fun is half-done.

Family and university fail him. Playing the "heroic outcast," Percy conveys his vibrant anger for failed leaderships in most of his later works. Wholly uninfluenced in his lonely walks through tragic London, he longs for an aristocratical thunderstorm and transitions to vent alone in Wales. In Shelley's sharp, emergent writings, he is marking out two great forces—the force of progressive improvement and the conquering force of all appearances. Echoing his admiration of Tom Paine, Percy is attempting to announce the place of "freedom" amongst the mutual forces of "Necessity" and "Mutability."

As Shelley is nearing nineteen, he is considered a wandering radical. Dramatically paranoid—in case he is too maimed and left for dead from a brutal beating—he begins to always carry concealed vials of laudanum. During this period, Shelley writes: "You talk of a future state. Imagination is the proof demanded, but we are very much prejudiced in favor of what we earnestly desire. So many analogies seem to favor the probability of this hypothesis. On the supposition of this plan, congenial souls *must* meet, having fitted themselves for nearly the same mode of being, they cannot fail to be near each other. Freewill *must* give energy to this infinite mass of being to constitute virtue."

Shelley is warned to fully forsake his radicalisms—or be fully forsaken. In *fuller* rebellion after his expulsion—and finalizing his severance from his wealthy family—Percy elopes with Harriett Westbrook. His father is outraged that the Shelley baronetcy will not acquire any additional lands from this marriage—stalling the calculated expansion of the Shelley estates. To Shelley's parents, he had become a mad viper, and his influence must be deleted, erased from their home and hopes. They are fearful that his lawless actions—without antidotes—will not only corrupt his siblings and household but will also detrimentally affect the system of the aristocratic class in England. Though his father now forbids Percy Bysshe's name to be spoken, Harriett— "with two *Ts*"—transfers the affections of his first family to his second, perpetuating Shelley's name to remain "Bysshe."

He writes to Harriett, "turn / Those spirit-beaming eyes and look on me / Until I be assured that Earth is Heaven / And Heaven is Earth." When Percy first met her, he gifted Harriett his inspired, violent, macabre works. From Oxford, in further correspondence to her, Shelley dedicated his first lyrical collegiate essay. She was well bred, amiable, and accommodating. For Percy, Harriett's hair was as pretty as a poet's dream, and her cheerful complexion was the tint of the blush-rose shining through the lily.

At Oxford, with glee, Shelley discovered the *incendiary* writings of Godwin, affecting his personal and social spheres as much as his mind. He avowed that *he* would be devoted to these lucid ideals—*and* that so would his Harriett. Although Shelley's father supported Percy's writings before Oxford—in mounting intolerance—his father insisted that this vow to Godwin's works has commenced his heir's *recalcitrant* sallies of folly and madness, culminating in his son's imprudent *misalliance* with the daughter of a retired coffeehouse merchant.

~A BOYO'S HEAVY CARGO

American titan Mark Twain—Daddy-o *Sammy Clems*—wrote: "Shelley was nineteen. He was not a youth, but a man. He had never had any youth. He was an erratic and fantastic child during eighteen years, then he stepped into manhood, as one steps over a doorsill. He was curiously mature at nineteen in his ability to do independent thinking on the deep questions of life and to arrive at sharply definite decisions regarding them, and stick to them— stick to them and stand by them at cost of bread, friendships, esteem, respect, and approbation. For the sake of opinions, he was willing to sacrifice all these valuable things, and did sacrifice them; and went on doing it, too, when he could at any moment have made himself rich and supplied himself with friends and esteem by compromising with his father at the moderate expense of throwing overboard one or two indifferent details of his cargo of principles."

(11.) *tale of the cake-maker's knight*

~IN THE THICK
"Novelists like himself 'have *love* as a main concern' since our interest lies outside 'the economic struggle' or 'the life of violence,' as conditioned to some extent by our lives from sixteen to twenty-one."

SCOTT
Engaged, Percy and Harriett are loosed, fleeing northward, marrying in the capital of Scotland as Shelley turns nineteen. They were in *the pink*—like their frank and fair Scotchwomen in this pious land of bakers. The newlyweds then travel for two years throughout the British Isles, disseminating Shelley's extremist social assessments. Not suffering having his wife become a cake-maker, Shelley initiates his project in grooming the mind and values of his bridal disciple. Throughout their expeditions, Percy's budding anger and despair grows as he witnesses the horrors, cruelty, and degradation that are instituted through trenchant poverty.

Astonished, Shelley asserts, "I had no conception of the depth of human misery until now—thousands huddled together in one patch of animated filth. A remedy must begin." Shelley prides in his destiny at having been born during the fervor of the French Revolution. Shelley asserts, "The rich grind the poor into abjectness, and then complain that they are abject. They goad them to famine and then hang them if they steal a loaf." Defending free, uncensored discussion, Shelley is suspected of disseminating militant egalitarianism. For the government, aristocracy, and priesthood of the British Isles, "freedom of the press" is too obnoxious to be able to exist.

~BUT WHAT IS LIGHT?

"The beholder saw he was beautiful, but could not discover in what *it* consisted."

SCOTT

Yet, Percy's viable form of mediation is targeted to able laborers, lecturing classical liberalism—that *laws* should not be confused with *rights*, that laws should not discourage the practice of truth. As Shelley learns that Bonaparte is the great favorite of the Irish, he begins to envision that Napoleon is the current vessel of "Necessity." Like the Roman ideal of the union of the social classes, Percy yearns for expectant Napoleonic reform throughout Europe.

"From my irradiated creed against this world's cold schools, I thirst for unbending action." Authoring his tracts in hurried, frantic passions, his youthful imagination is driven to redress oppression and injustice, proclaiming "titles are tinsel, glory a bubble, and excessive wealth a libel." From a mild persecution complex, Shelley's compositions arrive with ease. Witnessing the Irish dehumanized, Shelley is compelled to imitate the oratory writings of Thomas Paine. Resolute in Ireland and Wales, Percy engages in distributions of his foolhardy political writings, further broadcasting his fragmentized works into the sea to be found in boxes and bottles. As the British are seizing American ships, Percy is suspected of occultisms of the Illuminists. Royal agents spy on him, composing a dossier of Shelley's activities thought subversive.

~ON THE REDCOATS' RADAR

"Shelley's mental activity was infectious; he kept your brain in constant action. Its effect on his comrade was very striking. The Poet delighted to see the seeds he sown, germinating. Shelley said he was the sparrow educating the young of the cuckoos."

~ROYAL ESPIONAGE RECONNAISSANCE CONCLUSION

"Attend our will: *Romeo must not live.*"

SCOTT

Since Shelley *is* a minor, the Home Office lacks grounds to prosecute him for sedition. In Dublin, Shelley enjoins Harriett in advancing his *philanthropy* of exhorting the Irish to awake and arise from their wretched, unheeded groans into the daring social transfiguration of his developing vision. Percy's literature decries "the rich" exploiting "the poor"—

the manipulations driving English societies between anarchy and despotism. Shelley advocates that the infamous revelries of the rich—"industry"—contaminate the peaceful vales, deforming the loveliness of nature with human *taint*.

Although his quixotic quest is authoritatively quieted, leaving all of Ireland's windmills—his sweet little nothings—as he has found them, it becomes Percy's singular ambition to influence ardent contempt for failed *leaderships*—as far as their curse is found—scorning each abhorrent mismanagement of mankind. He is commanding, but his commands are so generous, so simple, and so devoid of offense that it always takes some irony of time for others to discern that Shelley himself is a sort of tyrant.

Although Percy already considers his metaphysical differences of opinion to be his future disqualification from Parliament, his father would've been expecting his son—as he was approaching twenty years old—to follow him in sitting with his party and inheriting his seat. However, Shelley's scandals with Oxford and Harriett—and now his tireless exertions in Ireland and Wales—damage Mister Shelley's political career, losing, and never regaining, his seat in governance.

During his second year of marriage, ricocheting between North Wales and London, Percy, still *considered* agitational, becomes fearful that continual entities pursue him for incrimination—bent *stalking silhouettes* sent to deter his budding insurrection.

While incautiously dispensing his writings in Wales—assuming he has avoided his hostile shadow of informants—Percy escapes two bullets *shot* from a silent conspirator, fearfully fixing his conviction in his own importance. Hounded, yet elevated, Shelley simplifies that governments hate poets and must make poets their enemies because poets intrepidly write transparent *truth*.

(12.) <u>*yare*</u>

ZELDA

Remember? You had that shadow backstory going somewhere. Have it there—your daydream beginning in the apostasy of the little blue-eyed neglected boy. Remember? In his little town with the little thought that there hung colored balloons and sensation in the night somewhere—twinkling gorgeous *things* that had nothing to do with God—if he'd get off his little Blatchford porch?

Get him out there to partake of that glistening and give it to him. With all the wonder that his little cobalt peepers can collect, scribble him seeing his destiny ship come in—in the dirty midst of his digging clams and fishing salmon. What's that other one from that pair of shorts—they were *yare*—that you wrote out at the yacht club lake? There was that manifesting of a mysterious *tough* with an alter ego. Well, have *him* clean up and wear a gold tie for his act. Then, give *it* to him—get him his auric gal with her dangerous auric voice.

SCOTT

Gold tie—*great*—Scott's golden noose and the man, young Jimmy Clams, who had to die—twice. We can title it "The Deliberate Opposite—an Inspiring Misreading," or "See *What*? She Said." Sidenote—the other tag team that Our Mediator of the Med was willing to gamble the future on was "the Moor" and

Desdemona. Whereas it is, the *"Great Us"* happens to lie *here* though—this book. Yes, look here. I saved you the spot—like our denouement's dance—how her story reads into all this—how we're sleepless and *here*.

~ENKINDLED

"Nature decayed around me, and the sun became heatless. Rain and snow poured around me. Mighty rivers were frozen. The surface of the earth was hard, chill, and bare, and I found no shelter. Oh, earth! How often did I imprecate curses of the cause of my being! The mildness of my nature had fled, and all within me was turned to gall and bitterness. The nearer I approached to your habitation, the more deeply did I feel the spirit of revenge enkindled in my heart. Snow fell, and the waters were hardened, but I rested not."

SCOTT

Zelda—in her infinite empathy—looks at Scott, then back at the passage, seeing the controlling idea of these scenarios is our hopefuls trying to get back to some clear, clean point—impossible—to reset things, to get back to a golden moment from a golden day.

ZELDA

A book—*your* book—can't be wandering recollections and distant dazes, Scott-o. That's bathtub gin—a lazy, cold trout stream of bathtub gin rolling right through this villa's living room. Rather, scratch 'em up a Scotch-spangled ballad of urban wilderness cries. Give them something from your top shelf—you know—established wealth and its dearest warfare with fast fortune. Tip them your hat of gold—Great Fitzgerald and his great money question. Now we've got it. The materialism and immorality of the old guard—right?—and the have-nots who overestimate *possibility*—and how we're so different. The "anything-can-happen" man—your social class lesson story—Scott's ruin of the upstart, the inferior outsider, who's illusion—Scott the Reacher's great illusion—that class equality can be bought and sold. Now we've got it. You're absolved. Jellybean in peace, heartbreaker.

SCOTT

Your intimate insights woo me to your world. They'll call it, "Court and Break—the Restored and *Betrayed*." No, a Fitzgerald dying fall and mystery—like eggnogs, like mint juleps—are the preference of this touched typist, more than a Wentworth eavesdropping and his sleight-of-hand, last-minute love letter. I'll call it, "Old Gold's Old Foreshadow." Give Scott a hero, and Scotch will give you a casualty.

~HIS NEW ONE

"'See here,' I would say, 'this is a novel by Fitzgerald—you know the fella who started all that business about flappers. I understand that his new one is terribly sensational—the word "damn" is in the title. Let me put you down for one.' And this would be approximately true. I am not in love with sensationalism, but I must plead guilty to it in this instance. And I feel quite sure that, though my books may annoy many, they will bore no one."

SCOTT

Still, these loves—*this is it*—weren't trying to buy their way into the heaven of cultural memory, but, in their languishments, they could not have peace without a certain person—at the mercy of *their one* who could not remain possessed. The money question? It's inescapable. There're always the supremacies of the proprietors.

This ominous *question* festers in its nuisance. This bane isn't my cup of kiss-and-forget. It's no great secret that I cherish an abiding animosity—with the smoldering hatred of a peasant—toward the leisure class of sprawls, working them so that I can share their mobility. But, our "haves" with their noble money isn't the only land your Fitzgerald socializes. Not everyone born on the outside dies on the outside. There's also wonder . . . and all the *great* powers like it.

ZELDA

Like love? Well, here's the sentimentalists in the great city of the great love. Well, count our stars—and our stripes—if this isn't the big ol' jackpot. So, it's *love* that has a price, love that can be bought and sold under the *gangrene* lights? I'll Parisian play along. I'll be the "doomed Romantic" and acquiesce, feigning to be filled with disquiet at the idea of your suffering, away from you, in the inroads of your misery and grief. You'd have me roll my Jane Austen eyes, slowly, playfully, like a sage convinced that a man is blind to the thousand minute circumstances that call forth a woman's sedulous attentions, these manifold conflicting emotions that would render me mute. "O, I'm yours, but make me yours. O, what love must abide and endure." Then, you'd close me, having me bid you a tearful, silent, female farewell.

"You live, and my power is complete! Come on—my enemy—we have yet to wrestle for our lives, but many hard and miserable hours must you endure until that period shall arrive!" Good God. Give me a drink, my *punish'd*. Rather, I'll get it and get back to my swimming and dancing—my French flying lessons. Zelda, *away*! You type, old sport. Utterly inspired, diddle us a good dinner.

SCOTT

Well, *save* me. Save me her waltz and last kiss if she isn't the truest—having me diddle, diddle, diddle to the haste of her must-have squirrel coat to droop over her debutant-sized brass knuckles, rectifying the chaste rights of women, *vindicated*.

ZELDA

The rights of "woman," scholar boy. Who, what can I even evoke in your obsessive mania of this?—what you're at, this performance—except that I'll just be, be a part of something different, what you can't make yours. Asinine. I can instruct as well—without dropping out. Surely, you *know* my darling diaries like dollars. Don't take a fake monopoly of what's ours of theirs. Divorce these lazy Riviera distractions. They'll just want to all see right through it—through you—right to our ruin. Status quo, Scott-o. This is the old drink that will drown you when you fall into it.

So, don't pawn the hubcaps, Hubby. Be a little more magnanimous and restore "yourself" *to your self* and write me a book all about it—with beautiful, young, sugar *me* on the front page. We'll endure this trickling as long as we know we'll get that valve-in-the-sky splashed open again—when Heaven will just have to turn this faucet back on, so long as it'll be flowing and rolling through at least one of our *thinkers* and through one of our *tickers* and through one of our trousers' pockets.

SCOTT

Hmmm . . . persuasive. I'll title this pile of stock, "In the Wake, What Foul Dust Floated." Now, back to the prestigious. The stage-man's pledge is high, folks. Vote for high-bouncing Scott. He won't betray your shallowness. In the great fear of poverty, in the great worship of success, and with all faiths shaken—like cocktails—vote Scott. To the delights of consumption, to the new woman, nostalgia, cynicism—I'm your oracle—Scotch's your romance, your man.

ZELDA

Keep it clear in the election—my abject party boy—who's the icing and who's the cake for your appointment as the loud, heady host when you land us a real ball—my real waltz—back across the pond on our great sprawling American lawn. Still, if only people could travel as easy as words—and be so easily revised. I wish that we had become people—at least paper people—so we could be revised like words.

Folly, adieu! It's *my* skidoo year—you had yours in New York. Now, it's mine "to away." So, away, away to the gay of the day. Your Gloria flitters tither—clean as the streams and wind—and criticism of your Rosalind ends in her abiding beauty, my amorousness!

SCOTT

Once again, her restless, reckless Scott begins the great novel. "Zelda" will play the opulent misfortune, Mrs. Daisy Fay Buchanan, the delicate flower fairy who's confused that she's a machine-gun-battalion's artillery. Now, it was Daisy who wanted to decide, and not somebody else—for her to pull the levers, and not be pulled. She wanted to buy now and not be bought—"the daisy-star that never sets." Her love *was* for sale, but no longer. Like seasons that lead nowhere, she had already put all *that* behind her.

There was Daisy in her next luxurious summer with her Miss Jordan. Her husband, Tom the Great

Cannon, and their daughter—were around and around. Cousin Nick would be right across the Sound for her carelessly crafted summer. After she shoved her Jordan and her Nick together for her seasonal play things, Cousin Nick would invite Cousin Daisy to tea to meet his mystery friend. Yet, this curious friend and this curious Daisy had met before in their own curious Southern mystery.

For the undisciplined satirist, it was Daisy Fay Zelda's world—as long as she was young, and as long as she was beautiful. Boyishly, she wanted something, something—some strong work to perform, to be a dilettante-power upon the earth, the heir of many willful years and many men—to craft her own pedestal and be announced as a career out of cocktails, the heroine for the next generation of shopgirls before she was empty as an old bottle, before she was obsolete, pseudo-wise, and nursed to an utter senility by the men she had broken. The world would not wait motionless and breathless. The living world was going ahead—drinking and discussing, drinking and arguing—a fire without warmth.

Now, *to it*, roaring Riviera distractions—the grand Britisher bio and great American novel—the doubled stuff of mirrored life.

(13.) *Queens of Necessity*

~IDEALISM'S IDOL

"He lives by a law which is not visible to vulgar eyes. He enters into the world of spirits. He compares the greatest things, sets eternity against time, and chooses rather to be forever great in the presence of god when he dies—than to have the greatest share of worldly pleasure whilst he lives."

SCOTT

Circuiting back to England, Shelley becomes devoted to the firm basis of rational liberty, crafting an aesthetic of social poetry from which critical rage and insubordinate hope must force others' impulses to think of *change* as necessary. As an enthusiastic disciple in London—with the literary reign of freedom and justice in his head—Percy solicits his Enlightenment hero. His idol is Godwin, the living reformist who authored the novels and political philosophy that Shelley absorbs and painstakingly translates into his own radical lyrics, initiating his own delicate career. Neglecting Harriett, Percy's esteemed vocation becomes professing his collective anarchist creed in verse, the translation of Godwin's principles—his radiant vision of universal benevolence made manifest in actual liberty via actual equality.

Entrenched in his correspondences, Percy disagrees

with the educational booklets from Godwin's company. Percy argues that youth should not be the host of a classical education, contending that *words* are the very *things* that so eminently contribute to the growth of prejudice and establishment of violence—the learning of unacquainted terms before the mind is capable of attaching correspondent ideas—*words* that solidify uncritical partisanship and socially superstitious hatreds.

~TAROT-CARD KNIGHT

"He looked on political freedom as the direct agent to effect the happiness of mankind. Generally serious, he yet was capable of fun, and he had the ease of manner, the contempt for ceremony, and the perfect politeness, which is the hallmark of the young aristocrat. What's more charming than a saint who is at the same time a man of the world? At the Godwins', the girls called Shelley 'Elf-King' or 'the King of Faery;' he was also known as 'Ariel' and 'Oberon.' Sometimes falling into a poetic vision, he forgot that he was expected at a tea party."

SCOTT

Nevertheless, Shelley—still *lawful* heir to grand-Bysshe's estates—avows to alleviate Godwin's financial burdens in exchange for both establishing Shelley's ongoing literary fostering and Godwin's participatory connections with other Romantics and philosophical radicals. Before Godwin will guide Shelley through his collegiate course of histories and philosophy, Godwin issues his condition to

Percy—to cease authoring pamphlets—Godwin warning him, "You are preparing a scene of blood, and when the calamities come, you will have to share the responsibility." Godwin counsels Shelley to first become a scholar before he publishes any more pages—and to *seek* reconciliation with his outraged father. Believing that Shelley has started these ventures, Godwin's aim shifts to raising the loans for their mutually beneficial futures.

Boldly, Shelley informs Godwin, "I always go on until I am stopped and I never am stopped." Like Godwin, Shelley advocates the ideology of *Necessity*, the idea of the "unseen power" surrounding as an atmosphere "in which some motionless lyre is suspended, which visits with its breath our silent chords, at will," an "untamable wildness and inaccessible solemnity"—the imageless force of ultimacy.

Godwin theorizes that "if Alexander the Great had not swum in the Cydnus River, and if Shakespeare's mother had fallen from a ladder during her pregnancy—then the whole subsequent history of the world would be different." Godwin compels Shelley to believe that "to an uncorrupted mind, truth will reveal herself—proposition by proposition."

~ARCHETYPAL TRANSCENDENTALISTS

"One easily projects pain from their parents into foreign modes of disbelief. Many of the best of our aging British minds are shifting to pantheism."

SCOTT

As Necessitarians, Shelley and Godwin advocate that existing disparities are entirely the result of needless social arrangements, advocating the tireless aspiration of human improvement as a determinism of historical inevitability. For Godwin and Shelley, there are no natural grounds for social classes—all people having a common nature and sharing a great substantial equality.

While the rich are getting richer, the ardor of these seasons in hotels deteriorates. Without house or security, Harriett is discontent with their roving marriage. As Shelley's marooning artifice is piteously failing, Harriett becomes pregnant. Aware that his distancing authorship is growing into a dissociative phantom, Percy agrees to settle outside Windsor Forest in their last home for a more familial, leisurely year. While studying under Godwin in London, Shelley considers this to be the happiest months of his life. Centralizing his writings, Shelley coalesces his confused experiments into a magical lyrical framework.

"He was definite in his object. He thought it was time for society to come to particulars—to know what they would have." In perpetual, mindful motion, Shelley begins to see his work as Necessity's vessel—to deliver political potency via soldiered poetry. Now considering Bonaparte to be a tyrant betraying the beauty of the revolution, Shelley pens his warning that "one able and amiable benefactor of mankind might *convert* and be its bane with the worst purposes of chance-given powers of command." Percy will convert the prose of his heroes into inspired verse.

Positioning between the forbearance of quietism and afar from *taking arms*, Percy completes his polemical view of poetical speeches. Twenty years old in London, Shelley prints and distributes anonymous copies of *Queen Mab*—his revolutionary, visionary attack on the powers that feed on gold and blood, the "priestcraft" idolatries of *the religiosi* and the "kingcraft" shams of tyranny—considered by many contemporaries to be the best activist poem from their age of turbulence, earning Shelley both countercultural prestige and lasting infamy.

Mab is the queen of fairies who births dreams to deliver to people their hopeful desires as they sleep. Percy addresses *Mab* to enthusiasts "yet unvitiated by the contagion of the world" to have her vision path to utopia planted in their breaths, tears, tortures, and joys of her dreams, declaring sleep as its own world and wide realm of wild reality, asserting that life is twofold—that *sleep* is the misnamed boundary between death and existence.

Rather than delivering his previous political disseminations via paper boats and hot-air balloons, Shelley's queen of the fairies—and the spirit of her disciple—travel through the world of dreams on her charmed chariot, harvesting their strawberry scenes of small societies without rule, war, religion, or meat. Being too ardently against each existing establishment known in English—and under threatening pains of severe prosecution by the Vice Society for aggressive propaganda—Shelley's *Queen Mab* is not published, remaining anonymous.

To avoid risk in being prosecuted for religious and seditious libels, Shelley addresses his poetics to Queen Harriett. "Harriett! Let death all *mortal* ties dissolve / Be, but *ours* shall not be mortal." Shelley's task is to institute the power of reasoning to attempt to ensure that the near future will not repeat the ignorant chariots of the tragic past. "The vermilion / And green and azure plumes of Iris"—his Queen of Spells casts her utopian, fairytale rainbows from her magic car. "O Thou bright Sun! / And, gleaming lovelier as thy beams decline, / thy million hues to every vapor lendest, / And, over cobweb lawn and grove and stream, / Sheddest the liquid magic of thy light." Glamorizing Godwin's theories into readied courage-porridge for the poor, Shelley poeticizes his fantasy ride in the chariot of the queen of Necessity, showing chains of events that *might be* if "the good and sincere" could burst these manacles of custom that fetter their minds and bodies.

~WE WILL ALL BURN

"Like a spirit from another sphere, it was the cardinal article of his faith that if men were but taught and induced to treat their fellows with love, charity, and equal rights, this earth would realize paradise and make men brothers. In his unworldliness, he met enmity with amity. His sympathy was excited by the misery with which the world was burning—sufferings of the poor and the evils of ignorance. His fervent call on his fellow-creatures was to share alike the blessings of the creation and to serve, in love, each other in the noblest works that life and time permitted."

SCOTT

Appealing to the literary peers of his era, Shelley sends copies of his *Queen Mab* to America and sends a copy to Lord Byron. During this same year, Godwin meets Lord Byron twice, and—out of admiration—Byron assists Godwin with a publisher. Pirated throughout the West, *Mab*—"the daemon of the world"—circulates as the basic text amongst the freethinking, self-taught working class and trade unions—which will later haunt Percy's future paternal ventures for justice. Six months later, Byron's own long poetic work will prove poetry's public potency and will make lasting literary history—selling his astronomical ten-thousand copies in one little aristocratic day.

~GIN AND OLIVE SANDWICHES

"In St. Raphael, the wine was sweet and warm. It clung like syrup to the roof of my mouth and glued the world together against the pressure of the heat and the dissolution of the sea.

'How's your exhibition?' they said. 'We've seen the

reproductions.'

'We love those last pictures,' they said. 'Nobody has ever handled the ballet with any vitality since—'

'I thought *that* rhythm—being a purely physical exercise of the eyeball—that the waltz picture would actually give you, by leading the eye in pictorial choreography, the same sensation as following the measure with your feet.'

'Oh,' said the women, 'what a wonderful idea!' 'Oh,' wailed the guests; 'the world is terrible and tragic, and we can't escape what we want.'

'Neither can we—that's why there's a chip off the globe teetering on our shoulders.'

'May I ask what it is?' they said.

'Oh, the secret life of man and woman—dreaming how much better we would be than we are if we were somebody else or even ourselves, and feeling that our estate has been unexploited to its fullest.'

'When I revert to the allegorical school, my Christ will sneer at the silly people, who do not give a rap about his sad predicament, and you will see in his face that he would like a bite of their sandwiches if somebody would just loosen up his nails for a minute—'

'We shall all see it.'

'And the Roman soldiers in the foreground will also be wanting a bite of sandwich, but they will be too jacked up by the dignity of their position to ask for it.'"

SCOTT

Shelley dedicates the inspiration of his celebrated utopian work to his Harriett. "Though garlanded by me, / Thine are these early wilding flowers. / Press into thy breast this pledge of love, / And know, though time may change, and years may roll, / Each flowret gathered in my heart, / It consecrates to thine, / Whose eyes I have gazed fondly on / —And loved mankind the more— / And whose is the love, that gleaming through the world, / Wards off the poisonous arrow of its scorn."

This summer—naming his first child after his dream heroine from *Queen Mab*—Shelley's fair-haired daughter, Ianthe, is born. Writing her a tender sonnet, he vaunts that Ianthe is the very image of Harriett's loveliness. Percy prophecies that the dark blue eyes of his daughter—spirit of light, life, and rapture smiling—will again, amid ruin, ever reawaken, giving joy unto the faithful bosom of the Shelley heritage.

"The tear for fading beauty check, / For passing glory cease to sigh; / One form shall rise above the wreck, / One name, Ianthe, shall not die." In his warmth and fondness toward Ianthe, Shelley sings his own song lyrics of nonsense, which is what pleased her the most and lulled her when she was fretful. "I love thee—*Baby!*—for thine sweet sake."

~A NEW IDEA

"Thus 'Ovid' and Miss Westbrook clasped hands over

the cradle. The idea of bringing up a new being that he might save from prejudices was delightful to him."

~DADDY DAD DADS

"'The hotelman called Daddy a Prince! And to think, Mummy—that would make *me* a Princess. Imagine them thinking anything so silly. If I were a Princess, I should always have my own way. I am making myself as spoiled as I can.

The shadows seemed to move. Only babies were frightened of shadows or of things moving at night. I have not many experiences to relate. There couldn't be anything hiding in the shadows. They just appeared to move that way. Was that the door opening?' 'O—o—oh,' she shrieked in terror.

'Sh—sh—sh,' her father assured her, holding out the promise of warmth and comfort to his daughter. 'Did I frighten you?'

'No. It was the shadows. I'm sometimes silly when I am all by myself.'

'I understand. Grown people are too, very often.'

'Daddy, she said, her only piece of advice that she had to give me was this: "Don't be a backseat driver about life."'

'Did you understand?'

'Oh, *no*,' sighed his daughter—gratefully and complacently.'"

(14.) *primroses*

~HONEY-DO LIST

While you're making a real go at it like a thinking crow on a country morning, pecking in every crevice for a jewel—raffling through the sock drawers to make a F. Scott-nest of every little stowaway of my dear diary's seedy darlings—could you *smooth* the dints and kinks out of my stockings before you scutter off from your co-conspirator's armoire?

~FABLES ARE FOR LOVERS

"You have led me to discover that I write worse than I thought I did. There is no stopping short. I must improve, or be dissatisfied with myself. As you like a moral in your heart, let me add one. As I was walking with Fanny this morning, I found a pretty little fable directly in my path. Your moral to review will be 'there is no end to our disappointments when we reckon our chickens too soon.'

In a grove near London, there was a poor Sycamore growing up amidst a cluster of Evergreens. Every time the wind beat through her slender branches, she envied the foliage of her neighbors that sheltered them from each cutting blast. The only comfort this poor, trembling shrub could find in her mind (as *mind* is proved to be only *thought*, let it be taken for granted that she had a mind—if not a soul) was to say, 'well, spring will come soon, and I too shall have leaves.' But so impatient was this silly plant that the sun could not glisten on the snow without her asking of her more experienced neighbors if 'this' was not 'spring.' At length, the snow began to melt away, the snowdrops appeared, and the crocus did not lag long behind. The hepaticas next ventured forth, and the mezereon began to bloom.

The sun was warm—balsamic as May's own beams. 'Now,' said the Sycamore, her sap mounting as she spoke, 'I am sure *this* is spring.' 'Wait only for such another day,' said a fading Laurel, and a weather-beaten Pine *nodded* to enforce the remonstrance. The Sycamore was not headstrong and promised to wait at least for the morrow—before she burst her rind.

What a tomorrow came! The sun darted forth with redoubled ardor, the winds were hushed, and a gentle breeze fluttered the trees. It was the sweet southern gale—which Willy Shakespeare felt—who arrived to rouse the violets whilst every genial zephyr gave birth to a primrose. The Sycamore no longer regarded admonition. She *felt* that it was spring, and her buds—fostered by the kindest beams—immediately came forth to revel in existence.

Alas, poor Sycamore! That morrow, a hoar frost covered the trees and shriveled up her unfolding leaves, changing in a moment the color of the living green. A brown, melancholy hue succeeded, and the Sycamore drooped, abashed. A taunting neighbor whispered, bidding her in future to distinguish February from April. Whether the buds recovered and expanded—when the spring actually arrived—this *fable* sayeth not."

— Wollstonecraft to Godwin

~WELL FLAVORED FRUIT

"I have got hold of a book now that makes me stop to take a breath and think—Shelley's *Queen Mab*. I got the volume with a lot of new books in English, which I took in exchange for old French ones. Not knowing the names of these authors, I might not have looked into them—had not a pampered, prying priest smelt this one in my lumber-room. After a brief glance at 'the notes,' the priest exploded in wrath, shouting out, 'infidel, Jacobian, leveller! Nothing can stop this spread of blasphemy but raising the stake-and-faggots. The world is retrograding into a cursed heathenism and universal anarchy!'

However, to my taste, the fruit is crude, but it is well flavored. Though it requires a strong stomach to digest it, the writer is an enthusiast and has the true spirit of a poet. He aims at regenerating—not like Byron, *levelling* mankind. They say he is but a boy and that this is his first offering. If that be true, we shall hear of him again."

(15.) *love that carves*

SCOTT

Their young marriage has sojourned Scotland, Ireland, and Wales. After they revisit the lakes where they had married, Percy enters adulthood and his hopes commence to plummet. In Windsor—contentedly settled from rambling and happy as a mother—Harriett's intellectual pursuits dwindle, refusing to continue as her Bysshe's philosophical neophyte. Anxious dissatisfactions arise as Harriett pressures reconciliation with Shelley's past, stressing him for the *resources* of his forsaken lineage.

Though his father demands Percy's social renunciation of his follies by which he has forfeited his proper family, Shelley counters, without compromise, that in this—his *trial* of intellectual uprightness—he will not disavow what is *true* and will not degrade himself as a miserable slave of publicity. Shelley considers his father's ultimatums as infamous and empty concessions that will foster hollow duties—duties that his brilliant daughter will not inherit. As Mister Shelley gloats on his son's poverty, Percy responds, "Depend on it—no artifice of my father's shall seduce me to take a life interest in the estate."

Percy becomes frustrated with the machinations of Harriett's scheming family—the Westbrooks—

and Harriett becomes frustrated with Shelley's too frequent group of effete, armchair musing radicals. "From the dismaying solitude of myself, I have escaped into all that philosophy and friendship combine"—his menagerie of an outcast aristocrat, an eminent tinker, and some sentimental butchers and medical students *retailing* their philosophies. Indeed, each spouse ceases to stimulate the other. Through Percy's sentimental libertarian friends, Harriett begins to loathe Godwin and will soon slander him as a wicked enchanter. Their restless marriage soon becomes grim. Although in quiet fray, Shelley initially resigns to "duty's hard control" that will cast him "again into the boundless ocean of abhorred society," Percy distills his educational experiment to cultivate Harriett to be a gross and despicable *superstition*.

~SENSIBILITY'S SENSE

"But Harriett's mind was his very own handiwork. He had formed it, trained it, cultivated it. He was accustomed to think of it as his echo. On suddenly discovering that this other-self had *detached* itself from him—and could sometimes even make fun of what he said—he was surprised and profoundly hurt."

SCOTT

Since debtor's prison is Godwin's surreal fear, it becomes essential to leverage Shelley for his release from financial bondage. To satisfy the underwriting of his lenders to become Godwin's benefactor,

Shelley agrees to obtain a binding marriage license. As Godwin is introducing Percy into his own radical London set, this ceremonial second marriage will appease Harriett's family, having her legitimized as the legal recipient of Shelley's reluctant inheritance. Feeling victimized wherever he is, Shelley disenchantingly boasts to his new audience that "love acts upon the human heart precisely as a nutmeg grater acts upon a nutmeg." Yet, during their *last* season together—as Harriett, "his beauteous half," and Percy remarry through the Church of England— Harriett feels the fluttering within her from their second child.

Her Bysshe alone knew the blessings of her loving look and gentle words, but also her cold command— that he must live in her sunshine or be doomed to fall beneath her scorn. Shelley thirsts for pity, and Harriett's attempts to mend her Bysshe with *hate* will be fatal. Of his growing "rash and heartless union with Harriett," Shelley writes, "Bid the remorseless feeling flee; / 'Tis malice, 'tis revenge, 'tis pride, / 'Tis anything but thee; / Oh, deign a nobler pride to prove, / And pity if thou canst not love."

The more he writes, the more he despairs—imputing his "poetical temperament" in *unfitting* him from marriage, considering Harriett's inabilities to feel poetry and to comprehend philosophy to be the incurable dissensions that are disuniting them. "Chain one who lives and breathes this boundless air, / To the corruption of a closed grave?"

"Alas! That love should be a blight and snare / To those who seek all sympathies in one; / Such one I sought in vain—then black despair, / The shadow of a starless night, was thrown / over the world in which I moved alone." "Love," Shelley accuses, "how *it* sells poor bliss / For proud despair! / But these, though soon they fall, / Survive their joy, and all / Which *ours* we call."

With chilled affections, pregnant Harriett tires of accommodating Shelley's eccentricities and maneuvers to return with infant Ianthe to her parents. Shelley laments his lapsed state: "Duty and dereliction guide thee back to solitude"—"Away, away! to thy sad and silent home; / Pour bitter tears on its desolated hearth; / Watch the dim shades as like ghosts they go and come, / And complicate strange webs of melancholy mirth."

Percy finds consolation in Virgilian nights, visiting the breakers of vows living on Dante's moon. Encouraging himself to gravitate from his own *Purgatorio*, he writes, "With fortitude, I must feel like a brother, a father, and a husband, but I must still act a man—and growl and scratch—rather than disgrace myself by effeminate lamentation."

~GHOST STORY

"'I will not attempt to describe the sleep of glory and bliss which bathed my soul in paradise during the remaining hours of that memorable night. Words would be faint and shallow types of my enjoyment, or of the gladness that possessed my bosom when I woke. I trod air. My thoughts were in heaven. Earth appeared heaven, and my inheritance upon it was to be one trance of delight.' 'This it is to be cured of love,' I thought. 'I will see her this day, and she will find her lover cold and heedless—too happy to be disdainful—and yet how utterly indifferent to her!'

'But, *how*, revered master, can a cure for love restore you to life?'"

SCOTT

Shelley blames his misfortune on the cruel *custom* of women being less educated than men. Justifying himself, Shelley declares to develop a system that synthesizes Wollstonecraft with *Mab's* Godwin and Paine. Although Shelley *does* consider his prized Harriett to be striking, capable, and kind, Percy pines for his ideal, feminine, *intellectual* beauty—for the marriage of his *mind's* own love. Feeling sunk into a premature state of exhaustion, Percy severs their faltering communion, leaving to live a life of separate maintenance.

In the conflictual poignancy of remorse, Shelley's severe mental struggle in this severance unbalances his reasoning. In this breach, Percy begins his pose as a widower in his scattered social circles. Wandering and watching a swan rise from a shore, Shelley writes, "Thou hast a home, / Beautiful bird! Thou voyagest to thine home! / Where thy sweet mate will twine her downy neck / with thine and welcome thy return with eyes / Bright in the luster of their own fond joy."

Without Shelley's unswerving influence and sensitivities, the gossip of their separation is readily condemned as a dereliction of duty, the ceaseless chatter from a country in which the custom of marriage cannot be dissolved—a murmuring country of whispers where cases of confirmed insanity still mark difficult grounds for annulment. Slapdash, Shelley feels as if he is subsisting through an itinerant, lucid dream from which he knows will fade into the cold, sober light of a nearby morning.

In his "little debt-factory of a bookshop," Godwin is quickly discovering that Shelley-the-adult lives to be given what he wants—when he wants it—irrespective of consequences. Percy is London's archetypal Peter Pan, imagining himself the leader of the lost boys and their fairies. Though, to sustain his family's livelihood, Godwin momentarily endures Shelley's reckless ideologies of endless gratifications. Still and all, Percy's mind prides in his new doubled pledge that his next educational experiment will not fail. In utter conscious disregard of social obligations and in irresponsibly meddling with wild, emotional forces, Shelley's "impish scandals" will harm every dear member of Godwin's household.

"Like the insect that sports in a transient sunbeam," Percy inaugurates this pivotal season with living at a nearby inn for a month in order to dine many nights in the warmth of the amiable Godwins. *Thus*, as from a shadow into its source of light, Percy becomes hypnotized by the daughter of his political idol and academic mentor. Shelley's mind suffers "like a little kingdom in the nature of an insurrection" in the violence of sudden, irresistible convulsions, declaring Mary's fierce, wild, and passionate intellect, opening himself into the second bloom of his youth through his *sordid* encouraging of Godwin's daughter.

He is convicted, surrendering himself to Mary, vowing to be his own executioner in seeking any course of retreat. He asserts to have been misled, long wounded, and deserted by his first love, Shelley wooing his new girl with enchantments of learning the Italian poets together—dreaming eventualities of living all over Italy as endless lovers.

~SAINT LAMBKIN

If a virgin brings two unshorn lambs to the altar of the Basilica of St. Agnes in Rome, the nuns will weave their wool into cloth, and the virgin– rewarded—will dream of her future husband on the darkling evening preceding the Day of St. Agnes.

SCOTT

Altering his original dedication and transferring his intellectual affection, Percy inscribes his private hardcover copy of *Queen Mab* to Mary. Writing out a poem of affirmation on its rear flyleaf, Mary pledges her life to Shelley through his sacred gift. As he stalls in London for the final sorting of Godwin's loan—delaying his departure to Harriett—Mary makes her determined play, honestly declaring herself to Shelley. While Godwin is reconciling with Harriett, Percy dedicates to Mary his new edition of the work that caused his dismissal from Oxford, transferring to Mary his previous accomplishments as an accepted proposal for their nuptial engagement.

In this critical love triangle, Harriett—in bitter dejection—recognizes the ironically successful method of Mary and Percy now threatening their own suicides if deprived of each other—just as she had sealed Shelley for herself through this *device* three years ago at Mary's same age "dying in love for him." Harriett hadn't meant it, and neither does Mary. For Percy, it is either a sure suicide or a sure elopement—our mercurial, passionate Shelley advocating his *higher* law of the heart, prescribing his philosophy of disinterested love in which the remorseless, unsatisfiable ethos of *Eros* must be the triumphant conqueror of life. Zealously, Percy offers Mary his bottle of laudanum—and himself his small pistol—covenanting their escape into death's sanctified reunion.

Shelley believes Mary to be the double embodiment of both of her idealistic parents—his surety of Mary's promissory excellences. In the cemetery near Godwin's, Percy and Mary had fallen in love in ecstatic meetings at the grave of Wollstonecraft—

awestruck with eager lips and in speechless swoons of joy, awestruck in the solace of all sorrow, whispering their ardent hearts to each other under this arbor of willows. Enthralled, they had lived out their rapturous month of incarnate romance that Mary cherishes as *sublime*, as if knowing that there are only a few things—*love's first glow*—that ever happen to anyone that carve one's heart deep enough to harbor all the multitudes of poisons that must be borne—rooted and committed—in devotion to *another*.

(16.) <u>*a noodle*</u>

DAISY

"That huge place *there*?"

JAY

"I keep it always full of interesting people—night and day—people who do interesting things.

I know—we'll have the 'boarder' play the piano."

EWING

"I'm all out of practice, you see. I'm all out of—"

JAY

"—Don't talk so much, Ewing, old sport. *Play!*"

SCOTT

Play!

"In the meantime . . . in between time . . . oh but honey . . . but in any way, dear, we'll stay as we are . . ."

NICK

They had forgotten me. I went down the marble steps into the rain.

"In the meantime . . . in between time . . ."

SCOTT
"We'll stay as we are." Tap. Tap. Tap. Click.

TOM
"Did you see that?"

SCOTT
demanded Tom.

JORDAN
"See what?"

NICK
He looked at me keenly, realizing that Jordan and I must have known all along.

TOM
"You think I'm pretty dumb, don't you?"

SCOTT
he suggested.

TOM

"Perhaps I am, but I have an—an almost second sight, sometimes, that tells me what to do. I've made a small investigation of this fellow. An Oxford man! Like hell he is! He wears a pink suit."

JORDAN

"Listen, Tom. If you're such a snob, why did you *invite* Gatsby to lunch?"

TOM

"Daisy invited him. She knew *him* before we were married—from God knows where!"

NICK

We were all irritable now with the fading ale—and, aware of it—we drove for a while in silence.

Tolerance has a limit. When I came back from the East last autumn, I felt that I wanted the world to be in a uniform moral attention forever. I wanted no more riotous excursions with privileged glimpses into the human heart.

The *thing* that preyed on my friend—old Gatsby— the foul dust that floated in the wake of his dreams, floated, floated . . . temporarily closed out my interest in abortive sorrows and short-winded elations.

The past has a life of its own. I used to be a marine. The helmet I wore is now packed away in some crate for someone else to find. And yet now, the present—unallied—seems to be a campfire tale, its uncertain atmosphere consumed in morphing *drek*, as if its hopefuls are haunted by a clay man. It wears different *hats* and tries to be different . . . *people*.

The *past*, though, is a tad more solid. It is a single window that can be opened and closed. When we were gnawed at by rats in the muddy dugout trenches, we longed to regain federal holidays and picture shows and spats—and we did. We know our past, but we do not *know* what today is. A *noodle*—people think they know what a brain looks like until they see a brain. Then, they feel that the best thing to do is to get very drunk.

SCOTT

Mr. Scott—dictate! A memo declination—yes—in memorandumry!

~There ought to be some way to drink faster, if we could only discover it.

~Faster and faster till we're back at the beginning.

~We'll learn our lesson.

~Drunk at twenty . . . wrecked—and human—at thirty . . . mellowing, then dead at forty . . . harmonious mathematics.

Signed, —your Dapper Drek

~Postscript—a nightcap and a day drink . . . yes, the test of intelligence is to hold two opposed ideas in the mind at the same time and still retain the ability to function. One should be able to see that things are hopeless and yet be determined to make them otherwise. This is philosophy that wears well when one *sees* the improbable, the implausible, the *impossible* come true. Life is something you dominate if you are any good. Life yields easily to intelligence and effort—or to what proportion can be mustered of both.

~AWFUL SNOB

One of his friends of an earlier day, replying to a question I had asked, told me: 'Yes. I know Scott very well. He is an awful snob.' Another reported that at the present time he was sequestered in a New York apartment with $10,000 sunk in liquor and that he was bent on drinking it before he did anything else. Still another related the story of how, in New York, Fitzgerlad became bored with his guests and called the fire department. When the firemen arrived and asked where the fire was, Scott pounded his stomach and dramatically announced: 'The fire is right here. Inside me.'

SCOTT

Forever dissatisfied, one must hold in balance the sense of the *futility* of effort and the sense of the *necessity* to struggle. If this can be done through the common *ills*—domestic, professional, and personal— then the ego can continue as an arrow shot from spectral nothingness . . . to spectral nothingness . . . with sure force.

Now, to it—*egoists* shot and shot, shooting through the stuff of life—through good parents and their good children, through their shot glasses and fine minds . . . through the hearts of their loves.

(17.) *fire where flowers should be*

~4ᵀᴴ DOWN IN THE 4ᵀᴴ QUARTER

"'What would you that I should do?'

'*I!* —Oh, nothing, but lie down and say your prayers—before you die. But, were I *you*, I know the deed that should be done.'

I drew near him. His supernatural powers made him an oracle in my eyes, yet a strange unearthly thrill quivered through my frame as I said— 'Speak!—teach me—what act do you advise?'

'Revenge thyself, man!—humble thy enemies!—set thy foot on the old man's neck and possess thyself of his daughter!'"

PERCY

Thy accents sweet fell like dew on half dead flowers. Thy dark eyes threw their soft persuasion on my brain, charming away its scorned load of agony, curbing my soul's mute rage from preying upon itself as its own devouring cage. What is excellent and sublime—

MARY

—If liberty is not the name of blind love and equal justice, then—from a white lake into the open gate of death—gather thy repressed blood into thy heart to blot heaven's false blue portrait and sink headlong through aerial golden light—winged sublime as a wild swan athwart the thunder-smoke path of your dawn unmade, making not the memories that make the mind a tomb, if liberty is not the name. What is excellent and sublime—

PERCY

—interests my heart. I ardently desire the acquisition of knowledge and long to enter the world. I believe myself destined for some great enterprise. From my infancy, I was imbued with high hopes and lofty ambition. There is something at work in my soul which I do not understand. I am practically industrious—painstakingly—a workman to execute with perseverance and labor. Besides this, there is a love for the marvelous, a belief in the marvelous, intertwined in all my projects, which hurries me out of the common pathways of men, even to the wild sea and unvisited regions of the heart.

The labors of men of genius, however erroneously directed, scarcely ever fail in ultimately turning to the solid advantage of mankind. The innermost world is to me a secret, which I desire to divine. It is the secrets of heaven within earth that I desire to learn. From the outward substance of things, the inner spirit of our natures and the mysterious soul of man occupies me.

My inquiries are directed to the metaphysical—those undiscovered solitudes of the heart. Paradise can be what beams from a golden heart. What may not be expected in a country of hearts of eternal light?

The sun can be forever visible to the soul, its broad disk just skirting its horizon and diffusing a perpetual splendor. A sailor of the soul, I may there discover this wondrous interior power. I shall satiate my ardent curiosity. These are my enticements and they are sufficient to conquer all fear of ruin or death. I will pioneer a new way, explore our unknowns, and unfold to our world our deepest mystery—ourselves.

In putting to stirring verse the politics of our Godwin, I entrench my pen in holding ever-living tension, holding darkness as I hold light. In the paradox of our tragic titan hero, the Promethean complex of our contemplation, the agent of this tension, pressing between being our *descent* to the awareness of the hard knots of our nature and our *ascent* to the creative civilizing fires of our industrious toils. I also risk all in this overreaching of all our own tyrants, defying them with the impartial reforms that must be inaugurated and invested in our English isles. Mary, I sense in your eyes that you also yearn to make yourself the Fire-Bringer.

I have one want I have never been able to satisfy. I have no true friend of deep intellect, such as you. If I am to glow later in the enthusiasm of success, there will be none to participate in my joy. If I am assailed by disappointment, no one can endeavor to sustain me in dejection. I commit my thoughts to paper, but it is a poor medium for such feelings!

MARY

Young people are very apt to substitute words for

sentiments and clothe mean thoughts in pompous diction. Industry and time are necessary to cure this. Writing *well* is of great consequence in life. It teaches a person to arrange their thoughts and forms the only true basis of rational and elegant conversation. In your passions, I find the same value of my mother's mind as Blake found for her aspirations.

"I went to the Garden of Love, / And saw what I never had seen: / A Chapel was built in the midst, / Where I used to play on the green. / And the gates of this Chapel were shut, / And "Thou shalt not" writ over the door; / So I turn'd to the Garden of Love / That so many sweet flowers bore; / And I saw it was filled with graves, / And tomb-stones where flowers should be: / And Priests in black gowns were walking their rounds, / And binding with briars my joys and desires."

PERCY

As she and he, I envision that it is our own beneficiaries who will make their quotes of us. Till then, I fear—my beloved girl—little happiness remains for us on our present earth of injustice. Yet, all that I may one day enjoy is centered in you. Chase away your idle fears. To you alone do I consecrate my life and my endeavors for contentment. Can man be free if *woman* be a slave? You have stolen into my heart and you've dared to whisper paradisiacal dreams of love and joy, but the apple is already eaten, and the angel's arm is ablaze to drive me from old hopes. Yet, Mary, I would die to make you happy.

MARY

Such life and a bit more life—before death—I shall need no other happiness.

PERCY

Joyous treasure of mine own heroes—now that I find *you*—

—Yet, your eyes search mine to discern some other attachment. No, none on earth. I alone love only you, my Mary, and look forward to our union with delight. Let the day therefore be fixed, and on it, I will consecrate myself, life or death.

MARY

My Shelley, it's as if the springs of existence suddenly give way. How happy and serene all nature can appear—an amphitheater as for us! What a divine day! Am I rescued—this happy moment—in this golden moment? It's as if all the joy of life could be had in a pair of eyes at a single point on a single day.

PERCY

Here breaks in the power that dawns the confidence that the impossible can be repeated. "We look before and after, / And pine for what is not: / Our sincerest laughter / With some pain is fraught; / Our sweetest songs are those that tell of saddest thought. / The amorous birds now pair in every brake, / And build their mossy homes in field and brere; / And the green lizard, and the golden snake, / Like unimprisoned flames, out of their trance awake. / The earth doth like a snake renew / Her winter weeds outworn: / Heaven smiles, and faiths and empires gleam, / Like wrecks of a dissolving dream. / The lamps of Heaven flash with a softer light; / All baser things pant with life's sacred thirst; / Diffuse themselves; and spend in love's delight, / The beauty and the joy of their renewed might."

MARY

Ask him who lives, "what is life?" Ask him who adores, "what is God?" *Lover*, what is love? What is love?

PERCY

It is that powerful attraction toward all that we conceive or fear or hope beyond ourselves when we find within our own thoughts the chasm of an insufficient void and then seek to awaken *in all things* that are a community with what we experience within ourselves. From the instant that we live and move, we thirst after our own likeness—the meeting with *an understanding* capable of clearly estimating the deductions of our own and with *an imagination* which should enter into and seize upon our own subtle and delicate peculiarities which we have delighted to cherish and unfold in secret.

MARY

"Art thou pale for weariness / Of climbing heaven and gazing on the earth, / Wandering companionless / Among the stars that have a different birth— / And ever changing, like a joyless eye / That finds no object worth its constancy?"

In the motion of the very leaves of spring, in the blue air, there is then found a secret correspondence with our heart. As soon as this want or power dies in one, one becomes a living sepulcher. Then, at length, *Time*—itinerant executioner—after our loving, we will know you.

PERCY

"All things that we love and cherish, / Like ourselves must fade and perish; / Such is our rude mortal lot— / Love itself would, did *they* not."

Life, the great miracle, we admire not, because it is so miraculous. What is life? Thoughts and feelings arise, with or without our will, and we employ words to express them. Yet, how vain it is to think that words can penetrate the mystery of our being. We are on that verge where words abandon us, and what wonder if we grow dizzy to look down the dark abyss—of how little we know.

Whatever may be, there is a spirit within man at enmity with nothingness and dissolution, change and extinction. This is the character of all life and being—and wanted more than morning and the manna bread of being, this bread and morning I break here in your beauty and afar and ever after. Launching me enshrined in my Mary-gold mania, I shatter as your jeweler—my Helen and Athena and Hera incarnate all—

MARY

—warmth for tender virtue, gentle muse of your gentle art—life made most marvelous.

Love does save us. My orating *skylark*, teach me half the rapturous gladness you must know, and such harmonious madness—a melodious, melodious flow!—from my lips would I offer the awestruck world to show.

~CURSE PEN AND PAPER

"'Your company infinitely delights me. I love your imagination, your delicate epicureanism, the malicious leer of your eye—in short, everything that constitutes the bewitching tout ensemble of the celebrated *Mary*. Alas, I have no talent—for I have no subject. Shall I write a love letter? May Lucifer fly away with me if I do! No, when I make love, it shall be with the eloquent tones of my voice—with dying accents, with speaking glances, and with all the witching of that irresistible, universal passion. Curse on the mechanical, icy medium of pen and paper. When I make love, it shall be in a storm—as Jupiter made love to Semele and turned her at once to a cinder. Do not these menaces terrify you?'"

– Godwin to Wollstonecraft

(18.) *under the fedoras*

~SUPPOSING PLATONIC

"We are unfashioned creatures but half made up . . ."

SCOTT

He had come so far—the yacht man, combat command, Oxford, Wolfsheim, the racketeering, the mansion, the car, the shirts, the invite to tea. He'd already started the fire that would consume him alive. Opulence, deceit, drive . . . there's a wrong way, a new way, and an old way to wealth.

This new way is for one to desire that one "deserves" to aspire. Though, *while* they're running, dark horses are what liberty is—old sport. Get *arrived* and stay *arrived* . . .

Winning is the old way. His whole life, *Tom* had won. He knew that even when the quantity is the same, the quality could never be. Hence, again, Tom wins.

NICK

Integrity is the wrong way. "*No*, I wouldn't shake his goddamned hand." The case rests in its simplest form—the reports from the next morning—grotesque, circumstantial, eager, and untrue. Can such a thing be reduced *to* and then forgotten *as* "mad man"—mad man?

~DEAD AMERICAN IN AN URN

"Space wondered less at the swift and fair creations of God when he grew weary of vacancy—than *I* at this spirit of an angel of the mortal paradise of a decaying body. So, I think, let the world envy while it admires—as it may."

NICK

It's the Midwest in me—the returning trains of my youth, the street lamps, the bells, the shadows of holly wreaths, and some complacency in them—which perhaps is what has made me subtly unadaptable to Eastern life.

West Egg Village now crouched under a sullen, overhanging sky and lusterless moon. I wanted to leave things in order, not just trust its established indifference. Before I left for Wisconsin, there was an awkward, unpleasant thing to be done.

I saw Jordan Baker and talked over and around what had happened to us together. For a minute, I wondered if I wasn't making a mistake. Then, I quickly thought it all over again—the past has a life of its own—and got up to say goodbye.

JORDAN

"You did throw me over. It was new for me, and I felt a little dizzy for a while. Well, I met another bad driver, didn't I? I mean it was careless of me to make such a guess. I thought you were rather an honest, straightforward person. I thought it was your secret pride."

NICK

"I'm thirty. I'm five years too old to lie to myself and call it honor."

She didn't answer. Angry and half in love with her—and tremendously sorry—I turned away.

With a single dream, he disappeared among the yellowing trees. As the parvenue's optimisms split into Platonic particles, he must've looked up at an unfamiliar sky as he found how raw the sunlight was upon the scarcely created grass of a new world—material without being real, where poor ghosts breathe dreams like air.

~TRAVEL WELL
"To be nailed down into a narrow place; / To see no more sweet sunshine; hear no more / Blithe voice of living thing; muse not again / Upon familiar thoughts, sad, yet thus lost— / How fearful! To be nothing! Or to be in the void world, / The wide, grey, lampless, deep, unpeopled world!"

SCOTT
As logic and bullets and social rules sank, his dream

rose, blossoming undeniable from chlorine and salt dismantling his senses. In his last twilight from *Queen Mab,* they were young and bright in Louisville, and he had escaped being a sell-sword. Time could not frame him—the man who became dream—and he married her right there on that lawn before he would ever have to buy a pool that blood and littered-leaves would have to fill—before his words would have to dissolve in a claw-footed tub of tears and first truths. She was eighteen again and again, and all the fisherman and soldiers and bachelors envied him. She was deathless his, and it would always stop raining. Nick would always visit for tea and ride their rivers with them on their hydroplane that was always new. Time would never find them.

~AT THE BOTTOM OF IT ALL

"And now his limbs were lean; his scattered hair, / Wilted by the autumn of strange suffering, / Sung dirges in the wind; his listless hand / Hung like dead bone within its withered skin; / Life and the luster that consumed it, shone / As in a furnace burning secretly / From his dark eyes alone."

NICK

I called up Daisy half an hour after we found him—called her instinctively and without hesitation—but she and Tom had gone away early that afternoon and taken baggage with them.

Jay Gatsby had broken up like glass against Tom's

hard malice, and the long secret extravaganza was played out. One afternoon in late October, I saw Tom Buchanan. He was walking along Fifth Avenue in his alert, aggressive way. He saw me. Smiling, he made at me—holding out his hand.

TOM

"What's the matter, *Nick*? Do you object to shaking hands with me?"

NICK

"Yes. You know what I think of you."

TOM

"You're crazy, Nick—"

SCOTT

—he said quickly.

TOM

"—Crazy as hell. I don't know what's the matter with you."

NICK

"Tom, what did you say to him that afternoon?"

TOM

"I told him the truth . . . crazy enough to kill me if I hadn't told him . . . his hand was on a revolver in his pocket every minute he was in the house—"

SCOTT

—he broke off defiantly.

TOM

"What if I did? That fellow had it coming to him. Arrogant, smiling bastard, he threw dust in your eyes—just like he did in Daisy's—but he *was* a tough one.

NICK

There was nothing I could say, except the one unutterable fact that it wasn't true. I couldn't forgive him or like him, but I saw that what he had done was—to him—entirely justified. It was all very careless and confused. They were careless people, Tom and Daisy. They smashed up things and creatures and then retreated back into their money—or their vast carelessness, or whatever it was that kept them together—and let other people clean up the mess they had made.

On the white steps, an obscene word—scrawled by some boy with a piece of brick—stood out clearly in the moonlight, and I erased it, drawing my shoe raspingly along the stone. One night, I did hear a car and saw its lights stop at his front steps, but I didn't investigate. Probably, it was some final guest who had been away at the ends of the earth and didn't know that the party was over—

SCOTT

—that the *Great* Gatsby was once again Gatsby, *just Gatz*—a "Mr. Nobody from Nowhere."

NICK

The lawn and drive had been crowded with the faces of those who guessed at his corruption—and he had stood on those steps, concealing his incorruptible dream. His dream must have seemed so close that he could hardly fail to grasp it.

He did not know that it was already behind him ... greatest of all human dreams for a transitory enchanted moment ... something commensurate to his capacity for wonder ... beating—the future receding into the distance—against the current, borne back ceaselessly into the past.

~DARKNESS AND DISTANCE

"It's not the same town without him—so *say* many of us. A scandal is only a scandal, but he could turn a Sunday School picnic into a public holiday. Yet, we were all young then—and as I look around at my white-haired compatriots, I wonder that the old days have gone. Ah, that was aways back—before the Arms Conferences, when Fatty Arbuckle was still respectable, and when bobbed hair was considered daring. *Sic transit.* We are old men. I realize at last that our work is behind us, and our day is done."

(19.) *the men who became dream*

~LOVE LETTER
"Which is best, to pass one's life in the natural vegetative state of the potters we saw in the morning turning a wheel or treading a lay, *or* to pass it like these players—in an occupation to which skill and approbation can alone give a zest—without a rational hope of ever rising to either?"

—Godwin to Wollstonecraft

SCOTT
Shelley survives his overdosing after his deranged suicide pact with Mary fails. Told of Percy's shocking development with Mary, Godwin is appalled—but temporizing, he expostulates with Shelley to return to virtue. Godwin pleads with him to give up this licentious love that is disturbing all their households in an inconvenient phase of madness. The loan is at hand, but its basis—Percy being an heir, adult, and married—must be preserved against betrayal, securing Godwin's bookshop through the Shelley baronetcy. To maintain the integrity of acquiring Shelley's obligation, Godwin writes a pair of letters to attempt to have Mary placed abroad—away from Percy.

Godwin writes to Shelley "I cannot believe that you would sacrifice your own character and usefulness or the happiness of your meritorious wife to fierce impulses—or the spotless fame of my child." Godwin writes reassuring letters to both Harriett and Percy, encouraging their ties of affection as spouses and as parents. While pregnant, Harriett shelters herself in the idea that Godwin's Mary is a passing infatuation. Harriett writes to her, requesting Mary to have Percy calm himself and subdue his transient desire.

~TUT TUT TUT

"Brain and heart consider the situation and resolve that it would be a right and manly thing to stand by this girl-wife and her child and see that they were honorably dealt with, and cherished and protected and loved by the man that had promised these things—and so be made happy and kept so."

SCOTT

After Mary had flung her young glory at the man who embodies her mother's passions and the spirit of how she wishes life to be, Percy is surprised that Mary had felt like a prisoner to Godwin's drastic educational plans. Mary is ready, and Shelley will propose his scheme. Consequently possessing their parabolic pearl—*each other*—Shelley and Mary will commence their renegade life together. They will rapidly elope for forty days on the continent. Shelley will journal, "She was in my arms, we were on our road to Dover." They will advance from England's white cliffs and will glory in the rise of the sun over France. On the day that Mary had returned to Godwin's from

Scotland, the Allied forces—without the redcoats—had dethroned Bonaparte, announcing civil freedom in France. This temporary peace from the entry of the Coalition soldiers into Paris will open the desirous possibilities for their spontaneous escape.

~CUSTOM CONCERN

"But custom maketh blind and obdurate / The loftiest hearts; he had beheld the woe / In which mankind was bound, but deemed that fate, / which made them abject, would preserve them so."

SCOTT

Shelley will witness that the revolutionary Parisian dreams have become "a bleak poverty" and he will reject Napoleon's system that has exiled *virtue* into the dusts of France. As they will pass through destroyed villages, Percy will exclaim "Liberty must at length prevail!" Shelley and Mary will heat their imaginations, preparing expectations for captured Paris and the Swiss playground from their favorite works of Mary's parents, visiting where Fanny and Wollstonecraft had lived before Godwin's.

Even so, Mary will begin to weigh her future costs. Although reciting verses of Wordsworth will arm them for the approaching grandeur of the Swiss Alps, Mary will be plagued by what she will be trading for her short felicity in Paris—for a few happy moments amidst Notre Dame and orange trees, amidst the boulevards and mesmerizing horizon of another world.

Their recollections of this trip will sustain them through the stiff social forces and many complex seasons of their youthful union. Shelley will write, "Fountains of crystalline water play perpetually among the aromatic flowers and mingle a new freshness. The pine boughs are instruments that wake the new music of delightful melodies. The very winds breathe health and renovation—and the joyousness of youthful courage." Mary will laugh to herself—treasuring her first printed piece—when another traveler will try to provoke Percy. "Oi, you're a *stick* of a John Bull—with all that beef about—an odd Bull that don't know how to eat *bull*." As they will deplete their purse, they will pass through the pleasing Swiss lands of milk chocolates, timepieces, cheeses, and Godwin's best anecdotes.

~PHILOSOPHER IN THE LOVER

"A worm in the bud—at fifteen, I resolved never to marry for interested motives, *or* to endure a life of dependance. But be assured, when I find a man that has anything in him, I shall let my everyday dish alone. I want to see you—and *soon*—I have a world to say to you. When I am happy myself, I am made up of milk and honey. Fanny—my little Lambkin—was so importunate with her 'go this way Mama, me wants to see Man' this morning. You tell me, William, that you *augur* nothing good, but Fanny wishes you a good morning. Now I have an inclination to be saucy and tell you that I kissed Fanny because she put me in mind of you this morning."

—"What say you, may I come to your house about eight, *to philosophize*? Let me assure you that you are not only in my heart, but my veins, this morning. I turn from you half abashed—yet you haunt me, and some look, word, or touch thrills through my whole frame. When the heart and reason accord, there is no flying from voluptuous sensations. Can a philosopher do more? I am sunk in the quicksand of Love. I would fain live in your heart and in the employ of your imagination. Am I not very reasonable? I do not like to lose my Philosopher even in the Lover. I want to have such a firm throne in your heart that even your imagination shall not be able to hurl me from it. I had felt sublime tranquility in your arms. Hush! Let not the light see. These confessions should only be uttered when the curtains are up and all the world shut out. I shall be wise and demure, *cher ami*."

—Wollstonecraft to Godwin

SCOTT

Departing on the Rhine, Mary will console herself by being primed with an authorial angle about the anxious terrors of returning home—about a boy born in a war hospital who grows to be a Faustian alchemist from a folktale. Upon the slander and scandal of their elopement, Mary and Percy will be ostracized from nearly all their relations throughout the British Isles.

Returning—pressured and harassed—Percy will continue his divided, uncivil elopement with the body and mind of his Mary Godwin. "Our natures are now so intimately united that I feel as if I were an egoist whilst I describe her excellencies that contrast these complications of self-projection that dominate my mind with delusive subjectivities. The very essence of love is liberty. Love is consequent upon the perception of loveliness, which withers under *constraint* and fades under *obedience*."

Life will become difficult for Harriett in her parents' home—and detrimental rounds of "The Blame Game" will cause lasting damage. Harriett and Shelley will both be hurt, and they will both invent the same sort of wounding excuse. Godwin will be imputed. Shelley will feel that he was extorted. "She only married me for the money and title. Now that she sees *her* hopes upset, she punishes me for her mistake. A heart of ice . . . a lump of ice!" Harriett will write, "Money is vying with Love," and her accusation against Godwin will be that "now *money*—and not philosophy—is the grand stream of his actions."

Shelley will write Harriett, "I was an idiot to expect greatness or generosity from you—that when an occasion of the sublimest virtue occurred, you would not fail to play a part of mean and despicable selfishness." Feeling that Godwin's financial enslavement to Shelley is the main source of her disaster, Harriett will plot to ruin Godwin, claiming he has debased his noble soul. Harriett will write her apostasy of his *Political Justice*. "The very great evil that book has done is not to be told. The false doctrines therein contained have poisoned many a young and virtuous mind."

Although Shelley will inquire about Ianthe, harried, Percy will become less vexed by the detestable implications of his blame and will repudiate all feelings of personal guilt and social condemnation—*the past has a life*—writing conclusive letters to Harriett, terminating any lingering emotional intimacy. "In the confidence of my undesigning truth, I am now united to another. In the treachery of your cavil of unworthy bickering and superstitious weakness, you are no longer my wife. The conviction that wedlock is indissoluble is studiously hostile to human happiness—inaugurating the acrimony and all the little tyrannies of its housebreaking in its *assurance* that either victim is without appeal. Love can never be wrong, but the hostility of Marriage makes us hostages of its disillusionments. It depraves and degrades the human mind and fills all human life with hydra-headed woes."

Harriett will refuse to meet with Percy. Shelley will continue his letters. "I have a certain price. It is confidence and truth. Are *you* above the world, and to what extent? My attachment to Mary neither could nor ought to have been overcome. Our spirits are united. We met with passion. She has resigned all for me. It would be *just* to consider with kindness that woman whom my judgment and my heart have selected as the noblest and the most excellent of human beings."

Harriett will bring her blistering complaint to her husband's father. "This is a vampire. Mary was determined to seduce him, and Godwin's *Political Justice* poisoned his virtue with its evil doctrines. Our Bysshe has become profligate and sensual. Here *I* wait, awaiting another infant into this woeful world. The man I loved is vanished. Everything goes against me. I really see no termination to my sorrows." Harriett will incriminate Godwin with the vulgar slander that Godwin had sold—had pandered—his Mary to Percy. Shelley will write his response. "If it be indeed true that your perversity has reached this excess . . . wanton cruelty . . . it is obvious that I can no longer consider you but as an enemy. How happy I should have been if I had done you injustice." Latterly, after securing his pledged loan, Shelley will withhold half of it from Godwin to ensure his own ulterior divisionary scheme.

Godwin will be lambasted by previous literary rivals, shaming his radical principles of *justice* with their new caveat. The rampant libel will be that this disgraced philosopher has sold his daughter to Shelley to avoid debtor's prison. To protect his remaining family members, Godwin will comply with the cruel ritual of social shunning. Although Mary has possessed an excessive attachment to her father, the Godwins will reject and disown our new scandalous London couple.

Godwin will remain adamant in spurning Mary for more than two years. Mary will recollect, "Until Shelley, I may justly say that Godwin was my God." Mary will write to Shelley, "My father is plagued out of his life. Hug your own Mary to your heart. Perhaps she will one day have a father. Till then, be everything to me, love. Press me to you." Of his Mary, Shelley will write, "She feels as if our love would alone suffice to resist the invasions of calamity. She seems insensible to all future evil."

~"THINK I'M IN LOVE"

"What was the use of keeping it? There wasn't a way to hold onto the summer—no hopes to be salvaged from a cheap French photograph. Whatever it was that she wanted from him, he took it with him to squander. You took what you wanted from life—if you could get it—and you did without the rest."

SCOTT

Once Godwin is informed that Shelley has retracted his financial obligations, Mary's father will feel bitterly betrayed, intensifying Shelley's own mendacity toward his philosophical mentor. Amidst their first autumn, Mary will write to her Shelley, "why will not Godwin follow the obvious bent of his affections and be reconciled to us? Papa might be happy if he chose." All too soon, the loving veil will be removed that had shielded Mary from the social pressures of debtor's prison and the acrimony of the press. Before our heroine will secretly depart to the continent for her volitional elopement, our daring, dreaming Mary and her darling father will dispute the outlandish request of their roving dinner-visitant.

(20.) *Caedmon*

~DOWRY BEQUEATHED

"He had said she was as pretty as two little birds, but what had he said to her when she was a little girl? Once, he had said, 'If you want to choose, you must be a goddess.' That was when she had wanted her own way about things. It wasn't easy to be a goddess away from Olympus. There was nothing in the mackerel sky but cold spring rain, and she ran from the first drops of the bitter drizzle. 'We are certainly accountable,' she thought, 'for all the things manifest in others that we secretly share. My father has bequeathed me many doubts.' Panting, she went down the already slippery, red clay road."

MARY

"All that we wish to stay, / Tempts and then flies. / Worlds on worlds are rolling ever / From creation to decay, / Like the bubbles on a river / Sparkling, bursting, borne away."

GODWIN

No father could claim the gratitude of his child so completely as I should deserve yours. You seek for knowledge and wisdom—as I once sought with such passion—and I ardently hope that the gratification of your wishes may not be a serpent to sting you, or worse. I implore you, Mary—thwart yourself. Cease. Turn the heavy sails of your life to a mindful purpose.

Continue *us*. Is there no other side? Do only his persuasions hold any sway? Enjoin wisdom to balance your new hopes against your swelling obstacles.

MARY

Papa, Father, he is a being formed in the very poetry of nature. His wild and enthusiastic imagination is chastened by the sensibility of his heart. His soul overflows with ardent affections, and his friendship is of that devoted and wondrous nature that the world-minded teach us to look for only in the imagination. Good Father, *Papa*, this Shelley sees me and he praises. My poet writes to me.

"There seems set a crown of distinction on her head—her gestures, sublimating. Her brow is clear and ample, her hazel eyes cloudless, and her lips and the molding of her face are so expressive of sensibility and sweetness that none can behold her without looking on her as of a distinct species, a being heaven-sent—mine to protect, love, and cherish—bearing a celestial stamp in all her features for all my praises. Her saintly soul will shine like a shrine-dedicated lamp in our peaceful home. Her sympathy will be ours.

Her smile, her soft voice, and the sweet glance of her celestial eyes will ever shimmer to bless and animate us. She will be the living spirit of *love* to soften and attract, who—when I might become sullen, rough through the ardor of my nature—will be there to subdue me to a semblance of her own gentleness, a gentleness as never tinged by dogmatism. She dispels all my illusions. I do not think that there is an excellence at which human nature can arrive that she does not indisputably possess. Her very motions and tones of voice—how persuasive—I do remember well the fresh May hour which burst my spirit's sleep. The sublime and rapturous moment cannot be painted to mortal imaginations. Endless kisses steal my breath, and no life can equal such a death."

Papa, he is forever busy, and the only check to his enjoyments is my sorrowful and dejected mind. I try to conceal this as much as possible, that I might not debar him from the pleasures he lives before my eyes and for my heart. But, Papa, in only such a short time, I know my Percy possesses a quality that elevates him so immeasurably above any other person I have ever known—his brilliant, intense eyes, the pride of his high chin and knowing grin, his urgent, passionate logic and lyricism. Shelley's mind!

He has such an intuitive discernment, a quick and never-failing power of judgment. He penetrates into the causes of things. There is an unequalled clearness and precision about him. Papa, he has that faculty of expression and a voice whose varied intonations are soul-subduing music! His feelings are profound. He possesses a coolness of judgment fitted for illustrious achievement. *He* is a strange and harrowing story of a frightful storm that embraced such a gallant vessel on its course and wrecked it—*thus*—at the steps of our own home.

GODWIN

Thus, strangely are our souls constructed, and by such slight ligaments are we bound to prosperity or ruin. Although you also have as much genius, Mary, we are the prey of feelings unsatisfied, feelings unquenched. I am ever a father, and still acute is being this widower. Mary, there is always scope for fear so long as anything I love is remaining, as if I am ever behind them.

Yes, to praise is the thing—for praise prevails and good to goodness adds. And yet, hereupon, is our hero at our door the new tranced tongue, the new Caedmon? Daughter, he baits you with our own concepts. "Everywhere I see bliss, from which I alone am irrevocably excluded. I was benevolent and good. Misery made me a fiend. Make me happy, and I shall again be virtuous." Is this not youth's wooing jest, my Mary, seducing so much to seem possible—this breathless, charming, chameleon poet? Do not be taken in the knavery of his handsome promenade of *adventure*.

~ALCHEMY

"'I don't see why my daughter has to choose her companions from the scum of the earth.'

'Depending on which way you look at it, the scum might be a valuable deposit.'"

MARY

"You will think as I do when you are as old." Did

you not find the same resistance to *your* father's knowledge? Dearest Father, but also listen for what you can't see. Shelley describes how melancholy is *soothing* as a joy that elevates in the warm sun, a garden of roses—in the smiles and frowns of one fair—and the fire that consumes my own heart. He has called forth my better feelings. He again taught me to love lost aspects of nature and the cheerful faces of children. Excellent friend, my Percy! He invents tales of wonderful fancy and passion. At other times, he repeats my favorite poems and draws me out into arguments that bound me along with feelings of unbridled joy and hilarity. He speaks of a power mighty as your Necessity, and I now cease to fear or to bend before any force less almighty than that which orders the elements. He is a high challenger of the highest conventions—keeping honorable and wise and good and true.

GODWIN

Why is every power of the social constitution, every caprice of the multitude, and every insidious project of the noble *thus instantly* in arms against so liberal and *grand* an undertaking of one man? This poet is a nightingale who sits in darkness and sings to cheer its own solitude with sweet sounds. He entrances himself in his own softness. He says many things for the sake of saying them well in the mock dignity of the ass in the lion's skin. Poets fabricate—for others' memories—pretended effusions of the heart, confining the term "romantic" to the preserving of artificial, falsified feelings.

Who is hunting who, my Mary? He enters this house as its benefactor and leaves it as an endless poison. Shelley is madly desirous of glory. A man worthy of you must have a double existence. He may suffer misery and be overwhelmed by disappointments, yet when he has retired into himself, he will be like a celestial spirit that has a halo around him, within whose circle no grief or folly ventures. Mary, this is clever youthful idealism promising the impossible. He is eloquent and persuasive, and once, his words had even power over my heart, but trust him not. Watch in the care of your own sight and freedom. He lives on vegetables—a vampire posing as an herbivore.

Audience is his lust. Observe that when his inherited time arrives, he won't renounce his seat of the baronetage in Parliament and he'll have his blinding, mischievous confusions heard and scorned. Would you also create for yourself—and for your small world—an endless enemy? Shelley does not need anyone the way any other needs him. You love the man that does as he wants—being born of the one woman that did as she wanted—but to what width is your freedom?

MARY

Alas! Best of fathers, my *Papa*, how partial you appear to know *me*—my feelings and passions alongside my mind you've molded. Do so, if you will, but I will not. You may give up your purpose, but mine is assigned to me, and I dare not. Such is "the" world. Fatal legacy! Will only *rationality* save us? It is cowardice that nurses the children of unhappy marriages—the dull virtue of the cheaply virtuous.

A more common degree of penetrating observance might have shown me that the secrets of feigned domestication cut off their possessor from the dearest ties of human existence—henpecked and housebroken—rendering him no longer able to receive the overflowing of a kindred heart. The most heroic sentiments are arrived of a mind made more feeling and of an intelligence more within the affections. How you reason and philosophize about *love*—Do you know if I had been asked, I could not have given one "reason" in its favor? Yet, I have as great an opinion as you concerning its exaltedness and "love" very tenderly to prove my theory.

GODWIN

In your *first* love story, seek from both stations of mental integrity. Your mother's intuitive perceptions of the beauty in others' minds improved my own anxious desire to not be deceived during times of reflection. Her bold, sound, and robust receptions of true emanations from others were made firm through her cultivated, picturesque imagination, guiding me to fix my own responsive, oscillating skepticisms.

Yet, it is seldom that the justice deserved in esteeming the best qualities of the illustrious dead does not become the public subject of thoughtless calumnies and malignant misrepresentations. In Paris, with

Fanny's father, your mother had *hoped* to emigrate to his native wilds of America. Yet, her fruitless images of prospective independence, happiness, and domestic felicity gave pungent *agony* to the sensibility that was destroying her. She tried to kill herself twice—as you know. Mary, like the sorrows of a female Werther, pleasure could transport her, and disappointment could be indescribable. Seek both stations.

I first fell in love with your mother reading her *Letters* —from Scandinavia—her passage on stretching her hand to the roaring torrent of a cataract in the northern wilderness. To me, your mother was like a mystical serpent recapitulating on a sunlit rock. Casting her slough, she could appear again in the brilliant and sleek elasticity of her happiest age. Her tender, bewitching smile could win the heart and soul of almost any who beheld it. Affliction had tempered her heart to a softness almost more than human. As she died, she told me—in her tears always mine—I was the sweetest and most kind man . . . Mary of my Mary, be moved by nothing less than these sacred forms of warmth.

MARY

I ever shall, Papa. Yet, it is from this clarifying doubled warmth that Mother also greatly defended that the familiar charities within the terms "sibling," "spouse," and "parent" become empty titles in the destructive commerce of sacrificing pleasures to business or to the chase of wealth. My Shelley is already my knight. He defends mother's strong position that hereditary honors do change man into an artificial monster with faculties that unfold benumbed—and that true happiness can only be enjoyed by equals.

It is brave to receive love. Cowardice dissuades it. I stand alongside my Shelley and I am not diminished. Do you not perceive how we fit one another? What variable finds *you* in such factored distress? To my Shelley do I link all my future.

GODWIN

Daughter, treasured duty of my heart, you are my dear one—and without contradiction. Yes, I authored that marriage is a systemic institution of fraud—that a thoughtless and romantic youth of each sex mingle together, seeing each other for a few times, and under circumstances full of delusion then vow to each other eternal attachment. Yes, I authored that such men who carefully mislead their own judgments—in the daily affairs of their life—must have crippled responses in every other concern. What else is to be proven of such fraud—the frustrations and disappointments that force our conversions for the worse? Do we not have all the years of Europe to teach us of favoring the generosity of love and its tenderness?

Yet, Mary, I see *and hear* goodness in you that will be abused. It is he who is unfit. As my own apprentice in our home, he rants around—driven to spoilt, eccentric mutterings, like a Macbeth musing apathetic witch-crafts to another scornful madman. Here, he persists in his false, bookish taste in poetry, obsessed with a perpetual sparkle and glittering. It is pristine, hypocritical prattle, refusing to combine his evanescent, volatile essence with anything solid. It is admitted Shelley is brilliant, but it is more to admit pity that he is wicked. He has become a vagabond of turbulent and fearful stealth, avoiding his dishonors and his creditors. You are deceived to believe that a good whole can be framed from parts so inflammatory—ever skulking on and on about magic and death.

Has he not already absconded from his first elopement? Percy does not face his burdens as he should, scribbling about them instead. One from such a cruel and thoughtlessly savage history cannot be trusted. Does his heart hold any form of shame? Free love is *honey*. It is the distortion and mischief of jaded, inflated fantasists! You are betrayed from the first. Just see! Shelley feigns talons, keeping a weapon about him, but—rather like a sickly song bird—eats only raisins and nuts, drinking only liquor or laudanum. Hideous deceptions—just *see*, Mary. Just . . .

~MAYBE COMANCHE

"'She's the wildest one, but she's a thoroughbred.'

'*Thoroughbred*! They must mean that I never let them down on the dramatic possibilities of a scene. I give a damned good show.'

'Alabama, you're positively indecent. You know what an awful reputation you've got, and I offer to marry you anyway and—'

'—And you're angry cause I won't make you an honest man.'

'You'll be sorry.'

'I hope so. I like paying for things I do. It makes me feel square with the world.'

'You're a wild Comanche. Why do you try to pretend you're so bad and hard?'

'Maybe so. Anyway, the day that I'm sorry, I'll write *it* in the corner of the wedding invitations.'

'I'll send you a picture, so you won't forget me.'"

(21.) **Jimmy Clams**

SCOTT

The whole golden boom was in the air. I was pushed into the position of both a spokesman of—and typical product of—this same moment. There was going to be plenty to tell about it. Sentimental, then resentful, it's like "the alcoholic" when he gets sober for six months and then can't stand any of the people he's liked when drunk. All the stories that came into my head had a touch of disaster in them—that the lovely, young creatures would helplessly find ruin and that there is an ultimate, inward price for all the fragile, impermanent splendors.

Speak easy. Speak easy. *Tap. Tap. Tap.* Yet, in a decade of decline and decay, how can such characters avoid such corruption from such settings? Speak low. Speak low. *Tap. Tap. Tap.* Well, there's Catholicism and Calvinism, or there's gin and olive sandwiches.

~VYING MINGLED LIGHTS

"Through the sea-change of faces and voices and color under the constantly changing light, there were the romantic speculations, the whispers . . . 'he's a cousin of Kaiser Wilhelm's—that's where all his money' . . . 'fat chance—just a German spy during the war' . . . 'couldn't be—was in the American army' . . . 'not at all—killed a man who had found out he was nephew to Field Marshal Von Hindenburg—and second cousin to the devil' . . . 'nah, it's an enchanted life—really lives in a boat like a house secretly moving up and down the Long Island shore' . . . 'it's San Francisco wealth—God's truth—to chests of jewels throughout Europe, living like a young rajah.'"

SCOTT

"I told you there was something off with that swindler, that crazy fish, Gatsby," said Tom. "The wool is he's either some damn spy or a bootlegger—a piper. Though, my hunch is he's some *criminal*—a killer—for that conman Semite."

NICK

I've been drunk for about a week now, and I thought it might sober me up to sit in a library. Here, I remember that none of my English professors at Yale ever suggested that books were being written in America. Poor souls, they were as ignorant as I was—and after this summer—possibly more so. Jay's high shelves were paneled with carved English oak, and I found his father walking up and down excitedly in Gatsby's Gothic library, priding in his son and in his son's possessions.

HENRY GATZ

"Such a mad act as that man did should make us all think. Hardly know where I am when I hear about a thing like this. Where've they got Jimmy?"

NICK

"I didn't know what you'd want, Mr. Gatsby—"

HENRY GATZ

"Gatz is my name. *Gatz*."

"You needn't bother to ascertain. I've ascertained. They're real, absolutely *real*—have pages and everything—bona fide pieces of printed matter, *all*."

SCOTT

From printings I've gravitated toward on lively bookshelves, I've ascertained that the dealings of Death are of a somewhat feminine freewill. She smokes incessantly and hazardously, always burning herself—also sheets, bedspreads, and holes in her clothes. Lackadaisically, she drops cigarettes in cuffs of trousers, and they burn. We have to hunt the floor and wastebasket to find where the smoke is coming from. We never find it. She pretends she needs tubes of medicine to put on her burns, and carpets are not pleased. Some fine day, I'll give her one of Zelda's long harlequined cigarette holders.

NICK

Fatherly Gatz had reached an age where death no longer has the quality of ghastly surprise. When he looked around him now for the first time—and saw the height and splendor of the hall and the great rooms opening out from it into other rooms—his grief began to be mixed with awed pride.

HENRY GATZ

"He had a big future before him, you know. He was only a young man, but he had a lot of brain power. If he'd of lived, he'd of been a great man. He come out to see me two years ago and bought me the house I live in now. Of course, we was broke up when he run off from home, but I see now there was a reason for it. He knew he had a big future in front of him. It just shows you, don't it? It just shows you. Jimmy was bound to get ahead—always had resolve."

SCOTT

From printings that've found me from enchanted bookshelves, I've ascertained that the dealings of Time are of a somewhat masculine freewill. When he's sobered, he's a stoic. Whereas, when old sport Time goes for the bottle at the back, all the boys and tomboys feel the tug to uncork a jug and toast to clocks. Yet, since the war, he's gone to less meetings. He thinks it's a damn riot when he wabbles down the street with his hands out, pretending—with bona fide resolve—to be blind and oblivious.

NICK

He was already too far away, and I could only remember—in a resentment of *time* itself—that Daisy hadn't sent a message or a flower. *Jimmy*—the poor son of a bitch.

Human sympathy has its limits, and we were content to let all their tragic arguments fade with the city lights behind. I was thirty. Before me stretched the portentous menacing road of a new decade.

SCOTT
Keats . . . Shelley—their promise ran out on them before they could fall into the safety of the bleak, cruel pit of thirty. Jay was just a pair of years passed, and he got *his* after he got Daddy-o-Gatz his new house. Nick and Tom were thirty, and someone had to die. Nick and Jay had survived the war, but Jay wouldn't survive Tom.

They were all in their "big futures," their clocks wound full swing with doomed, prismed light as Zelda and I live through our own certainty of being marked. Only playing "Babylon" in the evenings seems to satiate and hold off our sure augury.

NICK
Thirty—the promise of a decade of loneliness, a thinning list of singles to know, a thinning briefcase of enthusiasm, thinning hair. But there was Jordan beside me, who—unlike Daisy—was too wise ever to carry well-forgotten dreams from age to age. As we passed over the dark bridge, her wan face fell lazily

against my coat's shoulder, and the formidable stroke of thirty died away with the reassuring pressure of her hand.

As a coupe flashed by us with a flurry of dust, and hard brown beetles kept thudding against the dull light, we drove on—*toward death*—through the cooling twilight.

(22.) *freedom*

~WELL-NIGH

"And, so, if our women gave up decorating themselves, we'd have *time* to turn our sad eyes on the bleak telegraph wires, on the office buildings (like homes of trained fleas), on the barren desolateness of city streets at dusk—time to realize too late that almost the only *beauty* in this busy, careless land (whose every acre is littered with the waste of the day *before* yesterday) is the gorgeous, radiant beauty of its girls."

SCOTT

While Harriett is confined with their expectant successor, she lives in a "dreadful state of suspense" once Percy ceases to return her recurrent letters. Latterly, seeking to redefine their life on their own terms, he and Mary strive to live "to the hilt." Even so, in their Parisian playland, Shelley sells his valued watch-and-chain to get them to Switzerland, and Mary is pregnant with their own daughter—vomiting each day of their return up the Roman-fortressed Rhine. In the penniless and pregnant culmination of their vilified elopement, they arrive "home" to the cold doom of London.

~BLOOD MERIDIAN

"How speed the outlaws? Stand they well prepared /

Their plundered wealth, and robber-rock to guard? /
To view with fire their scorpion's nest consumed?"

SCOTT

Disgraced and wistful, Mary fondly remembers it was during the revolving season of their youth that she and Fanny would girlishly gather blackberries and apples—"apples red"—and dream of what awaited them. Shelley sells his prized solar microscope and evades the harassing *emissaries* of his creditors, of his spouse, and of his father. Especially fearful, Percy has Mary live apart from him, drifting her through four different ragged apartments in their new freedom. Harriett and Mary suffer mutual ruinations. "Harriett sends her creditors here, nasty woman," Mary reports, "and now we shall have to change our lodgings."
For eight disparaging months, Mary abides through this series of discreet and shifting locales throughout London during her forced separations from her Percy "Elf" Shelley.

~POCKET CAKES

"Shelley sent round to his colleague. While waiting for the money, he took out the pocket-Shakespeare he always carried and read aloud from *Troilus and Cressida* to Mary. It made them forget their hunger a whole day through. Next morning at breakfast time, Shelley's colleague—penniless himself—sent them cakes. If life was difficult, there was some joy in suffering together."

SCOTT

During this ruinous period of poverty, Mary and Percy—reduced to necessities—sell their remaining personal possessions, entrenching their outcast position. Severely ill, abject, and in danger, Shelley writes an urgent appeal to Harriett. "Money affairs are in a desperate state. If November arrives without further success, I must go to prison. I am without hope or resource . . . We have even now sold all that we have to buy bread . . . Before I could sell the last valuable, Mary very nearly perished with hunger."

By the close of this year of departures, Fanny delivers baby clothes and blankets to Mary for Christmas. Fanny helps prepare the layette and attempts to ease the strained pains between Godwin and Mary. "I confess to you," Shelley writes, "that I am shocked and staggered by Godwin's cold injustice." Gracefully, Fanny—illegitimate herself—encourages Mary to believe that it's not a wicked *thing* to be having Shelley's child. Yet, Fanny does insist that Mary is paying too heavily for her freedom—reduced to a wraith in horrible confinement, flitting through poor, damp rooms of beggars.

~PUT MONEY IN THY PURSE

"Well, so, now I am to write a "goodnight" with the old story of what I wish I could say to you. Yes, my love, it has indeed become an old story, but I hope the last chapter has come. If you but get money, love, which indeed you must, we will defy our enemies and our friends. For aught, I see they are all as bad as one another—and we will *not part* again. Is that not a delightful axiom? It shall cheer my dreams."

SCOTT

Must "ruin" always be the *shadow* of love? Only seven months ago, tartan-clad Mary had returned from Scotland to her Godwin, to her Fanny, and to her awaiting to live her life—anchored in the springtide fortitudes of ghost stories and poetry. By this autumn, while Mary is seventeen, pregnant, rejected, and in deficient want, Percy's legal heir—little Charles Shelley—is born to Harriett. Hounded and unsuccessfully soliciting his "colleagues," Percy is progressively unable to support either worsening household.

~OLD DAD'S RESOLVES

"Be happy. Resolve to be happy. You deserve to be so. Everything that interferes with it is weakness and wandering. A woman like you can, must, and *shall* shake it off. Afford no food for the morbid madness and no triumph to the misanthropical gloom of your afternoon visitor. Call up with firmness the energies which I am sure you so eminently possess."

— Godwin to Wollstonecraft

(23.) *a lyre of stars*

MARY

In the remembrance of our first bright summit, I wept like a child. Now, dear mountains and my own beautiful lake!—how do you welcome your wanderer? Your summits are clear, and the sky and lake are blue and placid. Is this to prognosticate peace, or to mock at my unhappiness? My days are devoted to love and idleness, but despite my earthly paradise, I feel a frustration born of guilt. I am free to write and create as I please, but I am pregnant with this constant whisper that I am nowhere closer to achieving my dreams than a child. I could not figure to myself that romantic woes or wonderful events would ever be my lot. Has this mind, so replete with ideas, imaginations fanciful and magnificent, formed a world that has perished? Or—existence depending on the life of its creator—has this mind perished? Does it now only exist in my memory? Marked, my wings of desire backslide unsacramental—unborn of the spirit, I am born again in the flesh—my christening unmade, backsliding, I am marked.

Beautiful Percy, don't you see that I also am the Romantic—this legislator of this world—with my peculiar prose as much as with your splendorous poems? But our lives can also be beautiful—not just our art. We can start again—a ravine in renewal—like before all the deteriorations, this evil heap we've made. Even a hell has hills where love—love staring—might touch us, a new mist.

Our past is a shared restless youth-fire longing to be loosed—from the causes of our parents and schools, of the clergy and gentry, and their arsenal of artisans—when we thought to order all our own steps without others controlling our fire, convinced we'll do it best, outshining all others' attempts into a jealous envy, laughing into a sweet sleep each night into each other—no matter our circumstance. Tell me, my dearest victor, my knight, answer me, I conjure you, by our mutual happiness, with simple truth—do you not love another?—your lovely self?—feigning as the victorious legacies of Wollstonecraft and Papa in your verses, your daydream "revolution"?

Yes, Papa does continue as the grieving love of her life, bearing her torch, in which I—appointed—have now joined him in this parade of Godwinian authorship, needing desperately their acceptance—and yours—needing the same sympathy that each of you would extend to any other, save your youth-treasured Mary, like unformed clay that hasn't dried, or isn't yet its own. "Oh, be naught equitable to every other, and trample upon me alone."

It is no great effort to discern *how I came to think of* and to dilate upon so very hideous an idea. It is not singular that, as the daughter of two persons of distinguished literary celebrity, I should very early in life have thought of writing. The memory of Mother has always been the pride and delight of my life. The admiration—of others for her—has been the cause of most of the happiness I have enjoyed. Her greatness of soul and Papa's high talents have perpetually reminded me that I ought to degenerate as little as I could from those from whom I derived my being. I felt as if I must prove myself worthy of my namesake. I have awakened from subsisting as their stagnant afterbirth—brought back to life as more than the material of the great, dead mother, Godwin's great, dead wife.

Although I embark to emulate Mothers' passion and defiance, I also helplessly mimic her stretched polarities—lively as they are lethal—where also sits my own heart's love. Percy, you were forever inciting me—to judge how far I possessed the promise of better things hereafter—to "obtain literary reputation," anxious that I should prove myself worthy of my parentage and enroll myself on the page of fame. Although, yes, my now inspired scratching is a minor testament to Mother and Papa, it is—in its majority—my indictment of your callous carelessness, our offspring of fresh grief at your own hands.

It is this incitement that has made this my progeny of so hideous an idea—your summons as the core and substance of this *tale* that has made us outcasts forsaken—the saddening origin of my lovelorn authorship in a form presentable to this world—rather than another domestic case to dismiss, disaffectedly—one you may care more mindfully for.

~CHAOS WORTHY

"I do not like the man in the book. The world in which I *trust*—on which I seem to set my feet—appears to me to exist through a series of illusions. These illusions need—and occasionally get—a thorough going over ten times or so during a century."

MARY

Everything must have a beginning. Invention, it must be humbly admitted, does not consist in creating out of void, but out of chaos. The materials must, in the first place, be afforded. Though it can give form to dark, shapeless substances, it cannot bring into being the substance itself. Invention consists in the capacity of seizing on the capabilities of a subject and in the power of molding and fashioning ideas suggested by it. Creation can occur through destruction. All destroyers are creators. What magnanimous Prometheus designed in his uncritical heart would be the "Great Doom," what would isolate his tyrant's hate—unabated—in each camp of all creatures, each demographic of us, thereafter. Why must all around you lessen—decreasing—as your own greatness expands? Yet, Percy, my epic poem made real, my Perseus, you are ever my hero—all.

All myths are tragic, but the doom of our love doesn't have to be this social martyrdom, this living Promethean punishment, suffering as a Persephone and Hades—or, me fated as Demeter mourning—that you repetitiously goosequill scratch—convinced—deep etching our mythic curse on large pages—like fabric to coat all our barren furniture—in these empty, migrant rooms. Weeping in our fires within, while we still know that we *can* heroically choose, we could be, can be again like an Aphrodite and Adonis, a Psyche and Eros—or, best—a Eurydice and her Orpheus in a deathless song that sinks subterranean, an oracle that can't help but be found as the renown of its age—as a lyre of stars embroidered in the sky—even with each choice tragic, but in these decisions—desirably *so*. Yet, you narrate us as a gelding—forfeitable—in stooping to help our brothers and sisters in all our causes.

Yes, no good deed goes unpunished well, but it is easier, it would be more bearable without what is most surely our wounded ego being chastised, projecting us as a false Icarus or Sisyphus for others, or us as social buttresses—some contemporary Themis or Atlas? Must we be as these penalized Titans, and not still love as lovingly possible?

You are my precious Perseus, yet there is only one Mary, my Mary of my life, and each Mary like her, praying for the world—of the poor for heaven and a haven for pagans—Mary-me trying to reach out to you before you sell your mind to archaic Greece. Gladly punished, I hold your heart, yet you are restless until you hold all the world on your back, constricting all that I bear into pining—like an old Penelope weaving, or a Galatea waiting to be real for her Pygmalion. Rewrite me in your spirit—not as your torturing punishment, your Pandora sent—not as your Eve of our Fall, trapping us in cold institutions that force us to these shifting London rooms and this bare bassinette in wait.

Isaac was chosen. You are chosen. Are we your Hagar and Ishmael? You must choose. Banished, we are surely lost. Death's appetite seems curious for the displaced. Send us the way to not be sent away. How many more days can living remain? Send an angel, or a fairy. Send rain. Send for us.

(24.) <u>on the carpet</u>

SCOTT

I've written ever since I can remember. I wrote short stories early in school, I wrote my Midwestern plays and poetry in prep school, and I wrote stage comedies and short stories for Princeton, but one day I picked up a trendy book while riding on a train. After I had read about a hundred pages, I thought 'if this fellow can get away with it as an author, I can too.' His books seemed to me to be as bad as possible. The principal thing he did was to make *inessentials* seem important, but he was one of the near best-sellers. After I closed *that* for good, I dug in.

We didn't know what New York expected of us. We scarcely knew anymore who we were and hadn't a notion what we were. We became a small nucleus ourselves and gradually we fitted our disruptive personalities. Or rather, New York forgot us and let us stay. Perhaps, everyone thinks they are apart from their milieu. Our denouement commenced when I realized that the City was mostly a rather lost and lonely people. We thought we were apart from all that. As I prepared to get roaring, weeping drunk for a decade at my own mediocrity and inabilities, I was adopted.

New York adopted me as the archetype of what it wanted. This is what it now is—what they . . . wanted me to write them . . . their archetype scribbling them symbols. Well, here's where I tried. No one is born with technique—relentless, inexorable toil. There are no halcyon days for a writer. *Tap. Tap. Tap.*

Adopted, their archetype shifts from his against-the-clock pace—with revolt and discovery—to a more conscious experiment of form, my new slow care—decoding the signals, engaged—crafting this Modernism myth of romance—its deceptions and powers, its corruptions that lay beneath the sparkling social surfaces, the nature of its darkness that surrounds the glowing light.

So, on the subject of, apropos of, regarding, about, with a view of, in the interest of, en route to, toward, to—once again—"*to* Zelda"!

NICK

We witnessed the death of a man's dream, and no one knew it. How pleasant it could have been—mint juleps. But how things really work, things are more brutal than books. I think Tom wanted to let his victory seep in—big dumb ape—standing there, smirking handsomely with that travel bottle of whiskey that he never even opened.

TOM

"You must be crazy!"

SCOTT

—*exclaimed Tom automatically.* Gatsby sprang to his feet, vivid with excitement.

JAY

"She never loved you, do you hear?"

SCOTT

Gatsby cried.

JAY

"She only married you because I was poor and she was tired of waiting for me. It was a terrible mistake, but in her heart, she never loved anyone except me! I told you what's been going on, going on for five years—and you didn't know.

—No, we couldn't meet, but both of us loved each other all that time, old sport, and you didn't know."

TOM

"Oh—that's all . . ."

SCOTT

Tom tapped his thick fingers together.

TOM

"You're crazy!"

SCOTT

—*he exploded.*

TOM

"And I'll be damned if I see how you got within a mile of her unless you brought the groceries to the back door. But all the rest of that's a goddamned lie. Daisy loved me when she married me and she loves me now."

JAY

"No—"

SCOTT

—*said Gatsby, shaking his head.*

TOM

"She does though. The trouble is that sometimes she gets foolish ideas in her head and doesn't know what she's doing."

JAY

"Daisy, that's all over now. It doesn't matter anymore. Just tell him the truth—that you never loved him—and it's all wiped out forever. *You never loved him.*"

NICK

She hesitated. Her eyes fell on Jordan and me with a sort of appeal, as though she realized at last what she was doing—and as though she had never, all along, intended doing anything at all. It was too late.

DAISY

"*There*, Jay—"

SCOTT

—*she said*. But her hand—as she tried to light a cigarette—was trembling. Suddenly, she threw the cigarette and the burning match on the carpet.

DAISY

"Oh, you want too much! I love you now—isn't that enough? I can't help what's past."

SCOTT

She began to sob helplessly.

DAISY

"I did love him once—but I loved you, too."

TOM

"Even that's a lie—"

SCOTT

—*said Tom savagely.*

TOM

"She didn't know you were alive. Why—there's things between Daisy and me that you'll never know, things that neither of us can ever forget."

JAY

"You don't understand—"

SCOTT

—*said Gatsby, with a touch of panic.*

JAY

"You're not going to take care of her anymore."

TOM

"I'm not?"

SCOTT

Tom opened his eyes wide and laughed.

JAY

"Daisy's leaving you."

TOM

"Who are you anyhow?"

SCOTT

—*broke out Tom.*

TOM

"Don't you call me old sport!"

SCOTT

Gatsby said nothing.

TOM

"Walter could have you up on the betting laws too, but Wolfsheim scared him into shutting his mouth. That drug store business was just small change—"

SCOTT

—continued Tom slowly.

TOM

"—but you've got something on now that the bankman's afraid to tell me about."

SCOTT

Jay began to talk excitedly to Daisy, denying everything, defending his name against accusations that had not been made. But with every word, she was drawing further and further into herself. So, he gave that up. Only the dead dream fought on as the afternoon slipped away, trying to touch what was no longer tangible, struggling unhappily, despairingly, toward that lost voice across the room.

NICK

I looked away—I knew the secret. Time could not frame Daisy. She was eighteen again and again, and all the fisherman and soldiers and bachelors envied Jay. She was deathless his, and it would always stop raining. Time would never find them.

TOM

"Go on. He won't annoy you. I think he realizes that his presumptuous little flirtation is over."

~ZELDA'S HOUSE RULES

"They rose to leave the pleasant place.

'We've talked you to death.'

'You must be dead with packing.'

'It's death to a party to stay till digestion sets in.'

'I'm dead, my dear. It's been wonderful!'"

NICK

They were gone, without a word, snapped out, made accidental, isolated like ghosts even from our pity.

After a moment, Tom got up and began wrapping the unopened bottle of whiskey in the towel.

TOM

"Nick?"

SCOTT

—*he asked again.*

NICK

"What?"

TOM

"Want any?"

(25.) *the latest thing*

SCOTT

Click. Tap. Tap. The music had died down as the ceremony began, and now a long cheer floated in at the window.

DAISY

"We're getting old. If we were young, we'd rise and dance."

JAY

"Not exactly."

TOM

"Oh, yes, I understand you went to Oxford."

SCOTT

Another pause. A waiter knocked and came in with crushed mint and ice, but the silence was unbroken.

JAY

"It was an opportunity they gave to some of the officers after the Armistice. We could go to any of the universities in England or France."

DAISY

"Open the whiskey, Tom—"

SCOTT

—*she ordered.*

DAISY

"And I'll make you a mint julep. Then you won't seem so stupid to yourself. Look at the mint!"

TOM

"Wait a minute—"

SCOTT

—*snapped Tom.*

TOM

"I want to ask Mr. Gatsby one more question."

JAY

"Go on—"

SCOTT

—*Gatsby said politely.*

TOM

"What kind of a *row* are you trying to cause in my house anyhow?"

SCOTT

They were out in the open at last, and Gatsby was content.

~ROW, OLD SPORT

". . . it is the loves over thirty—as proof of their vitality—that have led to operas, and *Anna Karenina*, and also murders in the *Daily News*."

DAISY

"He isn't causing a row."

SCOTT

Daisy looked desperately from one to the other.

DAISY

"You're causing a row. Please have a little self-control."

TOM

"Self-control!"

SCOTT

—*repeated Tom incredulously.*

TOM

"I suppose the latest thing is to sit back and let Mr. Nobody from Nowhere make love to your wife. I want to know what Mr. Gatsby has to tell me."

JAY

"Your wife doesn't love you,"

SCOTT

—*said Gatsby quietly.*

JAY

"She's never loved you, old sport. She loves me."

~PALE WHITE LIGHT

The shadow pair, too, stroll through the place. Suddenly, the west *flares* with pale white lightning. Simultaneously, both couples turn to each other in the terrible revelation of the bolt of lightning.

'Did you see?' she cried in a whisper. 'Did you see them? They're us! They're us! Don't you see?'

(26.) *star-spangled chaw and grog*

SCOTT

Years later, Percy the Great and his own "*Nick*"—his own mesmerized narrator and matey—will muse on pirating their own dream of their own yare American "*hydroplane.*"

PERCY

"There's not a drop of the old Hellenic blood here. *These* are not the men to rekindle the ancient Greek fires—their souls are extinguished by *traffic* and by superstition. Come away!"

MATEY

—*and away we went.*

"It's but a *step* from these ruins of worn-out Greece to the New World. Let's board that American clipper there."

~OLD FLAG-WAVERS

"And, O thou stern Ocean deep, / Thou whose foamy billows sweep / Shores where thousands wake to weep / Whilst they curse a villain king, / On the winds that fan thy breast / Bear thou news of Freedom's rest! / Can the daystar dawn *of love* / Where the flag of war unfurled / Floats with crimson stain above / The fabric of a ruined world?"

PERCY

"I had rather not have any more of my hopes and illusions mocked by sad realities."

MATEY

"You must allow *that* graceful craft was designed by a man who had a poet's feeling for things beautiful. Let's get a model and build a boat like her."

PERCY

"It is an intriguing prospect. We'll not tarry long though."

MATEY

The idea so pleased the Poet that he followed me aboard the clipper.

The Americans are a social, free-and-easy people accustomed to take their own way—and to readily yield the same privilege to all others. So, our coming on board—and examination of the vessel, fore and aft—were not considered as intrusion. The captain was on shore, so I talked to the deck officer—a smart *specimen* of a Yankee. I commended her beauty.

YANKEE

"Now we have our new copper on, I expect she has a look of the brass *sarpent*. She has as slick a run, and her bearings are just where they should be."

MATEY

"Likewise, we wish to build a boat after her model."

YANKEE

"Then, I calculate you must go to Baltimore or Boston to get one. There is no one on this side the water can do the job. We have our freight all ready and are homeward-bound," he explained, pointing to the sea. "We have elegant accommodation, and you will be *across* before your young friend's beard is ripe for a razor," he mused.

"Come down and take an observation of the state cabin—plenty of room to live or die *comfortably* in . . ."

~GEO'S PUFF

"Sublime tobacco! which, from east to west, / Divine in hookahs, glorious in a pipe, / When tipped with amber, mellow, rich, and ripe."

MATEY

The Yankee then pressed us to have a chaw on real old Virginian cake, *i.e. tobacco*, and a cool drink of peach brandy. I made some observation to him about the Greek vessel we had visited.

YANKEE

"Crank as an *eggshell*—too many sticks and top hamper. She looks like a bundle of chips going to hell to be burnt."

MATEY

The Yankee would not let us go until we drunk under the star-spangled banner—to the memory of Washington and to the prosperity of the American commonwealth. I seduced Shelley into drinking the glass of weak grog. Then, the Poet raised his toast.

PERCY

"As a warrior and statesman, he was righteous in all he did, unlike all who lived before or since. He never used his *power* but for the benefit of his fellow-creatures.

He fought / For truth and wisdom, foremost of the brave; / Him glory's idol-glances dazzled not; / 'Twas his ambition, generous and great, / A *life* to life's great end to consecrate."

YANKEE

"*Stranger*, truer words were never spoken. There is dry rot in all the main timbers of the Old World—and none of you will do any good till you are docked, refitted, and annexed to the New.

You must log that song you sang. There ain't many Britishers that will say as much of the man that whipped them. So, just set these lines *down* in the log—or it won't go for nothing."

MATEY

Shelley wrote some verses in the book, but not those he had quoted.

—*And, so, we parted.*

~NEW FLAG-WAVERS

"Brothers! between you and me / Whirlwinds sweep and billows roar: / Yet in spirit oft I see / On thy wild and winding shore / Freedom's *bloodless* banners wave."

(27.) *the warring British*

SCOTT

Burr and Paine were both critical figures in the American Founding, they both suffered similar exiles from their home countries, they both plotted cabals against their countries, they both attempted to meet with Napoleon in Paris, and they both opposed General Washington. Washington had refused Colonel Burr's appointment as a brigadier general, and Burr despised Washington "as a man of no talents and one who could not spell a sentence of common English." Knowing Burr's preference for the contemporary philosophers of England, Burr's eminent political enemy—who *was made* a general by Washington—accused Colonel Burr of "perfect, rank Godwinism." To Burr's American peers, Godwin was considered a passionate lover of justice who had "waged a well-meant, ineffectual warfare against the State of Things."

~THE CROWN'S FAVORITE FUN

While tyrannies reign in France, Great Britain is in fear of losing its own aristocracy after losing its colonies in America, suppressing interior dissentions throughout its domain. Large crowds are prevented from gathering, public meetings are supervised, and Parliament alters acts to expedite the death penalty for treasonous crimes, which popularizes Godwin's *Political Justice* against its contemporary madness— and founds General Washington as a hero amongst

British intellectuals during the fervors "across the pond."

SCOTT

Antecedently, Godwin meets Wollstonecraft through the London circle that admires Blake and Paine. Godwin and Paine were raised in similar households and both had become dissenting preachers. Though, recognized early as a powerful political author, Paine is inspired to emigrate to British colonial America and completes *Common Sense* in one year—and in five more years, meets with the King of France to secure millions to fund the revolutionaries of the American colonies. In *The Crisis*, Paine writes, "These are the times that try men's souls: The summer soldier and the sunshine patriot will, in this crisis, shrink from service . . . Tyranny, like hell, is not easily conquered; yet we have this consolation with us, that the harder the conflict, the more glorious the triumph."

As Paine returns to London after the American Revolution is secured, Godwin helps Paine publish *Rights of Man*, which becomes Napoleon's favorite contemporary manuscript—and the book for which Paine is outlawed from England. Blake advises Paine to flee to Paris. The year that Shelley is born, Wollstonecraft publishes *A Vindication of the Rights of Woman* and follows Paine from London to Paris at the rise of the French Revolution. Although the first of these British advocates for extending the French example into England is Wollstonecraft—publishing her prominent *A Vindication of the Rights of Men* before

Paine's own major response—in both England and France, however, his *Rights of Man* is the most read political work ever written.

In France, Paine condemns Napoleon during his rise toward dictatorial emperorship. After George Washington is dead, Paine returns to America while Burr is Vice President, openly opposing Burr's political reputation. Conversely, on Wollstonecraft, Burr writes his wife, "be assured that your sex has in *her* an able advocate. *Vindication* is, in my opinion, a work of genius." Inheriting some of Paine's fame, Godwin publishes *Political Justice* two years after *Rights of Man* and is befriended by both Coleridge and Wordsworth. The year that Godwin and Wollstonecraft meet again in London—and become lovers—Godwin's first famous novel is dramatized.

Four months after Mary is born and Wollstonecraft dies, Godwin publishes his tribute to his dead wife—*Memoirs*. Subsequently, a revered set of the copied, totemic portraits of Godwin and Wollstonecraft are installed in Burr's office as the American Vice President. At length, after subsisting throughout his own vilifying scandals, Burr visits Godwin to pay him homage. Likewise, Godwin is interested, philosophically, to meet Burr—the grandson of Jonathan Edwards. Leaving America, Burr travels through Denmark with Wollstonecraft's *Letters* as his guide and reads *Memoirs* on his way to London. Across the pond, Godwin and Burr are contemporaries—born within one month of each other, and Paine dies the season after Burr arrives at Godwin's. Reaching the Juvenile Library, Burr brings a set of "little books" as gifts to Fanny and Mary. Over the course of four years, Burr will dine at Godwin's ninety times, discussing abolition, suffrage, Paine's works, free education, utility, duality, Hawthorne, and Poe.

In London, Fanny wins the honors of Burr. Before Fanny meets her next man of nobility—*Shelley*—Burr and Fanny enjoy engrossing walks together, discussing her mother's works and mutual intellectual interests, cheering Burr from his low moods. Godwin, penniless himself, raises money for Burr, selling valuable books and his own ring-watch. "This family truly loves me," Burr writes. Although Burr had been acquitted of Napoleonic treason, effigies of his likeness still burned across the pond. Burr buys Fanny a present and takes her on a picnic. He is taken with Fanny's talents in drawing, dancing, and reading music. In the company of other philosophers in London, Burr boasts, "It is only Fan I can trust."

Burr had raised his own daughter into adulthood on the precepts of Wollstonecraft's texts, and Fanny deeply reminds Burr of his esteemed daughter during their walks in London. Burr carts his portrait of his daughter around England—cradling it in his lap during his stagecoach trips—seeking a second to be made by the same portraitist as Wollstonecraft's. Nevertheless, Burr then leaves Europe as the American President declares a second war of independence with Great Britain. In a letter to Burr on his departure from England, Godwin writes,

"I wish I could persuade you that my method, the method I have laid down for doing good is—which I sincerely believe—the best." Still, later this tragic year, Burr's luck runs out—drawing the "Drowned Sailor" card. On her voyage to join Burr in his return from European exile—his treasured, devoted daughter dies, disappearing at sea. Burr will consider himself "severed from the human race" and will be buried at Princeton as a recluse. *Tap. Tap. Click.*

This Anglo-American war will inspire the patriotic "Defense" lyric, which will be set to the music of my star-spangled heritage at the height of The Great War, marching me, Lt. target-practice Fitzgerald of the 67th Infantry—and my Red Cross Kids—to imagine our valor against the Red Baron and his Iron Cross Huns. I'd been named after my distant cousin—Francis Scott Key. Yet, sometimes, I played him up so much that I played me down, scribbling out this working book-title, "Under the Red, White, and Blue." In the curious case of driving up on Cousin Key's monument, I jumped from the car, hid in the bushes, and yelled out, "Don't let Frank see me drunk!"

~RAMPARTS WE WATCHED

"'And why isn't it any fun to be an American?'

'Because it's too big to get your hands on. Because it's a woman's country. Because it's very nice and its various local necessities have made it impossible for an American to have a real credo. After all, an

American is condemned to saying, "I don't like this." He has never had time, and I mean *time*, the kind of inspired hush that people make for themselves in which to want *to be* or *to do* on the scale—and with all those arrogant assumptions—with which great races make great dreams. There has never been an American tragedy. There have only been great failures. That is why the story of Aaron Burr opens up things that we—who accept the United States as an established unit—hardly dare to think about.'"

SCOTT

The same year as Burr's departure from the Godwins, their heir apparent of the baronetage eagerly enters their lives. Harriett's *Bysshe*—her Shelley—and *his* Godwin first correspond through letters for ten months. Percy presents himself as a glittering-eyed knight errant and patron. Godwin presents *himself*—rather than the politics of Ireland and Wales—as the better cause and investment of Shelleyan social justice. As Napoleon is abdicating and being exiled, Percy's transition from Harriett to Godwin's home mirrors his own outward loss of hopes for reform. In his first visits at Godwin's, Percy instantly becomes interested in Fanny—the very girl from his favorite work by Wollstonecraft.

Alongside Fanny's long brown hair, pleasing figure, and flirtatious blue eyes, Percy discerns the beauty of her mind and her desire for intellectual accomplishment. Closer in age than Harriett, Fanny and Shelley are immediately attracted to each other, disagreeing about the primeval prejudice and social significance of class. Sharing a few evening walks, Fanny is attentive and receptive to Shelley's melancholic, idealist poetics and his other mental riches. To Fanny, Shelley becomes her "knight of the shield of shadow."

Together, they confer about political turbulence with Russia, the Papacy, and Prussia. They discuss the possibilities of liberty. Fanny shares Godwin and Shelley's belief about what Napoleon being deposed means. They muse that things must be back to the "bad old ways." Their *antihero* is dethroned, and tyranny is back in full force with the new king of France now seducing London. Mirroring these matters of statecraft, there are simultaneous household calamities. While Godwin is bound to his fine art of protecting the execution of his loan from Shelley, Percy is occupied in courting Fanny.

Although desirous—in glances, sighs, and gazes—Fanny mournfully declines Percy's inevitable, overwhelming, sensual invitation. Judiciously, Fanny also shares Godwin and Shelley's mindful habit of putting beliefs before relationships. Still, she flatters Percy, writing him that only in poets are "nature and art united," that only poets are "the eternal benefactors of their fellow creatures," and that only poets "make ordinary, everyday life bearable."

While Godwin is formalizing Shelley's marriage

to Harriett—and their heirs—he suffers Shelley's letters. Godwin is discerning that libertine Shelley can be just as mad and dangerous to know as the first young celebrity of genius emerging in England. Doing as they pleased amidst the social paranoias of all radicalisms, Byron and Shelley are each becoming glamorous, arrogant, and rebellious artists of the bourgeois. While Harriett Shelley is pregnant with their second child, Percy becomes estranged and frequently visits Fanny. Guarding her virtue—and his loan—Godwin sends Fanny to Wales, removing her from Percy's fanciful, captivating influences.

Solitary—where he had also wandered lovesick after Oxford—Fanny fantasizes about her Shelley as she rambles among the valleys and cliffs of Wales. Her bizarre Welsh holiday is her most treasured remembrances of her mild, sensible life. Percy's transcendental poetry calls to her. "Lovely the woods, waters, meadows, combes, vales, / All the air things wear that build this world of Wales." Fanny recites his words to herself and wants to live within them. Fanny envisions herself following Shelley to their *rescued* Paris in an affair of lusty trysts—as her mother had followed Paine to *their* revolutionary Paris in the thrill of a new, magical life.

Then, from a bleaker woodless landscape, Mary—the youthful daughter of Wollstonecraft *and* of Godwin—returns to London from her own transformative voyage in Scotland. There is love in London. Shelley is remarrying his pregnant wife in March. Through April and May, he is offering his affections to Fanny.

In the further awe of June and July, Shelley showers his amorous affections on Mary. In August, Shelley and Mary are traversing Western Europe as the warring British—"over the Land of the Free"—are capturing and burning the federal buildings of the youthful U.S.

~FAITH LIKE RED-COATED NAILS

"She thought that she herself would never have every single thing about her just right at once—would never be able to attain a state of abstract preparedness. Her sister appeared to be the perfect instrument for life. Her sister's voice droned on, cooing and affected, listening to its own vibrations.

'You taught me how to use my fork and how to dance and choose my suits—and I wouldn't come back to your father's house if I'd left *my Jesus*. Nothing is good enough for him.'

Sure enough, *he* never did. She had learned from the past that something unpleasant was bound to happen whenever 'the Savior' made his appearance in the dialogue. The savor of her first kiss was gone with the hope of its repetition. The bright polish on her nails turned yellow, and deposits of neglect shone through the red."

SCOTT

When his blossoming, pregnant Mary elopes with her viper-in-velvet aristocrat, Godwin sends for his wistful Fanny to return from Wales to be his anchor—to assist in managing his strained home while he is being denounced in the press. Fanny's cumulative woes are born. After this summer, she and Mary continue as sisters through letters to each other. In such a letter, Fanny muses from their mother, "Those charming talents which my soul instinctively *loves* produce misery in this world—abundantly more pain than pleasure. Why then do they at all unfold themselves *here*—where keen blasts blight the opening flower?"

Although Mary Godwin and Percy Shelley are shunned, neglected, and in squalor throughout their first winter in icy tenement rooms, they both feverishly write throughout their continued period of illegitimacy, tension, pregnancy, and forced estrangement. In stark contrast to their heart-rending settings, our cooped, inspiriting songbirds meet clandestine in coffeehouses and taverns—avoiding Shelley's bailiffs. Through reciprocal editing and encouraging, they share and debate—unhesitant—their passionate alternating views amongst their rivalrous authorial developments.

Shelley writes to Mary. "My admiration of your letter to Fanny—the simple and impressive language in which you clothed your argument, the full weight you gave to every part, the complete picture you exhibited of what you intended to describe—was more than I expected. How hard and stubborn must be the spirit that does not confess you to be the subtlest and most exquisitely fashioned intelligence! Among women there is no equal mind to yours! And I possess this treasure! How beyond all estimate is my felicity! Yes, I am encouraged. I care not what happens. I am most happy. Meet me tomorrow in St. Paul's. Adieu! Remember, love, at vespers before sleep." Shelley has his dear quarry—his prized intellectual beauty. Preceding his discovery of Mary, Percy had lamented, "some of us have loved an Antigone in a previous stage of existence, and can find no full content in any mortal tie."

Notwithstanding, Mary's emerging thesis becomes a stiff rejection of her social set's revolutionary dreams, refusing their unnecessary sufferings thought *essential* during *transition*. Mary asserts her anti-political policy of the organic, gradual evolution of domestic affections to rectify chaotic Promethean idealists. She principals her local pastoral of domesticity to remedy young minds subjected to isolation and to guard against their future social injustices as solitary outcasts.

Shelley wants to be best known for works of fear-craft—of obscene violence and shocking upheavals—rather than milder scenes of affectionate cares. Although Percy's conceptions of the best passions are his most noble voice in his verses, he is mostly averse to these expressions—unless highly idealized—casting aside many of his most beautiful effusions.

Mary commences to charge that Shelley barters his

sacrificed magnanimous lyrics to be the crowned ornament of his systemic martyrdom. Striking her first blow to his excessive, narcissistic project, Mary critiques that each increase in his type of ideal poetical consciousness will parallel an increase in despair—the pensive disease that spreads to colonize the spirit.

(28.) *urban pilgrims*

SCOTT

What *speciality*—what beyond—is seated within me? I've centered my difference to anyone else with a typewriter to "seeing"—that I see the sustaining in the transitory, see story in the crowd. I see the romantic egoist and his merits put to the test, the man who would not crack up, the man who goes after it—with blood and hope and hell—the man whose passion—his love—isn't a calculated faucet—isn't a cold social valve—the man that when the bed is in the ballroom and lit up under the lights . . . doesn't . . . well, he doesn't shit the bed, the ordered man who can take orders, can machinegun the enemy in the Old World, the man who can get the honor and the glory . . . and the money—new fires in the new jungle—and all for the allure of the grail with a girl's face and golden voice.

"I'll expose the bastard. *Old sport* nonsense. He can't get away with . . . He's not smart enough—in front of me, '*always so cool*' at my own table . . . in his clown car . . . Well, I suppose the latest thing is . . . utterly submerged . . . control of things . . . up to *us* . . . all the *things* that go to make . . . *go* into town . . . Then, let's . . ."

Thomas *Buchanan*—the tough as nails tight-end in his years at Yale—he could surprise when things were on the line. Tom—the atomizer-of-tomorrows—he *kills* me. He's the best character I've done—much cleaner than the innocent and poor. He's the Byronic *man*—old Geo himself—not his antihero personae. Tom wins. Touchdown.

From their hermitage of the Plaza Hotel, our urban pilgrims engage the savage parlor of a day suite, a devout place to have their confessionals and pious mint juleps.

TOM
"The thing to do is to forget about the heat—"

SCOTT
—*said Tom.* He unrolled the bottle of whisky from the towel and put it on the table.

JAY
"Why not let her alone, old sport?"

NICK
". . . sensitivity and intelligence are not enough to *get* love or happiness."

TOM
"That's a great expression of yours, isn't it?"

SCOTT
—*said Tom sharply*.

JAY
"What is?"

TOM
"All this *'old sport'* business. Where'd you pick that up?"

NICK
We were listening to the portentous chords of Mendelssohn's "Wedding March" from the ballroom below.

DAISY
"Still—*I* was married in the middle of June."

SCOTT
—*Daisy remembered*.

DAISY
"Louisville in June! Somebody fainted. Who was it fainted, Tom?"

(29.) *separate madnesses*

~MUTABILITY IS A WALTZ

"'Life without pretensions leaves us facing the *basic* principles, which are usually a good deal worse and harder to unravel.'

'But what of the consequences?'

'*Pronunciation* has made many an innocent word sound like a doctor's orders for a stomach pump.'

'And if a spade becomes a steam shovel, what do we do when it's time to spade the garden?'

'Then, we spade with the steam shovel in a case of necessity, but *necessity* is one of the rarest things in the world.'"

MARY

I confess that neither the structure of languages, nor the code of governments, nor the politics of various states possess attractions for me. Rather, the moral relations of things are what matter—the busy stage of life. The virtues of heroines and their actions are my mind's theme.

I dream to become one among those whose name is recorded *in story*—as a gallant and adventurous benefactor of our species—while yet remaining perfectly humane, thoughtful in generosity, and tender amidst my passions.

PERCY

Recorded *in story*—yes! Yet, can what is behind—the drive *vis-à-vis*, the busy stage—be confronted? "Whence," I often asked myself, "does the principle of life proceed?" It is a bold question and one which has ever been considered as a mystery. Thus, with how many things are we upon the brink of becoming acquainted if cowardice or carelessness did not restrain our inquiries? One who has never tried an experiment in his life is a fool. None but those who have experienced the enticement of the metaphysical can conceive of the invitation and its incentives. In other studies, you go as far as others have gone before you—and there is nothing more to know—but in a pursuit of "the meta," there is continual food for discovery and wonder.

Yet, alas, how great is the contrast between us! You are alive to every new scene, joyful when you see the beauties of the setting sun and happier when you behold it rise and recommence a new day. You point out to me the shifting colors of the landscape and the appearances of the sky. "This is what it is to live," you cry! How *I* enjoy existence! In truth, I am occupied by gloom and ennui. Without your pestering direction, I neither truly care to witness the descent of the evening star nor the golden sunrise reflected, which are alone rivaled through the reflections of your own vision.

MARY

The site of the awful and majestic in nature can

indeed always effect the solemnizing of our minds. We can contemplate the lake—the waters that are placid. All around can be calm. The snowy mountains, these palaces of nature, they will not be changed. As if by the silent working of immutable laws, nature elevates us from all the littleness of feeling and grief, subduing and tranquilizing.

~CHEMISTRY KNIGHT'S SLAIN CHIMERAS

"Convulsions in nature . . . excite our curiosity . . . awaken our astonishment . . . the agencies of fire . . . the conversion of dead matter into living matter . . . how different is man informed through the beneficence of the Deity, by science, and the arts . . . brilliant, though delusive dreams concerning the infinite improvability of man, the annihilation of disease—and even death."

PERCY

The blue lake and snow-clad mountains, they never change. My ambition will not be altered. Success shall crown my endeavors. Wherefore not? Thus far have I gone, tracing a secure way over the pathless seas of the spirit—the very stars themselves being witnesses and testimonies of my interiorizing triumph. Why not still proceed over the untamed yet obedient elements of our constitution, the body—this vehicle—itself? What can stop the determined heart and resolved will of man? I may one day be worn and woeful as your ancient mariner, yet I carry a pistol and dagger constantly about me—readied—ever on the watch to prevent artifice.

MARY

With both sense enough—not to despise me as only romantic—and affectionate enough—for me to endeavor to regulate my mind—are you mad, my metaphysician, or whither does your senseless curiosity lead you? Preventing *artifice*? Attachment to this ideal of presumption, or any of bent vain glory—without participation in the world of others—is the business of foxes, of flowers—fauna and flora—not men. It requires more philosophy and persuasion than I possess for even sainted patience to continue as judge.

PERCY

Am I required to exchange aims of boundless grandeur for realities of little worth? Metals cannot be transmuted, and sure elixirs are sure chimeras. Isolated, I had dared not expect an epical success, yet I could not bear to look on the reverse of the picture. Cultivated in tasking experimentations past—engaged arduous heart and rapturous spirit—a resistless, almost frantic impulse urged me forward.

Yet, together in our trials, it has been a most beautiful season. Contributing greatly to our convalescence, never did the fields bestow a more plentiful harvest—or the vines yield a more luxuriant vintage. I have felt sentiments of joy and affection revive in my bosom. It is as if my gloom has disappeared, and in our short time, I have become as cheerful as before. Yet, I am ever attacked by my fatal passion and ever adjudged in my fated vacillations.

MARY

Consider the convergence of our love and virtues to be *our* fate. They are the principle of *our* life. Recount how Sir Isaac Newton avowed that he felt like a child picking up shells beside the great and unexplored ocean of truth. Those of his successors in each branch of natural philosophy appeared even to my youth's apprehensions as Tyros engaged in the same pursuit. Tyros, our untaught peasant, beheld the elements around him and was acquainted with their practical uses. The most learned philosopher knew little more. He had practically unveiled the face of Nature, but her immortal lineaments were still a wonder and mystery. The most learned might dissect, anatomize, and give names, but do not speak of a final cause. Even causes in their tertiary grades were utterly unknown to them. They promised impossibilities and performed nothing. Life is larger than our language. Life mocks our labels and taunts our newest principles.

PERCY

And even so, I am still urged forward. My thoughts remain committed to the channel of their earlier bent, the causation amidst this seat of such beauty and strength—turned to the force of life given to a visceral animal as complex and wonderful as the human frame! Some miracle might have produced it, yet the awareness of its discovered stages can be distinct and deduced probable—the first fires in the first minds.

My Parnassian application has been so ardent and eager that the stars have often disappeared in the light of morning whilst I am engaged. Yet, after more days of nights and of incredible laborious fatigue, I will emerge from my subterranean grottoes in knowledge of the dimension of disentombment and other mysteries of time. Nay, *more*, I will emerge a conduit bestowing the animations of my mind.

Life and death appear to me as ideal bounds of ink, which I should first break through and pour a torrent of light into our dark world. I will retread the steps of knowledge along the paths of time and exchange the discoveries of recent enquiries for the dreams of the forgotten—and its power. Do I not deserve to accomplish some great purpose of qualified wonder? Certainly, possessed of dauntless courage, glory is my preference. Thus, life must be the undertaking of the ever voyage of discovery.

MARY

"Of some world far from ours, / Where music and moonlight and feeling are one" / "A power from the unknown God, / A Promethean conqueror, came—"

PERCY

"—Apollo, Pan, and Love, / And even Olympian Jove / Grew weak, for killing Truth had glared on them; / Our hills and seas and streams, / Dispeopled of their dreams, / Their waters turned to blood, their dew to tears, / Wailed for the golden years."

MARY

"Worlds on worlds are rolling ever."

~MOONSTRUCK DRUNK

"The waning moon, / And like a dying lady, lean and pale, / Who totters forth, wrapt in a gauzy veil, / Out of her chamber, led by the insane / And feeble wanderings of her fading brain."

PERCY

Yes, romantic, mad, and best—yours. I must. Though we are separate madnesses, though we are divided presumptions, I now see *how* you glow, and now you are her. Her slow waning hermitage is released, seeping through your grey matters, through your wet brain lobes, wadding into bales and knotting—my Selene coming into full mad mother fertile moon.

~MOON-VINES

"He had caught a crimson moth once in the moon-vines and pinned it over his mantle on a calendar. 'It's a very good place for it,' he said, stretching the fragile wings over a railroad map of the South."

MARY

I glow, and now he is hers. He yearns to cease being lost and he sits on an old porch—morbid—raising his empty laudanum bottle to peer at his moon, wondering how the old Bishop of Cloyne is a Berkeleian in his Episcopal prayers, how he knows—but cannot—that he's *in* an idea-dream, immaterial moon-dream driven.

PERCY

Within another's living reverie, being authored, being moved—being removed—being enough. Did you not call us together—in your epistle—a glorious expedition? We are an exaltation. And wherefore is it not now gloried? Not because the way is smooth as a southern sea, but because it is full of perils, because at every new incident, our fortitude is to be called forth and our courage to be exhibited, because danger and now death surround it—and *these*—we are to brave and overcome.

Oh! Be mad, my Mary, or be more than mad. It cannot withstand you if you say that it shall not. All that we find proceeding mutable, my love, we shall overcome—*our* principle of life avowed.

(30.) *money*

SCOTT

I would rather impress my image (even though an image the size of a nickel) upon the soul of a people than be known, except insofar as I have my natural obligation to my family—to provide for them. I would as soon be anonymous if I could feel that I had accomplished that purpose—and that is no sentimental yapping about being disinterested. It is simply that having once found the intensity of art, nothing else that can happen in life can ever again seem as important as the creative process.

Typing is my thinking—my start, my something to defend or contradict, what to damn, what to enlarge—my magic-lantern that forces out a portrait of a siren for those who breed and weep and slay and will be slain. *Tap. Tap. Click.* I don't let them past my clunking keys—their singing, hating, dancing, and being eternally moved. I write their disillusions and amusements and cynicisms and tans of summers yet to come.

NICK

Gatsby turned to me rigidly.

JAY

"I can't say anything in his house, old sport."

NICK

"She's got an indiscreet voice. It's full of—"

SCOTT

—he hesitated.

JAY

"Her voice is full of money—"

SCOTT

—he said suddenly.

~IN HER HOUSE

"'If she were my child, I'd slap her jaw.'

'You would, would you! Well, I'd slap your own jaw.'

'When I was your age, I was glad to get anything. My dresses were all made out of Dixie's old ones. You're a vixen to be so spoiled. Mamma's little angel! It's exactly like she said she wanted it.'

'I've never heard so much fuss.'

'Alabama, will you stop that dispute? I'm trying to take a nap.'

'My Lord! She always has to blame somebody else. If it isn't me, it's Mamma or whoever's near—never herself.'"

NICK

That was it. I'd never understood before. It was full of money—that was the inexhaustible charm that rose and fell in it, the jingle of it, the cymbals' song of it. High in a white palace—the king's daughter—the golden girl . . .

(31.) *greed*

~WHAT ZELDA SAID

Fitzgerald's heroines were audacious and ingenious, and his heroes were fabulous strangers from lands of uncharted promise. His tragedies were hearts at bay to the inexorable exigence of a day whose formulas no longer worked and whose ritual had dwindled to less drama than its marionettes. His *pathos* was the pleasure of inescapable necessities over the keeping of a faith. His poignancy was the perishing of lovely things and people on the jagged edges of truncated spiritual purpose. These were the themes that transcended the crassness and bitterness which so easily betrays the ironic pen and leads the conviction of tragedy too frequently astray in the briars of scathing invective.

JAY

"No, old sport."

NICK

"I hear you fired all your servants."

JAY

"I wanted somebody who wouldn't gossip . . . Daisy comes over quite often—in the afternoons."

SCOTT

The headiness is not between good and bad, but what is chosen to cherish—ideal and intentional, the surreal glory of fiction—the principle of inarticulate aspiration and with whom it will link its fate.

NICK

So, the whole caravansary had fallen in like a card house at the disapproval in her eyes. Jay was now calling up at Daisy's request—would I come to lunch at *her* house tomorrow? And yet, I couldn't believe that they would choose this occasion for a scene.

SCOTT

Sending Death her fated mail, Time also gives her chocolates and he likes to light her cigarettes.

Tap. Tap. Tap.

NICK

We drank in long greedy swallows. We had luncheon in the Buchanan dining room, darkened, against the heat, and drank down nervous gayety with the cold ale.

DAISY

"What'll we do with ourselves this afternoon and the day after that, and the next thirty years? But it's so hot—"

SCOTT

—*insisted Daisy, on the verge of tears.*

DAISY

"And everything's so confused. Let's all go to town! Who wants to go to town?"

SCOTT

—*demanded Daisy insistently.* Gatsby's eyes floated toward her.

DAISY

"Ah, you look so cool."

SCOTT

Their eyes met, and they stared together at each other, alone in space. With an effort, she glanced down at the table.

DAISY

"You always look so cool—"

SCOTT

—*she repeated.* She told him that she loved him, and Tom Buchanan saw. He was astounded. His mouth opened a little and he looked at Gatsby and then back at Daisy as if he had just recognized her as someone he knew a long time ago.

NICK

"Unfathomable Sea! whose waves are years, / Ocean of Time, whose waters of deep woe / Are brackish with the salt of human tears! / Thou shoreless flood, which in thy ebb and flow / Art treacherous in calm, and terrible in storm, / Who shall put forth on thee, Unfathomable Sea?"

TOM

"All right—"

SCOTT

—*broke in Tom quickly*,

TOM

"I'm perfectly willing to go to town. Come on—we're all going to town."

SCOTT

He got up, his eyes flashing between Gatsby and his wife.

TOM

"I'll get some whiskey."

SCOTT

Good times . . . The mint julep, the true American beauty . . . *tap tap tap* . . . the cocktail of accomplishment. For mint juleps, Time abides our wars for our rosewater. *Clink*. *Clink*. Here's to a sugary toast . . . to the julep birth of a mythopoeia . . . and crushed mint . . .

(32.) *cold grey surname*

SCOTT

Spending most of her winter in bed, Mary starts to sign her letters "Runaway Dormouse." Indeed, during their tense period of despairing hopes from both scarcity and their distancing union—Percy and Mary's unnamed baby daughter is to be born to them. "You must rise early to receive the Dormouse all fresh from grubbing under the oaks." Mary wonders what color eyes her little spirit will realize to alleviate the evil of these nights suffered in her horrid, forced apartments. Their bond is now permanent, and they distract themselves with their editing, copying, and matches of chess. Mary is joyful to have the child of Shelley, and Percy joys in joining the lineage of Godwin and Wollstonecraft.

Mary's baby arrives. "Maia's child stirs, she enters stern into life." She is a small, lovely newborn with soft auburn hair—tiny, like a fairy, like a cherub. She is pretty and she is eager. At her daughter's birth, Mary sends for Fanny—Auntie Fanny—to delight together in their felicity. Mary journals on Percy's affections, "My soul is entirely wrapped up in him. Seeing his love and tenderness draws tears more delicious than the smiles of love from his eyes."

After their first week as a family, they—all too quickly—relocate to desolate lodgings in ruinous

British weather. Shifting from their first winter to their first spring, Percy and Mary's daughter dies in the same ironic number of days that Mary was alive before Wollstonecraft died. It is acutely pervasive to Mary that by simply being born *herself*, that she had caused her celebrated mother to suffer and die. The first grandchild of either of her parents has now died—unnamed. Mary laments, "I think about the little thing all day."

At her daughter's death, Mary and Fanny bear this bereavement together. Their mutual grieving is the last moments of bonding that Mary and Fanny share as devoted sisters. Penitently, Percy—troubled and afraid—is further withdrawn from Mary. Nurtured away from him, Ianthe is turning two, and Shelley feels formidable agony from his failure to protect his other daughter—gasping, suffering with only the surname of her maker, and perishing inanimate. Paranoid and paralyzed with phantasmal images, Percy lights her last candle under the cold, grey sky of ice and silence, weeping over his infant's little lips and eyes that will no longer open. *There is no light.*

Shelley goes alone to the Serpentine, sails his paper boats, and reminisces. "It was a time of riots, France threatened war, and Mary saw everything through a mist of tears." Her father will not speak to her. Miss Godwin is disconsolate, feeling displaced, isolated, distraught, and betrayed. "As each flower and herb on Earth's dark breast rises from the dreams of its wintry rest, only the silver dew of young winds can feed *love's sweet want*—enchained in solitude, trembling and panting companionless."

Bereaving, Mary sighs to her journal, "My charming Shelley understands the elves better than he does women." Two dear adulterine months later, Mary will be pregnant with their next illegitimate child.

(33.) *vampire*

~MAGIC AND DEATH

"When I was younger, I wanted to travel the Americas to harness the mystery of the tiger salamanders—and the pale pink amphibian of the Aztecs—to learn the molecular machinery to regenerate what's lost."

MARY

Remember during one of our doctrines was "the principle"—the breath of the vitalists, the coordination of animate creatures to express adulthood—and whether there was any probability of its ever being discovered and communicated?

~ELECTROPHORUS ILLS

"The well known facts relating to the torpedo ray and electrical eel prove that galvanic electricity is capable of being excited by the agencies of living organs. These facts, compared with the phenomena of the production of muscular contractions by galvanism, lead to interesting inquiries concerning the relation of this influence to living action."

MARY

There was that experiment in which a preserved piece of vermicelli in its glass case began to move with voluntary motion, musing perhaps a corpse would be reanimated—that Galvani had given token of such things. Perhaps the component parts of a creature might be manufactured—brought together—and endued with vital warmth, harnessing a current of electrical fluid in the twitching of nerves and muscles—

~HER MATTERLESS MATTER

"The general connection of electricity with physiology and with chemistry, which is, at present, involved in obscurity, is probably capable of experimental elucidation; and the knowledge of it would evidently lead to novel views of the philosophy of the imponderable substances."

MARY

—Remember? But what's blood without a heart to mobilize it? That's what must've made me dream, my Shelley, that our little baby came to life again—that she had only been *cold*, and that we rubbed her by the fire, and she lived. I had awoken in the night, and she appeared to be sleeping so quietly that I would not awake her. Yet, my baby is dead, and I am no longer a mother.

~HOARFROST

"A lovely being scarcely formed or molded, / A rose with all its sweetest leaves yet folded."

MARY

Your care and attentions are indefatigable, but you do not know the origins of my sufferings, this limitless illness. Pity me, my Percy. Spring is our unlucky season. Yet, all that is required is *us*—you and I as an assurance—a basic truth I find in your sights blinded as you make magic in seeing the savage—as you find our baby who died like a flower in a poem that just couldn't open.

PERCY

"Awful doubt, or *faith* so mild, so solemn, so serene, that man may be—but for such faith—with Nature reconcil'd."

I fail your feelings rent by irreparable evil, the void that presents itself to your soul, and your despair exhibited on your countenance. It is long before the mind can persuade itself that she whom we saw those days and whose very existence appeared a part of our own can have departed forever—that the brightness in such beloved eyes can be extinguished, and the sound of a voice so familiar and dear to the ear can be hushed.

Robbed of all that I could give her, how can one atone? I am my father's Prince Hamlet with no ghost, no new hopes for Ophelia, and no climax of death—like justice—just a sad heir with verse and too rough a divinity shaping his ends. Today, Claudius wins. Today, the tempter in the council scoffs, pointing—

no more a world for a Coriolanus. Look! Here are a pair surely routed.

MARY

When I look back on our summer, it seems to me as if that almost miraculous change of my inclination and will was the immediate suggestion of the guardian angel of my life—the last effort made by the spirit of preservation to avert the storm that was even then hanging in the stars and ready to envelop me. Her victory was announced by an unusual tranquility and gladness of soul, which followed the relinquishing of my torments. It was a strong effort of the spirit of good, but it was ineffectual.

Destiny was too potent and her immutable laws had decreed my utter and terrible destruction. Chance, the Destroyer, has asserted its prosecution and omnipotent sway over me from the reluctant moment I turned my steps from Papa's door.

~ADAMIC BISQUE

"Who would suppose, from Adam's simple ration, / That cookery could have called forth such resources / As form a science and a nomenclature / From out the commonest demands of nature? / There was a goodly soup."

MARY

Our usurping summer, our fall and winter of curses,

and now our punishing spring—passing us away. During my labors, I have not watched the blossom or the expanding leaves, sights which before always yielded me supreme delight—as if blinded from so simple a cure. So deeply have I been engrossed in preparing maternity and these writings that the leaves of our year have withered before my exertions could draw near their loving aim.

I now appear rather like a slave doomed than an artist occupied in a favorite employment. The beauty of the dream has vanished—comfortless sky. Breathless disgust fills my heart. I see the scenes that were familiar to me in my happier time, scenes I had contemplated but the day before in the company of her—who is now but a shadow and a recollection. Nothing can now appear to me as it had done the day before. A fiend has snatched from me every hope of future happiness. I, the miserable and the abandoned, am an abortion to be spurned at, kicked, and trampled on. I am alone. All this time, no distinct idea has presented itself, but my thoughts ramble to various subjects, reflecting confusedly on my misfortunes and their cause. I am bewildered in a cloud of wondrous horror.

PERCY

I have been tempted to plunge into the silent lake— that the waters might close over me and my calamities forever. Yet, hesitating, delayed in soliloquies on being alone, perchance to cut out this heartache acid with a bodkin, taking arms against the pangs and shocks and dread, *or not to*, starving sicklied pale, auditing this piling pain to add up—it doesn't—to mean something more than a nothingness that's less than even death.

What would be your surprise when you expected a happy and glad welcome—then—to behold, on the contrary, tears and wretchedness? I can scarcely believe that one small being can be responsible for such joy. You hate me, but your abhorrence cannot equal that with which I regard myself. Nearly in the light of my own vampire—my own spirit let loose from its ribcage grave—I have, through my own force, destroyed all that is dear to me.

MARY

My zodiac spectrums brood in quiet conflict, crafting and unmaking me, like abiding the careless arrows released into Saint Sebastian—arrows subsisted—yet arrows that abate, that banish youth to another world. When tested, there is no help. I am ancient Job unhedged in my cathartic monologues, abandoned.

She dies, and I survive. *She* dies, and—again, in strange math—I survive. Their fruitless sacrifices are *me*, and I am poverty.

Why does man boast of sensibilities superior to those apparent in the brute? It only renders them more necessary beings. If our impulses were confined to hunger, thirst, and desire, we might be nearly free. But now, we are moved by every wind that blows, moved by a chance word, or by a scene that such a word may convey to us. Why do I live? I know not. It seems utter despair has not yet taken possession of me. My feelings are of rage. Alas! Life is obstinate. Life clings closest where it is most hated.

(34.) *out of reach*

SCOTT

Does some cruelty just allow him a little more time than other opportunists to climb? What about the gat in the drawer? Yet, some fine day, the dream—I will love *this person*—wakes up, puts on the coffee, and can only give what a cloud or light can give . . . symbol . . . from a sky that gives, from a sky that takes.

TOM

"A lot of these newly rich people are just big bootleggers, you know. Well, he certainly must have strained himself to get this menagerie together."

DAISY

"At least they're more interesting than the people we know."

SCOTT

Daisy began to sing with the music in a husky, rhythmic whisper, bringing out a meaning in each word that it had never had before and would never have again. When the melody rose, her voice broke up sweetly, following it, in a way contralto voices have, and each change tipped out a little of her warm human magic upon the air.

~DANCE THAT SPEAKS

"'What do you find in the air that way?'

There was an aura of vast tenderness and of abnegation.

'—Forms, child, shapes of things.'

'It is beautiful?'

'Yes.'

'I will dance it.'

'Pay attention to the design well. You do well the steps, but you never follow the configuration. Without that, you cannot speak.'"

TOM
"I'd like to know who he is and what he does—"

SCOTT
—*insisted Tom.*

TOM
"And I think I'll make a point of finding out."

DAISY
"I can tell you right now—"

SCOTT

—*she insisted.*

DAISY

"He owned some drug stores, a lot of drug stores. He built them up himself."

NICK

Daisy's glance left me and sought the lighted top of the steps where a neat, sad little waltz was drifting out the open door. What was it up there in the song that seemed to be calling her back inside?

What would happen now in the dim incalculable hours? Perhaps . . . one moment of magical encounter would blot out those five years of unwavering devotion.

JAY

"I feel far away from her. It's hard to make her understand."

NICK

He was silent, and I guessed at his unutterable depression.

JAY

"—The dance? Old sport, the dance is unimportant."

NICK

He wanted nothing less of Daisy than that she should go to Tom and say: "I never loved you." After she had obliterated three years with that sentence, they could decide upon the more practical measures to be taken. After she was free, they were to go back to Louisville and be married from her house—just as if it were five years ago.

JAY

"And she doesn't understand—"

SCOTT

—he said despairingly.

JAY

"She used to be able to understand. We'd sit for hours—"

NICK

"I wouldn't ask too much of her—"

SCOTT

—*he ventured.*

NICK

"You can't repeat the past."

JAY

"Can't repeat the past?"

SCOTT

—*he cried incredulously.* He looked around him wildly, as if the past were lurking here in the shadow of his house—just out of reach of his hand.

JAY

"I'm going to fix everything just the way it was before—"

SCOTT

—*he said, nodding determinedly.*

JAY

"She'll see."

NICK

He wanted to recover something, some idea of himself perhaps, that had gone into loving Daisy. His life had been confused and disordered since then, but if he could return to a certain starting place and go over it all slowly . . .

~NATIVITY

"—and there was the place where she had sat while somebody told her about Santa Claus, and hated the informer and hated her own parents that the myth should be untrue and yet exist, crying out, 'I will believe—'"

SCOTT

Return . . . past in present . . . certain starting . . . *tap tap tap* . . . such color . . . against the current . . .

(35.) <u>rock vulture chain</u>

SCOTT

Watching, listening to time and all my bones make their sounds, drinking, *wasting*, grinning, not waiting—and damn grinning some more . . .

~YES'M

"'Mamma, did you love Dixie very much?'

'Of course. I still do.'

'But she was troublesome.'

'No. She was always *in love*.'

'Did you love her better than me, for instance?'

'I love you all the same.'

'I will be troublesome, too, if I can't do as I please.'

'Well, Alabama, all people *are*—about one thing or another. We must not let it influence us.'

'Yes'm.'"

SCOTT

Percy Shelley does not attend Old Bysshe's funeral. Reading *Comus*—Milton's debate on deception and depravity—on the steps of his childhood home, Shelley accepts his father's ban. Although Percy is not admitted to the reading of the will, great fortune finds great lovers. By the end of their first spring, Shelley successfully secures a settlement for a permanent annual income when his father is made the baronet of his family's estates.

~SAPPY P.

"Dear home, thou scene of earliest hopes and joys, / The least of which wronged-Memory ever makes / Bitterer than all thine unremembered tears. / Misery! we have known each other, / Like a sister and a brother / Living in the same lone home, / Many years—we must live some / Hours or ages yet to come."

SCOTT

Shelley is made the heir when his parents and siblings gather at the reading of Sir Bysshe's will. Percy's brother—who will acquire three titles of his own—is nine years old, and Shelley will never meet his siblings again. Three of Percy's four sisters will never marry, and Percy will never inherit the Shelley baronetcy. Still, in his annuity, he now prides in his appearance of independence. Shelley's pressing debts are paid, and he now properly supports Harriett—and their daughter and son. *Tap. Tap. Click.*

Together, without fear of arrest, Percy and Mary regenerate, traveling the heart of the English Riviera, redeeming their lost time. While they're touring, Percy delights in Mary's fable about a cat that eats roses and becomes a woman, and on this magical voyage, his forsaken intellectual purposes find regeneration. Having endured the bitter, earlier cold of their first migrations, they holiday at the warmest seashore resort in the country to celebrate the anniversary of their elopement. Whereas Mary determines to learn the maddening method of penning successful persuasion, Percy roams the cliffs to spy a view of his fallen emperor pacing the decks of the anchored British warship—bound for Atlantic exile.

Godwin publishes two letters of outrage on the interference of the Allies in the free affairs of France—on their voting to depose Napoleon and on their continuing war of conquest. Godwin, remaining hopeful for advancing the principles of the French Revolution, mourns Napoleon's defeat at Waterloo. Although Shelley praised Napoleon's aggressive campaign in an early poem of his youth, Shelley is now mixed about his defeat—rationalizing a restoration of the monarchy to be far worse for the future of *freedom*.

Still, writing *her Bysshe* a tender, compelling, virtuoso love-letter, Mary motivates her roving Shelley to devote his full vigilance to securing their happiness. Celebratory, Percy and Mary move into their cottage home in Bishopsgate at the edge of Windsor Great Park. West of primal London, Mary—"the Maie," "the Pecksie"—is back. This fresh summer, they ramble the winding brooks of the Thames and relish an excursion to Percy's alchemist rooms and infidel library at Oxford.

On the return down the Thames and under the oak-shades of Windsor Great Park, Percy poeticizes in melodious ideal hues—hues softened by death and in the checked ardor of his optimisms. Mirroring his transitional loss of hopes for political reform from Napoleon's final exile, Shelley turns his art inward. Haunted, paranoid, Shelley writes *Alastor*, his great contemplative work of an avenging demon—the ruinous quest of a doomed, seclusive luminary. These cautionary verses are of the destruction of his pensive poet who spurns sympathy, roaming for solitude and the secrets of the birth of Time.

~EGOMANIA

"The wanton horrors of its bloody play, / Frozen, unimpassioned, spiritless, / Shunning the light and owning not its name / —The cause and the effect of tyranny— / Unblushing, hardened, despising its own miserable being, / Which still it longs, yet fears, to disenthrall."

SCOTT

With softer fear-craft, Percy pens with newfound reverence and surprising gratitude. Percy concludes *Alastor* with his poet being devoured by the wasteland specter that haunts the impossible, destructive ideal of cold tranquility. Shelley shines brightest in his own self reproof, submitting his *Alastor* as a soulful presentiment of "the desire of the moth for the star"—of the cursed, unfruitful, aloof, and morally dead who languishes miserably selfish, blind, and torpid.

~THE GRAY PICTURE OF DORIAN

As one reviewer considers *Alastor* "indecent," Shelley is counter-defended by another as a rather chaste author, putting his readers—more than any other form of thought—in the mind of a sober nun.

SCOTT

Entering their second year, Mary is pregnant with their son, William Shelley. When their treasured boy is born, he is named in honor of Mary's father—wishing to soften his rationalist heart. Yet, as Godwin still publicly rejects his Mary, he grudgingly also now rejects his grandson—his *nepos*. Mary and Percy nickname their lovely, coveted son "Wilmouse." At Bishopsgate, Fanny—uninvited—visits, adoring her magical nephew.

Close to the Thames and large trees of King's Park, Mary feels as if her life is beginning again in her fond "Garden of Eden" cottage home—her kind season of relief and greatest happiness. Here, Mary—"the Dormouse"—is overjoyed and writes little, doting on and investing all her loving efforts in her Wilmouse and in her Shelley. Percy's mind is more at peace, and he begins to speak in a softer, less shrilling discordance of excited moods. Shelley writes to his friend, "The freedom of my recent expeditions, rural exercise, and the commencement of several literary plans provide such favorable effects on my health that my habitual dejections and irritabilities almost desert me. The leaves of this forest shatter in the gusts of the east wind. Share our new happiness at our fireside." *Tap. Tap. Tap.*

The season entering their third year is named throughout Europe as "the year with no summer." Some catastrophe from the Dutch East Indies is later blamed for the dense mists, fogs, and rains of this sunless haunting. Percy, Mary, and baby Wilmouse depart Dover to vacation the Swiss waterfront at Lake Geneva. Traveling, Shelley offers reverence to the echoes of carnage on the Field of Waterloo—to the skulls and grave of France. Once in Switzerland, they will frequent the outrageous nearby company—and festive games—of the favored poet, the first overnight man of literary celebrity, L. B. (their *Albe*). As Napoleon was ushered under the Union Jack to his final island, Lord Byron was twenty-seven and became the most famous figure in Western Europe.

Indoors, their minds will be enkindled, and Shelley will journal, "we talk of ghosts." During this stay at Lake Geneva, Mary will experience her vivid, unsettling *waking dream* that she will use to ground her new literary narrative throughout the next nine months. Mary will describe this remarkable summer without a solstice as the very movement of first *stepping into* her life.

~CELESTIAL EYES

"No tumbling water ever spake romance, / But when my eyes with thine thereon could dance, / No woods were green enough, no bower enough divine."

SCOTT

Traveling, Mary writes, "we read Latin and Italian during the heats of noon, and when the sun declines, we walk in the garden of the hotel, looking at the rabbits, relieving fallen Maybugs, and watching the motions of a myriad of lizards who inhabit a southern wall of the garden. I feel as happy as a new-fledged bird and hardly care what twig I fly to. In my present temper of mind, the budding flowers, the fresh grass of spring, and the happy creatures about me that live and enjoy these pleasures are quite enough to afford me exquisite delight! To what a different scene are we now arrived—to the warm sunshine and to the humming of sun-loving insects!

—From the windows of our hotel, we see the lovely lake, blue as the heavens—which it reflects—and sparkling with golden beams. The various ridges of black mountains rise, and towering far above, in the midst of its snowy Alps, the majestic Mont Blanc lords queen of all. Such is the bright summer scene reflected by the lake."

~MONT QUEEN B

"The wilderness has a mysterious tongue
Which teaches—a voice, great Mountain—to repeal
Large codes of fraud and woe; not understood
By all, but which the wise, and great, and good

Interpret—or make felt—or deeply feel.
All things that move and breathe with toil and sound
Are born and die; revolve, subside, and swell.
Power dwells apart in its tranquility,
Remote, serene, and inaccessible:
Frost and the Sun, in scorn of mortal power,
Have pil'd: dome, pyramid, and pinnacle,
A city of death, distinct with many a tower.
Yet not a city, but a flood of ruin.
The breath and blood of distant lands—forever
Rolls its loud water to the ocean-waves."

SCOTT

Originating from a glacier on Mont Blanc—nearly the tallest peak in all Europe—flows the River Arve through the Chamouni valley of the French Alps, emptying into Lake Geneva, whence then flows the Rhone to reach the Mediterranean. As Shelley lingers on the Bridge of Arve in the palaces of death and frost, he finds a terrible magnificence of the adamantine hand of Necessity—its avalanches, torrents, thunders, and deadly glaciers—as the proof and symbols of its absolute reign. The terrible force of the Arve flowing through this French valley of Mont Blanc is the formative setting of Percy's ensuing, superlative work.

~ARISTO P.

"We have bought some specimens of minerals and plants—and two or three crystal seals—at Mont Blanc to preserve the remembrance. The most interesting of my purchases is a large collection of all the seeds of rare alpine plants. These I mean to colonize in my garden in England."

~ALABAMA UNBOUND

"He met Alabama under the pink explosive apple trees where Lake Geneva spread a net below the undulating acrobatics of the mountains. Ladies in lace with parasols, ladies in linen with white shoes, and ladies in tangerine smiles patronized the elements in the station square. She played in sibylline detachment watching the Juras wedge their inky shadows between the rushes at the water's edge. White birds flying in inverted *circumflex* accented the colorless suggestion of a bounded infinite."

SCOTT

Celebrating Percy's twenty-fourth birthday, Mary gifts him a Swiss telescope to course the asterisms of their causal fluctuations. Percy points out the heavenly bodies to Wilmouse in the twilight skies. Mary writes, "we now inhabit a little cottage on the opposite shore of the lake and have exchanged the view of Mont Blanc and her snowy aiguilles for the dark frowning Jura. The thunderstorms that visit us are grander and more terrific than I have ever seen before. We watch them as they approach from the opposite side of the lake, observing the lightning play among the clouds in various parts of the heavens—and dart in jagged figures upon the piney heights of Jura, dark with the shadow of the overhanging cloud, while perhaps the sun is shining cheerily upon us. One night we enjoyed a finer storm than I had ever before beheld. The lake was lit up—the pines on Jura made visible—and all the scene illuminated for an instant. When a pitchy blackness succeeded, the thunder came in frightful bursts over our heads amid the darkness."

~WHAT GREEN LIGHT WAS

There was the simple discovery of the love of electricity—illuminating the voltage in the glass globe by rubbing it with leather. Then, there was the complex discovery of electrical love—of the high-bouncing lovers leaping in a line to let the ungrounded jolt travel, giving the charged green light passage through the heart and into the next beloved.

~PHANTOM PHENOMENON

From our hearts through all our nerves commanded, the pure animating of vital electricity is the mediator of the mutable body and the necessity of mind. This voltage is the power that moves our blood and breathing, the force that propels the impulses of thought, and the authority behind action. We *feel* electric before we think electrical, knowing "love" is the arbitrator of such anatomy enlivened.

SCOTT

Their minds are ignited. Germinating, Mary is coalescing Godwin's narratives, Wollstonecraft's visions, and Shelley's philosophy. Mary's first ideas of Prometheus are from her father's own book by his press, and she chiefly recalls from her childhood that Godwin's Prometheus *makes* man. Percy's ideas of Prometheus are formed from Goethe's theories and Bacon's *Wisdom of the Ancients.* Shelley and Bryron are also enthusiasts of "Prometheus Vinctus," in which Aeschylus sums up existence as the contesting of "the supreme despot" and "the benevolent rebel."

Indeed, from this summerless salon, their *L. B.*—in his full bohemian upper-class bravado—unveils his Napoleonic elegy, "Prometheus." There's this snappy, mesmerizing line—"*the rock, the vulture, and the chain.*" "Until its voice is echoless / . . . Like thee, man is in part divine, / a troubled stream from a pure source / and in portions can foresee / his own funeral destiny / . . . triumphant where it dares defy."

While Mary and Percy travel through the glaciers of Chamouni, she contemplates the work of her inspired story, perceiving—"a furious desolation, this cataract *falls*, dashing dread against its banks from a colossal deity commanding its unearthly thunder—an avalanche of terror—and ordering its ravenous, marauding wolves to shoot through the fiercely whitened mountain of new woe." Pensively, Mary queries, "aren't the great ones—chained atop mountains—greatly mistaking the shadow of courage for the substance of wisdom?" Mary muses on the special vivifying oil in the old broken castle on the rock over the river and *the thing* created at it—said to be still roaming these mountains.

~BREAKING UP HAPPY HOMES

"It pressed down about the earth, inflating the shadows, expanding the door and window ledges till the summer *split* in a terrific clap of thunder. You could see the trees by the lighting flashes gyrating maniacally and waving their arms about like Furies."

SCOTT

During another storm, Mary ruminates, "whence is the origin of such lightning communicated—from the same realm as poetics, that haven of life-gifting forces? Is there some magical electrical oil in the thundering shocks that can grant reanimation to ceased tissues—as from a radiant cloud of morning dew through the waste air's pathless blue, the wave of life's dark stream?—"

~ARIEL THE ARSONIST

"Electricity appears to act an important part in most of the natural operations that take place upon the surface of our globe and in the atmosphere. Lightning, thunder, the aurora borealis, and many other phenomena of meteorology are caused immediately by this powerful agent. By the extensive action of electricity, various changes in living and dead matter are perpetually produced. It occasions, or accelerates, in many instances, the phenomena of fermentation, of putrefaction, and of the general decomposition of organized compounds."

SCOTT

"—Can such electricity somehow transmit that vital fluid that awakens life—a soul-like spark of phantasmagoria that can be injected . . . into death . . . rendered receptive? Asunder—*no*—the trees are split!

No. It is an omen inviting obliterating incineration and matterless char—a masquerading force of hopeless, hopeless bereavement."

~FROM FREE GENEVA, WITH FREE LOVE

"Write to me of the new literature and political affairs. What has become of my poem? I hope it has already sheltered itself in the bosom of its mother—Oblivion—from whose embraces no one can be so barbarous as to tear into it. Yet, how else can I dedicate a temple to *liberty*?"

SCOTT

While Mary and Percy are in Switzerland, Fanny writes to them about England's state of excellence in evil and misery. The harvests of Great Britain are failing, and the food prices are rising. In such national distress, there is fear of an explosive—"overdue"—revolution. Although Fanny was forced to be Godwin's emissary to Mary and Percy for the last two years, Fanny is now advocating her own letters.

"These papers may never reach you, yet I cannot forbear recording." In Switzerland, Mary receives two vulnerable letters from Fanny describing her tense, unhappy life. As Mary departs from France, she again contemplates their mother writing her brave domestic manifesto near this port town while raising little Fanny alone. This strange autumn, Percy, Mary, and Wilmouse return to London. During the next month, Mary receives her last letter from Fanny.

~FAN MAIL
Well, *hell*, who wants to hear what's sullen in London when you can holiday—and watch holiday lizards run all through a holiday wall?

(36.) *their imaginative world*

SCOTT

Imploring Mary to have Percy liberate her from Godwin's, Fanny insists that when *all* had deserted them *that she* had loved them all the more. Although she was poor, dependent, and betrayed, Fanny had loved their lost daughter, drenched sick from pouring rains to mourn with them, and would surely help raise and shelter Wilmouse—wanting most to be included in their home and in the haven of their imaginative world. The attempts of Fanny-the-Arbiter to keep her family together are ignored.

At twenty-two years old, being denied for the last time, Fanny briefly meets with Shelley before departing to Wales to kill herself. In their last communications, she warns Shelley that Harriett is spreading false reports against him, and her knight makes Fanny the empty promise of an independent income in his will. Meeting Shelley alone in London, she initially tries to beseech him for Godwin's restless demands. Shelley—unusually *thick*—is dully unaware of the pains being stomached in her chaotic home. To him, "the black outlook" is of the "backslider" Godwin complaining that he won't be able to finish his new book without more of Shelley's money. Fanny's pleas and intersessions on behalf of Godwin then become mixed with her own—in solemn urgency for her life.

Reading her last bleak sentences to each of them, Shelley and Godwin both desperately rush to locate Fanny. In a hotel, Shelley finds her dead, and his mind is damaged. Fanny is wearing her best for her last outing—her silk-lined, fur-trimmed coat and hat over her blue skirt and white blouse. Mourning, Shelley sketches an ideal burial site with stairs surrounded by three urns of drooping blossoms, remembering—in dire remorse—fond passages of Fanny in Wollstonecraft's books and his own part he now plays in tainting her mother's legacy with more outrage—more *scandalabra*. Although Godwin simplifies his belief that Fanny's suicide stems from Percy's sustained preference for Mary, Godwin will soon believe that reconciliation with Mary will be *necessary* to avoid an even darker autumn of death.

"Misery—her kindred, her friend, her lover—sits near an open grave and calls Fanny's vacant name alone." In her last letter, she asked Percy to bury her when he will have discovered her death place. On Fanny's lifeless body, Percy confirmed the Swiss gold watch that Mary had sent her and articles of clothes that were Wollstonecraft's. Fanny could no longer tolerate being silly notes in the side margins of these *authors*. Fanny wanted them to know that her eradication was the only way for them to hear her—ceasing to be their scapegoated burden. Fanny had no confidant. She wanted to be dissolved under a mound of leaves into opium, bones, wine, and spices. Alongside his rueful sketch of dark, drooping flowers, Shelley composes his memorial. "Thy little footsteps on the sands / of a remote and lonely shore,

/ the twinkling of thine infant hands / where now the worm will feed no more, / thy look of mingled love and glee / when *one* returned to gaze on thee— / these footsteps on the sands are fled, / thine eyes are dark—thy hands are cold, / and she is dead—and *thou* art dead."

Ten years earlier, Godwin began to reveal Fanny's origins to her. Having believed Godwin to be her father, Fanny then understands that she is an adopted orphan. In her teens, Fanny read about her disturbing past from her mother's early writings. On her nineteenth birthday, a year before she met Shelley, Godwin gave her an inscribed copy of the book he published of her mother's major works and his biography of Wollstonecraft. Her readings were counterproductive.

Through her last three years, Fanny felt the least loved and feared the new awareness of her inheritance—her fear of suicidal impulses. Subsequently, while Mary and Percy are in Switzerland, Fanny—from a visitor at Godwin's— is told new stories about Mary Wollstonecraft and about her own early life while living in France. Fanny memorized published passages about herself as an infant and young child. "She has an astonishing degree of sensibility and observation . . . she is all life and motion . . . she is a sweet little creature . . . she indeed rewards me . . . her little intelligent smiles sinking into my heart." Wollstonecraft's final pledge before finding love with Godwin was that despite her own deepest wounds, she would indeed live for her sweet infant—her Francoise, her little Fannikin.

~WANT SIX KISSES

"Give Fanny a biscuit—I want you to love each other. I send no amulet today, but beware of enchantments."

— Wollstonecraft to Godwin

SCOTT

Fanny's early literary pace was astonishing and she excelled in drawing. Socially, Fanny was open, clever, opinionated, and delighted in being pleasantly useful. Compared with Mary, Godwin wrote that Fanny "was more reflective, less sanguine, and more alive to the prosaic obligations of life." Yet, misunderstood, she had become "The Obedient Peacemaker," "The Servant," and "The Nuisance." Wanting so much to be wanted, Fanny was resented, bearing the slights, jilts, rejections, crossfire, harassments, abuses, and neglect of her group of geniuses who seemed to be succeeding in peddling fictitious, impossible futures.

~NO APOLOGIES

"All women can't be classic beauties, but almost any young woman can be pleasant to the eye. The competition is heavy and in the open. Man is vain of his accomplishments and he has never apologized for the fact that he is strong or clever—that he has made a fortune or invented a good mousetrap. If a girl is a better facial draftsman than her neighbor, why shouldn't the world make a beaten path to her door?"

SCOTT

Fanny's future became *blank*, and her life became scarcely worth having. Fanny wrote, "You will soon have the blessing of forgetting that such a creature ever existed . . . a being whose birth was unfortunate and whose life has only been a series of pain to those persons who have hurt their health in endeavoring to promote her welfare."

Fanny's father had been an adventurous entrepreneur and an author as well. Before she was born, her father was a roving American veteran who abandoned Wollstonecraft in France once she had become pregnant with Fanny. Godwin had found him, and he didn't want Fanny after the death of her mother. From then, Godwin had been her "papa" for eighteen years. Miss Frances "Fanny" Godwin was Mary's last living link to her mother—from which Mary vowed all the more to live into the heritage of her maternal birthright.

Before their mother suffered a painful, feverish death, Wollstonecraft had only married Godwin for her last five months, which Godwin had considered the happiest season of his troubled life. Yet, to the living, she tried to avoid being unfair. For the last two years, Fanny felt that she could neither leave Godwin's nor remain there. However, during her last season, the growing scandal between Shelley and Godwin—Harriett's wildflowers of wildfire—dramatically prevented Fanny from her prospect of joining her aunt, Wollstonecraft's sister, as a readied educator in Ireland. Hence, Fanny felt she would endlessly be deprived of a future. Fanny determined to discontinue to live to be such a disgrace to such an endearing mother. Although it seemed to Mary that Fanny's root circumstance was her loveless suspension between Percy and Godwin's discordant households, Fanny's uncertainty and timidity had slowly mutated to scorn. Fanny was forgotten, was unconsoled, and was failed. Fanny had lived invisibly through all she tried to help, and her last letters were her decisive pleas for love.

~THE FIRST TRIO

"And now, my dear love, what do you think of me? Don't you find solitude infinitely superior to the company of a husband? When I have finished my pilgrimage, I will discharge the penance of my absence. Take care of yourself, my love, and take care of—will it be *a William* or *a Mary*? Whatever I am, do not *you* be drowned. Do not give place to this worst of diseases! I remember at every moment all the accidents to which your condition subjects you and wish I knew of some sympathy that could inform me from moment to moment how you do and how you feel. Farewell, my love. I think of you with tenderness and shall see you again with redoubled kindness. Kiss Fanny for me. Tell Fanny I have chosen a mug for her. There is an 'F' on hers, shaped in a garland of alternating green and orange tawny flowers. Your William affectionately salutes the trio: M., F., and—

last and least, in stature at least—little W. Or, is it little M.?"

— Godwin to Wollstonecraft

SCOTT

Alone in Wales again—where she had dreamed of her life with her poet—Fanny kills herself with a suicidal dose of laudanum. In fear of stimulating notoriety to her sister's death—and their strained, treasured *namesake*—Mary keeps her epistolary correspondences with Fanny concealed from further damaging Godwin's standing in London. Mary alternates writing bitterly and sewing new cloth into her private mourning clothes—like stitching together a creature as ugly as the dead—piecing together the subplots of her new chapter about the adopted servant girl of Mary's fictional Swiss family—and her tragic death.

"Noninvolvement" had been decided. "Go not—disturb not—the silent dead," Godwin had tearfully written Shelley. Godwin remembers that he let Fanny care for the garden when she was little and that he would give her six kisses if Fannikin had kept some berries and beans for her papa. There is no known image of Fanny Godwin. At her death, no one claims her—the first child of *the* Mary Wollstonecraft. Assumed to be in an unidentified pauper's grave, the place of Fanny's burial is unknown. There is no lock of hair in remembrance of Fanny. The only thing left of her is tears. Shelley, discovering Fanny deceased—regretting having neglected Mary's sister—writes,

"Misery—O Misery, / This world is all too wide for thee. / Her voice did quiver as we parted, / Yet knew I not *that heart* was broken / From which it came, and I departed / Heeding not the words then spoken."

When Mary was young, she memorized an entry from Godwin's journal. "I will be back and look out the coach-window to see the trees at Camden Town, and Fanny will spring to meet me, knowing I would soon return to my Frances and never give her away—that she shall be nobody's little girl but her papa's." William Godwin—*the poor son of a bitch*, having raised Fanny since she was three—writes to Shelley, "Do nothing to destroy the obscurity she so much desired that now rests upon the event. It was—as I said—her last wish. Think what is the situation of my wife and myself now deprived of all our children but the youngest and do not expose us to those idle questions, which—to a mind in anguish—is one of the severest trials."

Overamplified, Shelley's increasingly heightened mental strains are unleashing the psychic imagery of his Gothic machinery. His appreciation of the abnormal is developing into his literary aesthetic of terror, allying the beautiful and the grotesque. Through the increased receptive powers of his awful hypersensitivity, Shelley believes he is perceiving the conscious entrance of invisible phenomena. Like the prey of the two alluring, glaring eyes of his Alastor, it is Shelley's own severe mind that now violently feels the brutal and monstrous of the unseen.

(37.) *kiss-me-at-the-gate*

NICK

As I went over to say goodbye, I saw that the expression of bewilderment had come back into Gatsby's face, as though a faint doubt had occurred to him as to the quality of his present happiness.

Almost five years! There must have been moments even that afternoon when Daisy tumbled short of his dreams—not through her own fault, but because of the colossal vitality of his illusion.

It had gone beyond her. He had thrown himself into it with a creative passion, adding to it all the time, decking it out with every bright feather that drifted his way. No amount of fire or freshness can challenge what a man will store up in his ghostly heart.

His hand took hold of hers, and as she said something low in his ear, he turned toward her with a rush of emotion. I think that voice held him most with its fluctuating, feverish warmth because it couldn't be over-dreamed. That voice was a deathless song. I looked once more at them, and they looked back at me, remotely, possessed by intense life.

JAY
"I'd like to show her around."

NICK

Before I could answer, Daisy came out of the house, and two rows of brass buttons on her dress gleamed in the sunlight.

DAISY

"That huge place *there*?"

SCOTT

—*she cried, pointing.*

JAY

"Do you like it?"

DAISY

"I love it, but I don't see how you live there all alone."

JAY

"I keep it always full of interesting people—night and day—people who do interesting things, celebrated people."

NICK

With enchanting murmurs, Daisy admired this aspect or that of the feudal silhouette against the sky. She admired the gardens, the sparkling odor of jonquils, and the frothy odor of hawthorn and plum blossoms, and the pale gold odor of kiss-me-at-the-gate.

~GLEAMING, ADMIRING

. . . Pendulous pink blossoms of the Chinese honeysuckle—just little pink blossom lips you just want to kiss and kiss some more.

NICK

It was strange to reach the marble steps and find no stir of bright dresses in and out the door and hear no sound but bird voices in the trees.

SCOTT

"There grew pied windflowers and violets, / Daisies—the constellated flower that never sets— / Like a child, half in tenderness and mirth, / Its mother's face—with Heaven's collected tears— / When the low wind, its playmate's voice, it hears. / With its dark buds and leaves, wandering astray; / And flowers azure, black, and streaked with gold, / Fairer than any wakened eyes behold."

NICK

We went upstairs—through period bedrooms swathed in rose and lavender silk and vivid with new flowers, through the kaleidoscopic spectacle of dressing rooms and poolrooms, and bathrooms with sunken baths.

Finally, we came to Gatsby's own apartment. He hadn't once ceased looking at Daisy, and I think he revalued everything in his house according to the measure of response it drew from her well-loved eyes.

Sometimes, too, he stared around at his possessions in a dazed way—as though in her actual and astounding presence, none of it was any longer real. Gatsby sat down and shaded his eyes and began to laugh.

JAY

"It's the funniest thing, old sport . . . I can't—when I try to—"

NICK

—He had passed visibly through two states and was entering upon a third. After his embarrassment and his unreasoning joy, he was consumed with wonder at her presence.

He had been full of the idea so long, dreamed it right through to the end, waited with his teeth set, so to speak, at an inconceivable pitch of intensity. Now, in the reaction, he was running down like an overwound clock.

DAISY

"It makes me *sad* . . . I've never seen such—such beautiful shirts before."

JAY

"If it wasn't for the mist, we could see your home across the bay. You always have a green light that burns all night at the end of your dock."

SCOTT

Daisy put her arm through his abruptly, but he seemed absorbed in what he had just said. Possibly it had occurred to him that the colossal significance of that light had now vanished forever. Now it was again a green light on a dock.

NICK

There was a small picture of Gatsby, in yachting costume, on the bureau—Gatsby with his head thrown back defiantly—taken apparently when he was about eighteen.

DAISY

"I adore it! The pompadour! You never told me you had a pompadour—or a yacht."

JAY

"Look at this. Here's a lot of clippings—about you."

NICK

They stood side by side examining it.

DAISY

"Come here quick!"

SCOTT

—*cried Daisy at the window.* The rain was still fading, but the darkness had parted in the west, and there was a pink and golden billow of foamy clouds above the sea.

DAISY

"Look at that. I'd like to just get one of those pink clouds and put you in it and push you around."

NICK

When clouds are small and shift to a tight patchwork of blue with white, like mackerel scales, "it's as right as rain on its way."

SCOTT

Gatsby flipped a switch. The gray windows disappeared as the house glowed full of light. Outside, the wind was loud, and there was a faint flow of thunder along the Sound. All the lights were going on in West Egg now. It was the hour of a profound human change, and excitement was generating on the air.

(38.) *devils believe*

~PROFESSOR MEPHISTOPHELES

"A novel interests me on one of two counts: either it is something entirely new and fresh and profoundly felt, or else it is a *tour de force* of exceptional talent. A great book is both these things."

MARY

"The clouds are no longer the charioted servants of the sun, the rainbow has ceased to be the messenger of the gods, and thunder is no longer *their* awful voice, warning man of that which is to come. We have the sun which has been weighed and measured, but not understood. We have the assemblage of the planets, the congregation of the stars, and the yet unshackled ministration of the winds—such is the list of our ignorance.

Nor is the empire of the imagination less bounded in its own proper creations than in those which were bestowed on it by the poor blind eyes of our ancestors. What has become of enchantresses with their palaces of crystal, of their dungeons of palpable darkness? What of fairies and their wands? What of witches and their familiars? And, last, what of *ghosts*—with beckoning hands and fleeting shapes—which quelled the soldier's brave heart and made "the murderer" disclose to the astonished noon the veiled work of midnight? These which *were* realities to our forefathers, in our wiser age . . ." *Scratch. Scratch. Scratch.*

"—But let it be twelve at night in a lone house—assisted by solitude, flapping curtains, rushing wind, long and dusty passages, and half open doors—to set whether there be such *a thing* in the world or out of the world. I have heard that when Coleridge was asked if he believed in ghosts, he replied that he had *seen* too many to put any trust in their reality. Yet, the true old-fashioned, foretelling, flitting, gliding *ghosts*—who has seen such a one? I have known two persons who at broad daylight have owned that they believed in ghosts—for that they had seen one. One of these was an Englishman . . . Fee-fi-fo-fum."

"Yet, is it so true that *we* do not believe in ghosts?"
Scratch. Scratch. Scratch.

~HEARTHSIDE WITH MEPHISTOPHELES

"Grim reader, did you ever see a ghost? / No, but you've heard I understand; Be dumb / And don't regret the time you may have lost, / For you have got that pleasure still to come."

"Come, I will sing you some low, sleepy tune, / Not cheerful, nor yet sad; some dull old thing, / Some outworn and unused monotony, / Such as our country gossips sing and spin, / Till they almost forget they live: lie down!"

MARY

"On his arrival, his friend questioned him as to the cause of the traces of agitation visible in his face. He began to recount his ghostly adventures after much hesitation, knowing that it was scarcely possible that his friend should give faith to his relation. No sooner had he mentioned the coffin—with the crown upon it—than his friend's cat, who seemed to be lying asleep before the fire, leaped up, crying out "then I am king of the cats," and then scrambled up the chimney—and was never seen more."

(39.) *hills where love*

~GREEN EYES IN THE GREEN MIST
"'And do you dream?' asked the daemon."

PERCY

Ghost stories—I do not think that the skeptics who profess to discredit these visitations really discredit them, or if they do—in daylight—are admonished by the approach of loneliness and midnight to think with more respect for the world of shadows. All ghost stories are love stories. At all times, I am rebuked. Under the shine of the very sun, my love stands admonished.

"Peace, peace! Learn my miseries, and do not seek to increase your own," thus spoke my prophetic soul. As torn by remorse, horror, and despair, I beheld those I loved—the first hapless victims to my unhallowed arts. I haunt and refute my own life—

MARY

—*my* loves like imaginary ink—this first pair from my papers? *Our* loves? This exaggeration goes too far. All are forever punished who peep through the keyhole of your heart. To believe the tale of such a life would force the requisite fabrication of a monstrous abomination on which to blame its veracity.

How close is virtue's path? Does not guilt call out from the good road? Is this how the vice-furies find us—slowly plodding all their ire—sure life snatching by sure life, like here—Victor's victims—like every *Prince Prudent* in his hopes against you—only *unhallowed* you? Your inhumane mind is possessed in frightful transferals of paranoia. You've come to haunt yourself as your own priggish pedant who you see behind you in your strange mirror.

PERCY

Through their remembrance, you were able to call forth feelings of my original better heart and bring forth merrier memories. My understanding becomes undisciplined without you. Your thoughts alone can waken mine to energy. I am a cold, dark, midnight river, and you are my illumination—my firm moonlight, flecking the starry sky in woven pearl. Your gentleness and affection warm and open my senses. Can I become again the same happy creature? But, here, now—this dreary November—all is blasted!

MARY

Can someone so loved be so erased—edited from the histories of all the hearts she lived amongst? I remember when we were little, and Papa took Fanny on his lap when Coleridge came to read his albatross poem. We were frightened. I clung to my father's arm, and Fanny hid her face in his chest. Later, when we were girls, we heedfully looked for the mariner's great bird when we went to the sea, but never saw any fly in.

She was a young teen when Papa proudly presented her during his meeting with Burr, impressing him with Fanny's intelligences. She was childhood's best memories—from gleaning strawberries together in spring up to our clever dinners at Papa's table when you started to frequent us—just dreams, *sentiments* that die with me.

Yet, *dwelling* on irresolvable uncertainties so long—the dark things—is an evil in itself. How much happier we can still be, believing our native land to be the world—than aspiring to become greater than nature allows.

PERCY

You have hope and the world before you, but my losses are irreversible and I cannot begin life anew. You've offered good effort for the goodness of my soul—but everything is now ineffective! I have been condemned by my own evil prosecution. "Man's yesterday may never be like his morrow." The same step into the same river is impossible, not remaining what it is from one moment—one step—to the next. The past cannot, again, reoccur recurrent. "Naught may endure but mutability!"

MARY

Yet surely, will not spring follow? We must take recess in the supplanted knowledge that the tyranny of our heartache will be shocked by all the other haunting griefs that will later arrive to replace it. Yet, we endure. Even a hell has hills where love—love staring—might touch us with life.

PERCY

You endure. Love can endure. However, instead of that serenity of conscience which allowed me to look back upon the past with self-satisfaction—and from thence, to gather promise of new hopes—I am seized by remorse and the sense of guilt which hurries me away to intense tortures.

I feel as if my soul is grappling with a palpable enemy. I feel mingled with horror. Alastor! This full tiresome weight of disappointment—this bifurcated self—is inescapable. "Like one, who, on a lonely road, doth walk in fear and dread, and turns no more his head; a frightful fiend doth close behind him tread!"

MARY

Inescapable. They hate Mother—with murderous disgrace to Papa and his sagacious kind. Her daughter—my sister of my life!—is dead. My baby, my girl is dead. For Harriett, they hate me. Is this all a little guiltless *boy* is to know—Wilmouse's mother rejected in all ways meaningful and his father maimed in endless vilifications? Is this how "love" finds our son?

"Who was I? Let me see that I excite the sympathy of some existing thing. I shall feel the affections of a sensitive being and become linked to the chain of existence and events. I ardently desired the acquisition of knowledge and longed to enter the world, to open a field for the plan of life—marked out in an enslaving passion. Overwhelm me and extinguish all fear."

And yet . . . even so . . .

PERCY

In forcing our freedom, I've found a frenzy that overwhelms—an abyss I've discovered that's deepened difficult to ascend. It's made my mind lightning, my Mary. All my *Merriment*, extinguish your distress that I do not consider *Love* to be *a god*. Love is confessed by many to be a great god. Yet, Love is neither mortal, nor immortal—but something intermediate. Love is communication between the divine and human—their attendant power to convey and render. Whilst we sleep and then wake, Love—like Mab—is the converse conceded us by the gods. There are many daemons, and *Love* is one of the more grand—the force of transmission between the divine and the mortal.

~LOW DAEMONS LOW

"Filling the house with gray-turning, gold-turning light, the shadow of a tree fell abruptly across the dew, and ghostly birds began to sing among the blue leaves." "The spectral birds, perched on the utmost spray, / Incessantly renewing their blithe quest, / With perfect joy received the early day, / Singing within the glancing leaves, whose sound / Kept a low burden to their roundelay."

PERCY

At waking and twilight, I find that the lowest order and most material of daemons are *birds*—and their presages of the overthrow of our pantheon. I hear what they commune to me—their melodious night songs released from the progressive lusts of hell, heralding its darkling snares. Death is its own love. It sings to me songs of graves, and I scribble of the inconstancy of fortune and instability of human life. I hear the birds, and *Misery* comes home, my Mary. As daemons hunger for communion, men appear to me as monsters thirsting for each other's blood.

Yet, my Mary, let me tell you of the *greater* daemon that is later conceded by the gods of each eradicated empire when *Love* is most enthroned—whilst the great gates of the great walls rattle in a yearning ferocity of such an ensnared *feast* set for its terror—readied for release.

~ALL AFIRE

Ariel: "With hair upstarting—then like reeds, not hair—was the first man that leaped; cried 'Hell is empty, and all the devils are here!'"

Prospero: "Why, that's my spirit!"

PERCY

In one last wind, all the birds fall dead, and the avenging, arisen *Power*—its hell on earth—is spread! It sings its own victorious advent song. Each comes to belief in its procession. Advancing, the food of men and women fails. They draw the breath of its decay. Spreading, the scent of blood lures them—gaunt and wasting—stalking like fell shades among their perilous prey. In their green eyes, a strange disease glows, moaning upon their gazing faces. The vines and orchards are burned so that the meanest sustenance is weighed with gold, and *Avarice* dies before the god it made. There is no animating fuel, and only what is loathed is found. In the marketplace, only stagnant vile matter—even human flesh—sits as remains for sale. It is weighed in small scales, and many a face is fixed in eager horror. The depths are barren—barren now are all the depths. In windless *heat*, each dried well chokes with rotting corpses and becomes a cauldron of green mist made visible at sunrise.

~THE ROOD IS ON FIRE

"And their baked lips, with many a bloody crack, / Sucked in the moisture, which like nectar streamed; / Their throats were ovens, their swollen tongues were black / As the richman's in hell, who vainly screamed / To beg the beggar, who could not rain back / A drop of dew. / Here the earth's breath is pestilence, and few / But things whose nature is at war with life— / Snakes and ill worms—endure its mortal dew. / But I am Pestilence; hither and thither / I flit about that I may slay and smother: / All lips that I have kissed must surely wither, / But Death's—if thou art he, we'll go to work together."

PERCY

Madness rages like poison through their bursting veins. Many see their own lean image everywhere. Then, ghastlier blistered selves appear beside them. Blind *contagion*, advancing, sheds its victims, shrieking in bloodlust. Lastly, they screech aloud, "we tread on fire!" They *shriek* as they are consumed. The great heat spreads. "Hell is become earth," gasps the last of the love in the last of the blood of the last boiling man—

from the last melting trumpet.
Desolation is deified. *Be* . . . not! Anathema! And like my words—*abolished*—they were no more.

Oh, Mary, there is *horror* after all Love's powers . . .

Part 2: Necessity

ARIEL: "Was't well done?"

PROSPERO: "Bravely, my diligence. Thou shalt be free."

(40.) *rain*

~DARKNESS AND DISTANCE

A blind man, feeling his way along with a walking stick, had come in the door, and Scott was watching him as if he were a unique fact. So, I paid the cigar man for both packages, and we went out into the street. I noticed that Scott was acting queerly as we stepped on the sidewalk. He seemed quite unsteady on his feet, and as I looked up, I saw that he had closed his eyes.

Silently, I watched him walk down the crowded street, feeling his way along by tapping against the sides of the buildings with his walking stick. A young woman, passing in company with a man, exclaimed, 'Oh look at that poor boy. How sad it must be to be blind.'

But Scott walked on, his eyes shut. He had almost experienced the sensations of a blind man for an entire block on a crowded street when, unluckily, two middle-aged women passed us by, and passing, one said to the other: 'Oh look at *that*.' And then, Scott opened his eyes.

SCOTT

Our hero reaches out into darkness and distance across the snaring egg-split bay . . . Well, who the hell says "no" to an invite to tea? He was ready, but had he thought it through about Buchanan's daughter with Daisy?

Had he thought past . . . had our good American quarterback planned his audibles? Who would Gatsby have to outgun? Would Daisy really mind the underground bonds business?

NICK
"Don't bring Tom—"

SCOTT
—he warned her.

DAISY
"What?"

NICK
"Don't bring Tom."

DAISY
"Who is '*Tom*'?"

SCOTT
—she asked innocently.

NICK

The day agreed upon was pouring rain. A greenhouse of flowers had arrived from Gatsby's. There was the sound of a motor turning into my lane. Under the dripping bare lilac trees, she arrived. Daisy's face—tipped sideways beneath a three-cornered lavender hat—looked out at me with a bright ecstatic smile.

DAISY

"Is this absolutely where you live, my dearest one?"

SCOTT

The exhilarating ripple of her voice was a wild tonic in the rain.

NICK

As she admired the flower arrangements in my bungalow, there was a gentle, dignified knocking at the front door. I opened it. Gatsby—pale as death with his hands plunged like weights in his coat pockets—was standing in a puddle of water glaring tragically into my eyes. In his silver shirt and gold colored tie, there were dark signs of sleeplessness beneath his eyes. With his hands still in his coat pockets, he stalked by me into the hall.

For half a minute, there wasn't a sound. Then from the living room, I heard a sort of choking murmur and part of a laugh followed by Daisy's voice on a clear artificial note.

DAISY

"I certainly am awfully glad to see you again."

SCOTT

A pause, it endured horribly.

NICK

Gatsby stared down at Daisy sitting frightened but graceful on the edge of the stiff couch.

JAY

"We've met before."

NICK

His eyes glanced momentarily at me, and his lips parted with an abortive attempt at a laugh.

DAISY

"We haven't met for many years."

JAY

"Five years next November."

NICK

With the automatic quality of Gatsby's answer, I had

them both on their feet with the desperate suggestion that they help me make tea.

Gatsby got himself into a shadow. While Daisy and I talked, he looked conscientiously from one to the other of us with tense unhappy eyes. I made an excuse at the first possible moment and walked out the back way for a huge, black, knotted tree whose massed leaves made a fabric against the rain.

SCOTT

While the rain continued, the murmur of their voices rose and swelled—now and then—with gusts of emotion.

NICK

I felt that silence had fallen within the house. I went in—after making every possible noise in the kitchen—but I don't believe they heard a sound.

They were sitting at either end of the couch looking at each other—as if some question had been asked or was in the air—and every vestige of embarrassment was gone.

Daisy's face was smeared with tears. When I came in, she jumped up and began wiping at it with her handkerchief before a mirror.

SCOTT

But there was a change in Gatsby that was simply confounding. He literally glowed. Without a word or a gesture of exultation, a new well-being radiated from him and filled the little room.

JAY

"Oh, hello, old sport—"

SCOTT

—he said, as if he hadn't seen Nick for years.

NICK

"It's stopped raining."

JAY

"Has it?"

SCOTT

And he repeated the news to Daisy.

JAY

"What do you think of that? It's stopped raining."

DAISY

"I'm glad, Jay."

NICK

Her throat—full of aching, grieving beauty—told only of her unexpected joy.

(41.) *acquiesce*

SCOTT

I open this leatherbound wastebasket, which I fatuously refer to as my 'notebook.' 'Crack!' goes the pistol, and off starts this entry. Sometimes, I have caught it just right. More often, I have jumped the gun. On these occasions, if I am lucky, I run only a dozen yards, look around, and jog sheepishly back to the starting place. But, too frequently I make the entire circuit of the track under the impression that I am leading the field and reach the finish to find I have no following. The race must be run all over again—a little more training, take a long walk, cut out that nightcap, no meat at dinner, and stop worrying about politics.

Cracking the spine of fresh verses gets things moving again. My mothering Maxwell—good "get-it-published" Perkins—got me the new one by the Wolfhound's best poet. In it, "the villagers" wanted to know about Death: "The owl whose night-bound eyes are blind unto the day cannot unveil the mystery of light. You would know the secret of death, but how shall you find it unless you seek it in the heart of life?"

Time, do as we wish. *Tap. Tap. Click.* Throughout this autumn, Mary, grieving, remains distraught about the death of her sister, aggravating her emotional wounds from the death of her infant daughter and the continuance of her estrangement from Godwin. Mary journals, "The idea of his quiet disapprobation makes me weep as it did in the days of my childhood."

~WITHOUT

"She sat alone that night without Bonnie. She hadn't realized how much fuller life was with Bonnie there. She was sorry she hadn't sat more with her when she was sick in bed. Maybe she could have missed rehearsals. Alabama threw the broken fan and the pack of postcards that she had left behind in the wastebasket."

SCOTT

Anonymously, through disheartening letters—even up to the week before her disappearance and dismal suicide—Fanny had merely, *tacitly*, remained as "The Liaison" amid Mary and their father. Though, in the crisis of losing their beloved Fanny, Godwin privately reconciles with his *living*, rejected daughter.

~OLD ANCHOR

"Every day she went to the old house—so clean inside and bright. She brought her father little special things to eat—and flowers. He loved yellow flowers. We used to gather yellow violets in the woods when we were young."

SCOTT

In alignment with his political philosophies, Godwin—having acquiesced—then coerces Shelley for his own subsidy of the settled annuity, prompting his baronet-in-waiting to still fulfill his solicitations. Provided a paltry funding for subsisting his household and business, Godwin endeavors his own new somber novel.

(42.) *obdurate*

MARY

I dismissed her imploring appeals. She required kindness—*sympathy*—and did not believe herself utterly unworthy of it. All my speculations and hopes are stilled. "Work without Hope draws nectar in a sieve, / And Hope without an object cannot live."

GODWIN

Her eyes had wandered in vacancy, for they had lost their charm and their delight. "Where was then / Wisdom the mirrored shield, or scorn the spear? / Or hadst thou waited the full cycle, when / Thy spirit should have filled its crescent sphere, / The monsters of life's waste had fled from thee like deer."

Without release, I harbored this longsuffering too much to her—the disgraces we were accused of—as if we had sold you to Shelley, as if to some James Harris, after you returned to us from Scotland and then so swiftly to the continent with him.

MARY

Fanny, my cherished one!—our cherished one! And now . . . my Shelly . . . *Love*—is man, indeed, at once so powerful, so virtuous and magnificent, yet so vicious and base? A glorious creature he was in his halcyon days, then so noble and godlike in ruin, feeling his own worth and the greatness of his fall.

GODWIN

It's been a rather dreary November, Mary. His constant and deep grief fills me with sympathy and compassion. He must have been a noble creature in his better days, being even now—in wreck—still magnetic and amiable. He is eloquent. Once his words had even power over my heart. Trust is a mystery.

In isolation, we'll never discover all the forces that determine us. Alas! Mary, when falsehood can look so much like truth, who can assure themselves of certain happiness? Admit my return. Is your disaster so irreparable? What have you put to mind and intend?

MARY

My first resolution was to quit forever my country, which—when I was happy and beloved—was dear to me, when man was susceptible of perpetual improvement. Yet, in my adversities, England had become hateful. What could I do? Yet, if I continued so obdurate, all would look on me as a wretch—doomed to ignominy and perdition. In an evil hour, I subscribed to a lie—and now—only am I truly miserable. And thus put, as I imagine, the seal to my fate. As if possessed of magic powers, he has obscured his deepest intentions from me. Whether from cowardice or prophetic feeling, my heart sinks within me.

I have read from a great philosopher that "*feeling* ripened into virtue embraces the interests of the whole human race and keeps aloof from the unmeaning rant of romance." Yet, Papa, great thoughts of great virtue *were* mine, "when first / The clouds which wrap this world from youth did pass. / But I am worn away, / And Death and Love are yet contending for their prey."

GODWIN

"Go and catch a falling star. / Tell me where all the past years are." From its complexities and misery, there is no elixir to life—not even in a story. Yet, in our anxieties of absolutes, we must choose. Our European religion of charity does not admit that we have a right to do what we will with our own. It is rigorous in prescribing the duties of the rich, as well as of the poor. The beacon and regulator of virtue is impartiality—that we shall not give exertion to procure the pleasure of *an individual* which might have been employed in procuring the pleasure of many individuals.

MARY

I sometimes vacillate between fear and love for him. Yes, it's certainly not order that my Shelley desires—nor freedom, *per se*. He requires life without restraints, which is unalike. He engineers himself to live without order until he's forced to be ordered—by toxic forces he despises. Without restraint, he attracts strong regulating powers to himself—as if he's fixed on a merry-go-round of prison recitals and funeral speeches.

"On both sides thus is simple truth suppressed." Yes, my Percy will will not yield until sainted in the poetical echelon, dramatizing the dire invention of his own "hamartia," wasting us all—we who will surely be forgotten. He dooms himself enslaved through all the days of our eyes entranced in him, ensnared in his lethal liberties.

GODWIN

"I was benevolent and good. Misery made me a fiend. Make me happy, and I shall again be virtuous." No. People are rendered ferocious by misery. It is always youth's wooing jest. "Therefore I lie with her and she with me, / And in our faults by lies we flattered be." For Percy, his companion must be of the same species and have the same defects. This being, he must—being what he is—create in you. Mary, persevere in your avoidance of his ambition and seek happiness derived from tranquility. He treats matter with his hubris—convinced it is his to mold—and by attempting to control, destroys both.

~JAMES "ROUSSEAU" HARRIS

Grasping for braggadocio, he boasts his vainglories. "I am part of the race's consciousness. I have influenced the language and youth. That's why I command the prices I do, *baby*. I occupy a lonely eminence—for it *is* lonely, being a bigshot. I can't imagine anyone defying me in the really big things. I *must* rule. Napoleon was like that, wasn't he? All the small writers look up to me. I am a topnotcher. I am the *maître*."

MARY

His species have I become. I took Mother from you, and Fanny has sacrificed herself in my late causes. We—only *now* less divided—are the living, and my bent is revealed. I see now that my resolve is to cover my Shelley with a love that veils his trivialities, his incivilities, and vilifications of his loveliness. Though I have caught my fallen star in my arms and now also burn with him, I have not been blinded. I see all the more through one light. I am his and what I will do is remain his.

GODWIN

"The serpent hisses where the sweet birds sing."
Yet, first and now, it is your father who sighs all too soon—of his best beloved—that "thou hast wept to know / That things depart which never may return: / Childhood and youth, friendship and love's first glow."

(43.) *the pursuing*

SCOTT

By the time of the war, I had decided that poetry was the only thing worthwhile. So, with my head wringing with meters, I spent the spring doing sonnets, ballads, and rondels into the small hours. I read somewhere that every great poet had written great poetry before he was twenty-one. I had only a year, and, besides, battle was impending. I must publish a book of startling verse before I was engulfed. By autumn, I was in an infantry officers' training camp with poetry in the discard and a brand-new ambition—I was writing an immortal novel.

If poetry had not gone out of fashion, I would have been a poet. But poets don't make any money today, so I couldn't afford to be one. And so now it's to this, I'll write prose on the same fine lines as Keats's poetry.

Click. Tap. Tap. Prose talent—assimilations and selections—is not only having the thing to say but the necessity of saying it in interesting ways. My gift is not discursive or intellectual. I have the harder gift—of the lyrical, wistful, and elegiac.

JORDAN

"She heard the name Gatsby for the first time in

years. It was when I asked you—do you remember?—if you knew Gatsby in West Egg. After you had gone home, Daisy came into my room and woke me up and said, 'What Gatsby?' When I described him—I was half asleep—she said in the strangest voice that it must be the man she used to know. It wasn't until *then* that I connected this Gatsby with the officer in her white car."

SCOTT

We want life on a higher plane. We know that life will deliver what we want—as young and soon as it will. Yet, like all my favorite burnout poets, the old muses seem to pull back what little they implant and leave their writer gnawing notoriously every day at what was there.

What I carry in my waking heart, I sometimes shake off in my dreams. The great promise is that something is going to happen, and after a while you get tired of waiting because nothing happens, except growing old, except growing within—when life writes you a brief postcard, "have been meaning to come in and see you. Manage things until I do. Till then, chin up."

NICK

Then it had not been merely the stars to which he had aspired on that June night. He came alive—to me—delivered suddenly from the womb of his purposeless splendor.

SCOTT

Is there only *promise*? Who's enough at anything? I take things hard. I emotionally stamp my pages with the authority of failure so that people can readily understand—so that they can read it blind like braille.

No one wants to be interested in a soldier who is only a little brave. So, I swim submerged—like a double agent—holding my breath all the time, extracting personal protozoa materials to transfigure into fictions, preaching to myself the boldness and the nerve that being a writer is the profession that wants the whole works, every covert particle.

Click. Tap. Tap. Death is careless, most beauties fade, and the snows that we want always melt—an ardent author's battleplan against impermanence is tenderness, is sweetness.

JORDAN

"He wants to know . . . if you'll invite Daisy to your house some afternoon and then let Gatsby come over."

NICK

The modesty of the demand shook me. He had waited five years and bought a mansion where he dispensed starlight to casual moths so that he could "come over" some afternoon to a stranger's.

JORDAN

"He's a regular tough underneath it all. You're just supposed to invite her to tea."

NICK

Unlike Gatsby and Tom Buchanan, I had no girl whose disembodied face floated along the dark cornices and blinding signs. So, I drew up Miss Jordan Baker beside me, tightening my arms. A phrase began to beat in my ears with a sort of heady excitement. "There are only the pursued, the pursuing, the busy, and the tired."

JORDAN

"And Daisy ought to have something in her life."

NICK

It made no difference to me. I'm slow thinking and full of interior rules that act as brakes on my desires. Dishonesty in a woman is a thing you never blame deeply.

"Suppose you met somebody just as careless as yourself?"

~A SUMMER'S INSIGNIA

"Through the summer, Alabama collected soldiers' insignia. By autumn, she had a glovebox full. No other girl had more, and even then, she'd lost some. So many dances and rides and so many golden bars and silver bars and bombs and castles and flags and even a serpent to represent them all in her cushioned box. Every night, she wore a new one."

JORDAN

"I hope I never will. I hate careless people. That's why I like you."

(44.) <u>*adjudged*</u>

~GET READY TO PAY A CARELESS AMAZING AMERICAN STINKO

Since I must make *money*, I must use writing in its least skillful form—*criticism* (four copper pennies per golden word). I've lifted the veil of these British classics and I find Mary rolling up her eyes, like in "The Reluctant Bride." So, my Lit-crit stands, get ready to pay up—*baby*—up and up, the Fitzgerald way.

SCOTT

Their contemporary Romanticism movement is Percy's self-proclaimed "spirit of the age" of individualism—that poets are the "unacknowledged legislators of the world," rallying against conservative institutions with enthusiastic theories of energizing social alleviations and reconciliations with the metaphysical.

Although Percy will be considered by their *interior* as the fervent literary architect and leading inspirator of their artifices of revolutions, yet, it is actually—mathematically—our will-be-Shelley, our Mary-with-the-magic, who *is* its colloquial more warranted Regent of Romanticism, per her unique pedigree in such daintily tallied credentials:

~independently exhausting her father's vast library in lieu of formal schooling;

~nurturing her indulgences in her ethereal waking dreams of the phantasmal and fantastical;
~her cultivation in her blended Leftist family;
~the anomaly of her competitive intellectual surroundings—her own parents' freethinking circle of radical authors frequenting their home in London;
~attuning young to the direct sensitivities of Blake, Wordsworth, and Coleridge, their founding candid experimentalists;
~then, to most embody their *Age*, her intimate influences from the paragons of her Shelley and his Byron—also, later from teatime with Keats himself—shaping and priming her extractions;
~and most considerably, lettered in her father's own anarchist writings, Godwin's numerous devotees, and his even greater master novels;
~and—moreover and *most over*—the memorizations of her mother's ardent texts and arguments for the experiment of educational equality in England.

Though, as the cumulative *successor* of the spirit of their movements, Mary defects—having charmingly "become infinitely indifferent to it"—supplanting *reputation* for her counter-revolutionary synthesis of realized *domesticity*. Philosophically and socially, she slowly loses a faith in the dangerous ideals of these radical writers, growing assuredly conservative amongst this "crazy fish" age of alterations—with prized sanity.

~HOW TO RISE JUST FINE

"Could a woman of delicacy seduce and marry a

fool? This ignoble mode of rising in the world is the consequence of the present system of female education. It is a maxim for some that the wisest thing a young woman of sense can do is to marry a fool. And they will learn by experiment the justice of their maxim. Women are certainly great fools, but nature made them so. I think—with a poor mad woman I knew—that there is God, or something very consolatory in the air. I have not time or paper, else I could draw an inference not very illustrative of your "chance-medley system," but I spare the moth-like opinion—there is room enough in the world. What a fine thing it is to be a man!"

— Wollstonecraft to Godwin

SCOTT

Now that Mary is authorial, she gravitates to the very trend that she had fled from in her stepmother, the very thing that the printings of her parents had dissuaded—what had made many others around her dismal—in the complaints of Fanny, in Shelley himself, and in Shelley's Harriett.

Through vision unexpected, Mary's schematic of basic familial serenity is a cooling stalemate to their Romantic crusades, dramatically evolving her critical counterforce. Mary's emerging tale embraces and cherishes a defense of her own dialectic—and to Godwin's own growing gladness in his dissenting daughter of his heart.

MARY

Do we wait to expose our stunted, heedless uncaring of others in the failure of a weird egocentric curiosity? Is it not better to nurture, compel, and command one's creativity to be life-giving—to give what each has been given to give to each of those whom each has been given to treasure? Is it not better to share all we are with those we've been given a shared life? At the necessary least—at the bottom of things—*rights* themselves must be shared. Is not *love* the Promethean heat—the voltaic spark—of a soul's giving? Other spurs seem artificial and will result in life that is artificial.

SCOTT

Through her unfolding chapters, she intends to accomplish much. Mary—the British beneficiary of her literary generation—offers a prophetic challenge to European humanism. She rejects the progressive Enlightenment ideal of inevitable improvement and also rejects the alternative anarchist faith in Romantic imaginations of personal perfection. Mary presents a disenchanted view against the centrism of self-delusional ambition. Amongst her individualists, Mary advocates improvement through the civil practices of self-sacrifice and mutual dependence. Similar to her mother—the *lesser* Godwin—our Marigolds propose that if well blossomed feminine virtues can triumph over the violent obstacles of masculinity, men may be free to express their better natures of generosity, sympathy, and compassion. Determined for *more* civility, not *less*, Mary insists that *social justice*—what's most beneficial for most people—can be developed through establishing paradigms of educational equality.

~IN THE DOCK

"There the large olive rains its amber store / In marble fonts; there grain, and flower, and fruit, / Gush from the earth until the land runs over; / But there too many a poison-tree has root, / And midnight listens to the lion's roar, / And long, long deserts scorch the camel's foot, / Or heaving whelm the helpless caravan, / And as the soil is, so the heart of man."

SCOTT

As their unearthly benefactor from the outside, Percy aims to reform the common circles, legislating their language and verse and thought. Mary wants her book to anticipate that his method will have his audience unexpectedly detest themselves more, committing forms of vengeance toward their empowering Remembrancer—toward Percy himself, their Promethean architect to punish, having enkindled the fire of the new knowledge of *new good* and *new evil*, having levied them their new consciousness as an undesirable burden. *Tap. Tap. Tap.*

Mary has her "modern" protagonist's inadvertent impositions on his *creature* not only foster the reciprocal drive to destroy its *father* for having done so—but further nurture his creature's collateral initiative to become *worse* and spill more blood. Mary has her allegoric pages predict how Percy's addressees—cursed with their unbearable Shelleyan forms of her father's ideas—will unwittingly resent unboxing their confusing new self-awareness. *Tap. Tap. Tap.*

When Shelley reimagines the sublime defiance of Lucifer's opposition to omnipotent tyranny as morally superior—the Promethean hero to celebrate from *Paradise Lost* in his antithetical literary circles—Percy is identifying himself and his cause as the current manifestation of the "Romantic Fallen Hero." *Tap. Tap. Tap.* In sublime disapproval, his capable Mary pens her own devotion—her undermining reprimand to the hypocrisies of her bright Hellenized lover—through her own cautionary parody of patriarchal delusion. *Tap. Tap. Click.*

(45.) *godless*

SCOTT

In steady course, throughout their elopement, perpetual social comparisons between Harriett and Mary are ongoing defamations of all three families. Before their third autumn closes, a month after Fanny's suicide, Mrs. Harriett Shelley—while pregnant with her third child—drowns herself in the Serpentine River at Hyde Park.

Harriett became sadly incapable of rebuilding her life Before she throws herself from the bridge into the Old Reservoir, Harriett had been "missing" for three weeks. Her costly emancipation from her family's oppressive influences became hopeless, finding herself increasingly *unfit* for the burden of life. After an additional few more mysterious weeks, Harriett is found floating dead with an esteemed ring on her finger. An article in *The London Times* is published on her fatal catastrophe.

~DEFENSELESS SILENCE

"How does one see the invisible? It is the fabulist's secret. He knows how to detect what does not exist. He knows how to see what is not seeable. It is his gift, and he works it many a time to poor dead Harriett Shelley's deep damage."

SCOTT

As Harriett wrote, she wept for her children. "Too wretched to exert myself, lowered in the opinion of everyone, why should I drag on a miserable existence? Is it wrong, do you think, to put an end to all one's sorrows? I often think of it—all is so gloomy and desolate. Shall I find repose in another world? Oh grave, why do you not tell us what is beyond thee?"

~RING OF DEATH

"There wasn't any use of getting another. The apartment was no good anyway. Life at home was simply an existence of individuals in proximity. It had no basis of common interest. She felt like a gored horse in the bullring, dragging its entrails."

SCOTT

Harriett's discovered suicide note is addressed to her husband. "Do not regret the loss of one who could never be anything but a source of vexation and misery to you and not one ray of hope to rest on for the future. I was unworthy of your love and care. My dear Bysshe, if you had never left me, I might have lived, but as it is, I freely forgive you and may you enjoy that happiness which you have deprived me of—so shall my spirit find rest and forgiveness. You dear Bysshe, *may all happiness attend you* is the last wish of her who loved you more than all others. *God bless you* is the last prayer of the unfortunate Harriett S."

~THE DROWNING POOL

"They were silent for a while, each with a separate thought. His thought was that he would never know what her thought was—that it must be left unfathomed and, perhaps, unfathomable in that obscure pool in the bottom of every woman's heart."

SCOTT

It is the most terrorizing letter of Shelley's life. "She has destroyed herself." Harriett's lonely suicide cuts through him. "What madness." Morbidly sensitive, Shelley harshly reproaches himself at the shocking catastrophe. Shelley writes, "That time is dead forever, child! / Drowned, frozen, *dead* forever. / We look on the past / Under the bitter breath of the naked frozen sky / And stare aghast / At the specters wailing pale and ghast / of hopes that thou and I beguiled."

"This name which during a few years had meant the whole world to him—for the future he must associate with all that is basest and most vile." Shelley is severely altered, suffers recurrent low moods, and confesses, "I know not how I have survived." "Ought I to have sacrificed my sanity and my life to one who was unfaithful to me—and second-rate?" Shelley's reasoning opposes his heart. Attempting to deaden his feelings, Shelley's regiment will be to "take a great glass of ale" each night. Loathingly, he looks back through his suds of beer, "The serpent is shut out from Paradise. / The wounded deer must seek the herb no more / In which its heart's cure lies. / The widowed dove must cease to haunt a bower / Like that from which its mate with feigned sighs / fled in the April hour."

~OPHELIA'S ADIEU

"Every age has its cares. God knows I have mine. This world is a scene of heavy trials to us all. I little expected ever to go through what I have. Tell me how you are in health. Do not despond—though I see nothing to hope for when all that was virtuous becomes vicious and depraved. So, it is. Nothing is certain in this world. I suppose there is another. Adieu, dear friend, may you still be happy."

SCOTT

Harriett wrote that she wanted Shelley to keep their little Charles. "As you form his infant mind, so you will reap the fruits hereafter." Nevertheless, after Harriett's death, Mary and Percy anxiously await the official decision for the custody—of Ianthe (three and a half years old) and her brother (two-year-old heir apparent)—naively attempting to appear institutionalized to sway the High Chancellor's impending decree.

Shelley appeals to Mary, "In the thoughts of how dear and how good you are to me—how wise and extensively beneficial—remember my poor babes. How tender and dear a mother they will find in you—darling Wilmouse too. My eyes overflow with tears." Percy then writes the parents of Harriett.

"There is no earthly consideration which would induce me to forgo the exclusive and entire charge of my children. They have only one parent, and that parent . . . is awakened to a sense of his duties and his claims, which at whatever price must be asserted and performed."

While Percy is securing their formal home in Marlow, Mary writes to Shelley. "These Westbrooks—they have nothing to do with your sweet babes. They are yours, and I do not see the pretense for a *suit*. I shall soon to the upholsterer—for now I long more than ever that our house should be quickly ready for the reception of those dear children whom I love so tenderly. Then, there will be a sweet brother and sister for my William who will lose his preeminence as eldest and be helped third at table. You tell me to write a long letter, and I would, but my ideas wander and my hand trembles. Come back to reassure me, my Shelley, and bring with you your darling Ianthe and Charles."

~THIRD AT TABLE

"'Where is Dixie?'

'She's out with some friends.'

Sensing the mother's evasiveness, the little girl draws watchfully close—with an important sense of participation in family affairs.

'Things happen to us,' she thought. 'What an interesting *thing* to be a family.'"

SCOTT

In the magic of Wilmouse's first birthday, Mary muses that the astrological influence of their son's constellation might sway their tense litigation. Justly and exclusively entitled to the custody and care of his children, Percy boasts, "So, I am here, dragged before the tribunals of oppression and superstition to answer with my children, my property, my liberty, and my fame—for having exposed their frauds and scorned the influence of their power."

The Westbrooks have "clandestinely placed" his children "in some place unknown" and refuse "to deliver them up" to their father. Shelley petitions to take possession of and educate them "virtuously and properly" in "a manner suitable to their birth and prospects in the world." Shelley answers that he and Harriett "were disunited by incurable dissensions" and that they "agreed in consequence of certain differences between them to live separate and apart." He denies that he deserted his wife. Although Harriett's father is also providing financially for Shelley's children, Percy's argument is that *he* is their natural guardian—and he has been abiding by Harriett's wishes during their tender years. Though Shelley is implicitly anxious in his affections for his children, he contends that he will dutifully provide for their proper educations—a fact he presumed was established.

Furthermore, to counter the Westbrook's complaint of *Queen Mab*—in which the Creator of the Universe is "blasphemously" "derided" and "denied"—Percy's philosophical argument is that Deism is the religion of almost all the *Literati* of Europe—independent writers whom possess custody of their own children. Expressly, his legal argument emphasizes that he never "published" *Queen Mab*—that "unpublished idealistic poetry" has nothing to do with paternal rights.

Yet, after these anxious months, Percy Shelley—on adjudged grounds of *immorality*, as "godless and unfit"—is restrained from the custody of his own daughter and son, in which he considers himself victimized in a manifestation of traumatic injustice. It is ordered that he had deserted his wife and that he had unlawfully cohabitated with the daughter of the author of *Political Justice*. He will never see his first children again. In such a barefaced comeuppance, Shelley loses an observable portion of his confidence and becomes less openly wild. "Tyranny"—civil and religious—is upon him. Confirming the mortgage to settle in their new home, Shelley is now horrified about what despotisms might also oppress his charmed Wilmouse—and Percy's circle of authorial friends compiled in *royal* dossiers.

~DEVIL ELDON

"No words can express the anguish he felt when his elder children were torn from him. In his first resentment against the Chancellor, on the passing of the decree, he had written a *curse* in which there breathes, besides haughty indignation, all the tenderness of a father's love, which could imagine and finally dwell upon its loss and consequences."

SCOTT

For Percy, the Capital of Great Britain is becoming Babylon. "Lovers, haters, worst and best, / All are damned—they breathe an air / Thick infected, joy-dispelling; / Hell is a *city* much like London." Bluntly, Shelley proposes, "We have love-songs, why should we not have hate-songs?" Personifying the tyrannical authority of the High Chancellor's order, Percy writes, "His big *tears*, for he wept well, / Turned to mill-stones as they fell. / And the little children, who / Round his feet played to and fro, / Thinking every tear a gem, / Had their brains knocked out by them."

Mary's guilt is palpable in being party to the loss of these babes and to the destruction of the lives of Harriett, Fanny, and Godwin. Amongst the turmoil of these deaths and defeats, Mary continues to confide in her mother at Wollstonecraft's gravesite. "I had a dream tonight of the dead being alive." On the second anniversary of suffering her daughter's death, Mary grieves in the belief that Fanny has now joined her infant in also haunting her life.

~GOD BLESS YOU

"What misfortune can equal death? Change can convert every other into a blessing, or heal its sting—death alone has no cure. It shakes the foundations of the earth on which we tread. It destroys its beauty. It casts down our shelter. It exposes us bare to desolation. When those we love have passed into eternity, 'life is the desert and the solitude' in which we are forced to linger—but never find comfort more."

(46.) *invisibility*

~SMILING AND SLOW

"Now stench and blackness yawns, like death. O, plead / With famine, or wind-walking Pestilence, / Blind lightning, or the deaf sea, not with *man*! / Cruel, cold, formal man; righteous in words, / In deeds a Cain. No, Mother, we must die: / Since such is the reward of innocent lives; / Such the alleviation of worst wrongs. / And whilst our murderers live, and hard, cold men, / Smiling and slow, walk through a world of tears."

MARY

Suffocating grief is upon me as a snake, which fold-by-fold presses life from me—a clinging fiend that clenches with deadlier hold in each attempt that I stir to live. So, grief will remain—*let it remain*—untold to the living. Yet, as one outside of time—as dreams in daylight—Mother approaches me and communes. I share with her the happiness of my pregnancies, and she delights in them as she would have while still with Papa. She whispers encouragements to me to exact virtues more noble than being in an anxious bondage of needing to inspire love from others.

Mother, always, another death I now know you through and your presence, persisting, this harming heist of the best of a heroic heart—both our first daughters now dead. Mother, when shall we be free from fear of treachery? Cherished darling *"Girl"* and my always Fanny, join Mother and commune in us, enheartening. Abide Papa in all his griefs and pursuits. Be summoned alive in my bent spirit, in our best little Wilmouse, and in this Shelley's other sweet ones, enliven! My confidants, we will have life in all our destructions, and—in reanimation—avenged!

They still try to humiliate, to shame you—the "hyena in petticoats." You haunt them. Live through me. My mothering muse, incite my fingers your power of death-challenging task. Quicken through me in each stroke and page. "Let them use us well, else let them know the ills we do—their ills instruct us so." We will live—created again—in this *Modern Prometheus* spurn. Equip me with process and patience to divine our galvanized revitalizing in this ink lasting, raising us who will not be dead.

Inspirit the brevity of our narrative volumes— again repeated novel. Spirited Mother, we meet and commune in you, authoring our laments reversed. Mother-me as your vessel—Mary in me affective, as when death and grief were but words which found no true echo in my heart. I call on you—spirits of the dead, my wandering ministers of my vengeance—to aid and conduct me in my work.

"We will each write a ghost story." His proposition was acceded to—one which would speak to the mysterious fears of our nature. I thought and pondered—vainly. "Write the ghostbooks." I felt that blank incapability of invention, which is the greatest misery of authorship—when dull *Nothing* replies to our anxious invocations. My imagination guided me, gifting the successive images, my answer—the fraud of his *world legislation*—a collaged monstrosity of disastrous contradictions awakened in toxic ambition.

Frightful must it be, for supremely frightful would be the effect of any human endeavor to mock the stupendous mechanism of the Prime Mover behind the world. His bent success would terrify the artists. He would rush away from his odious handiwork, horror-stricken. He would hope that, left to itself—myself—the slight spark of life which he has communicated would fade, that this *thing*, which had received such imperfect animation, would subside into dead matter. He might sleep in the belief that the silence of another new grave would quench forever the transient existence of the hideous partnered corpse—his captive lover!—which he had looked upon as the cradle of life.

The bitterness of betrayal is the shocking consciousness of the loss of time—urgency exterminated without returns. And yet, then shines compassion—Love, aid and conduct me!—radiant in the warm awareness of its compounding blossoming of the hope of lost time redeemed.

Children and all—her whole life on the scale—Harriett slew herself—*"a source of vexation and misery, unworthy of love, unworthy of care*"—Harriett, at last made a writer from such a pit of excommunication as is surely entrenching me. No, Mr. Shelley, I will not be abandoned and made an invisibility. I will not so easily be vaporized. I will learn these dialectics and I will instruct into my heritage without retreat, penning *the specter*—my omen—which has haunted my midnight pillow, suffocating. It is my Shelley who dream-copes with his pictures of his impressions— his beachcombed shards of affection and idea gathered amorphous—mirage facades needed to be sandbar-firm on my double shores narrow, ransoming his will that is itself held in his Grecian realm of Ideals and Forms, forced to scattered portrayals—a will that is possibilities that cannot be not possible.

~WARY P.

"The mixture of fact and fiction is calculated to ruin what is left of us—putting intimate facts in the hands of the enemies we've accumulated. My God, my books made her a legend, and her single intention is to make me a non-entity."

MARY

In his seemingness immanent, Percy plus people equals an impossible "we," he and I—the divides and divides of us wide. More, more than the flash floods of the flesh of your tongue, Shelley, wanting more than next to you—to hope to awaken together in I-spirit, in primal Platonic searching unsplit behind layers and peels impregnable, seeking our half-orange other each—our asunder that cannot integrate the fragmented divides and divides of us wide—our schism chasms that can neither be cross spanned nor conquered through this i-cortex outside, these i-cortices unassailable. Be instructed! It is your poor little Miss Mary who ascends these fallacies—your forgeries—my Promethean *dreamer*.

~AND THEN WHAT?

"Black shadows fell on the water, echoes of nothing poured down the hills and steamed over the lake. It began to rain. A Swiss downpour soaked the earth. The flat bulbous vines about the hotel windows bled torrents over the ledges. The heads of the dahlias bent with the storm.

The dancers, too, were thinking of the rain, and shivered a little through the bursting crescendo of the finale.

'I liked best the ones in black who fought themselves,' said Bonnie.

'It is *Prometheus* they're going to give,' he said, reading the program. 'I will tell you the story afterwards.'

'May I have the apricot jam?'

'Do you want to hear about "Prometheus," or not?' said her father impatiently.

'Yes, sir. Oh yes, of course.'

'Then,' resumed her father, 'He writhed there for years and years and—'

'That is in my *Mythologie*,' said Bonnie proudly. 'And

then what—after he was *writhing?*'

'Then what? *Well*—' her father glowed with the exhilaration of being attractive, laying out the facets of his personality for the children like stacks of expensive shirts for admiring valets. 'Do you remember exactly what *did* happen?' he said lamely to Bonnie.

'No. I've forgot since a long time.'"

(47.) *within and without*

SCOTT

That stuff about the "great vital heart of America" is corny. The American Dream is a state of self—it's fanciful, vulnerable illusions and loss; it's hopeful, unacademic cleverness and sophomoric magic; it's hope, foolishness, and romance, and it's the spirited exhibitions of perennially amusing undergraduates.

Click. Tap. Tap. Once Gatsby was eradicated, my Saint Nick must've thought he'd be able—at least once—to speak to the thing again—golden, but a *thing* again, a noun—after all its hopes were ravaged to the ground into lifeless anatomy . . . destiny would have silence as its commander.

NICK

He reached into his pocket, and a piece of metal—slung on a ribbon—fell into my palm.

JAY

"Here's another—"

SCOTT

—a photograph taken in Trinity Quad—with a cricket bat in his hand, a souvenir of his Oxford days.

JAY

"So, I thought you ought to know something about me. I didn't want you to think I was just some nobody. You see I usually find myself among strangers because I drift here and there trying to forget the sad thing that happened to me."

NICK

The city seen from the Queensboro Bridge is always the city seen for the first time, in this first wild promise of all the mystery and the beauty in the world.

~ON THE UPGRADE

"All over New York, people telephoned. They telephoned—from hotel party to hotel party—that they were engaged.

He and Alabama invited their friends to throw oranges into the drum at the Plantation and themselves into the fountain at Union Square.

Up they went, humming *The New Testament* and our country's *Constitution*, riding the tide like triumphant islanders on a surfboard. Nobody knew the words to "The Star-Spangled Banner." Possessing a rapacious, engulfing ego, their particular genius swallowed their world in its swift undertow and washed its cadavers out to sea. New York is a good place to be on the upgrade."

SCOTT

Anything can happen now that they've slid over this bridge—Nick thought—anything at all. Even Gatsby could happen—without any particular wonder.

NICK

There was the smile again, but this time I held out against it.

"—I don't like mysteries."

JAY

"Oh, it's nothing underhand."

NICK

I was within and without, simultaneously enchanted and repelled by the inexhaustible variety of life.

(48.) *grand shapes crowned*

PERCY

There is yet even a more disastrous future to be imparted to me! Some destiny of the most horrible kind hangs over me, and I must live to fulfill it. Oh! Stars and clouds and winds, ye are all about to mock me.

If ye really pity me, crush sensation and memory. Let me become as naught. But if not, depart, depart and leave me in darkness. "We rest; a dream has power to poison sleep. We rise; one wandering thought pollutes the day. We laugh or weep, embrace fond woe, or cast our cares away; it is the same: for, be it joy or sorrow, Man's yesterday may ne'er be like his morrow."

MARY

Compassion yields me when I see my fondest as a filthy mass who moves and talks. My heart sickens, and my feelings are altered.

What's the point if you can't take all the venom out of a bitten mess of the heart's flesh? Your grief has shaped you into matter aching heavy like a shooting star—descending as stardust—crashing some good green somewhere in any European place on my novel's map, whispering now to the virgins through the vines—in the olive groves—that youth vacillating is wicked as slavery, but that the full-bodied blood wine price pressed is your higher debt of only dreaming but one hermit-hope made vapors, and—behind you—bright hearts outspread into petals of muscles.

PERCY

Unveiled thus, not the tenderness of friendship, nor the beauty of Earth—nor of Heaven—can redeem my soul from woe. The very accents of love are ineffectual. The wounded deer dragging its fainting limbs to some untrodden brake, there to gaze upon the arrow which has pierced it—and to die—is but a type of me. The cold stars shine in mockery, and the bare trees wave their branches above me. Now and then, the sweet voice of a bird bursts forth amidst the universal stillness. All—save I—are at rest or in enjoyment. I, like the arch-fiend, bear a hell within me. And, finding myself unsympathized with, wish to tear up the trees, spread havoc and destruction around me, and, then, sit down and enjoy the ruin—the sick impotence of despair. I am malicious because I am miserable.

Why am I preserved so miserable and detested a life? It is surely that I might fulfill my destiny. Will death extinguish these throbbings and relieve me from the mighty weight of anguish that bears me to the dust? In executing the award of justice, shall I also sink to rest? The appearance of death is distant although the wish is ever present to my thoughts. I now often sit for hours, motionless and speechless, wishing for some mighty revolution that might bury me—my own destroyer—in its ruins.

MARY

"Whence are we, and why are we? of what scene / The actors or spectators? / Evening must usher night, night urge the morrow, / Month follow month with woe, and year wake year to sorrow. / Alas! I have not hope nor health, / Nor peace within nor calm around, / Nor that *content* surpassing wealth / The sage in meditation found / And walked with inward glory crowned"—

PERCY

—"Nor fame, nor power, nor love, nor leisure. / Others I see whom these surround— / Smiling they live, and call life pleasure;— / To me that cup has been dealt in another measure. / And in mad trance, strike with my spirit's knife / Invulnerable nothings. / Fear and grief convulse and consume me day-by-day / And cold hopes swarm like worms within this living clay."

MARY

My victorious, my greatest, my love, our vow is that whether Heaven—or *not* Heaven—are our principles the same, willed in our spirits' celebration, voyaging, giving, gaining. Yet, the power of the mask you sport, Percy—the high intellectual praised for his dire tragedies—is the mis-joining of our heads to our hearts—to our ruin. All we've written is our mausoleum. Is this how we're punished, pushed out, put out, excommunicated, like parents outside paradise, like Prometheus, like all origins, like lifeless clay, but slower and not all at acute once?

I hold the darkness to forget myself and my ephemeral—because human—sorrows. Alas! I prophesied truly and failed only in one single circumstance, that in all the misery I imagined and dreaded, I did not conceive the hundredth part of the anguish I was destined to endure. Destiny had endowed us with perceptions and passions. Then, it cast us abroad—as objects for the scorn and horror of mankind—from any other beings who wore the human form. We shun our fellow creatures as if we are now guilty of a crime.

Sometimes I grow alarmed at the wreck I perceive I have become. The energy of my purpose alone sustains me, but I am a blasted tree. The bolt has entered my soul—a miserable spectacle of wrecked humanity, pitiable to others, and intolerable to myself, the shadow of a human being. My strength is gone. I am as bones held together by destiny and ideas.

PERCY

Your blast has torn along me like a mighty avalanche and has produced a kind of insanity in my spirits that bursts all bounds of reason and reflection in a dance of fury. Why do you call to my remembrance circumstances of which I shudder to reflect, that I have been the miserable origin and author? The birth of that passion, which afterwards ruled my destiny, I find it arise, like a mountain river, from ignoble and almost forgotten sources. But, swelling as it has proceeded, it has become the torrent which, in its course, has swept away all my hopes and joys.

As if fixed—my fate—the lords of my imagination hold the darkness with a child's blindness for the alchemist's stone, for the curse of the elixir of life. By one of those caprices of the mind, which we are perhaps most subject to in early youth, I have given up my former occupations and all its progeny as a deformed and abortive creation.

Many times, I consider epical Satan as the fitter emblem of my condition. Yet, even in defeat, Satan has his companions in verse—fellow devils to admire and encourage him. I am abhorred and deserted and solitary. No mythical Eve soothes my sorrows nor truly shares my thoughts. I am alone. I have remembered Adam's supplication to his Creator. But where is mine? Has my soul not cried out from its depths?

MARY

Why do I not sink into forgetfulness and rest? Death snatches away many blooming children, the only hopes of their doting parents. How many brides and youthful lovers have been one day in the bloom of health and hope—and the next a prey for worms and the decay of the tomb? Of what materials am I made that I can thus resist so many shocks, which, like the turning of the wheel, continually renews my torture? Yet, I am doomed to live. Must not we live?

PERCY

I, who had ever been surrounded by amiable companions, continually engaged in endeavoring to bestow mutual pleasure, I am now alone.

Here am I who would spend each vital drop of blood for your sakes, who has no thought, nor sense, nor joy, except as it is mirrored also in your dear countenances, who would fill the air with blessings and spend his life in serving you—yet selfsame appear to others as the one who bids you weep, to shed countless tears! Happy beyond his hopes if this inexorable fate be satisfied and this destruction be paused—before the peace of the grave—will I have succeeded to your sad torments.

All pleasure seems to me sacrilege toward the dead. I am no longer that happy creature, who in earlier youth wandered on the banks of the lake and talked with ecstasy of future prospects. The first of sorrows that are sent to wean us from Earth have visited me, like whispering specters, their dimming influence quenching my last smiles. I no longer see the world and its works as they before appeared to me. Before, I looked upon the accounts of vice and injustice— that I read in books or heard from others—as tales of ancient days or imaginary evils. At least they were remote and more familiar to reason than to the imagination.

When Misery returns home, men appear monsters, and we move about in a dungeon more pestilential than damp and narrow walls, because the earth is its floor, the heavens are its roof, and its throne is of broken swords, scepters, and royal crowns trampled in dust.

When falsehood can look so like the truth, who can assure themselves of certain happiness? I feel as if I am walking on the edge of a precipice toward which thousands are crowding and endeavoring to plunge me into the abyss.

MARY

"No, no, go not to Lethe, neither twist / Wolf's-bane, tight-rooted, for its poisonous wine; / Nor suffer thy pale forehead to be kiss'd / By nightshade, ruby grape of Proserpine—"

PERCY

"—Make not your rosary of yew-berries, / Nor let the beetle, nor the death-moth be / Your mournful Psyche, nor the downy owl / A partner in your sorrow's mysteries / Already with thee! tender is the night, / And haply the Queen-Moon is on her throne, / Clustered around by all her starry Fays. / That I might drink, and leave the world unseen, /

And with thee fade away into the forest dim: / Fade far away, dissolve, and quite forget / The weariness, the fever, and the fret / Here, where men sit and hear each other groan / Where youth grows pale, / Where Beauty cannot keep her lustrous eyes, / Or new Love pine at them beyond tomorrow. / Now more than ever seems it rich to die."

MARY

I had been in the custom of taking every night a small quantity of laudanum for it was by means of this drug only that I was enabled to gain the rest necessary for the preservation of life. Oppressed by the recollection of my various misfortunes, I now swallow double the usual of "Medea's wondrous alchemy" and will soon sleep profoundly—dilated—an oceanic bliss in dissolution, a truce established between this present hour and the irresistible, disastrous future.

Allow me this faint happiness. Take me as your companion away from the joys of life and the smile of death.

"Whilst yet the calm hours creep, / Dream thou— and from thy sleep / Then wake to weep." Indeed, sweetest sleep does afford me respite from thought and misery. Living such lengths can be indeed hateful to me, and it is during sleep alone that I can taste old joy, sustained and inspirited by the hope of night— when in dreams, I hold converse with my companions and derive from that communion consolation for miseries and excitements as in regions of a remote world where no longer are the sun or stars, the winds, light, feeling, or sense—and in this condition must I find my happiness.

Some years ago, when the images, which this world affords, first opened—when I felt the cheering warmth of summer and heard the rustling of the leaves and warbling of the birds—these were all to me. Soon these burning miseries will be extinct. Lost in darkness and distance, I should weep to die to daylight. "Why fear and dream and death and birth / Cast on the daylight of this earth / Such gloom— Why man has such a scope / For love and hate, despondency and hope?"

Lulling my Shelley, the spell crept over me—like sweet turtledoves folded in the last knot that love could tie. I felt it as it came and I blessed this giver of oblivion—waited on and ministered to by the assemblance of grand shapes I had contemplated during the day. They all gathered round me and bade me be at peace.

There are two worlds of life and death—one that which we behold, but the other is underneath the grave, where do inhabit the shadows of all forms that think and move, half living, till death unite them, and they part no more.

All voluntary thought was swallowed up and lost to the commencement of my matron, Mab.

Anticipations and the past were blotted from my memory. In respites from Time's tyranny, my queen allows us to forget ourselves. The present was tranquil, and the future was gilded by bright rays.

(49.) *luncheon*

SCOTT

Love is an invincible burden. My mind was filled with one thought, one conception, one purpose. I seemed to have lost all soul or sensation but for this one pursuit. Time had altered her since he had last beheld her. It had endowed her with a loveliness surpassing the beauty of her childish years. There was the same candor, the same vivacity, but it was allied to an expression more full of sensibility and intellect. *Amour*—for her—was now expendable, a mere lever to release a mist of sand and glitter.

NICK

It never occurred to me that one man could start to play with the faith of fifty million people—with the single-mindedness of a burglar blowing a safe.

"How did he happen to do that?"

JAY

"He just saw the opportunity. They can't get him, old sport. He's a smart man."

NICK

As the waiter brought my change, I caught sight of Tom Buchanan across the crowded room.

TOM

"Daisy's been furious because you haven't called up."

NICK

"This is Mr. Gatsby, Mr. Buchanan."

SCOTT

They shook hands briefly, and a strained, unfamiliar look of embarrassment came over Gatsby's face.

~TOM, YOU OLD BYRON . . .

"Your arrogance should chastise you—your consideration for others' feelings, opinions, or even time is completely left out of your makeup. You trample on others' feelings continually with things you permit yourself to say and do—partly to the self-indulgence of drinking too much—is from the greatest egotism and sureness that you are *righter* than anyone else."

TOM

"How've you been, anyhow?"

SCOTT

Don't be a boy like Keats when you face the elites, Jaybird. If you will only begin to dramatize yourself as the man who would turn back—"about face"—*now* and hold the line, everything may turn out rightly . . .

NICK

"I've been having lunch with Mr. Gatsby—"

(50.) *elegant roughneck*

NICK

Although it is not a history of all aspiration and not the dream of all humans, the American *dream* is a place—maybe the last place—in the line of pioneers.

This novel is a case in point. Because the pages weren't loaded with big names of big things—and the subject not concerned with farmers (who were the heroes of the moment)—there was easy judgement exercised that had nothing to do with criticism, but was simply an attempt on the part of men who had few chances of self-expression to express themselves.

SCOTT

A poor boy in a rich town, a poor boy in a rich boy's school, a poor boy in a rich man's club—I have never been able to forgive the rich for being rich, yet it has colored my entire life and works. *Tap. Tap. Tap.* I've been a fish out of the tiled bathtub too much. I loathed the army and I loathed business. I was in love with change and I had killed my conscience. In uncritical worship, I wanted to be the exception to the great balancing rule of bachelors—"lucky in dice, unlucky in love." *Click.*

NICK

The secure position of his feet upon the lawn

suggested that it was Mr. Gatsby himself, who had come out to determine what share was *his* of our local heavens—of the silver pepper of the stars. I glanced seaward and distinguished nothing except a single green light, minuscule and far away—that might have been the end of a dock—and I was alone again in the unquiet darkness.

SCOTT

In his blue gardens, men and girls came and went like moths among the whisperings and the champagne and the stars.

~COMMUNION

"The big japonicas—with leaves like rusting tin, viburnum and verbena and Japanese magnolia petals lying about the lawns like scraps from party dresses—absorbed the quiet communion between them.

'I love little trees, arborvitae and juniper, and I'm going to have a long walk winding between like featherstitching and a terrace at the end.' Certainly the garden was to be very nice for whoever was being thought of."

NICK

Dancing, couples held each other tortuously, fashionably, and kept in the corners. Taking two finger bowls of champagne, the scene had changed before my eyes into something significant, elemental, and profound. Then, a man about my age looked at me and smiled.

JAY

"Your face is familiar . . . Weren't you in the Third Division during the war?"

NICK

"Why, yes. I was in the Ninth Machine-Gun-Battalion. I enjoyed the counter-raid so thoroughly that I came back restless . . . and decided to learn the bond business."

JAY

"I was in the Seventh Infantry. I knew I'd seen you somewhere before."

NICK

We talked for a moment about some wet, gray little villages in France—and how we'd sent the Huns back to their farms and beer to stew for a while, to stew on the rich empires getting richer. From the counter-raid to this mystery invitation—

JAY

"—I thought you knew, old sport. *I'm* Gatsby. I'm

afraid I'm not a very good host."

NICK

It was one of those rare smiles with an irresistible prejudice in your favor. It understood you just so far as you wanted to be understood. I was looking at an elegant young roughneck whose formality of speech just missed being absurd. Sometime before he introduced himself—with only machine guns in common—I'd gotten a strong impression that he was picking his words with care.

(51.) *the most advanced people*

SCOTT

Nick—their "Elucidator"—was always determining the forces that made people. People—well, he'd figured *that* out. He was American—so, "The Bonds Business" was next.

NICK

I'd known Tom in college. We were in the same Senior Society. I always had the impression that Tom approved of me and wanted me to like him with some harsh, defiant wistfulness of his own. Daisy was my second cousin. Now, I came to know them together.

Daisy laughed a charming absurd laugh, and I laughed too.

DAISY

"I'm paralyzed with happiness."

NICK

She laughed again, as if she said something very witty. Daisy held my hand for a moment—looking up into my face—promising that there was no one in the world she so much wanted to see. That was a way she had in her low, thrilling voice.

~THE PROMISE OF "IT"

"The childish voices droned through the clarity, conversing intimately.

'What is this "it" I saw in the papers?' said the eight-year-old voice.

'Don't be silly, it's only sex appeal' answered the voice of ten.

'Only beautiful ladies can have it in the movies,' said Bonnie.

'But sometimes don't men have it too?' said the little boy disappointed.

'Father says everybody does,' called the older girl.

'Well, Mother said only a few. What did your parents say, Bonnie?'

'They didn't say anything, since I had not read it in the papers.'

'When you are older, you will—if it is still there.'"

DAISY

"All right, what'll we plan? What do people plan?"

SCOTT

It was the kind of voice that the ear follows up and down as if each speech is an arrangement of notes that will never be played again. Her face was sad and lovely with bright things in it, bright eyes and a bright passionate mouth, but there was an excitement in her voice that men who had cared for her found difficult to forget. It was a singing compulsion, a whispered *"listen,"* a promise that she had done exciting things— just a while since—and that there were exciting things hovering in the next hour.

NICK

Miss Jordan Baker seemed to have mastered a certain hardy skepticism. Yet, sometimes Daisy and Jordan talked at once—unobtrusively and with a bantering inconsequence that was never quite chatter—as cool as their white dresses and their impersonal eyes in the absence of all desire. They were here—and they accepted Tom and me—making only a polite, pleasant effort to entertain or to be entertained. They knew that presently dinner would be over, and a little later, the evening too would be over—and casually put away.

DAISY

"It's very romantic outdoors. There's a bird on the lawn that I think must be a nightingale. He's singing away. It's romantic, isn't it, Tom?"

TOM

"Very romantic."

NICK

I've heard it said that Daisy's murmur was only to

make people lean toward her, an irrelevant criticism that made it no less charming. Yet, for Tom, two shining arrogant eyes had established dominance over his face and gave him the appearance of always leaning aggressively forward. "Just because I'm stronger," he seemed to say, "and more of a man than you are."

TOM

"I've gotten to be a terrible pessimist about things. This fellow has worked out the whole thing. It's a fine book and everybody ought to read it."

NICK

Tom and Daisy had spent a year in France—for no particular reason—and then drifted here and there unrestfully wherever people were rich together.

Daisy took her face in her hands—as if feeling its lovely shape—and her eyes moved gradually out into the velvet dusk.

DAISY

"We don't know each other very well, Nick, even if we are cousins. You didn't come to my wedding."

NICK

"I wasn't back from the war."

DAISY

"That's true . . . Well, I've had a very bad time, Nick, and I'm pretty cynical about everything. You see everything's terrible anyhow . . . Everybody thinks so—the most advanced people. And I know. I've been everywhere and seen everything and done everything."

SCOTT

Her eyes flashed around her in a defiant way, rather like Tom's, and she laughed with thrilling scorn.

DAISY

"Jordan's going to play in the tournament tomorrow over at Westchester. Nick, you're going to look after her, aren't you? She's going to spend lots of weekends out here this summer."

NICK

"Is she from New York?"

DAISY

"From Louisville. Our white girlhood was passed together there. Our beautiful white—"

TOM

"Did you give Nick a little heart-to-heart talk on the

veranda? Don't believe everything you hear, Nick."

DAISY

"I forgot to ask you something, and it's important. We heard you were engaged to a girl out West."

TOM

"That's right. We heard that you were engaged."

NICK

"It's a libel. I'm too poor."

SCOTT

The future recedes before us, we boats borne back to the past.

DAISY

"But we heard it—"

SCOTT

—*insisted Daisy, surprisingly opening up again in a flower-like way.*

DAISY

"We heard it from three people, so it must be true!"

NICK

"You make me feel uncivilized, Daisy. Can't we talk about crops or something?"

SCOTT

—pretending to be a hick.

My millionaires were going to be as beautiful and damned as Hardy's peasants. My point of vantage was the dividing line between the two generations. In life, these things hadn't happened yet, but I was pretty sure *living* wasn't the reckless, careless business these people thought—this generation just younger than me.

As a matter of fact, "the American peasant" as *real* material scarcely exists. He is scarcely ten percent of the population, isn't bound to the soil at all as the English and Russian peasants, and, with any sensitivity whatsoever, he is in the towns before he's twenty. Isn't it a fourth-rate imagination that can find only that "old property farmer" in all this amazing time and land?

(52.) *magnify*

SCOTT

While Shelley is securing what is to be their final home in England, Mary writes, "Ah, were you indeed my winged Elf and could soar over mountains and seas and could pounce on the little spot—a house with a lawn, a river or lake, noble trees, and divine mountains that should be our little mousehole to retire, and for the Dormouse to take long rambles among green fields and solitary lanes as happy as any little animal could be in her native nests."

Three months later, Mary describes the official Shelley family home—Albion House on the Thames—in the rural village of Great Marlow. "Our house is very political and poetical. You will have plenty of room to indulge yourself in and a garden which will deserve your praise when you see it—flowers, trees, and shady banks." Albion House is pseudo-gothic with pointed windows and battlements, and its library is as large as a ballroom. Its pleasure-ground is made up of "beautiful walks, uplands, valleys, wood, water, steeples issuing from clumps of trees, luxuriant hedges, meads, cornfields, brooks, nooks and pretty looks."

There are many visitors to their formal home where statues "as large as life" of Venus and Apollo guard and inspire their exquisite library. While preparing

Marlow for Mary and Wilmouse, Shelley joins the same writing circle as Keats. As the lives of Shelley and Keats begin to intersect, Keats is contemplating a work concerning the overthrow of the Titans. As Shelley and Keats crisscross each other in their careers, Keats begins to picture his later Romantic epic to be centered on the deification of Apollo.

~SINCERELY JOHN KEATS, ALIAS "JUNKETS"

"Does Shelley go on telling strange stories of the death of kings? Tell him there are strange stories of the death of poets—and that some have died before they were conceived. Does Mrs. Shelley cut bread and butter as neatly as ever? Tell her to procure some fatal scissors and cut the thread of life of all to-be disappointed poets. Remember me to them all."

SCOTT

Keats feels that he is in a body too small for his spirit. Before he finds literature, his favorite outlet is fighting—boxing *anyone* for lively sport. Tempering his enthusiastic boisterousness in a private academy, Keats studies English and Latin for eight years. Wanting to do the world some good—and a university degree being *un*necessary—he joins an apothecary shop to become a surgeon's apprentice. Alongside his medical training, he also heavily studies poetry for his next five years. As Mary and Shelley are eloping from Godwin's, Keats composes his first poem. Although Shelley also had youthful aspirations to become a surgeon, Keats's fellow apprentices rather shame him to embarrassment on his budding abilities as a poet. While Mary and Shelley are in Geneva with Byron, Keats obtains his license to practice surgery and publishes his first poem. When Fanny kills herself, Keats's next poem is published—as he dresses wounds in a London hospital. When Harriett kills herself, Shelley and Keats are honored in their mentor's celebrated, literary manifesto that aims to reanimate English poetry.

With bright gusto, Shelley and Keats are enthusiastic to advance English poetry as more fluent, more flexible, and as more gorgeous. Advocated in this publication helps Keats to transition from his surgical skills to writing full-time. "I find I cannot do without poetry. I began with a little, but habit has made me a leviathan." As Mary is completing her Gothic masterpiece, Keats's first book of poems is published, including "On First Looking into Chapman's Homer," likening his literary discovery to explorers encountering the awe of the New World, which Shelley especially admires. Percy's pamphlet on reform—to increase suffrage throughout the Kingdom—is also listed in this same advertisement for Keats's *Poems*. During this year, Godwin meets Keats three times. As a critic, having published his own eloquent defense for Chapman's *Homer*, Godwin greatly admires Keats's poem. Keats gifts Godwin his published poetry, paying him tribute for inspiring him since he was a schoolboy from Godwin's textbook *Pantheon*, which has led Keats to pursue his poetic remythologizing—reframing the mythoi that will make him famous. *Pantheon* is also the book from which Mary has learned Godwin's founding allegory of Prometheus.

Nevertheless, once Keats and Shelley meet in their rambles on the heath, they do not invigorate each other's creative passions. Keats is sensitive about his origins, and Shelley is somewhat overbearing. Keats is a few years younger than Shelley and is wary of him—shy to Shelley's hectic, argumentative nature. Although Keats is predisposed to find Shelley an odd philosophic fanatic, quietly, Keats perceives Shelley's inward light, easily discerning his better-minded abstract gifts—talents with little relation to Keats's poverty or his political reticence. Poles apart, Keats and Shelley's temperaments are incompatible, and there is no lightning of violent delights that will root any violent ends between them. Although they prefer each other's poetry more than each other's personalities, their legacies of future consolatory odes will soon be bound to one another in the hero-worship heaps of another country of departures.

~SWEPT

'"We couldn't go on indefinitely being swept off our feet.'

'Compared to the rest, you are happy.'

'We grew up founding our dreams on the infinite promise of the songs, silent films, and articles from American advertising. I still believe that one can learn to play the piano by mail and that mud will give you a perfect complexion.'"

SCOTT

With the apple trees in blossom, Shelley is content with his garden, his books, and his boat. Pensive on the Thames, Shelley reminisces that although Wollstonecraft, floating unconscious down this same river from Putney Bridge, had been rescued by fisherman years ago, Shelley bemoans that there was no hero—that there was no *love*—to pull Harriett from her man-made lake. Meanwhile, at Marlow, Mary suffers a nightmare in which she experiences Harriett arising—as a vengeful *revenant*—to torment Mary from the Serpentine. "As we kiss, we consume, and all will be a dream," Mary scrawls her curse, assured these new times will soon only be other anecdotes of reminiscence—doomed to be wonderless old-chestnuts of recollection.

"Ought we not to be happy—and, so, indeed we are—in spite of the Lord Chancellor's decision for the deprivation of our beloveds?" Saved since Switzerland, Mary sows their transplanted pile of Alpine seeds in her new *parabolic* garden near where the wild ivies climb in profusion throughout their lattice-work porch. Happily striving against her paranoias at Marlow, Mary makes jellies, reads her macabre novels, and edits the final draft of her fictive text.

Late in their third spring, Mary writes Shelley that

she has amused herself with rereading the verses that Byron had written amongst them the year before. "It made me dreadfully melancholy. The lake, the mountains, and the faces associated with these scenes passed before me. Why is not life a continued moment where hours and days are not counted? But, as it is, a succession of events happens. The moment of enjoyments lives only in memory, and—my Shelley—when we die, where are we?"

Their sufferings are purging them from their self-delusions. Throughout their fourth year, Mary and Percy thwart their discontents and withdraw their quarreling with each other throughout their collaboration with her novel's development. While in Marlow, they are both known for their charity and tenderness to local villagers. Percy continues his negligibly celebrated literary achievements while liberally editing—carte blanche—Mary's evolving drafts. At length, while also pregnant throughout this year with their third child—a girl—Mary completes her ominous, inconvenient manuscript. She alternatively titles her work *The Modern Prometheus*, guiding the allusion that her protagonist is to be interpreted as a mythically punished overreacher—the castigated benefactor of mankind who will be made noble in his *suffering*.

In Marlow, amidst their fourth autumn, Percy writes the anonymous preface to advocate Mary's novel. "Human dilemmas are stretched to magnify them in ways that mundane existence cannot. It affords a point of view to the imagination for the delineating of human passions more comprehensive and commanding than any which the ordinary relations of existing events can yield, endeavoring to preserve the truth of the elementary principles of human nature."

This same year, Godwin's own new novel, *Mandeville*, is published—an astonishing account of madness that results from social exclusion, betrayal, and disfigurement. In her last efforts for her family, this is the book being written that Fanny had enthusiastically solicited throughout London to ensure its completion—"for the world's sake." With a pervasive blackness, Godwin illustrates the breakdown of his character's personality via his own hounding, subconscious obsessions. Juxtaposing the diabolic with rational necessity, Godwin forms his argument for the exclusivity of the passions that mock all philosophy. Once published, Mary—also ardent of the worthy value of *Mandeville*—will find a way to directly advertise her father's novels through her own "modern" project. Indefatigable, Godwin begins his next novel of defiant imagination, securing his works as immortal classics.

Percy's published review of *Mandeville*—signed E. K.—contends that Godwin is in moral philosophy what Wordsworth is in poetry, that his new novel announces the most important class of truth, and that *against* Godwin there cannot be named a contemporary competitor who has not been *blinded* by fear, self-love, or the bigotry of faction. Shelley also privately writes Godwin. "I do not think that there ever was produced a moral discourse more characteristic of all that is admirable and lovely in human nature than that of the care of Mandeville's beloved to him as he is recovering . . . and, when at last, she weakly abandoned poor Mandeville, I felt an involuntary, unreasonable pang."

Closing this year, in a profound clarity against authoritative supremacy, Shelley composes his seminal sonnet "Ozymandias," offering a paradoxical softening for suffering domination. Mary writes of her Percy, "He was eloquent, but he was playful and indulged in the wild spirit that mocked itself and others—not in bitterness, but in sport." Shelley writes "Ozymandias" as his entry in a sonnet contest with his literary peerage of Marlow and signs the first printing of his master sonnet with an inventively affectionate pseudonym—"Glirastes," meaning "lover of dormouse." Conversely—with spirited pitches and pleas—in the reactionary literary-establishment of the Lord Chancellor's London, *Mary's* anonymous, accomplished novel is rejected, denied for publication.

(53.) *some force*

SCOTT

But what is light?

The great promise is that something is going to happen. Great American Dream, you always offer promise of another good time—as if just living might once again become a relevant estate.

NICK

Jazz and champagne lasted a few evenings, but we still had to wake up in the mornings. We had made the adjustment from the Victorian era to the bitter gallantries of the last war, finding a philosophy of tragic, truncating exaltation to tide over the heartbroken memories of men frozen in boxcars and drowned in mud on the lost frontier of foreign countries.

Now, God is billboards and monthlies. Tired, resigned, and no longer philosophic, we await the end with a list too full of suicides and too fraught with disasters to bring much light or lightness to this current pastime that plays out our remaining parts.

SCOTT

I had put the writing aside when I got a job in New

York, but I was as constantly aware of it during that desolate spring as of the cardboard in the soles of my shoes. It was like the fox and goose and the bag of beans. If I stopped working to finish the novel—I lost the girl.

It was back into the mind of the young man with cardboard soles who had walked the streets of New York—I was him again. For an instant, I had the good fortune to share his dreams, I who had no more dreams of mine own. And there are still times when I creep up on him, surprise him on an autumn morning in New York, or a spring night in the South when it is so quiet that you can hear a dog barking in the next county. But never again as during that all too short period when he and I were one person, when the fulfilled future and the wistful past were mingled in a single gorgeous moment—when life was literally *dream.*

WOLFSHEIM

"Several years. I made the pleasure of his acquaintance just after the war, but I knew I had discovered a man of fine breeding after I talked with him an hour—a young major just out of the army and covered over with medals he got in the war.

He was so hard up he had to keep on wearing his uniform because he couldn't buy some regular clothes. First time I saw him was when he come into Winebrenner's poolroom at Forty-Third Street and asked for a job.

I raised him up out of nothing—right out of the gutter. I saw right away he was a fine appearing gentlemanly young man, and when he told me he was an Oggsford—I knew I could use him good."

SCOTT

When Nick left his office, the sky had turned dark.

NICK

Jay had done extraordinarily well in the war. He was a captain before he went to the western front, and following the Argonne battles, he got his majority *and* the command of the divisional machine-guns.

There was something gorgeous about him, some heightened sensitivity to the promises of life— an extraordinary gift for hope—a romantic readiness such as I have never found. He came back from France when Tom and Daisy were still on their wedding trip. He made a miserable—but irresistible—journey to Louisville on the last of his army pay.

SCOTT

He stayed there a week, walking the streets where their footsteps had clicked together through the November night, revisiting the out-of-the-way places to which they had driven in her white car.

NICK

Just as Daisy's house had always seemed to him more mysterious and exciting than other houses, so his idea of the city itself—even though she was gone from it—was pervaded with a melancholy beauty, imbued in benediction over this vanishing illusion where she had drawn her breath. He stretched out his hand desperately—as if to snatch only a wisp of air—to save a fragment of the spot that she had made lovely for him.

SCOTT

And he knew that he had lost that part of it—the freshest and the best—forever.

The sky was darkling into many nights before from France and England. He was worried now—there was a quality of nervous despair in Daisy's letters.

NICK

Daisy was feeling the pressure of the world outside and she wanted to see him and feel his presence beside her to be reassured that she was doing the right thing after all.

SCOTT

Her artificial world was redolent of orchids—and pleasant, cheerful snobbery—and orchestras, which set the rhythm of the year, summing up the sadness and suggestiveness of life in new tunes. Through this twilight universe, Daisy began to move again with the season. She wanted her life shaped now, immediately. The decision must be made by *some force*—of love, of money, of unquestionable practicality—that was close at hand.

NICK

Doubtless, there was a certain struggle and a certain relief. That *force* took shape in the middle of spring with the arrival of Tom Buchanan. The letter reached Gatsby while he was still at Oxford.

~THE POOR BOY STORY

"Yet still I was too poor to marry, and she grew weary of being tormented on my account. She had a haughty but an impatient spirit, and grew angry at the obstacles that prevented our union. We met now after an absence, and she had been sorely beset while I was away. She complained bitterly and almost reproached me for being poor, and I replied hastily. 'I am honest if I am poor!—were I *not*, I might soon become rich!' This exclamation produced a thousand questions. I feared to shock her by owning the truth, but she drew it from me. And then, casting a look of disdain on me, she said, 'you pretend to love and you fear to face the Devil for my sake!'"

JORDAN

Daisy had a debut after the Armistice. In June, she

married Tom Buchanan of Chicago with more pomp and circumstance than Louisville ever knew before. He came down with a hundred people in four private cars and hired a whole floor of the Seelbach Hotel. The day before the wedding, he gave her a string of pearls.

I was a bridesmaid. I came into her room half an hour before the bridal dinner and found her lying on her bed as lovely as the June night in her flowered dress—and drunk with a bottle in one hand and a letter in the other. I was scared—I can tell you. I'd never seen a girl like that before. She groped around in a wastebasket she had with her on the bed and pulled out the string of pearls.

"Tell 'em all Daisy's change' her mine. Say, *'Daisy's change' her mine!'*" She began to cry—she cried and cried. I locked the door and got her into a cold bath. She wouldn't let go of the letter. She took it into the tub with her and squeezed it up into a wet ball and only let me leave it in the soap dish when she saw that it was coming to pieces like snow, but she didn't say another word.

We gave her spirits of ammonia, put ice on her forehead, and hooked her back into her dress. Half an hour later, when we walked out of the room, the pearls were around her neck, and the incident was over.

Daisy had her little girl, and they went to France for a year. Then, they came back to Chicago to settle down. Daisy was popular in Chicago. It's a great advantage not to drink among hard-drinking people. She could hold her tongue and time any little irregularity of her own. Perhaps her *amour* had faded, yet there was always something in that voice of hers.

~THE BAG OF BEANS

"'O Lord! Why can't I make money?'

Alabama understood vaguely why the keys rattled in his pockets where there was no money and walked the streets like a dizzy man traversing a log. Other people had money. He had only enough for roses. If he did without the roses, he would have nothing for ages and ages while he saved until she was gone or different—or lost forever."

SCOTT

On the last afternoon before he went abroad, he sat with Daisy in his arms for a long, silent time. It was a cold fall day with fire in the room. Now and then, she moved, and he changed his arm a little, kissing her dark shining hair. The afternoon had made them tranquil for a while as if to give them a deep memory for the long parting the next day promised.

They had never been closer in their month of love—nor communicated more profoundly one with another—than when she brushed silent lips against his coat's shoulder, or when he touched the end of her fingers, gently, as though she were . . .

~AN OMEN

"Her hands were folded on her bosom and her dark hair fell round her throat and pillowed her cheek. Her face was serene. Sleep was there in all its innocence and in all its helplessness. Every wilder emotion was hushed, and her bosom heaved in regular breathing. He could see her heart beat as it lifted her fair hands crossed above. No statue hewn of marble in monumental effigy was ever half so fair. Within that surpassing form dwelt a soul true, tender, self-devoted, and affectionate as ever warmed a human breast. With what deep passion did he gaze, gathering hope from the placidity of her angel countenance! A smile wreathed her lips, and he too involuntarily smiled as he held the happy omen."

(54.) *apricity*

SCOTT

Shelley was the convert of Godwin's writings, but to cement his own legacy, he was determined to be Godwin's son and heir. After Harriett's grim death—Mr. and Mrs. Percy Shelley are formally wedded in London. Mr. and Mrs. William Godwin are the official witnesses, fully redeeming their two households. Throughout the service, Godwin is beside himself, smiling with abandon. Percy is now the satisfied son-in-law of his favorite author. Shelley writes, "Indeed, Godwin throughout now shows the most polished and cautious attentions to us. He thinks no kindness too great in compensation for what has passed." Godwin writes, "It is a wonder a girl with not a penny of fortune should meet with so good a match . . . it is now her destiny in life to be respectable, virtuous, and contented."

Hoping that their mutual social stigmas would be removed from the last two and a half years, Godwin assists Percy in filing the marriage license to his Mary. Indeed, after the ceremony, Godwin's public crises do seem to cease, and he begins to regain his social affluences. After a while, Godwin takes on a new student from America, continuing his popular presence in the expanding empire of the States as a fountainhead for its frontier founders. Latterly, old Godwin also meets with his old Wordsworth-and-Blake-gang again.

Reaping the pleasant fruits of the new marriage, Godwin is his happiest since Wollstonecraft in the comfort, peace, and feasting that are reinvigorating the family. "We endeavor to forget the proceeding sorrows and to enjoy the flattering prospects that seem to present themselves to us now." In Marlow, Godwin is Mary and Percy's first guest. He admires their library and he dotes on his grandson, Wilmouse, his "mischievous young rogue." Shelley writes, "Yes, my quadruped has been metamorphosed since last visit into a featherless biped. He has ceased creeping and inhabits his father's house, walking with great alacrity." Godwin the Philosopher King prides in his little William—in his buttoning his boots and breeches—in answering all his first wondrous Wilmouse questions.

In the finale of their fourth summer, Mary and Percy's daughter, Clara Everina, is gladly born—the new legitimate child of the Shelleys. Little Clara, like her favored brother, is also named after members of Mary's ill-fated family—the living grandchild of Wollstonecraft's feminine lineage. In the fragility of these brief, happy hours, Mary and Percy are beaming—beholden—as they watch their beloved Wilmouse playing on the nursery floor and sharing his treats with Clara at her crib.

~AS MUCH

"'When your mother was young, she charged so much candy at the corner store that I had an awful time hiding it from her father.'

'Then, I will be as Mummy was.'

'As much as you can get by with,' chuckled her Gran.'"

SCOTT

In winter, Percy and Mary anonymously publish their earlier travel journals and letters as *History of a Six Weeks' Tour*, recounting their cherished, crucial elopement from London. In her preface, Mary writes, "Those, like river swallows, whose youth has been past in pursuing the inconstant summer adventures of delight and beauty that invest this visible world will be found anew in sailing enthusiastically with the authors down the castled Rhine—clothed with the freshness of a diviner nature—beholding the glaciers, icefalls, lakes, forests, and fountains of the mighty Alps."

~MERRY MERRY MARIGOLD

"Mary Wollstonecraft (the authoress) the wife of William Godwin, in giving birth to their only child, Mary (married to the poet Shelley) so that—at the time—such a rare pedigree of genius was enough to interest me in her, irrespective of her own merits as an authoress. The most striking feature in her face was her calm, grey eyes. She was very fair and light-haired, witty, social, and animated in the society of friends, though mournful in solitude. Like Shelley, she had the power of expressing her thoughts in varied and appropriate words derived from familiarity with the works of our vigorous old writers. This command of our language struck me the more as contrasted with the scanty vocabulary used by ladies in society, in which a score of poor Hackneyed phrases sufficed to express all that is felt or considered proper to reveal."

SCOTT

Mary has reached her paramount moment. In one inclusive spread, she is at once reinstated to her father, she is a published author, and she is married to her Shelley with their son and daughter. A few weeks before they were wed, Mary writes Percy, "Sweet Elf, I was awakened this morning by my pretty babe. The blue eyes of your sweet boy are staring at me while I write this. He is a dear child, and you do love him tenderly. He will be a wise little man for he improves in mind rapidly. I finished that tedious ugly picture I have been so long about—I have also finished writing that chapter, which is a very long one, and I think you will like it. Love me tenderly and think of me with affection whenever anything pleases you greatly." Mary sends Percy a thousand kisses.

(55.) _Echo-Narcissus chain_

~NOW, OR FOREVER

"'She's too good for you, you know?'

'Everybody's too good for everybody else. I can't wait to get drunk.'"

PERCY

The sunlight clasps the earth, and the moonbeams kiss the sea. What're all these kisses worth? If thou kiss not me? My May, _Maie_, you are my realm of ideals made now sublime.

MARY

Let us not bend to narrow and absolute answers, but do as we once wished—with full effort and purpose—walk arms open toward the extravagant and possible. Lull me again with your rhapsodic persuasions, your engrafted logics, the dues that are to this mind the keys I allow possible to these interior quarrels. As good reports issue from the birds throughout our days, let us open all the doors of our lives again and walk with renewed freshness upon what is. We are caught in the great celestial web, and let us not forget the divine knot that binds us from chaos. Our hearts' awakenings are the true work of our lives, and in it, let us continue our living work together in all the joy allowed!

PERCY

Look! Even the season guiding spheres, the heaven orbs—inviting—align, gathering their dusk bridesmaids at this late luncheon wedding on the dimming lawn, dimming. Renewing their vows—as we—the sweet moon sweeps over her horizon husband—their gold corona wedding bands curving, first from the left ring and then paced to the right—unhurried, exchanging their covenant vows, ours. How strange is this clinging love we have of life even in the excess of monotonous vexations.

MARY

So vulnerable to lethal heartbreak, are we not all blunted dull? Is this not what we flee from, our longing to be loosed from, our evening prayer? Lunar ambassador of tears, seasons, and longing—my hearth of spread spears and shield of death—you have grown rose-gold in my skull and pearl-fire within my chest. I can now pass my life in one heart—here, yours—a memorial of mountains I can scarcely repent. You are my Switzerland and my Rhine—our hearts battered into transparent verity and all curtains rent.

PERCY

In you, I see once more my blue lake and rapids—the divinest scene in nature and most dear to me in relieving the burdens of my mysterious woe born in the paroxysms of my childhood of torpor in which a prison was as welcome a residence. Misery had her dwelling in my heart, but in you I no longer talk the same incoherent manner of my crimes. Sufficient for me is the consciousness of them. By the upmost self-violence, I have curbed my imperious voice of wretchedness, which sometimes desires to declare itself to the whole world. Liberty itself would have been a useless gift to me had I not awakened to you.

Fulfill my destiny. I partake of you, and you compose me. In you, I am calm, I have manners, and I am a thing that *can* do good. Yet, I know your melancholy—the diffidence that in being my bride, there is a presentiment that my evil will pervade you—that we will become lost, and that my mad schemes will be the cause.

MARY

Surreal heaviness weights my heart, yet with no recourse higher, I take it all in—patient. Like the tree that knows it can't stop its branches from breaking when hope, the cover of love, is removed—uncovering what was given haven—there is revealed all that it hid, and the vision that gives is starved. You are sorrowful, my love. Ah! If you know what I have suffered, and what I may yet endure, let's endeavor to taste the quiet and freedom from despair that this one day at least permits us to enjoy. Be happy, my dear victorious Percy. My heart is contented. Live with me in the interchange of kindness. I vowed that I would dedicate my powers to thee and thine—have I not kept the vow? It is my heart made whole.

PERCY

We've passed Manhood's dark and tossing waves, and Youth's smooth ocean—smiling to betray—beyond the glassy gulfs we flee of shadow-peopled Infancy through Death and Birth to a diviner day. I would that thou and I—led by some strong enchantment—might ascend a magic ship whose charmed sails should fly with winds at wherever our thoughts might wend, and that no change, nor any evil chance should mar our joyous voyage.

Heavenly vivacity, I am again yours, charmed. My airy dreams of futurity, you have been my constant friend and companion. But, Mary, it is your happiness I desire as well as my own when I declare to you that our marriage would render me eternally miserable unless it were the dictate of your own free choice. Even now, I weep to think that, borne down as you are by the cruelest misfortunes, you may stifle—by pity or presumption—all hope of that love and happiness which would alone restore you to yourself. "Thus let thy power, which like the truth / Of Nature on my passive youth / Descended, to my onward life supply!"

MARY

However our togetherness realizes—and all is passed—I still, as an Echo and her Narcissus, choose only star-sent you alone, my Shelley. Darling Percy, a terrible love is still love. Percy, in your husbandry, you are my helpless double—both my Victor and his shadow. All I know is story. Story is all I can give you this year past, in which all youth has been used. Percy, story can be a purifying love, sanctifying—the education of marriage—and it *has*, from all other illusions in Papa's bookshop. Isn't it the majesty of it all—that we can start again like before—at any moment, any night, that it can all be reborn and new like before?

I know you know the depths of this splendor—the vital mystery—but withhold from no one, save me, sanctifying—ensuring me—from all illusion. More must be borne, but we must be poet enough to ascend our griefs. Percy, what life will there be when love is made death? Can we not reanimate with our love? In our trials, will we outlive all our love?

I am sure that we can touch redemption. Being *almost* saved is us fully lost, but we are not abandoned. Life is connecting vignettes of coloring events. Life is story. Yes, heavy tragic links forge our chain of themes, but I am sure it is fathering grace that binds, writing us patient—authors ourselves—into a more grand narrative where life makes sweet sense of us, a story where we will be lovingly healed.

You have poetical belief in this, always personifying any object new and emblematic, the living mechanics of story—your materialisms grounding things forever to every hearer. But it is the breath of story, the soul that more matters—the passionate metamorphosis unfolding—and the hard veneer of objects all the less. Love made life, my Shelley. Love has made you and I—gloried in our boy and girl—a cleaved life joined. Life together is what love makes, in love that is divinity's most self, and life—the culture and craft of this love.

PERCY

In union in mind in us, one harmony is—in irradiance—mixed. Mary—my dearest amity—you are the warmth of what home can be. Poor dear Fanny, if she had lived until this collateral moment, she would have been saved. For my house—in your living brilliance and thousand decencies that daily flow unfeigned—would then have been a proper asylum for her, her hopes made complete. You are resurrection, lighter than the feathers of wedding doves, lighter than finding that peace is these tears found in this green branch delivered to an aging weariness—born from destruction—that passes hard—passing—and can be purged into something maybe sacred—maybe—and born into this quiet jubilee of this silent tribulation passed—acquitted—salvaging me with more than was taken.

(56.) *a grail*

SCOTT

I had to have the alpha girl, the queen bee androgynous gal, the fluttery and daring and petite and young and pretty and unavailable, highflying live-wire doll. Well, I pay to see passion, and so does the public. There's no paradox to sorrow. We pay easy for communal catharsis.

~VERITABLY ALIVE

Mr. Fitzgerald is a novelist, but Mrs. Fitzgerald is a novelty.

SCOTT

Zelda knew no conventional bounds. She was alive with sultry excitement. She fascinated and her personality was always a vast surprise. Her very defects were stirring. She was a veritable witch of the Southland.

JORDAN

I was happier on the lawns because I had on shoes from England with rubber taps on the soles that bit into the soft ground. I had on a new plaid skirt also that blew a little in the wind. Whenever this happened, the red, white, and blue banners in front of all the houses stretched out stiff and said "*tut-*

tut-tut-tut" in a disapproving way. The largest of the banners—and the largest of the lawns—belonged to Daisy Fay's house. She was just eighteen, two years older than me, and by far the most popular of all the young girls in Louisville. She dressed in white, had a little white roadster, and excited young officers. All day long, the telephone rang in her house.

When I came opposite her house that morning, her white roadster was beside the curb, and she was sitting in it with a lieutenant I had never seen before. They were so engrossed in each other that she didn't see me until I was five feet away. The officer looked at Daisy while she was speaking in a way that every young girl wants to be looked at some time. Because it seemed romantic to me, I have remembered the incident ever since. His name was Jay Gatsby, and I didn't lay eyes on him again for over four years—even after I'd met him on Long Island, I didn't realize it was the same man.

Daisy went with a slightly older crowd—when she went with anyone at all. Wild rumors were circulating about her—how her mother had found her packing her bag one winter night to go to New York and to say goodbye to a soldier who was going overseas. She was effectually prevented, but she wasn't on speaking terms with her family for several weeks.

JAY

"She thought I knew a lot because I know different

things from her . . . Well, there I was, way off my ambitions—getting deeper in love every minute—and all of a sudden, I didn't care. What was the use of doing great things if I could have a better time telling her what I was going to do?"

NICK

Gatsby was overwhelmingly aware of the youth and mystery that wealth imprisons and preserves—of the freshness of many clothes—and of Daisy, gleaming like silver, safe and proud above the hot struggles of the poor.

He went to her house, at first with other officers from Camp Taylor, then alone. It amazed him—he had never been in such a beautiful house before or heard such a *voice* at night—rioting deliriously through life like a superimposed waterfall—half rhythm, half darkness.

He had come in contact with such people, but always with indiscernible barbed wire between.

SCOTT

"He wanders, like a day-appearing dream, / Through the dim wildernesses of the mind; / Through desert woods and tracts, which seem / Like ocean, homeless, boundless, unconfined."

NICK

He knew that he was in Daisy's house by a colossal

accident. So, he made the most of his time. He took what he could get, ravenously and unscrupulously. Eventually, he took Daisy one still October night, took her because he had no real right to touch her hand. He felt that every moment was precious. He wanted her youth—the fresh radiance of her mind and body.

He had deliberately given Daisy a sense of security. He let her believe that he was a person from much the same strata as herself—that he was fully able to take care of her. But he didn't despise himself, and it didn't turn out as he had imagined. He found that he had committed himself to the following of a grail. She vanished into her rich house—into her rich, full life, leaving nothing. From moments he could summon alive five years later, he felt married to her—and that was *all*.

I suppose young James Gatz had the name ready for a long time, even then. His parents were shiftless and unsuccessful farm people—his imagination had never really accepted them as his parents at all.

The truth was that parvenu Jay Gatsby—of West Egg, Long Island—sprang from his Platonic conception of himself—from his own heavens—in the service of a vast, vulgar, and meretricious beauty. So, he invented just the sort of Jay Gatsby that a seventeen-year-old boy would be likely to invent, and to this conception he was faithful to the end.

SCOTT

As a novelist, I reach out to the end of all man's variance, all man's villainy—as a man, I do not go that far. I cannot claim honor—but even the Knights of the Holy Grail were only "striving for it," as I remember.

NICK

It was a cool night with that mysterious excitement in it which comes at the two changes of the year. Jay and Daisy had been walking down the street when the leaves were falling and came to a place where there were no trees, where the sidewalk was white with moonlight. Out of the corner of his eye, Gatsby saw that the blocks of the sidewalk really formed a ladder and mounted to a secret place above the trees. "And now when the night was senescent / And the star dials pointed to morn / At the end of the path, a liquescent / And nebulous luster was born."

His heart beat faster and faster as Daisy's white face came up to his own. He knew that when he kissed this girl—and forever wed his unutterable visions to her perishable breath—his mind would never romp again like an immortal.

~CUP OF HEAVEN

"Each kiss a heart-quake; for a kiss's strength, / I think it must be reckoned by its length. / A long, long kiss, a kiss of youth, and love, / And beauty, all concentrating like rays / Into one focus, kindled from above; / Such kisses as belong to early days, / When heart, and soul, and sense, in concert move, / And the blood's lava, and the pulse ablaze."

NICK

Then he kissed her. At his lips' touch, she blossomed for him like a flower, and the incarnation was complete.

(57.) *inextinguishable*

SCOTT

Steadfast to her Shelley, Mary has refused to become an ostracized spinster—rebuffing, refusing to become snappish and resentful. Although Percy flees from his transgressions to his heroic literary mask—his rebellion to remain *the* Romantic—Mary fulfills Shelley's premise that literary discourse must be of an ethical nature. In her accusatory fable of presumption, Mary remains to her dedication that Percy will not be the monster to be abandoned alone—that Mary will be his willing fatalist, exciting the sympathy of her first audience—remaining unwaveringly his.

~SCRIBBLER

"Mrs. Shelley, who had always been what she calls a 'scribbler' from her early girlhood, was more tenacious of the project, and urged on by both Shelley and Byron, she at last completed the ghastly and powerful narrative, which, in spite of its technical imperfections, is certainly worth preserving, and will be undoubtedly read through by everyone who gets as far as the second letter."

SCOTT

A year after being married, Mary Shelley's novel is published anonymously in three volumes during their fourth winter—Percy having relentlessly advocated for her literary nursling throughout London. Godwin writes to Mary that she has cultivated her mind "in a manner most admirably adapted to make her a great, successful author." Joyfully, he asks Mary, "If you cannot be independent, who should be?" Mary's novel—entitled *Frankenstein; or, the Modern Prometheus*—is dedicated to Mr. William Godwin and his works.

~PROTOTYPE

"It is formed on the Godwinian manner and has all the faults—but many likewise of the beauties of that model. In the dark and gloomy views of nature and of man, it even goes beyond its great prototype. In return, it possesses a similar power of fascination, something of the same mastery in harsh and savage delineations of passion that are relieved in like manner by the gentler features of domestic and simple feelings."

SCOTT

Her influence from Godwin was considerable, not only his views concerning the innate goodness of man and the rational structure of ideal society, but also the idea of a hounded person haunted by the guilts of fruitless efforts to benefit mankind and from the sufferings that issue from its Pandora's box. One major review contended "this novel is an imitation of one that was very popular in its day—the *St. Leon* of Mr. Godwin."

Written when Mary was a baby, this mythic novel was Godwin's tragic fiction of an aristocrat's descent into a cursed wanderer torn between his rivaling desires for greatness and his necessary relational responsibilities—his work in which he eulogizes Mary's legendary mother as his equal. On the unfolding events leading to revolution, Wollstonecraft reasoned the anti-Prometheans as those who're "not able to distinguish the possible from the monstrous," insisting that "the limits of the possible have never been defined to stop the sturdy innovator's hand." When Shelley was also the same age as Mary, Godwin's *St. Leon* was the influence for his own gothic novel of a doomed, "miscreated" outcast.

~ODE FOR A NECROMANCER

"The book is obviously by a woman, but her methods of achieving an effect are entirely masculine. Even the defects in the book are masculine defects— intellectual curiosity in what amounts to a riot, solid blocks of strong words fitted into consecutive pages like bricks, a lack of selective delicacy, and, sometimes, a deliberately blunted perception. Read the scene where he goes to work in the machine shop and try to think what other women writers could have written it. This is not a perfect first novel—but it is honest, well written, if raggedy, and thoroughly alive."

SCOTT

Still, in the most famous review of Mary's anonymous

novel for social reform—in the bravado of a philosophical exposition—it is illustrated, "treat a person ill, and he will become wicked. Requite affection with scorn—divide him, a social being, from society—and you impose upon him the irresistible obligations of malevolence and selfishness, having been branded by some accident with disregard, and changed—by neglect and solitude of heart—into a scourge and a curse. He was an abortion and an anomaly. His original goodness was gradually turned into the fuel of an inextinguishable misanthropy. 'I was not born to hate them, but they have forced me to hate them.' We cry 'hold, hold, enough.' But there is yet something to come—and like the victim whose history it relates—we think we can bear no more, and yet more is to be borne."

However, before many of the reviews for *Frankenstein* are published, the Shelleys will have exiled themselves from the British Isles. Before the Shelleys depart from London, Mary writes her husband about the next location of their hopes. "If your feelings are decided enough on the subject—if Italy would not give you far more pleasure than a settlement on the coast—if it would, say so, and so be it. You glow with the thoughts of a clear sky—pure air and burning sun. You would then more enjoy life. Italy certainly holds forth a charming prospect."

More must be borne. Although the Master of Chancery admits that Shelley possesses an ardent mind and considerable talent, it is the admission of Percy's "Notes" from *Queen* Mab—advocating Paine's *Age of Reason*—that are the decisive evidence for the justification of the Court's denial, stressing Shelley's oppositional contempt of government and vilification of religion. There are now real fears of recent hangings for sedition and the disturbing fact that these "Notes" can now be used for other legal proceedings against Shelley. Harriett's family wants blood. To their own disbelief, the Westbrooks' ruse of religious objections against Percy also prevents their own continued custody of Ianthe and her brother. Subsequently, for the next eight months, a legal battle ensues for a plan to be ordered for their education and care.

Fearfully, the Shelleys leaving England will secure their familial safety of Wilmouse and Clara—beyond the tumultuous reach of British legal authority. Grim, "her hair streaming," the revenant of Harriett indeed haunts them from Marlow—to their doom. Once in Italy, the eventual appointment for the caregivers would be those from Shelly's party, ordering Ianthe and her brother to the warm London household of an eminent physician of Oxford who cares for veterans and the Duke of Cambridge. From their plan of education, they are ordered to "keep from perusal all books that tend to shake their faith," "discontinue the reading of novels," and be encouraged to study the "best poets" of Great Britain.

In Italy, three Shelleyan years later, Percy will write his colleague. "A droll circumstance has occurred.

Queen Mab, a poem written by me when very young, in the most furious style, with long notes against Christianity, and the king, and bishops, and marriage, and the devil knows *what*—is being published . . . against my desire . . . I apply for an injunction."

During these last four years together, Mary calls her Shelley her "Elf," "sweet winged Elf," "Ariel," "airy Elf," and her *E. K.*—her "Elfin Knight." To Mary, Percy commonly quipped—in adoration—that "on her hind paws, the Dormouse stood in a wild and mingled mood of Maieishness and Pecksietude."

(58.) *parasol*

~PROMETHEAN HEAT

"'Everybody gives you *belief* for the asking,' she said to Amory, 'and so few people give you anything more to believe in than your own belief—just "*not* letting you down." That's all. It's so hard to find a person who accepts responsibilities beyond what you ask.'

'So easy to be loved—so hard *to* love,' Amory answered."

MARY

We must be accountable for what we are causal. I had found myself fettered again to grief, indulging in all the misery of reflection, exteriorizing the horrid anguish that can no longer remain concealed. Then I spurred on myself, as an animal, striving so to forget the world, my fears, and, more than all, myself. My sufferings were augmented also by the oppressive sense of the injustice and ingratitude of their infliction.

Ceaselessly, each of our social allusions to the Titan seems to you now an embittering eulogy upon yourself. Percy, you once wooed me heroically, sermonizing that it was those who make themselves Prometheus are who must translate a ray of the divine wisdom from the haven of the gods, their one beam of truth and clarity that must be rendered to man from the source of the supreme celestial light, courting me that it is the tragic blind hopes from this singular fire that enkindles residence in the hearts of man, that it is the unique Promethean heat that misleads their zealous, ignited optimisms—like a somber torture to reason—having been augmented to be ravenous for ultimacy made impossible.

Did I solicit thee from darkness to promote me? Paranoia possesses you, fearing that your lone power is to be limited to its initial spark, the unrepeatable first heat, prevented from lasting subsisting ignition, recognizing your fear in promising blind hope. Yet, like fair veins that flow in sable marble, your overshadowing sorrow does not carve you less delightful. How sweetly sad thy melody attunes still my soul to tenderness.

I am Hope who remains in the old jar. See again. Like Byron writes, "thy godlike crime was to be kind." We must be poet enough to resist complete wretchedness. See again. Let us unstitch ourselves from the superficial patches we've amalgamated to excuse our consequences, ceasing to haunt all our loves to their exits, reversing our unexpectant tide.

We must resist. On what anvils and in what molds were our hearts set? Unbroken in such sufferings—is there nothing left for us but dying? No. We have trod unknown paths and dragged-out unknown things— most for the very best. Regardless of the exclusions of death that have marked our journey, have we not been marked more by the expansions of love? We are tempest tossed, but love me as you ever have—and may God preserve our children. Facing our dangers, our enemies shall not be too much for us.

It is my resolve to no longer hold up this paralleling mirror to your nature, but to reflect inspiriting light. If you like, Italy can be our South America that our creature vowed in its careful pact to its maker—that the heart is not like some old sock that is to be thrown away when it's torn, but the very thing of worth, the capacity for all affection in which there can be no greater. There's Galatea, her pearling softer and softer until real—who in all probability was to become a thinking and reasoning animal—who might refuse to comply with Pygmalion's compact made before her creation. They might even hate each other. Would her creator then hide himself, or even then desire to destroy her? How monstrous to mold like a god and then not be deity. We must resist and must foster what's best.

As we labor to make beautiful our art, we must labor all the more extreme to beautify our living, our lives to each other and our contemporaries. We must live beautiful. When we would want too much, we must bridle our deceptive ambitions of modernity. Life is obstinate and clings closest where it is most hated. Who's ever near as good as self-assumed? Nothing is more painful to the human mind than after mounting feelings have been worked up by a quick succession of events, these *feelings* transition to the dead calmness of inaction and decay sanity—certainly—which deprives the soul both of hope and fear. Yet, husband, we can level each other's troubled scales.

Isn't most of all we're scratching out of this conflict is to lilt to ourselves whether our parents are still alive, as light glints from our faces against the waters or other mirrors? Are we to stay in our morgues, cemeteries, and charnel houses to learn? Beloved one, I hope to see peace in your countenance and to find that your heart is not totally void of comfort and tranquility. Return. You will find a happy, cheerful home. You will find friends who love you dearly, to see you and be assured that you are well. No cares will cloud our countenances. Weep no more, my Shelley. Sigh no more.

Here waits our dearest Wilmouse—with sweet laughing cobalt eyes with dark lashes, curling hair, and rosy with health, two little dimples on each cheek—who shuns your powers of application. He looks upon study as an odious fetter. His time is spent in the open air, climbing the hills or desiring the lake. I fear that he will become an idler unless we permit him to enter on the profession which he has selected. At twilight, Albion becomes a little den of forest creatures where Blue Eyes jumps all about as a squirrel and stares with magical curiosity into the crib of the Dormouse's daughter. Though I have written myself into better spirits, my anxiety returns upon me as I conclude.

I cannot believe that I am the same creature whose thoughts were once filled with sublime and transcendent visions of the beauty and the majesty of goodness. Yet, one word from you—dearest loving husband—is necessary to calm our apprehensions. Return. Be our comforter. Come with feelings of peace and gentleness that will heal—instead of festering—the wounds of our minds. Enter your home with kindness and affection for those who love you. "How sweet is love itself possessed when but love's shadows are so rich in joy!"

The picture I present to you is peaceful and humane, and you must feel that you could deny it only in the wantonness of power and cruelty. My Perseus, my victor, banish these dark passions. Remember the friends around you who center all their hopes in you. Have we lost the power of rendering you happy? Clara is well and gets very pretty. How happy I shall be when my own dear love comes again to kiss me and my babes. Creating a loving, warm home can be the happy exhaustion of our talents for our happy seasons, fostering our passions and patiently anchoring our ambitions. Ah! While we love—while we're true to each other, here in this land of peace and beauty, we may reap every tranquil blessing! What can disturb our peace?

Let us only cling closer to what remains and transfer our love for those whom we have lost to those who yet live. Our circle will be small—bound close by the ties of affection and mutual misfortune. Farewell, first home—first glow. Farewell, Mother. Farewell, Papa. And when *Time*—my cherished one—shall have softened your despair, new and dear objects of care will be born to replace those of whom we have been so cruelly deprived. Let's to our Neapolitan days—to our Italy, my Heart! Without the smoke, fogs, and rains that conspire here to kill us, the red Italian sun will be your redemptive physician in our gentler, warmer climate and new, renewing colors.

—Your faithful pupil, affectionate transcriber, devoted philhellene, your Mary, Mrs. Shelley, like Prospero, overthrowing all her charms herself—watching her babies be happy in a tempest of catharsis—breaking her staff and drowning her London book, dispelling labyrinths of revenge outplotted, pardoning British deceptions now banished, crimes usurped in her rough magic releasing, shipping out from her terrible hurricane past, donning again her cap, her parasol for a rapier, and her hope for Naples.

(59.) *summer gypsy's sacred ink*

~CIN CIN! SALUTE!

Consider all the cocktails mentioned in this book drunk by me as a toast to the American Booksellers Association."

~SELF-ADDRESSED

"Dear Scott, well, you've damn well done it this time. *Now*, they'll never let you hide again. So, here's a cheap postcard with a fancy looking seashell on it—an anomaly who died a long time ago. The lines on your brain are like these pottery grooves and spines of this seashell—beaten at by an ocean's best waves. I think a lot of yourself will always be in *the hole* of that French coast penitentiary-villa, but now you've written yourself into the best old drinks that a Roman holiday can pour—during Prohibition. Drink. Drink deep. Like the perfect carnival ride, flow down the aqueducts toasting endless goblets of aperitifs. Keep liquid enough to not dry up into a hollow relic—into a pretty thing to be set on a pretty shelf.

— Mr. F. S. *Arriviste* Fitzgerald."

SCOTT

"France was a spoiled and revengeful child, which having kept Europe in a turmoil for two hundred years, has spent the last forty demanding assistance in its battles so that the continent may be kept as much like a bloody sewer as possible." Thus, *it* began in Paris, that *impression*—fleeting, chiefly literary, unprofound—that the world was growing darker. Still, of course, all life is a process of breaking down, but the blows that do the dramatic side of the work— the big sudden blows that come, or seem to come, from outside—the ones you remember and blame things on—don't show their effect all at once, but happen quickly. And yet, there is another sort of blow that comes from within—that you don't feel until it's too late, until you realize with sudden finality . . . you will never be as good a man again.

From our bedroom window here in Rome, I am moved by a glimpse of the Pope passing by and I can see the house where Keats died—the Keats-Shelley Memorial House that had opened when I was a kid. It's easiest to look back at enthusiastic beginnings— back to when they would let you win the World Series anyway you wanted. It was the gladdest year of any young man—revelry and marriage—the rewards of the year before. I remember riding in a taxi one afternoon between very tall buildings under a mauve and rosy sky. I began to bawl because I had everything I wanted and knew that I would never be so happy again.

London served strawberries in a gold dish, and Paris offered ice cream and dirty postcards, but we were pregnant. While leaves blew up streets, we waited for our child to be born. We were pregnant with Pie. I had sent *Beautiful and Damned* to Ober. We went abroad to the big capitals for a few months. I wrote to E. W., "damn—damn!—the Continent of Europe. It is of merely antiquarian interest. Rome is only a few years behind Babylon. France made me sick—its silly pose as the thing the world *has* to save. If we had let it be conquered, that would have been the only way to have saved the fleet of tottering old wrecks."

It was typical of our precarious position in New York that when our child was born, we played safe and went home to Saint Paul. It seemed inappropriate to bring a baby into all that glamor and loneliness. Scottie-Girl was now ours, and the second novel had now sold quite well. I then published my *Tales of the Jazz Age* and, on Long Island, I published my satirical stage play. It was a dud in the disagreeable world of the caprices of drama, but, hell, I thought *it* and then my Mr. Button curiosity were the funniest damn things ever written. It was clear they liked what I hated and hated what I liked, but this sort of awareness was very nothing to me.

We had run through a lot, though we had retained an almost theatrical innocence by preferring the role of the observed—to that of the observer. But innocence is no end in itself. As our minds unwillingly matured, we began to see New York whole and tried to save some of it for the selves we would inevitably become. It was too late—and too soon.

In a year, we were back and we began doing the same things over again and not liking them so much. In

Paris, we bathed Scottie in the *bidet* by mistake, and she drank the gin fizz thinking it was lemonade. So, back in ossified France—shaving a fairer exchange rate of this feverish life—I'd bought that Summer of the Riviera for myself—freed from my own authorial slaveries—immensely immersed until that *novel* novel of my soul was incarnate. They had come to object to my singular concerns of love and success, but—in God!—my mutabilities are all I had to write them. It was after that—and after I didn't need water anymore—that I had stopped giving, giving anything that required giving.

~INCARNATE

"'We will see,' the doctor said, staring out of the window impassively.

'I've got to have some water! Please give me some water!'

The nurse went on methodically straightening the dressings on the wheel table. 'Non c'e *acqua*,' she whispered.

The walls of the hospital opened and shut. The room smelled like hell."

~TENDER WILDFLOWERS OF HAIR THROUGH SCARS

"There're titles that seem to fit—and I had two others, but they seemed too light . . . Did the evolution of 'startling work' into 'accepted work' cease twenty years ago? . . . I thought it was a purpose of critics and publishers to educate the public up to original work. Nevertheless, Zelda and I are contemplating a careful revision after a week's complete rest. For Christ's sake, don't give anyone the dust jacket you're saving for me. I've written it *into* the book. Still, I think my novel is about the best American novel ever written and it's like nothing I've ever read before. It's been a fair summer. I've been unhappy, but my work hasn't suffered from it. I am grown at last."

ZELDA

I'd also imagined you there in the repair garage and in the other interims of us. Then, there they'd be—maybe on the bureau—the *letters* I'd send in sacred ink on blessed paper, and you'd read the commas, the blots, and the thumb-smudges on the margins.

SCOTT

My every little Latin thing! I hadn't realized you'd brought our *treasure* box trap to Rome. Well, open the thing, and let's drink our yesterdays. *Salute* to our mash notes! You can float us like a swan through the pines of the past, but float us lightly rural—like the summer gypsy you were named.

ZELDA

A last gloat in our last great city. *Cin Cin!* "Nobody's hands were on the Ouija but Mrs. Francesca's, who'd never heard of you, and *it*—the terrifying thing—told us to be married. Matrimony!

But, of course, I got scared and quit. She had told me theosophists think that two souls are incarnated together—not necessarily at the same time, but are mated since the time when people were bisexual. So, you see "soulmate" isn't exactly some formula from pulp magazines after all. It's really remarkable, even if you do scoff. I wish you wouldn't. It's so easy, and believing is much more intelligent.

Now, it's all just platitudes—like Momma, when she's a prude about what shouldn't be tried to be mixed: 'oil and water,' 'whiskey and tobacco,' 'prostitutes and gentility.' All philosophy is, more or less, platitudes now. It seems as if there's no new wisdom—and surely people haven't stopped thinking. Yet, I'm much too lazy to care whether things are done or not and I don't want to be famous and fettered. All I want is to be very young always and very irresponsible and to feel that my life is my own—to live and be happy and die in my own way—to please myself my own way.

Well, isn't it well that you didn't waste yourself wooing a mindless majorette, or some cheap popularity, or one of God's own good, little Gardenia Girls? All the fire and sweetness and strength grow so that nothing is lost. Things that are tremendously alive—just like blowing bubbles—they burst, but more bubbles are just as beautiful—and burst. So, don't mourn for a poor little forlorn, wonderful memory. Just come and tell me, and take me, and we won't worry anymore about anything."

~MASH-NOTE-CRAFT

"I like your last—may I call it *love* letter? Better than the first. I can give you a higher proof of my esteem than to tell you. The style of my letter will—whether I will or no. *It* has calmed my mind—a mind that had been painfully active all the morning, haunted by old sorrows that seemed to come forward with new force to sharpen present anguish. Well! Well, it is almost gone—I mean all my unreasonable fears and a whole train of tormentors, which you have routed. I can scarcely describe to you their ugly shapes—so quickly do they vanish. And, let them go. We will not bring them back by talking of them. Nay, *more* I cannot withhold my friendship from you—and will try to merit yours—that *necessity* may bind you to me. Now, will you not be a good boy, and smile upon me? I dine at half past four—you ought to come and give me an appetite for my dinner."

— Wollstonecraft to Godwin

(60.) *substantiality*

~DAMNED

In his festival conception of life, it was a terrible thing for him to love youth so much that he jumped straight from youth to senility without going through manhood, whining for lost youth's death-dance.

NICK

It was James Gatz who had been loafing along the beach that afternoon in a torn green jersey and a pair of canvas pants. He was ready to be Jay Gatsby. He'd had the name ready for a long time. For over a year, he had been beating his way along the south shore of Lake Superior as a clam digger and a salmon fisher. His brown, hardening body lived naturally through the half-fierce, half-lazy work of bracing days. He knew women early and he became contemptuous of them because they were hysterical about things, which in his overwhelming self-absorption, he took for granted.

A universe of ineffable gaudiness spun itself out in his brain while the clock ticked on the washstand, while the moon soaked—with wet light—his tangled clothes upon the floor. An instinct toward his future glory had led him, some months before, to a small college in southern Minnesota. He stayed there two weeks, dismayed at its ferocious indifference to the drums of his destiny—to destiny itself—and despising the janitor's work with which he was to pay his way through. Then he drifted back to Lake Superior, and he was still searching for something to do on the day that yacht dropped anchor in the shallows along shore.

~INEFFABLE ILLUMINANT

"He was bound for one of those immortal moments which appears so radiantly that its remembered light is enough to see by for years."

NICK

To young Gatz, resting on his oars and looking up at the railed deck, that yacht represented all the beauty and glamor in the world. I suppose he smiled—he had probably discovered that people liked him when he smiled. The clam digger was ready.

~WET YACHT LIGHT

"Thou must hold water in a witch's sieve, / And be liege lord of all the elves and fays, / To venture so."

NICK

Having had the name ready for a long time, he was employed in a vague personal capacity—he was in turn steward, mate, skipper, and secretary. The arrangement lasted five years during which the yacht went three times around the continent. He was left with his singularly appropriate education. The vague contour of Jay Gatsby had filled out to the substantiality of a man.

~AS YARE AS *ARIEL*

"No more to wait the twilight of the moon / In this sequestered vale of star and spire; / For one, eternal morning of desire / Passes to time and earthly afternoon."

(61.) _under the pink, white, and yellow_

~OF THEIR OWN MAKING

"With the streets free from automobiles, and morals free from movies, and, in a large portion of America, corners already free from saloons, what did it matter what these children thought as they lay awake on warm summer nights straining to catch the cries of newsboys? It was a romantic time to be a child, to be old enough to feel the excitement being stored up around them and to be young enough to feel safe. Formed in such a period of pregnant placidity, left free to wonder and dream in a changing age of little or no pressure exerted upon them by life, it is not amazing that when Time—having brought everything else out of the hat—produced his _piece de resistance_, "the war," these children realized too soon that they had seen the magician's whole repertoire.

This was the last piece of wizardry they believed in, and now, nearing middle age and the period when they are to be the important people of the world, they still hope wistfully that things will again have the magic of the theater. It is the result of a sort of debonair desperation—a necessity for forcing the moments of life into an adequacy to the emotions of ten years ago. The men, who at twenty-one led companies of two hundred soldiers must, it seems to us, feel an eternal letdown from a time when necessity and idealism were one single thing—and no compromise was ever necessary. A habituation to enormous effort during the years of the war left a necessity for trials and tests on them. It is a great emotional disappointment resulting from the fact that life moved in poetic gestures when they were younger and has now settled back into buffoonery. And with the current insistence upon youth as the finest and richest time in the life of man, it is small wonder that sensitive young people are haunted and harassed by a sense of unfulfilled destiny and grope about with a baffled feeling of frustration.

Perhaps, we worked too much over man as the individual so that his capabilities are far superior to the problems of life, and now we have endless youth of a responsible age floundering about in a morass of unused powers—and feeling very bitter, and mock heroic, like all people who think the element of chance in their lives should have been on a bigger scale. Outside of war, men of the hour haven't had a romantic opportunity near home since the last gold rush, and a great portion of young men feel that their mental agility or physical prowess can never be really measured in situations of their own making."

SCOTT

She dressed in white, had a little white roadster, and excited young officers. All day long, the telephone rang in her house. Her white roadster was beside the curb, and she was sitting in it with a lieutenant.

While she was speaking, the officer looked at Daisy—

my Zelda Fay—in a way that every young girl wants to be looked at. His name was James S. Key, Officer Gatzgerald—and Scott Fitz was ready to dance in a way that every young man wants to dance before he goes to die for the land of the free in France.

ZELDA

"If we were together, you'd feel how strong it is. You're so sweet when you're melancholy. I love your sad tenderness when I've hurt you. That's one of the reasons I could never be sorry for our quarrels. Those dear little fusses. There's nothing in all the world I want from you—apart from your precious love. All the material things are nothing. I'd just hate to live a sordid, colorless existence because you'd soon love me less and less. I'd do anything to keep your heart for my own. I don't want to live—I want to love first and live incidentally. Don't ever think of the things you can't give me. You've trusted me with the dearest heart of all, and it's so damned much more than anybody else in all the world has ever had. If you'd die, I'd have no purpose in life. I'd just be a pretty decoration.

I'm afraid I'm losing all pretense. Yet, as much as I could do anything without you, I have always been inclined toward the cheery atmosphere that boys radiate. The fire burns again, but the old bench looks so lonesome without us, making things mighty hard if I didn't know that we'd just have to have each other and I just had to wrinkle your shiny darling hair and just give you the biggest kiss of any on Earth.

This sweater is perfectly delicious, and I'm going to save it until you come, so you can tell me how nice I look. It's funny, but I like being 'pink and helpless.' When I know I seem that way, I feel terribly competent and superior. I keep thinking, those men who think I'm purely decorative are just fools for not knowing better. I love being rather unfathomable. You are the only person on earth, Lover, who has ever known and loved all of me. Men love me because I'm pretty. They're always afraid and they're always of mental wickedness. Men love me because I'm clever and they're always afraid of my prettiness. One or two have even loved me because I'm lovable. But you just *do*, darling—and I *do*—so very, very much.

~STARS FELL ON ALABAMA

Little Miss 1900 me didn't know my zodiac until Mrs. Francesca made me a Leo. He turned to me as strong as a century turns when I had the "Stars on Alabama" tune in my head. He looked at me madder than a meteor shower like he wanted to curse all the lazy fig trees. He knew a lioness couldn't like him more than it did.

ZELDA

I can't think of anything but of nights with you. I want them warm and silvery—when we can be all together all our lives, which will probably be long. I don't want you to see me growing old and ugly. I know you'll be a beautiful old man—romantic and dreamy—and I'll probably be most prosaic and wrinkled. As soon as we learn each other, we'll have to understand death. We will just have to die when we're thirty. But before then, we'll love each other, name all our children, and love each other and our children."

~THESE CHILDREN

"'And, so, goodbye. My mother and father will be very pleased and glad that you have been so kind and delightful about the nice time.'

She mounted the stairs contentedly. Alabama heard her purring in the hall.

'You must have had a wonderful time—'

—'I hated her stupid old party!'

'Then what was the *oration* about?'

'You said,' Bonnie stared at her parent contemptuously, 'that I was not polite the last time when I didn't like the lady. So, I hope you are glad *now* with how I was this time.'

'Oh, quite!'

"'*Consciousness*,'" Alabama murmured to herself, 'is an ultimate betrayal, I suppose.' She had asked Bonnie simply to spare the lady's feelings.

The child played often at her grandmother's house. They played at keeping house. Bonnie was the head of the family—and her grandma made an agreeable little girl to have.

'Children were not brought up so strictly when mine

were young,' her grandma said. She felt very sorry for Bonnie—that the child should have to learn so much of life before it began for her."

ZELDA

"The ring has wreaked havoc in Montgomery. Everybody thinks it's lovely, and I'm so proud to be your girl—you always loving me and that we'll be together for all of our lives. Today seems like Easter, and I wish we were together walking slow through the sunshine and the crowds from Church.

Everything would smell so good and warm, and your ring would shine so white in the sun—like one of the church lilies with a little yellow dust on it. We'd have to be together in this very room—the room where I am, or the room where you are—because it would be made for us to be in love in. I'd wish you'd just scribble it on the cover—what I live to hear you say. I can't tell you in ten words or ten volumes or ten years. I can't even tell you in a new way. I've tried so many times to think of a new way to say it—and it's still 'I love you, love you, love you.'"

(62.) *fairytale*

~FEAR AND LOATHING

"Zelda painting, me drinking, heavy sociability, a thousand parties and no work, drinking, loafing, again a thousand parties and no work, futile, shameful, useless, self-disgust, health gone."

SCOTT

Wisteria dripped chimerically through the gold end of day over the broad still Rhone. We warmed our sunburned backs and invented new cocktails—like the glass balls that make snow storms when shaken. We were too superior to use the guidebooks. It was exciting being lost between the centuries in the Roman dusk of the broken Old World. Yet, before we had left for Rome to fully revise the great heap of my great guts—aided in the great aggressions of my great wife—exasperating all the genius of youth, I had written to Perkins, "I wish I were twenty-two again with only my dramatic and feverishly enjoyed miseries. You remember I used to say I wanted to die at thirty? Well, I'm now twenty-nine and the prospect is still welcome."

ZELDA

Well, here's the one you've worn out swooning. Zounds! "Goofo, you've got to try to feel how much I do. I can't even hate these damnable people—

nobody's got any right to life but us. They're dirtying up our world, and I can't hate them because I love *you* so. Scott, do please what you think is best, but wait if you can—because God, or something, has always made things right, and maybe this will be. I could never do without you—even if you hated me and were a leper, even if you ran away with another, even if you starved me and beat me. I would still want you. I know—and I will always know it.

So, darling heart, our fairytale is almost ended, and we're going to live very happy afterward.

I'm so sorry for all the times I've been mean and hateful—for all the miserable minutes that I've caused you when we could have been so happy. You deserve so much—so very much. I will always be very, very happy with you—except sometimes when we engage in our delicate brunch debates—and even *then*, I rather enjoy myself. I'm absolutely nothing without you—just the doll that I should've been born. You're a necessity and a luxury and you're going to be the dearest husband to your dear wife."

SCOTT

We wanted to discover the ruins for ourselves—like Keats had, writing of spring and the unchangeable stars, like our Shelleys, teaching their favorite child about crumbling and beauty and power. "Can spring be far behind?"

~BRIGHT RUINS

Keats edits, coughing blood, "I will imagine you Venus tonight and pray, pray, pray to you, fair Star." Boarding his voyage to Italy, to die, Keats edits his sonnet to his beloved. "The moving waters at their priestlike task / Of pure ablution round earth's human shores." Keats ends his gentle poetry, "Pillow'd upon my fair love's ripening breast, / To feel for ever in a sweet unrest, / Still, still to hear her tender-taken breath, / And so live ever."

(63.) *going ahead*

~WHEN I DRINK, I THINK BACK

"I could go on for a long time quoting things that delight me: the beginning of Chapter Two and the night 'when we hunted through the great rooms for cigarettes'—for instance. Someone once said that the thing that was common to all real works of art was a nostalgic quality, often indefinable, not specific. If that is so, then Fitzgerald's is surely one because it makes me want to be back somewhere as much, I think, as anything I've ever read."

SCOTT

Once again, let's be recaptured—reinvented, reconciled. We could go back South—back to values and absolutes, this side of paradise. There's that fascinating Scopes ordeal in Tennessee, and there's the Parthenon in Nashville. Then, we could pop in on Alvin-old-sport-York at his general store, and you could sign him a copy of Jay Gatz impersonating his decorations from the Argonne. Yet, if rather back to Paris, are we to just escape—keep fleeing—our—

ZELDA

—our sufferings? Or, by them be purified, be atoned? Yet, Scott's idealistic aspirations were unsustainable. "'She'll see. I'll show them,' said Scott," playing his broken lute. They tried to penalize him for his sensitivities of the Romantics, deserting him. No matter! The victor belongs to the spoils. He wanted the world to wait motionless and breathless, but the world was going ahead—reading, forgetting, making stamp-books, *living*.

SCOTT

Forgetting, *yes*—our first caricatures. Well, we'll just have to play "Paradise" right here then. Yes, our young Blaine—his father was an ineffectual, inarticulate man with a taste for Byron and a habit of drowsing over the *Encyclopedia Britannica*. But, *Beatrice* Blaine, there was a woman! Early pictures taken on her father's estate at Lake Geneva and in Rome—at the Sacred Heart Convent—were an educational extravagance. Her youth passed in renaissance glory. She learned in England to prefer whiskey-and-soda to wine, her small talk was broadened during a winter in Vienna, a culture rich in all arts—barren of all ideas—in the last of those days when the Great Gardener clipped the inferior roses to produce one perfect bud.

ZELDA

Before our bland Blaine was summoned back to Lake Geneva, he had appeared—shy but inwardly glowing—in his first long trousers and purple handkerchief. He had formulated his first philosophy, a code to live by, a sort of aristocratic egotism. He marked himself capable of infinite expansion— for good or evil. Your caricature granted himself personality, charm, magnetism, and poise. He had a rather Puritan conscience that made him consider himself a great deal worse than other boys. There was also a curious strain of weakness running crosswise through what made him. He was liable to be swept off into surly sensitivities or timid stupidity. He was a slave to his own moods and he felt that though he was capable of audacity, he possessed neither courage nor self-respect. With vanity—tempered with self-suspicion—and a desire to pass as many boys to get to a vague top of the world, he drifted into adolescence.

SCOTT

They might want to forget him—but not our Rosalind. She had great faith in man as a *sex*. Women—she detested. They represented qualities that she felt and despised in herself. In her vivid, instant personality and her disturbing, eternally kissable mouth, she was the delicious, inexpressible, once-in-a-century blend.

ZELDA

Well, our *honeysuckle* couldn't just sit there and stare like a little materialist wretch of a caricature, she had to have a soul. She couldn't be rational and she wouldn't be molecular. It seemed to her that in reaching her longing, she would drive the devils that drove her, that she would be able—through her own medium—to command her emotions, to summon love or pity or happiness at will. Yet, once the adequate years are achieved for choosing direction, the die is cast, and the moment has long since passed which determines the future.

~METERED BELIEF

"The meter, being waltz time, which moves nostalgic twilights to their rendezvous, the world believes again in sentiment and turns to fairytale; whereas those years haunted by the more aggressive sadnesses of *march time* produce a more dynamic, tragic, spiritual compensation."

ZELDA

She quietly expected great things to happen to her, and no doubt, that's one of the reasons why they did—once again, and once again. "Then wear the gold hat, if that will move her; / If you can bounce high, bounce for her too, / Till she cry '*Lover*, gold-hatted, high-bouncing lover, / I must have you!'"

~GOLD INK-FILLING LOVERS

"I wear a charmed skin. Send me, the next time anybody comes, *my* bottle of ink. *You* can fill an inkstand. Fill it as high as your image at this moment fills my mind."

– Godwin to Wollstonecraft

"Fanny says, '*perhaps* Man come today.' I am glad there is no 'perhaps' in the case. As to another 'perhaps,' it must rest in the womb of time. Send me some *Ink*."

– Wollstonecraft to Godwin

(64.) *pastoral addendum*

ZELDA

Clink. Click. Shucks, I've got the corncob cure for your scattered chickenfeed memories—right here from your own humble biographer's farmhouse—a new mash note for Max to append to the end of your Anglo-Saxon *pastoral*:

In the knowing youth of his seventeenth Irish-Yankee year, Scott-to-the-Top had entered his wondrous Princeton, his glittering caste system—not quite for him—and in the wonder of his twentieth year, had left New Jersey in the presumption of his endless sense of expectation. Rather than grades, Scoffer stood on his short stack—soapbox—of his school-year stage efforts and bragged to that *E."Bunny" W.*, "I'm to become one of the greatest writers that ever lived and I'm going to have the top girl."

From his great American miscalculations to not hide behind a degree, F. Scotch Fake-Emeralds transitioned in pursuit of his mother's other hope—the ideal promise of her little Scott-Key's literary dreams—which he quickly partnered to the imperative of his paternal tide of *machismo* expectancy. Putting his Scott-Hancock on that patriot paper, he greatly volunteered for the greatest army, commissioned a second lieutenant in the infantry of the United States of American Boy Scout Warriors to end *all wars.*

Twenty-one years old that divine, migrating summer, Officer Scott "Some Force" Fitzgerald was stationed at his fourth training post, Camp Sheridan. In heavenly star-showered Alabama, he penciled and served as *aide-de-camp*, riding his horse and drilling his regiment like a weekend coming-of-age article—"A Boy and his Bugle." Through the hedges of mock oranges at the Capital's haughty Country Club, Scott-the-Social-Striver had his debut, saluting and falling for the legendary belle of all Montgomery society, a State Judge's own supreme wayward daughter. My very own Valentino sheikh boy—with his angelic, delicate good looks—scrawled his grinning alter-ego moniker, signing "Scot Fitz" to all his gin-fizz dancehall cards. "His eyes were blue and clear, his jaw was squared, his mouth was sensitive looking, and his hair was corn-colored and wavy—in the ways that average Americans associate features with beauty." Well, shine *his* shoes—and she danced the army polish right from them.

As his handsome noodle *boiled* in the obligation to secure his valor with the husbands of my sisters on the battlefield, he played well his rounds of "Sweet Talk the Girl" and "Hero with a Halo" to the Red Cross kids—and "Please the Parents" to dour old Daddy. Scott-Bugler would call on her daily, worshipping and wooing Miss Taboo Zelda with his plans to find his fame. "The emotions of his youth culminated in one emotion—the most ecstatic, exhausting, and momentous emotion of his life." In *her*—his golden-girl ideal—Scott had perceived an effervescent sense of romantic self-importance, one kindred to his expansive own.

Militarily that autumn, Scott's battalion was assigned to Camp Mills on Long Island to be blown anywhere about the world. The promissory regiment of Daddy's Scout Key—tough as their own amber alloy American buttons—marched aboard their transport with steel helmets slung at their sides to be departed, staring out tight-eyed into the abysmal Atlantic. However, before our Second Lieu was deployed to save the trenches of France himself, the curtains of the Armistice fell heavy on his ambitions. He had lived, but he was punctuated. His book was shut. Target practice was called off, his regiment's flag was folded, and the very alive violence of his Great War was over—and made confetti kissing every street.

~MARCHING ORDERS

"You think I am a stone, a clam: / You think that I don't care a damn, / Across the waves I kiss you! / None can compare with Zelda Sayre, / Zelda, fair queen of Alabam'."

ZELDA

Fluttering back, Scott Knickerbocker had been batting his way in a big ballgame. Preceding me, Scott-Snot hadn't made the third string Tigers' pigskin team. Especially rudderless before his roaring days, he rode out of Princeton on a bicycle, failing out of his collegiate East Coast aristocracy—*strike one* for my dashing strong-chinned officer's starched collar—and more dreams than the clouds you could see from the Country Club where the provincial ritual was for local belles to allow themselves to be wooed by emboldened camp soldiers. Well, he held up his blunder of an olive-colored uniform and stared it over with his two salty little blue limes for confused eyes. Vested with bedtime ideals of the Old South and Civil War—then, no badges, no medals for her star-spangled Scotter after all that marching and call to colors, his heroic ascending career as a leader of men was revoked—dismissed to remain stateside—*strike two* for our handsome cheap-sharper.

Before settling in New York City—and then back to old Saint Paul—after his *manly* discharge, Scott proposed to his zealous, uninhibited Zelda. "She'll see," said Scott—that *old sport*—to himself. He was in love with a whirlwind and had to spin a big enough net out of his head to try to catch her. Yet, the never-sleepy city of the Empire State and Follies had not recognized his Midwestern form of wholesome gold as "manifest destiny," and he rather began losing confidence that his *love* would reverse his failures, his shabby suits, his poverty, his mediocrity. His proposal of matrimony was accepted, then was unaccepted—with smiling common sense—at the plummet of his ad-boy and copy-man act (scribbling streetcar jingle slogans) in the Big Apple—*strike three* of the great American ballgame for the rich girl's comfortable purse.

All that was left was Scott-the-Slugger staring at cigarette butts and popcorn papers in his empty stands. *Hampered* in the holiness of deflated aspirations, it was Prohibition that functionally *opposed* him. He tried to get married and then he tried to drink himself to death—foiled by both the great State *and* the greater gender. The little tragedy was the sensible thing. Yet, the dreamer's rubber heart—tougher than boot leather—was somewhat resilient. I must allow that he—the Big Out—must've wanted more than the soul's water for what it is that a man wants in a woman—her drinking, smoking, and dangerous distraction. Furthermore, it must've been that he correctly fathomed her flamboyant self-worth.

Although he spent his first thirty *smackers* from his first story on a magenta feather-fan he had sent to sway me, I knew some fun to hold out for my O. Henry to bring me some *Chanel No. 5* hidden in a bouquet of ragged-robin. Well, our Romantic "egoist" sold his cheap stories to his cheap magazines, but didn't keep it his failed habit—in the deep throes of his *jellybeaning*, gifted with an imagination needing an aesthetic ideal. His formula was that an egoist must become a "personality"—a maimed amateur searchingly desirous of beauty beyond him in waking dreams of imaginary heroism.

"Again," he said to the keys of his secondhand, receptionist typewriter, grappling with his wrestling angel—a Mr. Bounds weaving patchwork—to bounce that engagement ring back to her proper for her proper reconsideration of his renown. Well, he had emerged and he mailed me a wonder of a bracelet that must've cost more than a counter of perfumes. Scott-Complishment was my social success on paper and *in* the papers, her Who's Who battle boy who could fire a decent rifle and write a decent book to announce the year *our* jazz rage was born to the world.

Zelda chewed gum and showed her knees and stole cigarettes. She was "surprisingly emancipated, daredevil, and iconoclastic for a woman born in the Cradle of the Confederacy—with war still in vivid memory." Though, her Montgomery had been rather a muddling through the messes of corsets, and impropriety, and chastity, and spitballs—and not waiting for some Prince Charming. She had moxie and honey-gold hair—and she was elusive and she could hop out of windows to do whatever she wanted. She knew that the melting sun was *only*— and no more than—the melting sun and she knew that only some sort of unsafe foolishness was the only poetry of living. "Come and kiss me sweet and twenty. Come and kiss me sweet and twenty." Zelda allowed Scott to marry her with his suitable drinking and suitable authoring income—the coroneted Fitzgeralds stepping out celebrities together from the bright Manhattan sun with all the iridescence of the beginning of the world—Scotchy having become all things to win the darling of all the South, the brightest rays of his paradisical Big City days.

~SCOTT-KHAN

"'Mamma, I don't see why Dixie had to go all the way to New York to marry a man from so near home.'

'He's a very nice man.'

'But I wouldn't have married him if I was Dixie. I would have married a New Yorker.'

'Why?'

'Oh, I don't know.'

'More conquering—'

'—Yes'm, that's it.'"

ZELDA

On a magic Scott-carpet from Dixie Land straight to Saint Patrick's Cathedral—for a thousand-and-one nights of fun—everything impossibly happened all at once: the money, the glamor, the honey, and the hijinks. She had seen the unholy ghost of Irony descend upon him, anointing his healthy, *flawed* state that made him more cheerful, pleasant, attractive, and somewhat more significant than anyone else. Yet, more wondrously, she was Beauty—born anew every hundred years—disguised as a jazz-baby ragtime vamp to be paid in love—completely classical, glowing, and the most living person he had ever seen.

They were in their second childhood, adventurous, going to life—getting lost in their minor gifts under their sardonic constellations. From the start, they were alien to most—the boy with the talent they all wanted and the charmingly odd bobbed-hair girl who always said something surprising. The young Fitzgeralds knew they either had to feed them, feed on them, or shock them.

Keeping her shining and smiling two years more, Scott-a-trot's second classic joined his titan rivals in the greatest year of the greatest English. He was twenty-three and told the press that his greatest ambitions were "to write the best novel that ever was and to stay in love with his wife forever." He bound a lock of her hair with a blue ribbon and pressed it inside the cover. In this gift of *Zelda the Beautiful, Zelda the Damned*, he had inscribed to her, "my dearest sweetest, without whose love and aid neither this book or any other would ever have been possible. From me, who loves her more every day, with a heart full of worship for her lovely self."

~THE BEAUTY OF THE BEAST

"The book ends on a tragic note—in fact, a note which will fill any woman with horror, or, for that matter, will fill any furrier with horror. For Gloria, with thirty million to spend, buys a sable coat *instead of* reddish Asian mink. This is a tragedy unequalled in the entire work of Hardy. Thus, the book closes on a note of tremendous depression, and Mr. Fitzgerald's subtle manner of having Gloria's deterioration turn on her taste in coats has scarcely been equaled by Henry James."

ZELDA

On Long Island, he had hung his trench helmet talisman on the wall and dreamed pages of soldiering in the dark. America's favorite retired lieutenant deployed his miniature soldiers for battle on the dining-room table so he could solve America's favorite problems. *His story*, to Scott, "history" was just animations of colors and relics and personalities—of how the rich stay rich. Two more years of youth depleted, and they would move their American English to the continental Riviera shores—to their eternal Carnival by the Sea. For *Ascot*, there was nothing left for the tough and tumble United States of Toddlers to discover—that for eager scribblers, "imagination" was the last American frontier.

He whined and wrote whatever he wanted and caught it wherever he went. Though—finally—he'd become the man with a jingle in his pocket and had gotten his girl, he'd halted his traumatic trusts in money and in the confection of love. Their last American tango—that ruthless reception of their stage play, that stillbirth—was surely one of Zelda's nine female lives of her burning bones. Although *they* would have to make new friends in new hotels to despise them more slow, she did procure Scott his little gold *Triangle* charm for his watch-chain to mark the times of their new mess. *Fie! Fie! Fi-Fi!*

~BIOGRAPHER'S MEMO

"A New Fuss on Old Us"—*by:* Zelda the Damned—

would be an attractive title for your honestly attractive addendum. Or, you might like "What Light Was" for this potboiler sketch.

(65.) *dependence*

~FRANKEN-SCOTCH

"Enthusiasm runs high in the nature of Fitzgerald. He's even enthusiastic in his dislikes and certainly he's whole-hearted over the things he enjoys. To be with him for an hour is to have the blood in one's veins thawed and made fluent. His bright humor is as infectious as smallpox—and as devastating to gloom." "This is the sort of book that will infuriate those who take anything seriously, even themselves. This is a book that mocks at mockery. This is the highest point so far attained by Anglo-Saxon sophistication. It is written by a man who has responded, I imagine, much more to the lyric-loves of lovers long-dust than to the contemporary seductions of contemporary British flappers."

SCOTT

Her audacious armor was her lawless wit. Heedlessly, she fancied—fresh and free—that her saucy charm and brassy sass would persist as her tameless, unlimited zest and daily-born boldness. Her . . . she—

ZELDA

—*he* wanted to join the turnkey banner of waving his redefining generation's defining moment as lapsed, wandering expatriates with the mementos of watching their world turn into tunnels of corpses and cracked tea cups.

SCOTT

Amused—*okay?*—and bemused. Are we inseparable?

~NECESSITY

Well, *doll*, you know that most people don't care about how their body moves, but, then, you know also that you want most people to care about how your own Dixie body moves. You depend on it.

SCOTT

How endless is our endless faith in all this? Isn't on what we depended already . . . behind us . . . unguarded?

We know it—the disintegrations. Inseparable until we're separate . . . all we are—all our aliveness—just procession toward, then recession from—the only eternal expression . . . Revolving, we're a revolving *slogan*, we're "*I* . . . *love* . . . *you*." I love you. I love you.

~WHITE POPPIES

"When will we be three of us again? Do you remember our first meal in the Biltmore when you said 'And, now, there'll never be just two of us again—from now on, we'll be three'? And it was sort of sad somehow and then it was the saddest thing in the world, but we were safer and closer than ever. 'O my love, O my darling.' That's what we said on the softness of that expansive Alabama night a long, long time ago. And, so, years later, I painted you a picture of some faithful poppies, and the picture said 'no matter what happens, I have always loved you so.' This is the way we feel about *us*. Other emotions may be superimposed, even the accidental may contribute another quality to our emotions, but this is our love—and nothing can change it. 'For that is true.' And I love you still—happily, happily, forever afterwards—the best one can."

(66.) *arrow irretrievable*

~SIEGE

"I think the novel is a wonder. It has vitality to an extraordinary degree, and *glamor*, and a great deal of underlying thought of unusual quality. It has a kind of mystic atmosphere. It is a marvelous fusion into a unity of presentation of the extraordinary incongruities of life today. And as for sheer writing, it's astonishing. The amount of meaning you get into a sentence, the dimensions and intensity of the impression you make a paragraph carry, are most extraordinary.

In no other way could you have been enabled so strongly to feel at times the strangeness of human circumstance in a vast, heedless universe. Among a set of characters marvelously palpable and vital—I would know Tom Buchanan if I met him on the street and would avoid him. And all these things, the whole pathetic episode, you have given a place in time and space, and by an occasional glance at the sky, or the sea, or the city, you have imparted a sort of sense of eternity."

"The long siege of the novel winded me a little, and I've been slow on starting the stories on which I must live. If it's as good as you say when I finish the proof, it'll be perfect."

— *to* and *from* Scott in Rome

ZELDA

We'll drink our letters into the late-late-late before we kiss 'em back into this little *ark* of our covenant. Then, with a *daisy* of a pair of hangovers, the curtains will open, and the fresh hardcover copies will fly every-good-where from that warehouse. While we're sunning ourselves silly here in Capri, "it's a man's book" will hit the stalls and boom—and with the women critics too. So, pucker up your earlobes, Hubby.

"In several sweeping syllogisms, life was a damned muddle—a football game with everyone off-side and the referee gotten rid of—everyone claiming whose side the referee would have been on. Progress was people shouting that they had found it—the invisible principle—writing a book, starting a war, founding a school." Of course, *life* had found me. I was the last belle and the first flapper.

~EPHEMERAL

"And she still lives, too—in all the restless souls who follow the season in its fashionable pilgrimage, who look for the lost spell of brown backs and summer beaches in musty cathedrals, who seek the necessity for solidity and accomplishment but never quite believe in it, in all of those who make the Ritz what it is and make ocean travel an informal affair of dinner clothes and diamond bracelets."

ZELDA

"I took a long drink from your flask. I didn't like it, but I liked the way it made me feel. I think most people are that way. Oxford and Cambridge men—I told you—they're the boys of Sewanee and the University of Georgia. There's no regret in not being born an Englishman. Style is hard to find anywhere, and most boys in most places aren't really worth dressing up for or doing sensational things for.

You know I'm old in some ways—in others—well, I'm just a little girl. I like sunshine and pretty things and cheerfulness—and I dread responsibility. I don't want to think about pots and kitchens and brooms. I want to worry whether my legs will get slick and brown when I swim in the summer—from summerland to summerland."

"A summer of love—so many people have tried that proverbial name. Summer is only the unfulfilled promise of spring. It's a season of life without growth. It has no day."

"The first layer of quiet falls, and the shades lengthen under the awnings and heavy-foliaged trees. In this heat, nothing matters. All life is *weather*—and in the wisdom of the South—a waiting through *the hot* where events have no significance for *the cool*—the cool this is, soft and caressing like a woman's hand on a man's tired forehead."

~PERHAPS

"Zelda wrote me a splendid letter from Rome. Your cable changing the title has come and has been followed. So, we shall go ahead full speed."

"After having Zelda draw pictures until her fingers ache, I know Gatsby better than I know my own child. Although it may hurt the book's popularity that it's *a man's book*, I hope to Christ you get ten times it back on *Gatsby*—and I think perhaps you will. Please have no blurbs of any kind on the jacket. I don't believe in them *one bit* any more. If my book is a big success, or a great failure (financial—no other sort can be imagined, I hope) I *don't* want to publish stories in the fall. After weeks of uninterrupted work, the proof is finished. We're moving to Capri. We hate Rome. I'm behind financially, so, I'll do short stories for money for now—and there's the never dying lure of another play. There's no use telling you my plans because they're usually just about as unsuccessful as to work as a religious prognosticator's are as to the End of the World. Send copies to all the liberal papers."

— *to* and *from* Scott in Capri

ZELDA

I had escaped the doom of provincialism, but the pride of a brighter, finer antebellum day has gone missing from my modulations. The novel was ready. They would read it. He had written me an iconoclastic love letter for all our enemies to intercept. Was I ready for the *whole* world? Certainly, I just wanted to go to fabulous places where there was absolutely no conception of the ultimate convergence of everything.

~PEDANTRY

"The book comes out today and I am overcome with fears and forebodings. Supposing women don't like the book because it has no important woman in it, and critics don't like it because it deals with the rich and contains no peasants borrowed out of Hardy?"

ZELDA

When everyone's eyes are on you, how many *choices* are there? Who conquers who, what force? Right and wrong are not all wrong and right. Timidity, appearance, *milk for blood*—all forces—gamble, resolve, I . . . I am a force. I'm born to be an Alabamian storm.

The hundred little demons and the hundred fluttering angels—all the whispers—all expectation is *conquer*, or, be conquered. There never was a middle. All else is convenience, excusing *urgency*. When bidden, must I love in all its madness? His eyes tell me to drive the arrow, irretrievable—further through my chest—to recenter all else around this small fire spear implanted from my *Ithuriel* without my planning. There is no other peace—he tells me—no path to somewhere else. "Take arms against all other persuasion" hasn't been *his* Europa for me. As if all friends and influence are to be made *his* arrow, *his* fire, the stars, all fate. And yet . . .

(67.) *zeal*

SCOTT

Recenter. Be the mark. Compete—*loverman*—to be a romance. Then, you cannot be stopped. Then, F. Scott, you will *know* in your own Keatzian heart and in your own Shelleyan noddle: If doubt can be defeated, can doom be undone?

~GRAND EXCEPTION

"To know an author, personally, is too often but to destroy the illusion created by his works. If you withdraw the veil of your idol's sanctuary and see him in his night cap, you discover a querulous old crone, a sour pedant, a supercilious coxcomb, a servile tuft-hunter, a saucy snob, or, at best, an ordinary mortal. Instead of the high-minded seeker after truth and abstract knowledge with a nature too refined to bear the vulgarities of life, as we had *imagined*, we find him full of egotism and vanity, and eternally fretting and fuming about trifles. As a general rule, therefore, it is wise to avoid writers whose works amuse or delight you—for when you see them, they will delight you no more. Shelley was a grand exception to this rule."

SCOTT

The lengthier works of the Romantics were the chief wonders amongst their age of visions. From Keats's constructive strolls with Shelley, they compete for six months to write a poem of *at least* four-thousand lines of verse. Shelley's entry is *Laon and Cythna*. In his fourth autumn with his Mary, Percy completes this epic—his longest, most optimistic, and most controversial work of his life. In the faces of his poor neighbors, Shelley solidifies his social surety that no golden age has arrived on any acre in Europe from either the reign *of* or the overthrow *of* Napoleon.

Among his woods at Marlow—Shelley's own green cloisters—he first imagines the expectant, patient prospects of the religion of nature eventually improving human nature. Conversely, anchoring his little boat amid the dimmer islets of the Thames, Percy pivots with his vision of the fallen tyrant—as if the *beau ideal* of European revolution has succeeded, as if the frustrated hopes of the early Romantics have been realized. His juggernaut *Laon and Cythna* is his tragic poetical myth illuminating the grim struggle against primordial oppression. Unjust and ruthless governance is recast and opposed in his polemic for revolt. Shelley illustrates with terrifying treachery his *idiom* that a fallen tyrant is still a tyrant. Versifying key observations from the fervor of braving revolution—in stanzas of calamity, hope, crime, and chaos—Shelley advocates that revolt can beneficially force opportunities for bearing the strained fruits of forgiveness, charity, and equivalence in its audacious survivors.

On the working axiom that "art inspires action," the passionate and optimistic verses of his Cythna are the center of his epic. Shelley conveys to Godwin he has "written it with all of his heart, leaving something of himself in it." In *Laon and Cythna*, Godwin himself is veiled as an encouraging sage, the hermitical mentor who inspires its early heroic thesis. Percy mirrors Godwin's disapproval of an "excess of a virtuous feeling" that results in mob government and also radiates his counterview of the "the errors and perverseness of a few" perpetuated by "the infantine and uninstructed confidence of the many" who confuse "superior rank with superior wisdom." Written in tandem with this epic work, Shelley, as "The Hermit of Marlow," also publishes "On the Death of British Liberty" and other sobering political tracts.

~FANTASIST

"Shelley felt a devout reverence for what he believed to be the truth—a moral Quixote. He was perhaps the last notable writer to affirm the Romantic fantasy, descended from the Renaissance, of personal ambition and heroism—of life committed to or thrown away for, some ideal of self."

SCOTT

However, as his Laon and Cythna lead their insurgence and come to *reject* further axial violence as progressive, Shelley unveils his bloodless, post-Godwinian argument for freedom—that liberty is the growth of partnerships between independent equals. Wollstonecraft is the estimable model for

Shelley's "shero," Cythna, advocating rights to "woman, outraged and polluted long." His Cythna is "the first new woman" in poetry, representing how Wollstonecraft envisioned *woman* to roundly emerge. In *Laon and Cythna*, Shelley establishes the true voice of his calling, giving his best in his verses on the bridal of his heroine—"tides of maddening passion roll, / and streams of rapture drown my soul"—and in the intellectual beauty of her education, supplanting his own strains of prejudice and unreason that he had written into *Queen Mab*. In rapt poetic trance, Percy's "fervid utterances overawe fervid souls—enthralled in freedom's fearless shout."

His revelatory narrative institutes his belief that the creative and passionate force of love is the missing link in the Necessarian chain, the chasm between reason and sensibility—as represented in his dual statues to his library of the God of Poetry and of the Goddess of Sex. Just as Percy and Mary had first sought to escape from tyranny and now stand to face it in their love of each other, Shelley depicts the dramatic situation of his valorous lead heroes of his epic.

As his evolving dialectic to mediate Mutability with Necessity, Shelley is influenced by the idealized union of Godwin and Wollstonecraft—his philosophers as lovers, merging their powers of passion with their powers of mind. Through the shared vessel of this courageous mode of equality-in-love, Shelley offers his own revolutionary means for reforming the world—of the imagination.

~MERIT FROM MARY

"Shelley promulgated that which he considered an irrefragable truth. He spoke of love as the law of life, which inasmuch as we rebel against, we err and injure ourselves and others. In his eyes, it was the essence of our being, and all woe and pain arose from the war made against *it* by selfishness, or insensibility, or mistake. In his *Laon and Cythna*, he created for this youth a woman such as he delighted to imagine—full of enthusiasm for the same objects. And they both, with will unvanquished, and the deepest sense of the justice of their cause, met adversity and death."

SCOTT

In the preface to his brave experiment, Shelley observes that "nothing indeed can be more mischievous than the bigoted contempt and rage of the multitude. Hopelessness lulls the oppressors of mankind into a security of everlasting triumph. Our works of fiction and poetry have been overshadowed by the same infectious gloom. But mankind appears to me to be emerging from their trance. In that belief, I have composed." "And like sunrise from the sea, / 'Let there be light!' said Liberty." Professing an anarchist creed, Percy's aim is to demonstrate a society being governed by Necessity through an extensive struggle between "the transient nature of ignorance and error, and the eternity of genius and virtue."

~SHOCKED DEARLY

"'*Shelley* that bright-eyed youth—so gentle, so thoughtful—for *us*? Oh, why did you not name him?'

'Because he thought you would have been shocked.'

'Shocked! Why, I would have knelt to him in penitence for having wronged him even in my thoughts. If he is not pure and good—then there is no truth and goodness in this world. His looks reminded me of my own blessed baby—so innocent—so full of love and sweetness.'

'So is the serpent that tempted Eve described,' I said.

'Oh, you wicked scoffer!' she continued, 'but I know that you love him. I shall have no peace of mind until you bring him here. You remember, sister, I said his young face had lines of care and sorrow on it—when he was showing us the road on the map, and the sun shone on it—poor boy! Oh, tell us about his wife—is she *worthy* of him? She must love him dearly—and so must all who know him.'"

SCOTT

From her months at Marlow, Mary is readying her shifts from fears of "sick destructiveness" and cares of "tyrant quelling" for the laboring poor. Shortly before Mary's lovely, critical novel about her Percy-the-Romantic is printed, Shelley publishes his overt and sincere verses about his splendidly beloved wife, dedicating this heroic, visionary epic to her through an appended poem. Percy opens his memorial, "So now my summer-task is ended, Mary, / And I return to thee, mine own heart's home, / As to his Queen some victor Knight of Faery," alluding to his own first *nom de plume*, Mary's other intimate name for her Shelley—"Victor." Within this preface poem, Mary and Percy Shelley have now both united within the literary fame of her parents—of her "beloved name"—continuing his *daisy* of a "once-again-to" his dreamy Mary.

(1)

"Over the world in which I moved alone

Yet never found I one not false to me,

Hard hearts, and cold, like weights of icy stone

Which crushed and withered mine, that could not be

Aught but a lifeless clog, until revived by thee.

(2)

Thou Friend, whose presence on my wintry heart

Fell, like bright Spring upon some herbless plain;

How beautiful and calm and free thou wert

In thy young wisdom, when the mortal chain

Of Custom thou didst burst and rend in twain.

When Infamy dares mock the innocent,

And cherished friends turn with the multitude

To trample: this was ours, and we unshaken stood!

(3)

Now has descended a serener hour,

And from thy side two gentle babes are born
To fill our home with smiles, and thus are we
Most fortunate beneath life's beaming morn;
And these delights, and thou, have been to me
The parents of the Song I consecrate to thee.
    (4)
And what are thou? I know, but dare not speak:
And in thy sweetest smiles, and in thy tears,
And in thy gentle speech, a prophecy
Is whispered, to subdue my fondest fears:
And through thine eyes, even in thy soul I see
A lamp of vestal fire burning internally.
They say that thou wert lovely from thy birth,
Of glorious parents, still their fame
Shines on thee, through the tempests dark and wild
Which shake these latter days; and thou canst claim
The shelter, from thy Sire, of an immortal name.
    (5)
One voice came forth from many a mighty spirit,
Which was the echo of three thousand years;
And the tumultuous world stood mute to hear it.
Truth's deathless voice pauses among mankind!
If men must rise and stamp with fury blind

On his pure name who loves them—thou and I,
Sweet Friend! can look from our tranquility
Like lamps into the world's tempestuous night—
Two tranquil stars, while clouds are passing by
Which wrap them from foundering seamans' sight,
That burn from year to year in unextinguished light."

SCOTT

After the poetry of Shelley and Keats are first endorsed, their culture vultures gather, circling, awaiting their next works in print. Once their competition epics are published, they are decimated by the partisan critics of the elitists, lampooning their literary promoter as the "King of the Cockneys." Keats and Shelley regroup, seeking literary shelter in their small, trusted circles of authors and intellectual confidants.

As they each discuss leaving England, Percy, Keats, and their scholarly sponsor compile the entries of their last poetical contest—each writing a clever sonnet on "the Nile." Feeling he will be met with animosity wherever he lives, Shelley inscribes, "And well thou knowest / That soul-sustaining airs and blasts of evil / And fruits and poisons spring where'er thou flowest. / Beware, O Man—for knowledge must to thee, / Like the great flood to Egypt, ever be."

As juxtaposed to possibly following the elder generation of Shelleys to America, Mary and Percy gravitate to their eager Grand Tour of traveling the states of the alluring Italianate Peninsula. Throughout their last season in England, the Shelleys play chess daily, enjoy museums, and have a box at the opera for both *Don Giovanni* and *Figaro*. In London, Shelley is described as a patrician-looking young cosmopolite, and Mary as "bending in a similar direction with her white shoulders unconscious of her crimson gown."

~LARKLET

"His tired eyes traveled to the door. His little granddaughter waited, frightened, in the hall.

'I want to see the baby.' A sweet, tolerant smile lit his face. His granddaughter approached timidly.

'Hello, there, baby. You're a little bird,' he smiled. 'And you're as pretty as two little birds.'"

SCOTT

Above all, in their fourth valiant spring, Percy and Mary are resolved, harmoniously, for their permanent departure to Italy. Although Godwin pays his final visit after the christenings of his little treasured ones, princely William and precious Clara, Percy has still *not* provided what he had first promised Godwin from more than five years ago—his old *"alakazam"* with no sea change for his debts. Stiffed by his "blood horse" of the English Baronetage, Godwin acknowledges he has "tried" Percy's "temper too far." Crossing the Channel, the Shelley family is vigorous, cheerful, and fully hopeful, embarking on their ambitious roving lifestyle and inevitable homes in Naples, Rome, Florence, and Venice—the "locus of the decadent" magnetism of Italy. Before departing, Shelley does not visit Ianthe or his first son, rationalizing their rift for Wilmouse and Clara in the posterity of his verse.

~FEARLESS FREE

"With fairest smiles of wonder thrown / Thou with joy shalt fill thine dearest playmate own. / The winds are loose, we must not stay, / Or the slaves of the law may rend thee away. / They have taken thy brother and sister dear, / They have withered the smile and dried the tear. / They have bound them slaves in youthly prime, / And they will curse my name and thee / Because we fearless are and free. / And their swords and their scepters I floating see, / Like wrecks on the surge of eternity. / We soon shall dwell by the azure sea / Of serene and golden Italy."

SCOTT

While en route to Italy through France, Mary writes from Lyons. "We see Jura and Mont Blanc again from the windows of our hotel, and the Rhone rushes by our window. The sun shines bright and it is a kind of paradise which we have arrived at through the valley of Death's shadows. We exiles and the children bear the journey exceedingly well and thus far we are fortunate and in good spirits."

Tap. Tap. Click. Mary had concluded her allegory in cautioning the presumption of her promising explorer and his hardy seadogs who had formerly been emboldened to find that place on our planet of eternal light at the passage of the Arctic. Rather than paradise—echoing Coleridge's *friendless* "water, water everywhere"—Mary's mariner discovers the starving Arctic desperations of her ambitious Victor, wisely discerning his own arrogant perversions of altruism in these isolating graveyards of ice.

Embarking as a hopeful benefactor of humanity, her mariner ordered his vessel's failed return once Mary unmasked an eternal darkness beckoning them— their summons of the green northern lights that unfold, writhe, and fade, unfold, writhe, and fade. In their withdrawal, Mary averted a full tragic playing out of this fiction as she delicately wrote her remand of fragile Romanticism and its fragile Shelley, needing to assuage the plague of abandonments and all the other losses suffered for the careless liberties of her good British dandy.

~AS IT IS

"His state of mind was despondent. Life had brought him so much suffering. His good intentions had been repaid by such evil results that he had taken a horror of every sort of action. He felt an intense but undefined desire to withdraw from the perilous throngs of men whose reactions cannot be predicted and who are swayed by such terrible gusts of passion. The regeneration of the real world now appeared to him so unrealizable that he no longer sought satisfaction therein for his loves and hatreds, but looked for it in the more docile and malleable world of the imagination. Shelley now saw the world as it is, the brown earth arduous to cultivate, the harsh faces of men, women full of nerves and hysteria—the cruel and obstructive society from which he longed to escape."

~HARRIETT-FOR-HIRE

"I saw a Fury whetting a death-dart."

SCOTT

Cheery Mary is lovingly unaware that by pressing onward in her zeal for Italy—spurring Shelley to the other side of Mont Blanc, over their mythical bereaving mountain—that she will unwittingly mimic her own Promethean reversal, that she will be ensnared in her awaiting Continental Sirens, circling, seemingly signaling to the catastrophic *feast* all the other witchy dark ladies of Hellenized prophetic irony—Furies, Fates, and harpies. We think we can bear no more, and yet . . .

~MEDUSA

"Of all the beauty and the terror *there*— / A woman's countenance, with serpent-locks, / Gazing in *death* on Heaven from those wet rocks."

(68.) <u>sophisms</u>

~AESTHETIC VIOLETS

"My revision will be made on an aesthetic basis. Legitimate stuff has cost me a pretty emotional penny to amass, and I intend to use it when I can get the tranquility of spirit necessary to write the story of myself versus myself."

PERCY

From the Oppressor of mankind, vomiting divine
Vilifying smoke into the bright air, Heaven's
Winged, sneering minion—pollinating the pollution
From the tyrannous, poisonous lips—dips
Its salivating vulturous beak in deific slander
To joyfully tear outward the persecuted heart
Of this again and again nonconformist
Into the exteriorized corrosive *shapelessness*
From the precipice of established despair . . .

Altogether in exile, henceforth, I'm to leave English society. Yet, already, I suffer daily the perpetual neglect, ostracism, or enmity as an outcast *object*— my name execrated by all who understand its entire import as the most imprudent and unaccountable of mankind. It seems to them that I've no more virtue to lose—and, so, they are determined to invent my misdemeanors for me. Yet, perhaps, I should have shrunk from persisting in this living solitude of heart—this task of opposing *myself* in these evil times and among these evil tongues to what I esteem misery and vice. Still, I am undeceived in the belief that I have powers deeply to interest—or substantially improve—my species.

~BRIGHT EYES

"My scavengers look towards me for their violence, / But I have no silent, oozing laceration watering my violets. / Yet, my vultures, foraging patient, who build your bowers / High in your parasitical Future's towers, / My withered hopes on hopes will be spread! / And my dying joys, choked by my unaided dead, / Will serve your scrounging, cold beaks for prey / And will satiate many a callous night—and many a cruel day!

PERCY

Contending amidst Time's mutable and serpentine antimyths, the lamp of love that furls night into day—*this* is the torch that penetrates, clasps, and fills the world, mirroring to each the fire of one's own thirsts. The knots of necessities that hold us to places make living *longer*, but not more. Rome breathes the voice of dead time. An intense and rapid frame of thirty years fully felt is easily the same as ninety temperate calendars. The time of the firefly and the time of the tortoise are enjoyed the same. Passion is the animating matter and measure of *time* amidst each life.

Italy! Yes! It is not mere health—but life—I should seek, and not for my sake alone, but of those to whom my life may be a source of happiness, utility, security, and honor—those to whom my death would be all that is the reverse. Yet, if I am to be safe from the hauntings of six years of agents, am I *ever* to find safety from the harassments *of self*?

~POP QUIZ

"And are you really, truly, now a Turk?"

PERCY

Like one in dread who speeds through the recesses of some haunted pile of mental flash-flood-drift and dares not look behind in the tumultuous rapids of his passage from his own sensation to his reflection, it is when I wake that my blood seems liquid fire. I clasp at the phantom of unfelt delights until my weakening imagination half possesses such a self-created, tormenting shadow. I wake and find again I am my own torturer. I confront my own primordial self—archetypes of my own ambivalences. I have failed in any loving of these aspects, and, in myself, they turn hostile. My melodrama is Othello chastising himself suicidal as his own adversary. I am become "the Split" . . . "the Strangler." In effect—not deed—I am "the Murderer," detesting impulses I cannot disobey and am borne away in my own waves within . . . but who is more innocent?

~LOVER DEMON LOVER

"'O hold your tongue of your weeping,' says he, / 'Of your weeping now let me be; / I will show you how the lilies grow / On the banks of Italy. / All so dreary with frost and snow, / O yon is the mountain of hell,' he cried; / 'Where you and I will go.'"

PERCY

To you first entering on life, to who *care* is new—to who anguish is unknown—how can you understand what I have felt and still feel? Natural selfhood is only overcome by imagination. Ah! It is well for the unfortunate to be resigned, but for the guilty, there is no peace. The agonies of remorse poison the luxury there is otherwise sometimes found in indulging the excess of grief. Yet, the guilty are allowed, by human laws—the blood that they are—to speak in their own defense before they are condemned. I commit my cause to the justice of my judges, yet I see no room for hope.

~QUELL: I DIE, I FAINT, I FAIL!

"Let the young and the brilliant aspire / To sing what I gaze on in vain; / For sorrow has torn from my lyre / The string which was worthy the strain, / And I am now ashes where once I was fire."

PERCY

The remains of the half-finished creature—who I had

destroyed, who she was before—my dearest cherished lay nearly *scattered* on the floor of this departure. However, I do refuse it, and no torture shall ever extort a consent from me. You may render me the most miserable of men, but you shall never make me base in my own eyes. I must be condemned, although I would pledge my salvation on my innocence. Such a complete remorse would extinguish every hope if I am adjudged the author unconscious of unalterable evils. So, I'm "the Double"—and am I to spend my brief existence in bent resolve to destroy the doppelganger creature of my ego? The heart does not die when it should, primitive and transcendental. It is difficult to remain just one person. I am my own albatross.

"Don't wait until all are dead"—they say to me—hugging me in their burial shrouds of infested plump worms. You charge me with the misuse of genius, that I've made a version of evil from good—eloquent yet disastrous—a living curse that contaminates. That I was again allowed, *I*, to breathe the fresh atmosphere—the cup of life was forever poisoned.

"With hands as pale as milk; / Lay them in gore, / Since you have shore / With shears his thread of silk. / Cut thread and thrum; / Quail, crush, conclude, and quell!" Still, I *warble*—like the dying swan—my enchanting tale of pleasing woe. Although the sun shone upon me as upon the happy and gay of heart, I saw around me nothing but a dense and frightful darkness, penetrated by no light but the glimmer of your two caring eyes that glare upon me.

It is even so—the fallen angel *becomes* a malignant devil. Yet, even so, I did not satisfy my own desires. Still, I desired and yet still desire love and fellowship—the way of the heart. Is there no injustice in this? All men hate the wretched. How, then, must I be hated, who am miserable beyond all living things! Much mentioned is vapors to me. On the whole earth there is no comfort which I am capable of receiving. I am, by a course of strange events, persecuted and tortured—as I am and have been—can death be any evil to me? Am I not also the one who saves the lost drowning girl and is then shot through by the rustic mob-hovel-mentals of the public creek of public opinion?

~VS. ME SELF

"The pavilion of Heaven is bare, / And the winds and sunbeams with their convex gleams / Build up the blue dome of air, / I silently laugh at my own cenotaph, / And out of the caverns of rain, / Like a child from the womb, like a ghost from the tomb, / I arise and unbuild it again."

PERCY

My Mary, am I to lead a harmless life, or am I "the Scourge" of our fellow-creatures? Am I also the author of your—*our*—ruin? I walk about the Isle like a restless specter, separated from all it can love, descending, descending miserable in the separation. I am hurried away by fury. Revenge alone endows me with strength and composure. It molds my feelings and allows me to be calculating and calm at periods when otherwise delirium or death would be my portion. Yes, a selfish pursuit has cramped and narrowed me, yet—stretching my gaze across the Channel—your gentleness and affection warm and open my senses.

I had before been moved by the sophisms I had created. The wickedness of my promise bursts upon me. I shudder to think that future ages might curse me as their pest, whose selfishness does not hesitate to buy its own peace at this price. "Who uniteth the hopes of what shall be / With the fears and the love for that which we see?" In your calm and serene joy, I ascend my horror and misfortune. Your affection for me overcomes again my dislike of this disturbed imagination. My love, you turn your thoughts toward the best method of eradicating the remains of my melancholy and you raise my mind from this dust in your rays of allaying kindness.

And now, with the world before me, whither should I bend my steps? Every country must be equally horrible. You want us to travel to seek happiness, but a *fatality* seems to pursue us. It is true—in the infected mouths of the mob—that we *shall* be as monsters—cut off from the world—but on that account, we *shall* be more attached to one another. "Of fellowship I speak such as I seek—fit to participate in proportion due." Prepare for me the reward of my tedious toil—this pilgrimage! I fear, my beloved girl, little happiness remains for us on Earth.

Yet, all that I may one day enjoy is centered in you. Chase away your idle fears. My pretty, pretty enigmatic Pecksie, to you alone do I consecrate my life and my endeavors for contentment. You have stolen kindness into my heart—an oblivion—and you've dared to whisper paradisiacal dreams of love and joy. Although the apple is already eaten, and the angel's arm ablaze to drive me from the presumption of any hope, yet, Mary, I would die to make you happy. Our union will not be barren of good. I shall need no other living ambition.

Titaness! Each cold-blood day, unknowing, I had been your mighty bird at *your* liver. Henceforth, I am thee—in thine principality! My Mary—my *Marina*—like an unseen star of birth avowed, your Ariel now guides you over the sea of life from your nativity burning unextinguished. Your guardian spirit, who, from life to life, must still pursue your happiness from enchanted cell to the throne of Naples, your Ariel lits you over the trackless sea—flitting on, your prow before, like a living meteor sends this silent converse *token*, like the silent moon, a delighted spirit's enlightening *glow* spoken.

~AT THE END

"They had, *someday*, to accept the tightening-up of

the world—to begin some place to draw-in their horizons. Alabama lay awake thinking at night: 'the inevitable' happened to people, and they found themselves prepared—as the child forgives its parents when it perceives 'the accident of birth.' 'We will have to begin all over again,' she said to Amory, 'with a new chain of associations, with new expectations to be paid from the sum of our experience—like clipping coupons.'

'Middle-aged moralizing!'

'Yes, but we're middle-aged, aren't we?'

'My God! I hadn't thought it! Do you suppose my works are?'

'They're just *as* good.'

'No, I've got to get to work, Alabama. *Work*. Why have we practically wasted the best years of our lives?'

'So that there will be no time left on our hands at the end.'

'You are an incurable sophist.'

'Everybody is—my Amory—only some people are in their private lives, and some people are in their philosophy.'"

(69.) *folie a deux*

~COMMUNION

"In Rome, it's when we visited the Temple of Vesta, the goddess of hearth and home—that's when I was sure something was very wrong."

ZELDA

While the moon rose and poured a great burden of glory over the garden—dim phantasmal shapes, expressing eternal beauty in curious elfin love moods—we turned into the trellised darkness of a vine-hung pagoda. We were just voices then—little lonesome voices. Tear-bright to cover our eerie green love for the dusk, wraith-like, we drift on out before the rain—blown with the stemless flowers—with our old hopes, dead leaves, and loves again.

I have completed my speculation upon my future happiness. I will not return gorgeous or accomplish beautiful or important things, and will not loll about in serene glory to be worshiped by the bourgeoisie of the land.

You will stop caring for me, and I will go on and on, dancing alone so that no matter what happens, I will still know in my heart that *we*—the emotional beggars of the earth—are a godless, dirty game, and that love is bitter and all there is.

~ORION'S KNIFE

"Your fable of today puts an end to all my hopes. *Humble!* For Heaven's sake, be proud, be arrogant! You are—but I cannot tell *what* you are. I cannot yet find the circumstance about you that allies you to the frailty of our nature. I will hunt it out."

— Godwin to Wollstonecraft

SCOTT

I was only happy a little while before I got too drunk. Afterward, there were all the usual penalties for drinking. The Romantics were my bromide—my own panacea—from going too far into myself. You were going crazy and calling it genius. I was going to ruin and calling it anything that came to hand. Everyone far enough away to see us outside of our glib presentation of ourselves guessed at my insane indulgence in drink and at your almost megalomaniacal selfishness. Each dive into myself became more strained with the attentions of futurities—of what could or would've been.

~THE GREAT

"His success was his own. He had earned his right to be critical. Alabama felt that she had nothing to give the world and no way to dispose of what she took away."

ZELDA

Linked with Bacchic diversions, we were no longer

important. When we shifted back to Paris, only one heat remained in my heart, and afterward, I hurt whoever tried to reside there. People and places became blurs. After the book, the flapper had become *passé*, and I gave myself to dancing, *my dancing*—that was all, flittering, skimming like cat's-steps in *Swan Lake*. Until our springtimes that should so derange our minds, we *fairies*—while Beauty summons us—who do run from the presence of the sun, follow darkness like a dream.

~ADIEU, ISADORA

"Later, after crossing back over the Atlantic for the last time, our ride to Switzerland was very sad. It seemed to me that we did not have each other or anything else. And it half killed me to give up all of the work that I'd done. I was completely insane and had made a decision—to abandon the ballet and live quietly with my husband. If I couldn't be great, it wasn't worth going on though I loved my work to the point of obsession. It was all I had in the world at the time."

ZELDA

Our ship returned us to our New England. Gliding up the river, the city burst thunderously upon us in the early dusk—the white glacier of lower New York swooping down like a strand of a bridge to rise into Uptown, a miracle of foamy light suspended by the stars. A band started to play on deck, but the majesty of the city made it trivial and tinkling. Whole sections of the city had grown rather poisonous. But invariably, I found a moment of utter peace in riding south through Central Park at dark. There again was what I'd lost, wrapped *cool* in its mystery and promise. Yet, the detachment never lasts long—as the toiler must live.

~MODERN WIZARDRY

Under the first good spell, she wanted life to be easy and full of pleasant reminiscences. Under the other spell, it could all go to hell—and, as well, anyone who tried to care.

ZELDA

With "the most determined little chin," I was voted "Most Attractive" girl in my sweet Alabama class. At the City Ball, I was beloved for my jester's take on "The Folly Dance," and at our Club, I was prized for performing "The Dance of the Hours"—and for my long, golden, golden hair. "But fortune," like Daddy would tell us, "as well as misfortune, comes with both hands full." Well, my brother had killed himself, and I lived in swirling, psychotic excesses—my *folie a deux*. The earlier some blossom, the earlier some bottom-out. Diamonds of earth's saltiness—you have them or you haven't, like health or brown eyes or honor or a baritone voice. The plate that fissures will only do to hold her crackers late at night or to go into the ice box under her leftovers.

Still, sometimes, there's a *blackness* in my brain. Sometimes, I feel better when I paint fairytales. And sometimes, I just want to walk and walk and walk—walk off and walk *on*—and the darkness lessens as I play "Is/Was" under my golden head of the fairest fairy hair. Approaching the borders of "The Ghost Town of First Going Dim," the light of the panicking artist must make its prisonbreak. The light must flee the covering *wiles* of the basket weavers selling their valedictions of lamps and candles.

Although, when a ripe mind starts its *rot* in the muddy fields it was planted, there is no rescue, not even from Daddy's dusty duo—not his *Meditations* from Marcus, and not his *Consolation* of Boethius. Nothing but *luck* protects you from catastrophe—not safety, not saving, not love, not faith, not good deeds, not sobriety, not standing up, and not sitting down—just Lady Luck. And hell, they won't get to outlawing gambling—so that we can find out while we're still dumb and young. Then, on our roulette wheel from Fortune's "faithless face," there'll gleam on the mind all the grime of her "prestige," the diseased grifter's con game of switching her paper cups with all the drunks—binding all the boozers into one mass to sing together "we are raised high, high, *high* to be brought low, low *low*.'"

(70.) *daydream rapture smoke*

~JUNK-HEAP MORALITY

"'The clean-book bill' will be one of the most immoral measures ever adopted. It will throw American art back into the junk-heap where it rested comfortably between the Civil War and the Great War. They'll attack the authors they detest because they can't understand their works. Also, those who are unintelligible to children and idiots will then be suppressed at once for debauching the morals of village clergymen."

SCOTT

The British literary establishment opposes *Laon and Cythna*. Concerning the reactionary propaganda against it, Coleridge writes that he hopes Shelley will sink "like lead to the bottom of the ocean." Though Shelley is bitten by the failed reception of his epic in the old-hollow-hat-hell of dampening England, *Laon and Cythna* is ploddingly admired elsewhere. Shelley replies with a brief verse to an acerbated critic, "I hate *thy want* of truth and love, / How should I then hate *thee*? / Of your antipathy, if I am the Narcissus, / You are free to pine into *a sound* with hating me."

"Love," Shelley writes, "is most pure, perfect, and unlimited where its votaries live in confidence, equality, and unreserve." "Thus," Shelley continues, "when the rich are no longer able to rule us by force, they will invent a new scheme and will rule by fraud." Following his daring heroines Mab and Cythna—as Wollstonecraft's crusader—Percy will craft his next female leader of his revolutionary epics from his exile in Italy.

Percy finds notoriety abroad in his celebrated *Laon and Cythna*. In their paradise of exiles, the auspicious Italian heat is restoring our Shelleys, and their budding lives are beginning to take on the daydream shape they had envisioned. Glorious Italy begins as their classical land of romantic, mystical beauty. The first moonrise over the Alps marries all their cherished memories from their first pair of departures, and they're enchanted by the first Italian town they encounter.

Percy writes, "no sooner had we arrived—than the loveliness of the earth and the serenity of the sky made the greatest difference in my sensations. I depend on these things for life; for in the smoke of cities, and the tumult of humankind, and the chilling fogs and rain of our own country, I can hardly be said to live." Fascinated with discovering wild violets, Shelley writes, "London—where there are no green caverns of foliage, no fireflies over cornfields, and no nightbird songs in the dark distance—all that London has in common with Italy is *moonlight*."

Their first Italian home is under a shady laurel arbor, where they enjoy walks through the woods, viewing the delightful foliage alongside the river and traversing ramblings paths cut into the mountains. On other evenings, Percy and Mary ride among the Apennines, "the kingdom of the sweet jonquils of the forest," lighted home—from above—by Venus and Diana. At night, the brightness of the moon dims the fresh pleasant fire of the lightning bugs making strange patterns in the Italian darkness. At their nearby Country Casino of Amusements, there are evening Italian dances, French quadrilles, and German waltzes.

~MUSIC LOVES COMPANY

"Whilst thus intent, Shelley stood before us with a most woeful expression. 'What's the matter, Percy?'

'Mary has threatened me.'

'Threatened you with what?' He looked mysterious and too agitated to reply. 'With what? To box your ears?'

'Oh, much worse than that. Mary says she will have a party. There are English singers here, and she will ask them—and everyone she or you know. Oh, the horror!'

We all burst into a laugh.

'It will kill me.'

'Music—kill you? Why? You have told me, you flatterer, that you loved music.'

'So, I do. It's the company who terrifies me. For pity, go to Mary and intercede for me. I will submit to any other species of torture than that of being bored to death by idle ladies and gentlemen.'"

SCOTT

Mary and Percy watch the operas in Turin and Milan—Bonaparte's late capital—and are entranced by the "infinitely magnificent" ballet of *Othello*. Shelley translates Plato's *Symposium*, and Mary transcribes it. "What a wonderful passage there is," Shelley writes, "in the *Phaedrus* from one of the speeches of Socrates praising poetic madness and how a man becomes a poet. As a preservative against the false and narrow systems of criticism, every new poet should impress himself with this proud and sublime expression: 'No one in the world merits the name of *Creator* except God and the Poet.'" Affectionately, Mary and Shelley read and translate works of the best Italian poets. Their hearts find rest in the verses they share from Dante, Ariosto, Tasso, and Petrarch—whose preserved home and tomb they visit—and are both fascinated and inspired by the epic *Orlando Furioso*.

~VERONICA'S PAINTED VEIL

"Dearest Mummy, I was the hostess while Daddy put on his cuff buttons for a lady and a gentleman. Thus, my life is working quite well. Mademoiselle and the chambermaid said they never saw a box of paints so pretty as the one you sent. I jumped of joy receiving my paintbox and made some pictures of people at the beach, of us playing croquet, and of a vase with flowers in it I drew from life. When we Sunday, I go to 'catechism' to learn of the horrible sufferings of Jesus Christ. — Your loving daughter."

SCOTT

During their first Italian summer, Mary initiates warm correspondence with a novelist who will become a baronet in two years, Sir Walter Scott— who published *Rob Roy* two days before *Frankenstein*. Before Byron, Sir Scott was the most famous poet of English Romanticism. Godwin had met Sir Walter Scott in Edinburgh during the season before Shelley and Mary had left for Switzerland. Sir Scott publishes a very favorable review of *Frankenstein*. Afterward, Mary instigates their relationship, writing to Sir Scott, disclosing to him that *she* is the author of *Frankenstein*. After his review, her famous critic then works to spread this interest in his influential literary circles.

~THE DREAM IS GONE, BUT THE BABY ISN'T

This tale is fit into fictions "managed by marvelous and supernatural machinery" that describe "the mode of feeling and conduct" likely to be adopted, having opened its "new trains and channels of thought," that show us "the powers and working of the human mind." A "good illustration" "is the well-known *Saint Leon* of William Godwin," "assuming the possibility of the transmutation of metals and of the *elixir vitae*," deduces "the probable consequences of the possession of such secrets." "*Frankenstein* is a novel upon the same plan." "It is said to be written by Mr. Percy Bysshe Shelley, who is son-in-law to Mr. Godwin—and it is inscribed to that ingenious author."

This "extraordinary tale" discloses "uncommon powers of poetic imagination" "without exhibiting that mixture of hyperbolical Germanisms with which tales of wonder are usually told." "His descriptions of landscape have in the choice requisites of truth, freshness, precision, and beauty." There are lines where "the author possesses the same facility in expressing himself in verse as in prose." "If Gray's definition of Paradise—to lie on a couch, namely, and read new novels—comes anything near truth, then, no small praise is due to him, who, like the author of *Frankenstein*, has enlarged the sphere of that fascinating enjoyment."

The strange stage is set. The ground sea is heard, and the glaciers shift. Having become "embayed among the ice at a very high latitude," the "young man" is "recalled to life" after found "extenuated by fatigue, wrapped in dejection and gloom of the darkest kind." He had "engaged in physiological researches of the most recondite and abstruse nature" "in order to trace the minute chain of causation which takes place in the change from life to death, and from death to life. In the midst of this darkness, a light broke in upon him."

Sir Scott describes Shelley's "Promethean art."

"Although supported by the hope of producing a new species that should bless him as his creator and source, he nearly sinks under the protracted labor and loathsome details of the work he had undertaken—and scarcely is his fatal enthusiasm sufficient to support his nerves or animate his resolution." He had "collected the instruments of life around him," but now that he had finished, "the beauty of the dream vanished."

"The demonical corpse" "became a thing such as even Dante could not have conceived," and "Frankenstein pays the penalty of his rash researches into the *arcana* of human nature." Compelled "to a conference and a parley," it is relayed how the monster "becomes ferocious and malignant—in consequence of finding all his approaches to human society repelled with injurious violence." Although he "imagines he sees the justice due to the miserable being," he hesitates on "the right he had to form" this being—or another—and he sees his promise as "criminal."

SCOTT

Composing much in their "first fine careless rapture," Percy and Mary's creative powers—in renewed vigor and sensibility—are fresh and strong. Once Shelley befriends an engineer and commissions for an entertaining kaleidoscope to be constructed at their home—applying his new, probing, technical aptitude—Shelley is inspired to detail mechanical designs for producing European steam engine yachts.

Exhilarated, Shelley writes, "Mary and I ride the tops of the mountains, winding through forests and over torrents where the verges of the green ravines afford scenery magnificently. We pass through low cultivated lands with their vine festoons and large bunches of grapes—just becoming purple—on low trellises of reed among olive copses and between high mountains crowned with the most majestic Gothic ruins that frown from the bare precipices."

Nevertheless, their nemesis—tyrant Jupiter—is rising. Its festering thunderstorms fade away their evening fireflies, and its sudden battering hail halts the ways home of their lost nocturnal birds. Slightly wistful, Shelley writes, "Light clouds hang upon the woods and mountains, and my thoughts forever cling to Windsor Forest and the copses of Marlow." Apprehensive, Shelley continues, "Wanting a certain silver and arial radiance, diversified clouds bring thunder in the middle of the day with hail about the size of pigeon eggs. Over these forest-covered rifts, the pale summer lightning spreads through the sky." *Scratch. Scratch. Scratch.*

(71.) *burial island*

~GREEN SKIN SHEDDING

"'Where is *the green* your friend, the Laker—meaning Coleridge—talks such fustian about?' 'Who ever saw a green sky?' asked Byron. Shelley was silent, knowing if he replied, Byron would give vent to his spleen. So, *I* said, 'The sky in England is oftener green than blue.' '*Black*, you mean,' rejoined Byron."

SCOTT

Eagerly invited, Shelley goes to Lord Byron's in Venice to rekindle their mutual pursuits in L. B.'s marble apartment—filled with books, animals, pistols, and the best of billiards tables. Shelley prepares to instruct Byron on his translations of *The Symposium, The Republic,* and *Faust.* The domes and turrets on Shelley's approach to Venice glitter in long lines over the blue waves as "one of the finest architectural delusions in the world." Though, worse to Shelley than witnessing the dungeons of ancient tyranny during his approach is the present occupation of Venice under the swaggering troops of the last Holy Roman Emperor, the father-in-law of brutal Napoleon.

Arriving to the water-city, Shelley writes, "The gondolas are things of a most romantic and picturesque appearance. I can only compare them to moths of which a coffin might have been the chrysalis." In Venice, Byron notifies Shelley of London. "As you are addicted to posey, go and read the versicles I was delivered of last night—that is, if you *can*. I am posed, but I am getting scurrilous. Here's the letter of the Britisher to read. You are blarneyed in it, ironically."

~SHE-LOW

Shiloh—the primordial capital before Jerusalem—was destroyed by the Philistines, defeating the ancient Israelites and stealing their *ark* filled with miraculous artifacts from freedom's founding Exodus. Byron nicknames Shelley "Shiloh," sounding similar to "Shelley" when pronounced in Hebrew. Lord Byron ironically applies his expositions of scriptural passages to Shelley being a *placenta*—that his "Shiloh" is "the birth of the era of the Leader of Peace." Byron grins and quotes to Shelley that "The scepter shall not part until *Shiloh* comes, and unto him shall the gathering of the people be"—and tranquility.

SCOTT

L. B. invites Shelley to ride his elite horses across the desolate, empty beaches of the Lido—a long, sandy, barrier island as Venice's first defense from pirates and storms. Loving wild and solitary places, Shelley writes, "Nothing grows here but sea-wrack and thistle." "Upon the bank of land which breaks the flow / Of Adria towards Venice: a bare strand / Of hillocks, heaped from ever-shifting sand, / Matted with thistles and amphibious weeds, / such as from earth's embrace the salt ooze breeds."

As Shelley confides that others feign to appear *mild* when they are angry with him, Bryon quips, "Yes, they want to grasp a small knife and quietly murder the sweet and smiling child *trying* to play 'Jesus Christ.'" Regardless, as they contend in firing Byron's pistols, Percy warns Byron, his *Albe*, of becoming like Napoleon—of brazenly biting off more than he can chew—that *Albe* is not far from *Elba*. Living a lavish scandal in Venice, L. B. is now as famous as Napoleon himself. Remarkably, Byron does heed his Shiloh's sincere, cautionary intervention. Shelley and Byron agree that their productive dialogues along the Lido are more meaningful and superior to those from two years ago in Geneva. On the secluded Lido, they discuss their poetic ambitions and philosophize on the nature of man. Byron has man at the mercy of his passions, and Shelley contends that "the good" in man may be made better. In their Socratic debates, Shelley, as a progressive evolutionist, remands Byron as a pessimistic behaviorist.

~THE PURPLE BELL

"'Men are filled with hatred of one another—and to expect or hope for anything else is the mark of the visionary.' 'Why?' asked Shelley. 'You appear to believe that man is the victim of his instincts without being able to direct them. My faith is quite different. I think that our will creates our virtue. Though wickedness may be natural, that does not prove it to be invincible.' Then, Byron points near the patrician city—juxtaposed with the setting sun suffused with gold and somber purple. '*That,*' Byron said, 'is the madhouse. Every evening, when I cross the water at this hour, I hear the bell clanging the maniacs to vespers. Always the same Shelley!' laughed Byron. 'Infidel and blasphemer! *You* who can't swim, beware of providence! But you spoke just now of vanquishing our instincts. Does it not seem to you that this spectacle is rather an image of our life? Conscience is the bell that calls us to virtue. We obey it like the madmen without knowing why. Then, the sun sets, the bell stops, and it is the night of death.'"

SCOTT

From their memorable horse-backing throughout the beaches of the Lido, Percy writes his conversational poem of his contending, dialectical views with Byron—weaving his device of the inexplicable *plight* of a maniac. "He is heartedly and deeply discontented with himself, contemplating in the distorted mirror of his own thoughts the nature and destiny of man. What can he behold but objects of contempt and despair?" Percy's passionate maniac rants and hisses, imitating an Adriatic storm. Through the lyrics of his *maniac,* Shelley copes with his intense disappointments concerning Harriett, expunging the mixed complexities of their marriage—and her gloomy suicide. Although Percy strains to reclaim the maniac in his poem "from the dark estate of the caverns of his mind," the cynicisms of "experience" overcome the enthusiasms of theorized progress in his poem, complementing creativity more to pain than to improvement. "Love changes what it loveth not. /

That your eyes never had lied love in my face! / That, like some maniac monk, I had torn out / The nerves of manhood by their bleeding root / With my own quivering fingers! So that never / Our hearts had for a moment mingled there / To disunite in horror!"

~RAMBLING GAMBLER

"'You sit here and discuss your sports and your young ladies and your—' He supplied an imaginary noun with another wave of his hand."

SCOTT

Alternatively, along this island strand of hillocks and thistles, Shelley also envisions Harriett having fallen victim to "British fiendishness," "whose trade is over ladies / To lean, and flirt, and stare, and simper / Till all that is divine in woman / Grows cruel, courteous, smooth, inhuman / —Crucified 'twixt a smile and whimper." Compounding these revealed devastations, Shelley also discloses to Byron that Fanny's suicide has damaged him more than Harriett's—but that both will remain the chastising "twin thorns in his sides." Shelley and Byron also share their wounded feelings for the causes of their exiles—of "Babylon" arising in London. Riding along the sands of the sea, they discuss Shelley's two children cruelly taken from him. Byron confides that had he been in England at the time of the vile Chancery affair, "His Lordship" would have moved Heaven and earth to have prevented such devastation—and would've gotten his "pound of flesh" of *the merchant*.

~THE TEMPTATION OF THE . . . COUSIN

"If Byron's reckless frankness and apparent cordiality warmed your feelings, his sensitiveness, irritability, and the perverseness of his temper cooled them. I believed in many things, and believe in some now. I could *not* sympathize with Byron—who believed in nothing. 'As for love, friendship, and your *enthusiasm*,' said Byron, 'they must run their course. If you are not hanged or drowned before you are forty, you will wonder at all the foolish things they have made you say and do—as I do now. *Ay*, the Snake has fascinated you. I am for making a man of the world—of *you*—whom he is for molding into a Frankenstein monster.'"

"Goethe's Mephistopheles calls the serpent that tempted Eve, 'My Aunt—the renowned Snake.' As Shelley translated and repeated passages of *Faust*, as he said, 'to impregnate Byron's brain' when he came to that passage—'My Aunt, the renowned Snake'—Byron said, 'Then you are her *nephew*.' Henceforth, he often called Shelley 'the Snake.' His bright eyes, slim figure, and noiseless movements strengthened—if it did not suggest—the comparison. Byron was the *real* snake. His wit or humor might force a grim smile—or hollow laugh—but they savored more of pain than playfulness and made you dissatisfied with yourself and *him*."

"Byron goads Shelley, 'The Fool would tell us to laugh *now*—before the impending clouds spill all their infections as well. But,' Byron prods Shelley, 'you are "the Snake" and you must suffer.'"

SCOTT

Percy plays "The Good Snake" and aches well into his next skin. Travelling, Shelley writes to his wife, "Well, my dearest Mary, are you very lonely? Tell me truth, my sweetest, do you ever cry? If you love me, you will keep up your spirits and, in all events, tell me truth. I shall be flattered by cheerfulness from you and such fruits of this absence as were produced when we were at Geneva. Wilmouse and little Clara, our blue-eyed darlings, must be kissed for me—with my name." After a ride on the Lido, Shelley writes Mary, "And your sweet voice, like a bird / Singing love to its lone mate / In the ivy bower disconsolate; / O Mary dear, that you were here; / The Castle echo whispers 'Here!'" Shelley compels Mary to join him in Venice. "Here, here, Mary, hear!" Longing for Percy, it is Mary's twenty-first birthday as she prepares Clara and Wilmouse for their hurried voyage to Venice.

In high spirits, Shelley writes, "I have been obliged to decide on all these things without you. I have done for the best. My own beloved Mary, you must soon come and scold me if I have done wrong—and kiss me if I have done right. For I am sure I do not know which, and it is only the event that will show." In such a quick, erratic bustle of moving her children, Clara develops a fever, and Mary is reminded of the doomed traversing—in extreme temperatures— that haunted the death of their first child. Though, optimistic, Mary tries to find similar excitement in Othello's enticing tales to woo Desdemona—hopeful for her reunion with Shelley in *their* adventurous Venice.

~OF COURSE

"The word 'sick' effaced itself against the poisonous air and jittered lamely about between the tips of the island and halted on the white road. 'Sick' turned and twisted about the narrow ribbon of the highway like a roasting pig on a spit and woke her, gouging at her eyeballs with the prongs of the letters 'S-I-C-K.'

'Yes—what's left,' she sobbed. She lay there, thinking that she had always meant to take what she wanted from life. Well—she hadn't wanted this.

'You must come here to save her. It is serious. We have no one to count on but you and Jesus.'

'So much promise, she would perhaps have been *something* . . . in time—'

'—And *Holy Angels*, so young!' murmured the Italian. Only—of course—there wasn't any time."

SCOTT

Mary is entering Venice. "The elements above are observed in a state of tremulous convulsions while the surface of the waters remain calm." Again, a bright summer will morph into a dim autumn. Mary writes, "It's pleasant to visit—its appearance is so new and strange—but the want of walks and variety must render it disagreeable." Traveling to Venice, sweet Clara relapses, and her fever returns. Clara Everina Shelley, little *Ca*, born into their great home in Great Marlow, had compassed the mighty Alps—and from her deep lucid eyes that close to bleak sleep, she had gazed with infant wonder on the gleam of lightning and on the grace of stone-wrought deities and saints.

~GHOST LIGHT

"Somehow, she got her girl well enough to board the train. She bought them a spirit lamp for the voyage.

'But what will we *do* with it, Madame?' asked Mademoiselle suspiciously.

'The British always have a spirit lamp,' explained Alabama, 'so when the baby gets croup, they can take care of it. We never have anything, so we get to know the inside of many hospitals. The babies all come out the same—only, later in life, some prefer spirit lamps and some prefer hospitals.'"

SCOTT

In the height of summer, Mary and her Clara are in a gondola crossing into the Grand Canal. Three weeks after Clara's first birthday, suffering heat and fatigue, Mary helplessly holds her close in the anguish of convulsive twitching from her fever. Hope is over. She dies silently. Cared for in carriages for half her life, Clara dies in a dirty hotel, waiting for a doctor who doesn't arrive. Mary writes, "In this dreadful state of weakness that succeeded her illness, she began to cut all of her teeth at once, pined a few weeks, and died in my arms."

In the morning, Shelley boards his melancholy gondola with her little corpse. Percy silently contemplates the odd providence of the bedlam in London that has vouchsafed the lives of his first two children from such pandemonium. With the lapping of the oar of the gondola during this last trip to the Lido—the lapping oar of the chrysalis of the *death's-head* moth, the lapping oar dipping into this Styx — Mary's moan echoes in Shelley's mind, "Will this ever be a world for a girl?" There—amongst his treasured archipelago of the Adriatic—Shelley buries Clara in the little cemetery beach for foreigners.

Beset in paranoias and reduced to despair, Mary feels as if she were being punished by a wicked, pursuing spirit, and Percy laments that the hellish elements themselves—first the cold and now the heat—have taken his two daughters delivered from Mary. Shelley laments, "Forget the dead, the past? Oh, yet / There are ghosts that may take revenge for it, / Memories that make the heart a tomb, / Regrets which glide through the spirit's gloom, / And with ghastly whispers tell / That joy, once lost, is pain."

Byron attempts to distract the subdued Shelleys after Clara's death with tours of the palaces, museums, and bridges of Venice. Godwin tries to witness the spirit of Prometheus, writing to Mary, "I sincerely sympathize with you and the affliction—the severe trial of your constancy and firmness. You should, however, recollect that it is only persons of a very *ordinary* sort—and of a pusillanimous disposition—that sink long under a calamity of *nature*."

Mary writes, "Our little girl, an infant in whose small features I fancied that I traced great resemblance to her father, showed symptoms of suffering from the heat of the climate. Teething increased her illness and danger. We had scarcely arrived at Venice before life fled from the little sufferer, and we returned to the villa to weep her loss." Here, at Este, their villa's garden stretches to the foot of a ruined castle—the Gothic home of owls, bats, and Echo. Behind this villa from Byron, the Euganean hills rise—where Shelley composes his memorial poem for Clara. "In the deep wide sea of Misery, / Shines obelisks of fire / Pointing within constant motion / From the altar of dark ocean / To the sapphire-tinted skies; / As the flames of sacrifice / From the marble shrines did rise / As to pierce the dome of gold / Where Apollo spoke of old."

Reluctantly, Shelley is accepting that his flowering cannot "grow young again." Even so, trying to hold both truths in his mind, Shelley's writing is vacillating his dual defenses for the hopeful and the hopeless. Needing to reunite his mind to a freedom from such anathemas, Shelley starts to compose his transcendental *Prometheus Unbound*. After discussing the legendary epic Byron is about to write—*Don*

Juan—they conspire for the evolution of their elite epics.

Alone, Shelley briefly visits Rome. "Behold me in the capital of the vanished world!" Astonished by the aqueducts, Shelley writes, "I have never seen a more impressive picture in which the shapes of nature are of the grandest order, but over which the creations of man—sublime from their antiquity and greatness—seem to predominate." In museums, paintings by Raphael and Guido are being restored from being pierced by French bayonets. "Paintings are evanescent. The material part of these works must perish and can only survive in the mind of man. Sophocles and Shakespeare can be reproduced forever because books are the only productions of man contemporaneous with the human race, transmitted from generation to generation. Men can become better and wiser. The unseen seeds can produce plants more excellent from which they fall."

Percy is thinking of Clara when he writes about a painting by Guido. "She is leaning over her child, and the maternal feelings, in which she is pervaded, shadow forth on her soft and gentle countenance and affectionate gestures. It is only as the spirit of love—almost insupportable from its intensity—is brooding over and weighs down the soul." "I am disturbed and distracted in the death of my little girl. There is no malady, bodily or mental, which does not either kill or is killed."

After mourning Clara's death, the Shelleys initiate their restless, unhappy travels—from which they never cease throughout Italy. From their Euganean Villa, they go to Naples, bitterly retracing how Clara's sickness might've been avoided, to have remained firm in making their home in Naples—rather than having amused the whimsical invite to Venice from Byron.

~O SOLE MIO

'Signorina will like Naples,' he said surprisingly. 'The city's voice is soft like *solitude's.*'

The cab clumped away through the red and green lights set about the brim of the bay like stones in the filigree of a Renaissance poison cup.

'Well, I've got to live here,' said Alabama, 'So that's all there is to it.'

SCOTT

In full view of the lovely bay, their Neapolitan home is opposite the Royal Gardens—with the foreshadowing Vesuvius of Pliny in the distance. Mary and Wilmouse play in the streets amongst paper lanterns, laughter, marketing, and the music of guitars. Mary feels some relief in the final city of their first Italian year, writing "Naples stands glittering like a gem—a piece of Heaven fallen upon earth." Mary is pregnant with their fourth child. Yet, for Percy—feeling estranged from all that he enjoys—Naples appears as a sad, gloomy, potent cloister. Writing two of his best poems, Percy's plan is to publish "all his saddest verses raked up into a heap." Courageous and melancholy, Percy writes his most affective work—his disparaging 'Stanzas Written in Dejection near Naples.' After Percy finishes his first act of the dialogue verses for *Prometheus Unbound*, the Shelleys explore the excavated ruins of Pompeii and mount the haunted, sepulchral terrains of Vesuvius, beckoning them toward immortal Rome.

(72.) _dark swan quills_

SCOTT

Mary and Percy climb Vesuvius on mountain mules, crossing vast streams of hardened lava as if it were once a sea of liquid fire changed by enchantment and horrible chaos. "Vesuvius is, after the glaciers, the most impressive exhibition of the energies and irresistible strengths of nature I've ever seen. There are fountains of white sulphureous smoke and several springs of lava which gush precipitously over high crags and roll down molten rocks in a cataract of quivering fire." In Pompeii, the Shelleys lunch on oranges, figs, and medlars under the portico of the Temple of Jupiter—from which Shelley longs for the Acropolis of Athens.

~DAZZLING

"'Don't you want to hear about the Greek temples—all bright reds and blues?' she insisted.

'Si, Signora.'

'Well—they are white now because the ages have worn away their original, dazzling—'"

SCOTT

In Roma, the Shelleys visit the Forum, the ruins of the Colosseum, the Pantheon by moonlight, the Pope pontificating at Saint Peter's, and fireworks that break colors across the dark skies. Mary spends her mornings with her Wilmouse, sketching palaces and the Colosseum. "It has been changed by time into the image of an amphitheater of rocky hills overgrown by wild olive, myrtle, and fig, threading little paths throughout a labyrinth of ruin." From the vestiges of temples, Shelley writes, "Rome is a city, as it were of the dead, or rather of those who cannot die and survive the puny generations and make sacred to eternity. Such is the human mind, peopling vacancy with its wishes."

~FUTURE PAST

"Go to Rome, but seek not to find even a dim shadow of the city of the consuls, nor even the silent burial place of her bygone heroes. Traces of the altered faith gather around. Gloomy records of martyrdom and interminable portraitures of saintly miracles stand side-by-side with the relics of Roman glory and Roman power. Each are interesting—and both may be good—but they accord ill. The manners of the Romans of our days—their worldliness and covetousness—disturb the solemn emotions we desire to indulge among these time-eaten ruins.

Shun daylight in Rome. Avoid the garish sun which displays the ill-assorted marriage of ancient with modern. Wander forth beneath the moon's illusory rays. Then, the undergrowth of the puny sons of the latter years fades in the shade of night till Rome grows out of Rome. In the mirror of her past, she becomes the sepulchre of antiquity—and as such, becomes lonely in this venerable conservatory of old Time's rarest treasures."

SCOTT

Iconic spring portraits are painted of Shelley posing thoughtfully with a swan quill and of Wilmouse holding out a peony. Wilmouse has childish glee in his happy descriptions of the paintings of livestock in the Vatican. His parents pride in his individual personality. Mary writes, "Our little Wil is delighted with the goats and the horses and the broken sculptures of men, and the ladies' white marble feet." Percy writes that his *Willman* "has become affectionate and sensible, that his spirits have an unusual vivacity, and that it is impossible to find a creature more gentle and intelligent—that he is an astonishment to all the Italians he meets." With his tender parents, he had seen the majesty of Lake Geneva and the wonders of their all else—together. Glowing with angelic life, Wilmouse—communicating now in more Italian than English—asks his parents about the ruins and the mountains, asking why people build things and then destroy them.

More to be borne, the golden augury of grief—the strange evening star of the dead—returns with the revolving year. As Wilmouse falls ill with convulsions similar to Clara's, Mary scrawls, "the misery of these hours is beyond calculation—the hopes of my life are bound up in him." Percy and Mary keep vigil for sixty sleepless hours, "sixty miserable death-like hours," trying to comfort him. Mary writes "Grim death approached—the boy met his caress / And while his glowing limbs with life's warmth shone, / Around those limbs his icy arms were thrown." During their summer in the Eternal City, William "Wilmouse" Shelley—child of their shared hearts—dies.

The shattering sorrows of Percy and Mary join the echoes of the surrounding wrecks and rubble of Rome. Shelley writes to his friend, "Your little favorite had improved greatly—both in mind and body—before that fatal fever seized him."

Named after Godwin himself, Godwin later pauses over the sentiment of little William—that "it was impossible to find another creature more gentle and intelligent." Godwin writes to them and tries to reason them out of their misery. One of their friends writes them, "We must all weep on these occasions, and it is better for the kindly fountains within us that we should."

In bitter, stinging tears—like ashes—Mary recalls her earlier letter written in happy expectation to her husband. "I wish Wilmouse to be my companion in my future walks. To further which plan, will you send down, if possible, by coach, a trapper hat for him? It must be a fashionable round shape and have a narrow gold ribbon. I am just now surrounded by babes. Wilmouse is scratching and crowing, amusing himself with wrapping a shawl round him, and Miss Clara is staring at the fire. Adieu, dearest love!"

In her own *dejection*, Mary now writes, "Since his death, 'the loadstar of our life,' *Rome* is no longer Rome. Exceeding grief now changes all the things hoped for and done within. I am sick of it. I am sick of seeing the world in dumb show. The place is full of English, rich, noble—important and foolish. I am so devoured by ill spirits that I hardly know what or where I am. If I would write anything else about myself, it would only be a list of hours spent in tears and grief. We've now lived five years together. If all the events of the five years were blotted out, I might be happy." Mary is a mother without children once again, and remaining in Rome is unbearable. "We suffered a severe affliction in Rome by the loss of our eldest child, who was of such beauty and promise as to cause him deservedly to be the idol of our hearts. We left the capital of the world, anxious for a time to escape a spot associated too intimately with his presence and loss." Clara and Wilmouse eradicated, Mary discontinues her journal of horrid misfortune after she writes, "to have won and thus cruelly to have lost." In lasting shock—thinking of her own mother, of Fanny, of Harriett, and her own fresh woes—Mary contemplates suicide. Percy suffers strange waking visions, and—for a spell—their lives become a sort of living death wish.

Shelley laments the loss of his son. "Will it rock thee not, infant? 'Tis beating with dread! / Alas! What is life, what is death, what are we, / That when the ship sinks we no longer may be? / What! To see thee no more, and to feel thee no more? / To be after life what we have been before? / Not to touch those sweet hands? Not to look on those eyes, / Those lips, and that hair—all the smiling disguise / Thou yet wearest, sweet Spirit, which I, day by day, / Have so long called my child, but which now fades away / Like a rainbow, and I the fallen shower?"

With desperate courage, Shelley composes, "We look on the ghosts with aspects strange and wild / Of the hopes whom thou and I beguiled / To death in life's dark river. / Their stream is unreturning. / We two yet stand, in a lonely land, / Like tombs to mark the memory / Of joys and griefs that fade and flee / In the light of life's dim morning."

Mary writes her confidant, "By our hap, how blind we mortals are when we go seeking after what we think our good. We went from England comparatively prosperous and happy. The climate has destroyed my two children. May you never know what it is to lose two only and lovely children in one year—to watch their dying moments and be left brokenhearted, miserable, and never know one more moment's ease from wretchedness. It is useless complaining. It is not kind to transmit misery. William was so good, so beautiful, and so entirely attached to me that in his last moment he appeared in so abounding spirits—his malady appeared so slight a nature. The blow was as sudden as it was terrible. But all this is all nothing to anyone but myself, and I wish I were incapable of feeling it—or any other sorrow. Time is a weight to me, and I see no end to this. I regret that I can feel these ways because they force me to regret Rome."

~OVER THE TRACKLESS SEA

"Shelley took Mary away to a pleasant villa in the country, but she was indifferent to everything. Always she saw little feet running over the sands at Naples, hearing delicious childish phrases expressing mingled love and glee. Motionless, gazing away in a sort of torpor, she only roused herself to talk of the tomb in Rome. She wanted for her beautiful boy a block of white marble and flowers."

SCOTT

Suffering these sorrows, Shelley writes his best prose in his letters from Italy, finding comfort near his son's grave in a little lawn "overgrown by windflower anemones, wall-flowers, and violets, whose stalks pierce the starry moss, and with radiant blue flowers—whose names I know not—scatter through the air the divinest odor."

They commission a tomb for Wilmouse, a pyramid monument "built of the most solid materials and covered with white marble." "This spot is the repository of a sacred loss, of which the yearnings of a parent's heart are now prophetic. He is rendered immortal by love, as his memory is by death. I envy death far less than oppressors. The one can only kill the body, the other crushes the affections." Percy continues his lamentation, dedicating commemorative verse to memorialize this grave of his favorite child. "Follow where all is fled! Rome's azure sky, / Flowers, ruins, statues, music, words, are weak / The glory they transfuse with fitting truth to speak. / Go thou to Rome / At once the Paradise, / The grave, the city, and the wilderness. / Grey walls moulder round, on which dull Time / Feeds, like slow fire. / And one keen pyramid with wedge sublime, / Pavilions the dust of him doth stand / Like flame transformed to marble. And beneath, / A field is spread, on which a newer band / Have pitched in Heaven's smile their camp of death, / Welcoming him we lose."

Expiating his Italian calamities, this shrine of flowerets marks Shelley's inception for "Ode to the West Wind," envisioning the autumnal advent—in mantic cantos—as his own apocalypse. "I talk of moon, and wind, and stars, and not / Of song; but, would I echo his high song, / Nature must lend me words ne'er used before." Shelley imagines melding with the West wind to awaken the world with his words, to "Scatter, as from an unextinguished hearth / Ashes and sparks, my words among mankind!"

Tap. Tap. Click. They flee northward from Rome to vouchsafe the one happiness that swells between them. The rough seas on the western coasts fill their dreams with dread, and the Shelleys will protect and nurture their last-born child in the tranquility of

Florence. Shelley writes, "The babe is at peace in the womb / The corpse is at rest within the tomb / We begin in what we end—."

(73.) *bravely, my diligence*

SCOTT

In nostalgic yearning, Shelley muses, "O that I could return to England. Health, competence, tranquility—all these Italy permits, and England takes away. Still, I shall return some fine morning—out of pure weakness of heart. From my tower window, I now see the magnificent peaks enclosing the plain—is *nothing*. It dwindles into smoke in the mind when I think of some familiar forms of scenery over which old remembrances have thrown a delightful color. How we prize what we despised when present! The ghosts of our dead associations rise and haunt us in revenge for our having let them starve, and abandoned them to perish."

Seasoned to their sixth autumnal season, the only surviving child of the Shelleys—Percy *Florence*—is born and given his Italian nickname, *Persino*. In the cold of winter after five hateful months without a child, Mary has her fine baby boy who grows easily to a cheery, chubby little cherub—as healthy and rich as the Old World's olive oil. Although Shelley considers his new son to be "the image of poor William," Shelley—on the day of Persino's birth—channels his joy and envisions an industrious endeavor in inventing yachts powered by steam. Mary proudly writes, "The little boy takes after me, and has a nose that promises to be as large as his grandfather's. I have not yet seen his form, but I impute it to be the quintessence of beauty—extracted from all the Apollos, all those of Bacchus, all the loves, and all the dawns I carried him through. In his lively chief perfection, he smells me out and quiets when I take him."

"We removed to Pisa. We seemed to take root here and moved little afterwards. We feared the south of Italy and a hotter climate—on account of our child—our former bereavement inspiring us with terror." Wary, Mary writes, "We are tired of roving and we want our books. Until the abominable *idol* is overthrown, England cannot be free and true. Will not England fall? How will the equinoctial gales blow? You see what a John—or rather Joan—*Bull* I am now. Now I know we are not travelers, we are exiles. Although the lightning of misfortune will pierce through our tight-closed lids, let us shut our eyes. I am tired of wishing or hoping." What's left to learn?

~SOPHOCLES THROUGH THE TREES

"I squatted under the lofty trees, and opened his books. One was a volume of Sophocles and the other was a volume of Shakespeare. 'Is this your study?' I asked.

'Yes,' he answered, 'and these trees are my books—they tell no lies. Sometimes they rave and roar, shriek and howl, like a rabble of priests. In a tempest when a ship sinks, they catch the despairing groans of the drowning mariners. Their chorus is the eternal wailing of wretched men.'

'The sighs you talk about are breathed by a woman near at hand—a forsaken lady.'

'What do you mean?' he asked.

'Why, that an hour or two ago, I left your wife, Mary Shelley, at the entrance of this grove in despair at not finding you.'

He started up, snatched up his scattered books and papers, thrust them into his hat and jacket pockets, sighing, 'poor Mary! Hers is a sad fate. Come along. She can't bear solitude, nor I society—the quick coupled with the dead.'

Those well-recalled days, Mary was like Miranda craving social contact. Percy was like Ariel, fine with being a *sprite* in his cell of solitude.

To stop Shelley's self-reproaches, Mrs. Shelley, with her clear grey eyes and thoughtful brow, began in a bantering tone, chiding and coaxing him: 'What a wild *goose* you are, Percy. If my thoughts have strayed from my book, it was to the opera and my new dress from Florence—and especially the ivy wreath so much admired for my hair, and not to *you*, you silly fellow! When I left home, my satin slippers had not arrived. These are the serious matters to gentlewomen—enough to ruffle the serenest tempered. As to you and your ungallant companion, I had forgotten that such things are. But, as it is the ridiculous custom to have men at balls and operas, I must take *you* with me. Though, from your uncouth ways, you will be taken for Valentine, and he for Orson.'

We talked and laughed, and shrieked, and shouted

as we emerged from under the shadows of the melancholy pines and their nodding plumes—into the cool purple twilight and open country."

SCOTT

Mary writes, "Shelley's favorite taste is boating. When living near the Thames, or by the Lake of Geneva, much of his life was spent on the water. On the shore of every lake or stream or sea near which he dwelt, he had a boat moored. Singularly, Shelley's incessant boating does him a great deal of good." Sailing like a fetching *witch*, Mary and Percy give their sailboat, the *Ariel*, its first full run in open waters before late storms cover the sea with giant, purple warship creatures—drifting beneath the surface like opalescent apparitions. "Swift and beautiful, it's quite a vessel. We drive along this delightful bay in the evening wind under the summer moon until Earth appears another world. If the past and future could be obliterated, the present would content me. My only regret is that the summer must pass."

"The gales and squalls hailed our first arrival. The howling wind swept round us, and the sea roared unremittingly. At other times, sunshine and calm invested the sea and sky, and the rich tints of Italian heaven bathed the scene in bright and ever-varying tints. It was *thus* that short-sighted mortals welcomed Death, *she* having disguised her grim form in a pleasing mask! Living on the seashore, the ocean became as a plaything: as a child may sport with a lighted stick—till a spark enflames a forest and spreads destruction over all—so did we fearlessly and blindly tamper with danger and make a game of the terrors of the ocean."

~THE VEIL & MAGIC MANTLE

"Shelley attempts to learn to swim. When not eager to be pulled from the water, Shelley says, 'It was a great temptation. In another minute, I might have been in another planet. I always find the bottom of the well, and they say "Truth" lies there. In another minute, I should have found it.'

'But as you always find the bottom,' I observed, 'you might have sunk "deeper than did ever plummet sound."'

'I am quite easy on that subject,' said the Bard. 'Death is "the veil," which those who live call "life." They sleep, and it is lifted. Intelligence should be imperishable. The art of printing has made it so on this planet.'

'Why,' I asked, 'do you call yourself an atheist? It annihilates you in *this* world.'

'It is a word of abuse to stop discussion, a painted devil to frighten the foolish, a threat to intimidate the wise and good. I use it to express my abhorrence of superstition. I took up the word as a knight took up a gauntlet—in defiance of injustice.'"

~SECOND MATE SNAKE

"Shelley and his 'captain' of the *Ariel* determined to

man the schooner themselves. Shelley was awkward as a woman in all things appertaining to boats, but full of good intentions. He tangled himself up in the rigging, read Sophocles while trying to steer, and several times just missed falling overboard. But never in his life had he been so happy. 'Shelley! You'll never do any good with him until you shear the wisps of hair that hang over his eyes, heave his Greek poets overboard, and plunge his arms up to the elbow in a tar-bucket.'"

SCOTT

Waves were mountains high. "Call on the Twins of Jove—to appear on their yellow wings and lull the blasts and strew the waves." "Get up Shelley, it is all coming down." "No." "Reef your sails! You are lost!" Before Persino is three years old, heavy seas from a sudden severe storm on the Mediterranean engulf the *Ariel*. "Then, what is life? I cried"—atop his desk in fresh ink—is Shelley's last written lyric. In his own tempest, Percy drowns in the Gulf of Poets off the Italian Riviera—one lovely victim more to the true ruler of their sunny, demonic shores in the depths of Death's unrequited adoration—the one who was Mary's: her choice, her life, her hope, the one who awakened and satisfied her mind. Staring through clustered mirages of luminous reflections from a sea of infinite night, Mary records, "how void, bare, and drear is the scene of life!" Waves engulf the *Ariel*, filling its open hull with dark sea water, ripping off its masts and false stern, and leaving her shattered planks rotting on the shore of one of the Ionian islands.

~JITTERY P.

"Of presentiment, the only one he ever found infallible was the *certain* advent of some evil fortune when he felt peculiarly joyous."

SCOTT

"The spell snapped. It was all over," Mary confides. "The hour they left in their schooner, the coming of an intense evil brooded over my mind and covered this beautiful place and genial summer with the shadow of coming misery. This vague expectation of evil shook me to agony, and I could scarcely bring myself to having let them go. They made it, but they had not made it *back*. From that time, we could scarcely doubt the fatal truth. Yet, we fancied that they might have been driven towards Elba or Corsica—and so be saved."

~ACTS LIKE FILTHY RAGS

"'Maybe,' continued the Mate, 'but she will soon have too much breeze. That gaff topsail is foolish in a boat with no deck and no sailor on board. Look at those black lines and the dirty rags hanging on them out of the sky. They're a warning. Look at the smoke on the water. The devil is brewing mischief."

SCOTT

"There was a sea-fog," Mary indites. "Shelley's boat was soon after enveloped, and we saw nothing more of her. Although the sun was obscured by mists, it was oppressively sultry. The thundersquall commenced, and our lips quivered." "I am convinced that the two months we passed in our last home were the happiest which *he* had ever known. His vessel bore out of sight with a favorable wind, and I remained awaiting his return by the breakers of that sea—those about to engulf him. In the wild beautiful Bay, his days were chiefly spent on the water. At night, when the unclouded moon shone on the calm sea, he often went alone in his little shallop to the rocky caves and wrote his last production, his domineering *Triumph of Life*." From the *Ariel*, Shelley had written "My thoughts arise and fade in solitude, / The verse that would invest them melts away / Like moonlight in the heaven of spreading day: / How beautiful they were, how firm they stood, / Flecking the starry sky like woven pearl!"

For the last three years, in the unrest of his exhaustive attritions of authoring—frail and impermanent as drops of dew—Shelley's mind never lost the image that he had found in the painting "The Raft of the Medusa." A large portion of his last poem—left open on his desk—is Shelley's study of Napoleon leading the splendid, appalling, and sad pageantry of the conquering chariot of *Life*. From this baffling riddle of *Triumph*—out of all the false and fatal turbulence of the miseries of humanity's history—Percy offers no *finale* of reasoned surprise, but an acceptance in apprehending, like a shadow play, the kaleidoscopic powers of light as the mediator of Necessity.

Shelley and Byron were both adept in writing, in billiards, in yachting, and at pistol shooting. Percy's last night of pistol shooting ends with a suspect Italian soldier being stabbed, causing a legal scandal that delays Byron from joining Shelley's departure. During the week that Shelley died, he was described as "having an invincible juvenility about his face—except in his eyes—and his glossy brown locks were now mixed with some grey." Still, throughout his last month, Percy suffered violent nightmares. One evening during his last weeks, he saw a phantasm out on the terrace of their final home, and *it* asked him, "How long do you mean to be content?" Setting out, Shelley boasted to his "captain," "If I die tomorrow, *this Bysshe* will have lived more than his grandfather."

~EURO CRABS

"On the floor lay one with soiled, tattered garments, unkempt locks, and a wild matted beard. His cheek was worn and thin. His eyes had lost their fire. His form was a mere skeleton. Chains hung loosely on fleshless bones."

"'I'm sure everything's as demoralizing as could be expected.'

'Don't mind, sir. The European crabs never bite anybody but poets—since Shelley.'"

SCOTT

The fate and poetic promise of Keats were with Shelley until his last moments, drowning with the book that Keats had sent him. When Shelley is found, his right hand and arm are locked in his waistcoat. In the leather pocket of his sailing jacket is the volume of Keats—opened at *The Eve of St. Agnes.* "The face and hands, and parts of the body not protected by dress were fleshless. The tall slight figure, the jacket, the volume of Sophocles (the same from his woodland study under the whispers of the plumes of pines) and Keats's poems in the other, double-backed, as if in the act of reading had been hastily thrust away—were all too familiar to me to leave a doubt on my mind that this mutilated corpse was any other than Shelley's. The flesh, sinews, and muscles hung about in rags." Mary is a veritable widow. "The spot where the body of Signore Shelley lay was marked by the gnarled root of a pine tree near a rude hut built of young pine stems. The place was well chosen for a poet's early grave. Some weeks before, I had ridden with Shelley and Byron to the very spot, which I have since visited in sad pilgrimage."

~LIFE-DEATH-LIGHT

"All solid and fluid substances become luminous when heated to a temperature corresponding to about 850 degrees."

SCOTT

"I got a furnace made of iron-bars and strong sheet-iron, supported on a stand, and laid in a stock of fuel—as such things as were said to be used by Shelley's much-loved Hellenes on their funeral pyres," and of Shelley's Laon and of his Cythna. At the funeral of Shelley's "captain," Byron is beside himself in disbelief. "The materials being dry and resinous, the pinewood burnt furiously. As soon as the flames became clear, we threw frankincense and salt into the furnace and poured a flask of wine and oil over the body. All that now remained of my lost friend was exposed—a shapeless mass of bones and flesh." It was something out of Shelley's ghost story from years before. "The limbs separated from the trunk on being touched. 'Is that a human body?' exclaimed Byron. 'Why it's more like the carcass of a sheep, or any animal—than a *man*. This is a satire on our pride and folly.' Earlier, I pointed out the letters on the black silk handkerchief, and Byron looking on, muttered 'the entrails of a worm hold together longer than the potter's clay of which man is made.' Then, he cried, 'Hold! Let me see the jaw. I can recognize anyone by the teeth with whom I've talked. I always watch the lips and mouth. They tell what the tongue and eyes try to conceal.'" Nothing remained but dark colored ashes—with fragments of larger bones. Poles were put under the red-hot furnace, and it cooled in the sea.

~HOW LONG DO YOU MEAN TO BE?

"I repeated to myself all that another would have said to console me—and told myself the tale of love, peace, and competence, which I enjoyed. What a scene—the waving sea, the scirocco wind, the lights of the town, and our own desolate hearts that colored all with a shroud. All the agony we endured would be to make you conceive a universe of pain—each moment intolerable and giving place to one still worse. All was over. He had been found washed ashore. All this was to be endured. Days pass away—one after another—and we live thus. Burned to ashes, he shall be at Rome beside my child—where one day I also shall join them. I see the sticks that mark the spot where the sands cover him—and I live. Now, *it* is not of Keats, *Adonais* is Shelley's own elegy. All that might have been bright in my life is now despoiled. I shall take care of our child, and prove myself, and render myself worthy to join him. My weary pilgrimage begins."

~THERE IS NO LIGHT

"Collect my funeral pile and consume to ashes this miserable frame—that its remains may afford no light to any curious and unhallowed wretch who would create such another as I have been. I shall ascend my funeral pile triumphantly and exult in the agony of the torturing flames. The light of that conflagration will fade away, and my ashes will be swept in the sea."

SCOTT

The dead do not choose their voice. "I had no power to check the sacrilege. Even Byron was silent and thoughtful. A dull, hollow sound followed the blow of a mattock. The iron had struck his skull. The quicklime stained him in a dark and ghastly indigo color." "More wine was poured over Shelley's dead body than he had consumed during his life. This, with the oil and salt made the yellow flames glisten and quiver." Shelley's book of Keats was offered up to the flame that rose from his pyre. "The heat from the sun and fire was so intense that the atmosphere was tremulous and wavy. As the back of his head rested on the red-hot bars of the furnace, his brains literally seethed, bubbled, and boiled. Byron could not face this scene. The fire was so fierce as to produce a white heat on the iron and reduce its contents to grey ashes. I liberally rewarded the Italian soldiers for their allowance of these oceanside funerals."

Shelley's cousin writes, "The solemnness of the whole ceremony was the more felt by the *shrieks* of a solitary curlew, which, perhaps, attracted by the corpse, wheeled in narrow circles around the pyre. The bird was so fearless that it could not be driven away." "So piteous and so wild it screamed / round and round the reeking pyre. / His parted spirit hovering nigh, / *Transfigurate*! Comingle with the spangled sky, / Bask in nature's genial smile / And gladden all things through all time." As Shelley is being turned into the light of fire, the presaging curlew—with its pointed, sickled, reaping beak—swarms wild, haunting the pyre ablaze in harsh, daemonic caws of brass.

~THE CURLEW OF VESTA'S LAMENT

When the body first washed up, unrecognizable and torn, / Crabs had eaten its face and its two fellows, forlorn. / But in the jacket pocket, a book of poetry lay, / From one of his dearest companions, a friend from yesterday. / And the curlew circled high beneath the sorrowed sky, / singing its mournful cry. / From the first woe of the universe to the last that will be known, / The curlew cries a song for Percy Shelley, a woe-filled, haunting tone. / The Italians buried bodies, and lime was spread around, / The curlew knew the places where the souls were earthbound. / When the bodies were recovered, drawn back from the grave, / Those who loved them gathered, the curlew's cries so brave. / The bodies turned to ashes, but a heart refused to burn, / The curlew sung a dirge for a love that would not turn. / Its song, a melody of grief for a poet lost at sea, / Echoed through the ages, a timeless elegy. / Oh, the curlew sings forever of the heart that wouldn't burn, / A ballad of eternal woe for the poet who won't return. / Its song drifts on the wind, a requiem of the sea, / The curlew's song for Shelley, an endless, mournful plea.

SCOTT

Promisingly, the year before Shelley drowned, he wrote to his wife, "What is passing in the heart of another rarely escapes the observation of one who's a strict anatomist of his own. This is a tax—and a heavy one—which we must pay for being human. I hope that in the next world these things will be better managed. How's my little darling, and how are you getting on with your book? Be severe in your corrections and expect severity from me—your most sincere admirer. You *shall* still add higher renown to your name." At her preceding happiest—at Marlow five years ago—Mary had completed *Frankenstein* and her *Tour* with Shelley, ready to publish both. In Pisa, Mary is shed alive from the hemorrhaging at the terrifying miscarriage of her fifth baby—a dark presaging of the carnage to come. Losing her last baby a few weeks before she loses her Shelley, their little Persino almost loses both of his parents in less than a month.

Gathering his writings—salted by the sea air—solemnly, Mary will eulogize her vanished Shelley. "He had not completed his nine-and-twentieth year when he died. The calm of middle life did not add the seal of the virtues which adorn maturity to those generated by the vehement spirit of youth. The weight of thought and feeling burdened him heavily. You read his sufferings in his attenuated frame while you perceived the mastery he held over them in his animated countenance and brilliant eyes. He died, and the world showed no outward sign. But his influence over mankind, though slow in growth, is fast augmenting. And, in the ameliorations that have taken place in the political state of his country, we may trace in part the operation of his arduous struggles. His fearless enthusiasm, like other illustrious reformers, was pursued by hatred and calumny. Before the critics contradict me, let them appeal to anyone who'd ever known him. To see him was to love him—and, in his presence, like Ithuriel's Spear, it was alone sufficient to disclose the falsehood of the tale which his enemies whispered in the ear of the ignorant world. His spirit gathers peace in its new state from the sense that, though late, his exertions were not made in vain, and in the progress of the liberty he so fondly loved."

~THE MONSTER ACROSS THE ALPS

"Whilst he lived, his works fell stillborn from the Press. He never complained of the world's neglect nor expressed any other feeling than surprise at the rancorous abuse wasted on an author who had no readers. 'But for them,' Shelley said, laughing, 'I should be utterly unknown.' 'But for them,' I observed,' 'I should have never crossed the Alps in chase of him. My curiosity as a sportsman was excited to see and have a shot at so strange a *monster* as they represented him to be.'" "I had come prepared to see a solemn mystery, and as far as I could judge from the first Act—of "Franken-Shelley"—it seemed to me very like a solemn *farce*. I forgot that great actors when off the stage are dull dogs—and that even the mighty Prospero, without his book and magic mantle, was but an ordinary mortal. Yet, when Shelley joined us, he never laid aside his book or his magic mantle."

SCOTT

"Any man who breathed a syllable against the senseless bigotry of the two Georges was shunned as unfit for social life. To say a word against any abuse which a rich man inflicted—and a poor man suffered—was bitterly and steadily resented. He was sure to be assailed with the gentlest terms of the French revolution: 'Jacobian, Leveller, Atheist, Incendiary, Regicide.' Shelley's life was a *proof*. They caused his expulsion from Oxford, and for *them*, his parents discarded him. Every member of his family disowned him, and the savage Chancellor deprived him of his children—as the most heartless and mischievous of human beings." They all profited from their ventures against him.

As a poet, he was a follower of "the immortal Hour"—sent among men as summer lightning—as one of the grand episodes of Necessity's living poem. His greatest fault was his ignorance of his own worth. In a sullen letter to L. B., Shelley wrote, "I write nothing, and probably shall write no more. It offends me to see my name classed among those who have no name. If I cannot be something better, I had rather be nothing . . . and the accursed cause to the downfall of which I dedicated what powers I may have had flourishes like a cedar and covers England with its boughs. My motive was never the infirm desire of fame. This cup is justly given to one *only* of an age. Participation would make it worthless. Unfortunate *they* who seek it—and find it not."

"He was tall, but he was bent—from eternally poring over his books, which had contracted his chest. His features were expressive of his great sensibility—and decidedly feminine. At twenty-nine, he still retained on his tanned and freckled cheeks the fresh look of a boy with his long wild locks coming into blossom. To anyone disposed to try his hand at literature, Shelley was ever ready to give any amount of mental labor. His life harmonized with his spiritual theories. He left the conviction on the minds of his audience—that however great he was as 'Poet'—he was greater as an orator. His intellectual faculties completely mastered his material nature. He unhesitatingly acted up to his own theories—as Mrs. Shelley has observed, 'many have suggested and advocated far greater innovations in our political and social system than Shelley, but he *alone* practiced those he approved of as just.'"

Byron, leaving Italy for Greece—to his own death—"after commenting on his own wrongs, said, 'and Shelley, too, the best and most benevolent of men—they hooted him out of his country like a mad dog for questioning a dogma. He was grievously over-punished. Man is the same rancorous beast now that he was from the beginning, and if the Christ *they* profess to worship reappeared, they would again crucify *him*.'"

~BLOOM
"Dreadful, I pursued him toward the ocean and found there only his lifeless corpse. Day by day, I become weaker, and life flickers in my wasting form as a *lamp* about to lose its vivifying oil. I now saw that divine orb, gilding all the clouds with unwonted splendor, sink behind the horizon. It disappeared from a world where he whom I would seek exists not. It approached a world where he exists not. Why do I weep so bitterly? Why does my heart heave with vain endeavor to cast aside the bitter anguish that covers it 'as the waters cover the sea?' I go from this world where he is no longer—and soon I shall meet him in another. Farewell, the turf will soon be green on my grave, and the violets will bloom on it."

SCOTT

Although Mary gains beauty as she grows in years, her involuntary lamentations are perpetual. Clinging to the Italian solitudes of her myrtle-shaded streams and chestnut woods—spiritualizing ethereal matter—she sees her Shelley in the sunset hues that quiver in webs of soft light. "Whatever faults he had ought to find extenuation among his fellows, since they prove him to be human. Without them, the exalted nature of his soul would have raised him into something divine." Mary contemplates Percy unbound from his clay and shrine—his dark and light—made one with Nature. Mary writes, "the wife of Time no more—I wed Eternity. Alone, the stars behold my tears, and the winds drink my sighs."

(74.) *The Book of Esther*

~CHRYSALIS

"I want to write scenes that are frightening and inimitable. I don't want to be as intelligible to my contemporaries as Ernest is—bound for the museums. I am sure I am far enough ahead to have some small immortality if I can keep well. Sometimes I don't know whether Zelda isn't a character that I created myself. Every scribbler in Christendom is writing an immortal novel while I continue my ephemeral output. I shall crystalize some of this so-called personality of mine into a novel and preserve it against the short memory of man."

SCOTT

We were living there in a sort of idyllic state among everything lovely imaginable in the way of Mediterranean delights. I think Saint-Raphael was the loveliest spot I'd ever seen. We'd bought a little car, and Zelda and Scottie swam every day on a sandy beach. I was perfectly happy.

. . . If I choose to write *De Profundis* sometimes it doesn't mean I want friends praying aloud over my corpse . . . So, Ernest, with our being back in a nice villa on my beloved Riviera, I'm happier than I've been for years. It's one of those strange, precious, and all too transitory moments when everything in one's life seems to be going well.

ZELDA

Oh . . . that slimy *bogus* lowlife. Well, with a little more honesty of life and its humble triumphs—here's where I'm with it. I've jotted down my monologue. It's all atonement and confessional—so we can make a tomorrow.

"I vacillated. I found it impossible to merge *both* the Zeldas into just the one Scott Fitz. When my heads closed together, I knew I was no enigma. Rather, I knew it is very difficult to be two simple people at once with both the dodo who wants to have a law unto herself and also be the helpless birdie who needs to be loved, made safe, and protected—the Zelda that must have her birdcage door left unlatched, the princess in her tower fable who can climb down by her own magical hair, like wings."

Then, I shift my tone some. "His battered heart of sanity survived all my slings. Hell, Scott made and spent a million dollars and danced with Ginger Rogers—and he never *had* to apologize. But he did—because he was good."

I cue the curtain boy that it's almost time for tomorrow. "The dance was over, and there were no more fairies and no more gold to enter our ghost story. Yet, even if there isn't any me, or any love, or even any life, I love you. I wish I could write a beautiful book to break those hearts that are soon to cease to exist—a book of people who live by the philosophies and dances of popular songs."

~A CIGARETTE WITH DEATH

"The first thing Alabama thought of was that New Year's ball so many years ago. 'Death is the only real elegance,' she said to herself."

ZELDA

Letters, letters, letters—listen. "Next time we play 'Paradise,' I will *make* the jasmine bloom and all the trees come out in flower. We will eat pink clouds for dessert and bathe in the foam of the rain. You can win every golf game, and I will make you a new suit from a blue hydrangea bush and shoes from pecan shells. I'll sew you a belt from leaves like maps of the world, and you can always be the one that's perfect. Dear dearest, I suppose I will spend the rest of my time torn between the desire to master life and a feeling that it is, *au fond*, a contemptuous enemy. Sometimes I feel like a titan and sometimes like a three-month stillborn.

Although the world is a witch's cauldron, everything—luckily—dissolves. I want to fly a kite and eat green apples and have a stomachache—that I know the cause of—and feel the mud between my toes in a reedy creek and tickle the lobe of your ear with the tip of my tongue.

If Trouble bites, just rub his nose in it, give him a lump of sugar, and recite 'The Book of Esther' to him. He will soon subside. Though he may be a thoroughbred, remember his is a proletariat race. If Trouble *still* bites, give him a good kick in the ass for me. Anathema, anathema—etcetera, etcetera.

I sent you a flower. I wanted you to know that you'd love the smell of the sweetness. I think I like breathing twilight gardens and their moths more than beautiful pictures or good books because they're the most sensual. Something in me vibrates to a dusky, dreamy smell—a smell of dying moons and shadows.

So, I've spent today in the graveyard, and I can't find anything hopeless in having lived. All the broken columns and clasped hands and doves and angels mean romances—dead lovers and dead love—even in all their yellowish moss. In a hundred years, I think I shall like having young people speculate on whether my eyes were brown or blue. I hope my grave has an air of many, many years ago about it. Old death is so beautiful—so very beautiful. We will die together—I know."

~CUMULI

"The Fitzgeralds were an enchanting unity, traveling on the same golden cloud. It wasn't possible to love just one of them. You loved them both."

~SPLUSH!

A genuine pair enter unannounced, a wicked Sardine and her Stinko with spots of doggone liquor and double daiquiris spilt on his dopeless t-shirt.

SCOTT

Death is cheap, but we imbibe her with such romantic beauty so that youth will always have an escape hatch. Dear *dear* dearest, there *was* a favorite reply letter from your favorite authorial lowlife, and he offered his topping of sugar.

"You see, Bo, you're not a tragic character. Neither am I. All we are is writers. Forget your personal tragedy. We are all bitched from the start, and you especially have to hurt like hell before you can write seriously. You stopped listening—except to the answers to your own questions. That's what dries a writer up. We all dry up not listening. That's where it all comes from—seeing, listening. You see well enough, but you stopped listening.

You can think. But, say you couldn't think. Then, you must write. You are twice as good now as you were at the time you thought you were so marvelous. You can write twice as well. All we are is writers and what we should do is write. Of all people on Earth, you needed discipline in your work and instead you marry someone who wants to compete with you and ruins you. It's not as simple as that. I thought Zelda was crazy the first time I met her, and you complicated it even more by being in love with her. Long story—hard one to write. Always your friend, Ernest."

~THE PAST

"'Alabama, if you'd stop dumping ashtrays before the company has got well out of the house, we would be happier.'

'It's very expressive of myself. I just lump everything in a great heap which I have labeled "the past," and, having thus emptied this deep reservoir that was once myself, I am ready to continue.'"

(75.) *Perseán sword*

~HERMES'S CURVED HARPĒ

"In after years, Shelley being dead, Wordsworth confessed that he was then induced to read some of Shelley's poems, admitting that Shelley was the greatest master of harmonious verse in our modern literature." "Widely acknowledged as Shelley's *annus mirabilis*," the second year of his biochemical magnus on the Italian Peninsula "marked the confluence of his creative powers, his sociopolitical and artistic commitments, and his manipulation of genre and style in perhaps the greatest array of works and forms ever produced in a relatively short period by a single author in English literary history."

SCOTT

The history of my life is the history of the struggle between an overwhelming urge to write and a combination of circumstances bent on keeping me from it. Shelley's *annus mirabilis* was like holding out the head of Medusa and brandishing the borrowed sword of the gods. Only five years ago, the same as my *Paradise*, Percy's most important essay is published for the first time. For its contemporaries, the reactionary fear of prison was in the European air, stifling its arrival. Although incomplete, Shelley's pamphlet *A Philosophical View of Reform* is his clear, historical publicity on the deprivations of the working class, the inequality of wealth, and the poverty suffered by those whose lives are subjugated in continuing the wealth of others—that labor is the sole source of wealth. Employing scholarly "Utility" as Necessity, Shelley writes, "I have deserted the odorous gardens of literature to journey across the great sandy desert of Politics."

~STARRY ORPHAN

"I do not feel as if I were a man, / But like a fiend appointed to chastise / The offenses of some unremembered world."

SCOTT

Arguing for individual and institutional reform concerning militaries, debts, religions, juries, and to abolish no-work jobs, Shelley traces his history of the exterminations of previous cultures. Though eventually advocating the "system of government by the founders of the American Republic," Shelley restates Godwin's cautionary principle that "mankind has submitted to the 'mighty calamity' of government only to escape the worst evils of slavery." Shelley arranges his theory that improvising individuals mistakenly found the inequalities of the wealthy class through "the few" inheriting the unearned successes of their benefactors—to tyrannize the working class via exploitation and exclusivities, disregarding what would happen if their corporate, current "Atlas" of improvisors let the heavens fall. "On the contrary," Shelley exposes, "there's more injustice in casting the burden of the more heavy and more certain evils of life exclusively on *one* order in the community.

Surely it is enough that the rich should possess to the exclusion of the poor all other luxuries and comforts, and wisdom, and refinement—the least envied but the most deserving of envy among all their privileges."

"Mourn then, People of England. Clothe yourselves in solemn black. Let the bells be tolled. Think of mortality and change. Shroud yourselves in solitude and the gloom of sacred sorrow. Spare no symbol of universal grief. Weep—mourn—lament." Shelley's fervor mounts. "The poets, philosophers, and artists ought to remonstrate, and the memorials entitled their petitions—to *load* the tables of the House of Commons—might show the diverse convictions they entertain of the inevitable connection between national prosperity and freedom, and the cultivation of the imagination and the cultivation of scientific truth, and the profound development of moral and metaphysical enquiry. These appeals of solemn and emphatic argument from those who have already a predestined existence among posterity would appall the enemies of mankind by their echoes from every corner of the world in which the majestic literature of England is cultivated. It would be like a voice from beyond the dead of those who will live in the memories of men when they must be forgotten. It would be Eternity warning Time." Pressuring Parliament to institute reform without violence, the "seditious" seedlings from Shelley's pamphlet are reaped in the emergence of its inevitable political circles.

In Pisa, after Wilmouse dies, Mary and Percy trudge the tough path of their hearts back to society, dancing at a masked ball, attending operas, and riding horses. Shelley and Byron persist in their pistol shooting and philosophizing as Shelley concludes his paired dialogue poem of their speculatory caricatures. From his fearlessness of pursuing authorities, his isolations and freedoms in the Grand Tour cities, his imagination in swarms of societal turmoil, his less lavish living, his targeted condemnations from paranoid critics, his vacant income from authoring, his troubled, restless sleep, and to the deaths of his children, Percy channels his diverse, tindery fuels to ignite his consummate writings. During this year, in his "great array," Shelley is writing "against time" in the solitude of his urgent, personal idealisms. Convinced that political poetry is his necessary vocation, Percy asserts himself as on the side of "the people"—the working class—discounting the *fact* that he's not a "wage-earner" while Byron *is* generating a steady income by being for "freedom"—the Romantic against Romanticism—slaying his infidels in his verses. While Byron enjoys not being plagued as an evil sceptic and entertains his volumes of fan-mail, Shelley ignites his smoldering, magician cauldrons of each genre that will rage until he's drowned.

Indeed, Shelley, in his high year, effortlessly composes "the most *political* poem ever written," *The Mask of Anarchy*, a dazzling reactionary metaphor on "the murder of human rights," Shelley's brilliant retaliation to the recent massacre by horsed soldiers rampaging through an orderly crowd of Britishers in their Sunday clothes carrying silken banners, protesting for unity, strength, and common suffrage. "Slash, and stab, and maim, and hew / What they like, *that* let them do." Their slaughter "Shall steam up like inspiration, / Eloquent, oracular; / A volcano heard afar." In *The Mask of Anarchy*, Shelley vents his intense hatred for the inane despotisms that cannot protect people from "want and ignorance." "In popular tone, he writes for 'the people.' *Mask* might make a patriot of many whose hearts are not wholly closed against others. He wants to demonstrate that rights can be made equal—and more so, the great truth that 'the many,' if accordant and resolute, can control 'the few.'"

~SIGNED, ARIEL (IN HARPY FORM)

"Escapes, makes fiercer onset, then anew / Eludes death, giving death to most that dare / Trespass within the circuit of his sword."

SCOTT

Well, he's found *it* and he spends the rest of his time trying to shine, shine, shine it. But, what is light? What apricity wouldn't you give to go back to the impossible beginning? Well, today, it's the feeling of looking backward to that time—with the partner of my life—when we both were convinced that it was impossible that we would fail—*and* simultaneously, looking back in that mutual condition *not* believing or feeling that we had, yet, while also socially, sufferingly, convinced that in almost everyone else's mass-entity minds that we had. Long live the Press.

Shelley identifies the polluting thread running through and "propping up" the corrupted *polis*—that the social entity is the enemy against the individual, not allowing the singular man to have his cake and eat it too. The brightest are persecuted and held back so that mediocre talents and ordinary efforts stay promoted in a vicious cycle of power to limit the individual's reach of "hubris," limiting his extensions to morph, change, or affect the social entity. The individual, whose human rights must be murdered, is mutually exclusive to *their* ambitions, a disturbing threat to *what* the powers-that-be are attempting to achieve—their tiresome anthem of dominance to be sung out in the taverns of the poor.

~HERMENEUTICAL HOAX

"Swiftly gliding in, blushing like a girl, a tall and thin *stripling* held out both his hands. Although I could hardly believe as I looked at his flushed, feminine, artless face that it could be 'the Poet,' I returned his warm pressure. I was silent from astonishment. Was it possible this mild-looking, beardless boy could be the veritable *monster* at war with all the world: excommunicated by the Fathers of the Church, deprived of his civil rights by a fiat of the grim Lord Chancellor, discarded by every member of his family, and denounced by the rival sages of our literature as the founder of a Satanic school? I could not believe it. It must be a hoax."

SCOTT

Zelda and I toured Europe to finalize the editing of my second novel. As my sophomore effort was published, the first public staging in England of Shelley's *The Cenci* had its debut—a Romantic revenge tragedy, dramatizing a "knotty moral dilemma" that induces "restless and anatomizing casuistry in its audience." If this third book goes well, Zelda and I might catch it in a London playhouse next year.

As an antidote to her cheerlessness, Mary collaborates on *The Cenci* after their Wilmouse dies. Transitioning to stage drama, Shelley challenges himself to find competence in its plotting without the strengths of his metaphysical, abstract, theoretical, or ideal masteries of metered poetry. "This story of the Cenci is indeed eminently fearful and monstrous. On my arrival at Rome, I found that the story of the Cenci was a subject not to be mentioned in Italian society without awakening a deep and breathless interest. All ranks of people knew the outlines of this history and participated in the overwhelming interest which it seems to have the magic of exciting in the human heart."

Prefacing his "tragedy in five acts," Shelley asserts, "the highest moral purpose aimed at in the highest species of the drama is teaching the human heart—through its sympathies and antipathies—the knowledge of itself. If dogmas can do more, it is well: but a drama is no fit place for the enforcement of them." "The most atrocious villain may be rigidly devout and—without any shock to established faith—confess himself to be so. Religion pervades intensely the whole frame of society and is—according to the temper of the mind which it inhabits—a passion, a persuasion, an excuse, a refuge, but never a *check*."

In *The Cenci*, the Barberini Beatrice is Shelley's vestal angel of parricide. "It is in the superstitious horror with which they contemplate alike her wrongs and her revenge that the dramatic character of what she did and suffered consists. The crimes and miseries in which she was an actor and a sufferer are as the mask and the mantle in which circumstances clothed her for her impersonation on the scene of the world." Godwin writes to Mary, "I am glad to see Shelley at last descending to what really passes among human creatures. The story is certainly an unfortunate one, but the execution gives me a new idea of Shelly's powers. There are passages of great strength."

"And though / Ill tongues shall wound me, and our common name / Be as a mark stamped on thine innocent brow / For men to point at as they pass, do thou / Forbear and never think a thought unkind." Mary memorializes his drama. "Universal approbation soon stamped *The Cenci* as the best tragedy of modern times. From vehement struggle, to horror, to deadly resolution, and then to the elevated dignity of calm suffering, the poet dramatizes the intimate secrets of the noble heart of the unfortunate girl. It is the finest thing he ever wrote." Shelley's "loadstar" for his heroine was "the fanaticism of innocence." She "obeys blindly the fatality which drives her on and dies condemned—but not culpable in her own eyes." "It was with the greatest possible effort and struggle with himself that he could be brought to write *The Cenci*. Great as is that tragedy, his fame must rest not on it, but on his mighty rhymes, the deepfelt inspiration of his choral melodies." We're all suckers for something. I've chosen poetry—and its own "some sort of epic grandeur."

~CADUCEUS STAFF ASSAYS

"Time present and time past

Are both perhaps present in time future,

And time future contained in time past.

If all time is eternally present

All time is unredeemable.

What might have been is an abstraction

Remaining a perpetual possibility

Only in a world of speculation.

What might have been and what has been

Point to one end, which is always present.

Footfalls echo in the memory

Down the passage which we did not take

Towards the door we never opened

Into the rose-garden."

SCOTT

Prometheus Unbound is Percy's testament of the resilience—through wretched realities—necessary for the world to be made more humane. "All things are subject to Fate, Time, Occasion, Chance, and Change, but also Eternal Love."

At the death of his little Clara, Shelley commences his *Prometheus Unbound* in Byron's villa outside Venice. Both intoxicated in Roman passions and brought low in the death of his Wilmouse, Percy arranges more than half of his valiant epic.

Then, in the hopes of the Shelleys for Florence, is "the season at which new flowers and new thoughts must spring forth in Italy and in the mind." From Florence—the city of Petrarch and Dante, the sister-city Philadelphia of the Founders, of Zelda's Florence of the South, and of the influential Edinburgh of the Kingdom—Shelley executes the rejoicing conclusion of his masterful *Prometheus Unbound,* celebrating his newborn boy of all their hopes.

Echoing his earlier admirations of Paine and Godwin, Percy now finds his convincing acclimatizing for freedom amongst the force of Mutability and the power of Necessity. "I am one of those whom nothing will fully satisfy, but am ready to be partially satisfied in all that's practicable. We shall see. To achieve greatness, the poet must move between solitude and social mobility. The great thing to do is to hold the balance between popular and patience and tyrannical obscenity—to inculcate with fervor both the right of resistance and the duty of forbearance."

~LET'S

"Suddenly, Shelley raised his head, his face brightened as with a bright thought, and he exclaimed, joyfully, 'Now let us together solve the great mystery!'"

SCOTT

More than his best daydreams and nightmares, his *Prometheus Unbound* concerns the animating, poetical authorities of love. When love fails, all is lost, but when love is revived, the human mind can regenerate. The unifying supremacy of love is the mediating advocate, the mutual flowering of Mutability and Necessity in concord. "Time past and time future . . . the rose-garden . . . Only through time, time is conquered." Love bridges, abiding Mutability, compounding Necessity, transfusing and synthesizing these parental powers, mutating the space-moments of Death and Time made love. "A thing of beauty is a joy for ever: Its loveliness increases." The last doubt is annihilation. Will the beauty of love pass into nothingness? Love that regenerates the mind is "the loftiest star of unascended heaven, / Pinnacled dim in the intense inane / Yet not exempt from chance, and death, and mutability." Shelley's Prometheus will find the first death, but will the light in the mind of love learn something more than termination?

~AZAZEL OF ATHENS

"When my brain gets heated with thought, it soon boils and throws off images and words faster than I skim them off. If you ask me why I publish *what* few—or none—will care to read, it is that the spirits I have raised haunt me until they are sent to the devil of a printer. All authors are anxious to breach their bantlings."

SCOTT

His pamphlet he'd published as a minor at Oxford, rarely ever read, is weaponized against him the rest of his life and long after—material he'd refused to answer about its authorship. Similarly, distorting and censoring his ideas, Shelley continues to suffer material persecution for his themes in *Prometheus Unbound*—a unified literary target of the reactionary establishment, their conservative presses countering the hells that had turned the Continent into cemeteries. In *Prometheus Unbound*, Shelley remythologizes his treasured Greek drama into his mythopoetic philosophy of liberty as providential.

"The prominent feature of Shelley's theory of the destiny of the human species is that evil is not inherent in the system of the creation, but is rather an accident that can be expelled. Not deluded by the 'evil principle,' but oppressed and warring against *it*, Shelley believes people can be perfected by being willing to expel evil from themselves." His admiring, widowed Mary later summarizes *Prometheus Unbound*.

"Time falls from Saturn's throne of light and love. Saturn is the principle of good, Jupiter is the usurping principle of evil (wielding the dark scepter of the tyrant), and Prometheus is the regenerator—who, unable to bring mankind back to primitive innocence, uses knowledge as a weapon to defeat evil, leading mankind to a state of virtue through wisdom."
His chain is broken, his vulture is slayed, and he commences a happier reign than that of Saturn—from "a paradise within, happier far."

"From the annihilation of evil, nature resumes her primal beauty, the Moon is made bliss, and our planet is guided aright again through the realms of the sky—in such a way that we may find ourselves *unbound* when justly guided through the intricate paths of the wilderness of our minds." "Sphere of divinest shapes and harmonies, / Beautiful orb! Gathering as thou dost roll / The love which paves thy path along the skies. / Love, from its awful throne of patient power / In the wise heart, from the last hour of dread endurance and agony, springs / And folds over the world its healing wings."

Implying a biographical muse for each stage of his epic, Mary joyfully recapitulates her Percy's four acts of *Prometheus Unbound*. "He sets his most sublime imagining of freedom in the mountains of India—where Shelley believed civilization originated. Act One depicts the overcoming of the hatred for Jupiter and resisting the Furies' despairing temptations and hopeful visions for the spirits of the human mind.

Act Two is the quest for attaining transformation, understanding evil, and being liberated from doubts about ultimate reality. The freedom achieved in Act Three negates 'things as they were,' changing occurrences for the better. Subsequently, in Act Four, the cosmic dimension is healed in various forms of the energies of love."

~POLISHED GORGON-CROWNED AEGIS

"My friends say my *Prometheus* is too wild, ideal, and perplexed with imagery. It may be so. It has no resemblance to the Greek drama. It is original and cost me severe mental labor. Authors, like mothers, prefer the children who have given them most trouble—as Milton and his *Paradise Regain'd*. I have the vanity to write only for poetical minds, and must be satisfied with few readers."

SCOTT

Percy's radical convictions are entwined in his epic trilogy. Throughout his last year in England and his first pair of years in Italy, Shelley's crown is the second and third branches of his fantasy trilogy of the English Revolution. Like *The Paradiso*, *Prometheus Unbound* is third in the set of Shelley's epic Romance trilogy, concluding his argument for individual excellence from *Queen Mab* and *Laon and Cythna*. While hundreds of copies of *Queen Mab* are freely circulating, his second and third sections are austerely suppressed. In his *Mab*, Shelley names Necessity as the mother of the world and the spirit of nature.

"Even the minutest throb, the minutest molecule of light / That in an April sunbeam's fleeting glow / Fulfills its destined, though invisible, work, / The universal spirit guides." Shelley's poetry is the pastel colorings to veil Necessity as less materialistic, exalting one's feelings to be as necessary as one's senses. Necessity is the moveless wave of the one mind whose calm reflects all moving things that are. For Shelley, it is only the deathless elements of thought—will, passion, reason, and imagination—that can wield defiance against what Mutability weaves and has dominion over—worlds, worms, empires, and superstitions.

Vitalizing Godwin's theory that any societal change can only arrive through individual beliefs of men and women, Shelley insists that such individuals must promote their intellectual conversions in the active advocacy of agitation. Amongst the mass of the starving peasantry of Ireland—the poor "whom the morn wakens but to fruitless toil / and to ever hear his famished offspring scream"—Shelley fiercely opposes the "cold sophistry" of "the man of ease" who "confines the struggling nature of his human heart."

After escaping his assassin in Wales, the celestial tour of Shelley's daemon, Mab, reveals the world as distorted by corruption and exploitation. "The poor are set to labor for the pride of power—the miserable isolation of pride, the false pleasures of one-hundredth part of society." "Yet fear not; / This is no unconnected misery, / Nor stands it uncaused and irretrievable." Shelley's progressive inevitabilities of Necessity shimmer and trickle amongst the "kings, priests, and statesmen" whom "blast the human flower" and desolate "the discord-wasted land." Along bright beams of shadowed light, the flurried fragments, always present, are easily seen.

~WHILST, PEGASUS ARISES

"'I hope this accursed limb will be knocked off in the war.'

'It won't improve your swimming, but I will exchange legs if you will give me a portion of your brains.'

'You would repent your bargain. At times, I feel my brains boiling—as Shelley's did *whilst* you were grilling his.'"

SCOTT

For Percy, predetermining, guiding Necessity is what makes things feel "fixed"—like when the billiard balls at Byron's don't sprout devilish wings and take frightful flight after being struck with his cue. *Reason* is the presence of Necessity within, convincing us that hypocritical customs should be overthrown. For Shelley, ideals are fostered in the fused fatherings of Necessity and chaotic motherings of Mutability. In Percy's epic poetry, he is attempting a developmental reconciliation of reason and love to deal with the deterministic tensions between Necessity and Mutability.

Necessity is fixed far above the flux of time as if in a permanent and changeless reality that modifies the human plane through seeming mutabilities (evanescencies), compelling things toward their "hour with the omnipresent." We experience Necessity ("the all-mover's glory") through what we call "fate and destiny," but Necessity is without demands. It awaits its cast—the impassioned reason of minds.

To be "set free," Shelley has us as forced with situational opportunities "to apply reason and love"—nudging us from our archetypical fountains of all hopes and all fears. Shelley's epics have us to feel that Necessity is a living spirit, and that we *get* what we *make*. "The path of its departure still is free." Our infinity is the connections of all our finite parts. Percy pairs his humanist ardor with his insistence of suprarational intimations of "the pervading Spirit coeternal with the universe." Consequently, our strongest compulsion against "chance" is that we are in the only possible world—Necessity offering us the privilege of shaping "things as they are"—Shelley's idealism of merging determinism with freewill, making "minds" his battleground.

~VERGE

"O'er the wide wild abyss, two meteors shone, / Sprung from the depth of its tempestuous jar: / A blood-red Comet and the Morning Star / Mingling their beams in combat / . . . and thoughts within his mind waged mutual war."

SCOTT

In his forty-eight-hundred lines of *Laon and Cythna*, Shelley's goal is to reveal that when properly applying reason, we will discern that our freeborn souls are born bound and stifled under the heels of irresponsible leaders and perversions of oppressors—and, moreover, that violence merely reinforces what binds us. Shelley inspires that effectual love—when applied to reason—is the only mechanism of becoming "unchained." In *Prometheus Unbound*, this synthesis is the mental labors that must be individually pursued. Just as Shelley has been the "Laon" and will be the "Adonais" of his English Revolution, Shelley is now its "Prometheus," his representation of the potentials within people who are in revolt against repression. "We might be otherwise—We might be all / We dream of happy, high, majestical. / It is our *will* / Which thus enchains us to permitted ill. / Something nobler to live and die, / We have power over ourselves to do / And suffer what we know not till we try." Though, "stand warned," Shelley elucidates, "a shadow tracks thy flight of fire."

~HERMETIC HELM OF HADES

"The mythopoetical power is the influence which is moved not, but moves within the evanescent hues of this ethereal world. What is called poetry, in a restricted sense, has a common source with all other forms of order and of beauty according to which the materials of human life are susceptible of being arranged, and which *is* poetry in a universal sense. Startled with the electric life which burns within its words, the mythopoet attempts to idealize the modern forms of manners and opinion—and compels them into a subordination to the imaginative and creative faculty—arresting the vanishing apparitions which haunt the interlunations of life, veiling them, redeeming from decay the visitations of the divinity in man."

SCOTT

Significantly, "renewal" must arrive from Necessity with an additional strength outside of sheer *trusting* in resistance and love. Shelley's "Demogorgon" device must also turn its head towards generational destinies. Thus, Shelley concedes to the "deus ex machina" device from his treasured Greek dramas at the climactic summit of his trilogy—as did his two masters, Dante and Milton. Similarly, Shelley's Demogorgon in *Prometheus Unbound* sends his ardent ultimatum to his audience. The two polar chariots of Percy's Demogorgon appear from its apocalyptic caverns, illustrating the dual wisdom of Necessity. The chariot that arrives to Jupiter ruins the reign of his cruel, contemptible authority, and the chariot sent for rescue supplants his Titan's cursed nature with the ethic of love where the devastated vulture had been bedeviling its tormented victim.

Although "Eternity" will again release evil, unhedged, the empire over the enemy will be sealed via the revealed spells of gentleness, virtue, wisdom, and endurance. In imitation of his hero, Shelley insists there is victory only in individual expulsions of devious contaminations—allowing the utopian to replace hierarchy with harmony, power with delight-in-otherness, and authority with freedom, "unclassed, tribeless, and nationless."

~MERCURIAL WINGED SANDALS

"In the annals of authors, I cannot find one who wrote under so many discouragements as Shelley. Shelley could number his readers on his fingers. He said 'I can only print my writing by stinting myself in food!' The utter loneliness in which he was condemned to pass the largest portion of his life would have paralyzed any brains less subtilized by genius than his were."

SCOTT

Prometheus Unbound is Shelley's own favorite poem and best style—for his select class of gold-hatted readers. While Mary is withdrawn—writing and privately coping from the miserable losses of Clara and Wilmouse—Percy proclaims, "Let me find the seven purchasers of my seven copies, and they shall be the seven golden candlesticks with which I will illuminate the world." As *Prometheus Unbound* is being published, Beethoven is mesmerizing the theatre with his debut performances of *Overture to Prometheus*.

After only selling twenty copies, Shelley laments, "*Prometheus* was never intended for more than five or six persons." As an adult, he has earned less from his poetic works than from the sales of his two sensationalist gothic novels he published before his expulsion from Oxford.

~23 SKIDOO

"I can't understand about your stories. The school that you started and the vogue which you began are still dictating the spiritual emulation of too many people for your work to be irrelevant—and certainly the tempo of the times ought to bring you some success."

SCOTT

I'll title my brief on Shelley's defense for magic, "Can You Spare a Canto, Mack? (Docket #23: Percy Bysshe Versus the United States of Depression)." After his *annus mirabilis* passes, Shelley formulates his *Triumph of Life*—his cast of characters to be trampled: "creativity" and "charity." Creativity is imagination, poetry, and music. Charity is love, sex, and nurturing. Mystically optimistic, his synthesis of creativity and charity is light, "the fifth element" of Shelley's prestige. Light is the courage of the heart's mind. Light is the bright bursting of accepting Mutability with faith in Necessity, merging philosophy and passion into living relations. Light is as love-letters made real. Light makes the invisible seen. What is seen is veiled, but is revealed *in* its veiling. Light is the genesis of spectacle—beams that write and erase, simultaneously.

~ATHENS AFTER MATH

As painfully to pore upon a book
To seek the light of truth while truth the while
Doth falsely blind the eyesight of his look.
Light, seeking light, doth light of light beguile."

SCOTT

Concurrently, the glittering, mutable, misleading light of the Dog Star—the wilting heat of Orion's hound—interposes its counterlight, "Lucifer," into the bright guiding light of the star that was made for this planet that's peopled. "And the fair shape waned in the coming light / And as the presence of that fairest planet / Although unseen is felt by one who hopes / From Lucifer, amid the chrysolite." The moon dissolves in the light of the sun, but Lucifer challenges the first light. We experience our ideals as carried through this mingled light interfigured through both persisting stars. As a chameleon feeds on light, the veiling light covers, making things what they are not.

"One of the grandeurs of immortality," wished Keats, was that "we will completely understand each other." Accepting both our living fears and our living hopes, light is the path of time traveling between the mirrors of our eyes ceaselessly—from one cracked mirror to the next. Encountering the endless play of the "shape of all light" in *Triumph of Life*, Shelley swivels his last titanic interrogation from "what is life?" to "what should life be?"—continuing his Romantic quest of understanding with his ever-roving readiness to explore, envision, and improve.

~UNSINKABLE NUMEROLOGY

"'You are quite right; it is door No. 23?'

'We used to call it "the skidoo door," on account of the number. *That* is how I remember the number.'

'I do not understand *that*?'

'It is an American joke.'

'Will you explain it?'

'I could not explain it, my Lord.'"

SCOTT

For Shelley, Prometheus unlocks understanding the primal merger of light and counterlight—how one moves the weight of the other. Mutability carries the necessary, delivering the differentiated light through reason. To see, we must enter into the light of our ideals, abandoning ourselves into its differentiating games of how light plays *us* as its stage plays, exploring its uncertainties in our forced frustrations of unweaving, like plural Penelopes each, our fleeing memories, replaced and replaced, diminishing into forgetful sand—the dismemberings of disremembering to keep our "Ithacas" alive.

"We are such stuff / As dreams are made on." Like

dead, autumn leaves laced in morning dew reflecting the light of life from the wet ground, our memories are *fugues*—living musical tunes of loves and hates repeated in multifaceted patterns, playing, playing. Disentangling, we strike at unknitting our mythical Gordian knots. We sit on the ground with tales to recall the various flashes and shrieks in Time's lightning storms of us—"thoughts that do often lie too deep for tears." Although such solutions may somewhat immobile us—Shelley trumpets—this mystery left untried will be the realm of the dominion of all our ruin.

~AT THE END OF DAISY'S DOCK

"We know not / How much, while any yet remains unshared, / Of pleasure may be gained, of sorrow spared: / This truth is that deep-well whence sages draw / The unenvied light of hope, the eternal law / By which those live to whom this world of life / Is as a garden ravaged and whose strife / Tills for the promise of a later birth / The wilderness of this Elysian earth."

"These lights, this brightness, these clusters of human hope, of wild desire—I shall take these lights in my fingers. I shall make them bright, and whether they shine or not, it is in these fingers that they shall succeed or fail."

(76.) *withering will-o'-the-wisp*

~STARS *AND* STRIPES

"He was prejudiced in favor of the dead languages. He had an almost English dislike of the French and their literature."

SCOTT

When Shelley and Mary are first entranced in each other, Napoleon is abdicating as Emperor, and Shelley writes, "Time has swept in fragments towards Oblivion Napoleon's *pomp* from dancing and reveling on the grave of Liberty." "I know / Too late, since thou and France are in the dust, / That Virtue owns a more eternal foe / Than Force or Fraud: old Custom, legal Crime, / And bloody Faith, the foulest birth of Time." As several deaths ravage the Shelleys in Italy, Napoleon dies in exile. Eight months before Shelley himself dies, he composes his poem "Written on Hearing the News of the Death of Napoleon," a brief dialogue between himself and Vesta—"Mother Earth"—the goddess of the hearth.

> **SHELLEY:**
> "And livest *thou* still, Mother Earth? / Thou wert warming thy fingers old / O'er the embers covered and cold / Of that most fiery spirit, when it fled— / The last of the flock of the starry fold— / What, Mother, do you laugh now he is dead?"

VESTA:

"And the lightning of scorn laughed forth. / I was cloudy, and sullen, and cold, / Like a frozen chaos uprolled, / Till by the spirit of the mighty dead / My heart grew warm. 'Still alive and still bold!' / I feed on whom I fed. / In terror and blood and gold, / A torrent of ruin to death from his birth / Weave into his shame, which like the dead— / His dead fill me ten-thousandfold— / Shrouds me, the hopes that from his glory fled."

SCOTT

Although General Washington died when Percy was a boy, at Shelley's "Bona-Corpse Party" upon the death of Napoleon, he raises toasts to good Ole Geo— whose revolution is *still* succeeding.

Drinking to the memories of Washington and Napoleon, Shelley eulogies, "At once the tyrant and tyrannicide, / In his own blood—a deed it was to bring / Tears from all men—though full of gentle pride, / Such pride as from impetuous love may spring." Shelley raises glasses to the end of the Napoleonic Wars.

~RAISING ALE

"But feast tonight!—tomorrow we depart! / Strike up the dance, the festal bowl fill high, / Drain every drop!—tomorrow we may die."

SCOTT

"I stood upon a heaven-cleaving turret / Which overlooked a wide Metropolis—/ And in the temple of my heart, my Spirit / Lay prostrate, and with parted lips did kiss / The dust of Desolation's altar / And with a voice too faint to falter / It shook that trembling fane with its weak prayer." "When the lamp is shattered / The light in the dust lies dead, — / When the cloud is scattered / The rainbow's glory is shed." Shelley contemplates finding his own later liberty—and justice—in the States. Shelley's boating mate has the last toast. "How much is enough? Ole Napole could've easily suited his courage into a finer fit—say, a distiller or a fireman—like Virginia's own Geo." *Cin Cin!*

~MILKSOPS

"Mixing glasses of grog for him, I lowered to what sailors call 'water bewitched,' and he never made any remark. I once tried him of omission, and he quickly inquired, 'Have you not forgotten the creature comfort?' I then put in two spoonfuls, and he was satisfied. 'His English acquaintances in Italy were,' he said in derision, 'all milksops.' On the rare occasions of any of his former friends visiting him, he would urge them to have a carouse with him, but they had grown wiser.

Constantly active and starving his body, Byron keeps his brains clear. 'What's your complaint, how do you feel?' 'Feel! Why just as that damned obstreperous fellow chained to a rock, the vultures gnawing my midriff—and vitals too—for I have no liver. I don't care for dying, but I cannot bear this! Who wants to live? Not I. The Byrons are a short-lived race on both sides: longevity is hereditary. I am nearly at the end of my tether. I don't care for death a damn. It is her sting I cannot bear.'"

SCOTT

Since Venice, Albe and Shiloh continue frequent visits throughout Italy. Converting from his Napoleonic trend, L. B. aims to make some good with his influence—yet also to take aim with some choice others. "Few things surpass old wine; and they may preach / Who please, the more because they preach in vain. / Let us have wine and women, mirth and laughter, / Sermons and soda-water the day after." "They pronounce it as highly immoral and unfit for publication. I have a *conscience*—although the world gives me no credit for it. I am now repenting, not of the few sins I have committed, but of the many I have *not* committed. Now, my brain is throbbing and must have vent. Because *thou* art virtuous, thinkest thou there shall be no more cakes and ale? I've opined gin was inspiration, but *pretense* is stronger. Today, I had another letter warning me against the Snake. He alone, in this age of humbug, dares stimulate the current—as he did today on the flooded Arno in his skiff. Who reads Shiloh, yet? If *we* puffed the Snake, it might not turn out a profitable investment. If *he* cast off the slough of his mystifying metaphysics, he would want no puffing.'"

"Percy waved his wand, and Byron, after a faint show of defiance, stood mute. His quick perception of the truth of Shelley's comments on his poem transfixed him, and Shelley's earnest and just criticism held him captive." "Shelley indignantly answered, 'That is very good logic for a bookseller, but not for an author. The shop's interest is to supply the ephemeral demand of the day. It is not for him, but *you* "to put a ring in the monster's nose" to keep him from mischief.' Byron smiling at Shelley's warmth, said, 'He's right, if not righteous. All I have yet written has been for women kind. You must wait until I am forty, their influence will then die a natural death, and I will show the men what I can do.' Shelley replied, 'Do it *now*—write nothing but what your conviction of its truth inspires you to write. You should give counsel to the wise— and not take it from the foolish. Time will reverse the judgment of the vulgar. Contemporary criticism only represents the amount of ignorance that genius has to contend with.' I was then and afterwards pleased and surprised at Byron's passiveness and docility in listening to Shelley—but all who heard him felt the charm of his simple earnest manner. Indeed, Byron knew him to be exempt from the egotism, pedantry, foxcombry, and more than all, the rivalry of authorship—and that Shelley was the truest and most discriminating of his admirers." In Albe's last acts, he will take up the gauntlet of liberty for others. However, as his accurate oracle goes, L. B. will not make it to forty.

~A POLIS OF POLLUTION

"Oppressed by the burthen of his calamities, he had

lost every aspect of reputation and honor. And who can wonder, or, considering the poignancy of his sufferings, be surprised at the neglect of the world—seeing his works, one after the other, all dead from the Press. Others who did not possess a tenth of his genius were belauded by mercenary presses, and he was harassed by the public. Such lacerated his heart and made him at times doubt that the light which he followed was not a steady flame—but an *Ignis fatuus* of the imagination in which was no vividness or durability. And then, to look back onto the past to see all his dearest hopes blighted, his fond aspirations after immortality turned into a mockery—to see his life become aimless—profitless! How can we wonder at his despondency?

And yet, with all his despondency at the neglect of the world—his distraction of mind at the attacks of his implacable enemies, one may conceive the intense *enjoyment* he must have experienced at his creations. Self-absorbed, luxuriating in a world of his own, he annihilated matter and time. Hours fled like moments fledged with ever fresh delights. Even his sorrows (and who suffered more?) were but the drops in the Crucible—the sad mesh of humanity—and his poetical alchemy drew from them infinite purity and beauty. He had said, 'indeed the pleasure of sorrow is sweeter than the pleasure of pleasure itself.' Such might he have occasionally found, but there were times when his sorrow must have been almost more than humanity could bear. I remember his saying that four of his friends had committed suicide. He said that few people had not been tempted during some period of their lives to destroy themselves, and I have reason to think—that like Keats—he had contemplated such a termination to his ills. Shelley had said, 'I am regarded by all who know, or hear of me, as a rare prodigy of crime and pollution—whose look even might infect.' The fatal fanaticism in that article of Keats in the *Quarterly Review* also wounded Shelley's sensitive, spent spirit."

(77.) *bright dark star*

SCOTT

Keats's poetics catch fire when he and Shelley are featured in the "Three Young Poets" article after the suicides of Fanny and Harriett. Keats writes, "I am certain of nothing but the holiness of the heart's affections and the truth of the imagination. What imagination seizes as 'beauty' must be truth."

In this fearless early article, it's published, "We have spoken with the less scruple of these poetical promises because we really are not in the habit of lavishing praises and announcements—and because we have no fear of any pettier vanity on the part of young men who promise to understand human nature so well" and who "promise to help the new school revive Nature—'complete, powerful, and quiet.'"

As I was leaving Princeton, I learned Keats from Scribner's bio published on the centenary of his first volume of poems, the same year as *Prufrock* by T. S. There I was as I turned twenty-one, reading Keats as the onset to my *Romantic Egoist*. At his early, decisive review, Keats had just turned twenty-one. Between this first emboldening review and his malicious, impending reviews of vaticide, Keats emerges a wise writer, discovering the paradoxical transcendence from fuller engagement with finitude and suffering. Hence, bound together, Keats's and Shelley's condemned poetics will flourish after their deaths as the legends of their age.

~IF KEATS BE HIS REAL NAME TO SUCH RHAPSODY

"Poetry is the coyest creature that ever was wooed by man. She has something of the coquet in her—for she flirts with many and seldom loves one. There is not one poet of the present day that enjoys any popularity that will live. Each write for his booksellers and the ladies of fashion—and not for the voice of centuries. Time is a lover of old books and he suffers few new ones to become old. Posterity is a difficult mark to hit, and few minds can rend the arrow full home.

Wordsworth might have safely cleared the rapids in the stream of time, but he lost himself by looking at his own image in the waters. Coleridge stands bewildered in the crossroad of fame. His genius will commit suicide and be buried in it. Lord Byron is a splendid and noble egoist, but no spot is conveyed to our minds that is not peopled by the gloomy and ghastly feelings of our proud and solitary man. If a common man were to dare to be as moody, as contemptuous, and as misanthropical, the world would laugh at him. There must be a coronet marked on all his little pieces of poetical insolence, or the world would not countenance them.

However, the mind of Mr. Keats, like the minds

of our older poets, goes round the universe in its speculations and its dreams. His feelings are full, earnest, and original as those of the older writers were and are. They are made for all time, not for the drawing-room and the moment. His soul is an invisible ode to the passions. He knows that Nature is better and older than he is and he does not put himself on an equality with her. You do not see him when you see her. His mind has 'thews and limbs like to his ancestors.' Mr. Keats greatly resembles old Chapman and he excels in what Milton excelled—the power of putting a spirit of life and novelty into the heathen mythology."

~WHAT THINK YOU?

"Keats breaks out that he has composed a new line: 'A thing of beauty is a constant joy.' 'What think you of that?'

'It has the true ring, but is wanting in some way.'

An interval of silence, and again the poet: 'A thing of beauty is a joy for ever.' 'What think you of that?'

'That it will live forever.'"

SCOTT

While the Shelleys are in Marlow, Keats moves near Coleridge and initiates the productive literary hikes of the Hampstead Heath. Keats feels that his only relief from his vulnerabilities is to compose poems that force his contemplations to lift him from his stormy mists. In his first poetry contest with his literary circle, he opens his sonnet "The poetry of earth is never dead." Keats's poems are the Romantic longing for the unattainable, the passion for absolute beauty, and living completely in the immediacy of emotion—knowing melancholy dwells with the evanescent natures of beauty, joy, and pleasure. "There's no beauty without poignancy, and there's no poignancy without the feeling that it's *going*—men, names, books, houses—bound for dust, mortal." In a winter letter to his confidant, Keats conjures his theory of "negative capability," envying the authorial mode of being at peace with mystery against the nagging *needs* of clarity. When words—at best—are wagers of thought, "negative capability" is the harmony from doing without the irritable *need* to rationalize a writer's own half-knowledge of anxious indeterminacies, "when man is *capable* of being in uncertainties, mysteries, and doubts without any irritable reaching after fact and reason." Negative capability is Keats's writing method of discovering the independence to create, of dissolving social conflicts in mediations of beauty, of subduing the ego's rage for determinacy, and the basic Romantic insight of the fuller liberty found in thriving through the non-rational.

Wanting to stretch his poetic prowess and challenge the popularity of novels, Keats moves to the seaside of the Isle of Wight—hanging his portrait of Shakespeare over his desk—and composes his epic competition poem to Shelley's *Laon and Cythna*. His drive is to create a modern humanistic romance in poetics inspired by the love of nature that will rise to the mythic—for the real and ideal to be merged in a sensuous "fellowship with essence," uniting erotic love with spiritual love. After his seaside sojourn, Keats completes his epic romance after being invited to write and study for a season at Oxford.

As Keats's shepherd-prince reluctantly forsakes his idealized goddess of the moon—in the culmination of his vision in *Endymion: A Poetic Romance*, Keats's dreamer discovers that the beautiful foreign girl he has rather fallen in love with and marrying is indeed an incarnation, the earthly avatar of his goddess as the epical realization of "ideal beauty" in the "spiritualization" of his Endymion. As the Shelleys exile themselves to Italy, Keats's experimental romance is published. Although Wordsworth criticizes *Endymion* as "a very pretty piece of Paganism," and Keats's literary standing is defined by the Press as making "luxuriant song" out of his frustrated social disadvantages, Keats's brilliance stands, confounding time. "By old tongue of doom, / This dusk religion, pomp of solitude, / And the Promethean clay by thief endued, / By old Saturnus' forelock, by his head / shook with eternal palsy, I did *wed* / In the vesper hymn through dark pillars of sylvan aisles. / And as she spake, into her face there came, / Light, as reflected from a silver flame: / Ay, he beheld Phoebe, his passion! / She gave her fair hands to him, / And in a blissful swoon, 'twas fit from this mortal state he / —before three swiftest kisses—spiritualized be!"

Two duplicitous machines—forming the conservative construct of "public opinion"—now diminish the previously favorable reviews of Keats and savage his epic—vilifying Keats's publisher through his protégé, tarnishing Keats as the unhappy disciple of the new school of Cockney poetry. The first infamous review attacks Keats as an "'incongruous, uncouth, and unintelligible copyist"—and a "diffuse, tiresome, absurd, and impudent neophyte of gratuitous nonsense." "Of all the manias of this mad age," opens the second ruthless review, "the most incurable is *metromania*—the melancholy effect of turning the heads of we know not how many farm-servants and unmarried ladies; our very footmen now compose tragedies, and there is scarcely a superannuated governess in the island that does not leave a roll of lyrics behind her in her band-box." "Here, we find Mr. Keats from the uneducated and flimsy striplings of the rising brood of the land of Cockaigne—the pitiably ridiculous, fanciful dreaming tea-drinkers of Cockney poetasters."

"As for Mr. Keats's *Endymion*—adopting the loose, nerveless versification and rhymes of the Cockneys—no man, whose mind has ever been imbued with the smallest knowledge or feeling of classical poetry or classical history could have stooped to profane and vulgarize every association in the manner which has been adopted by this 'son of promise.' A small poet, Mr. Keats is only a boy of pretty abilities, which he has done everything in his power to spoil. It is a better and a wiser thing to be a starved apothecary than a starved poet. So, back to the shop Mr. John, back to 'plasters, pills, and ointment boxes'—and good-morrow to 'the Muses' son of Promise.'"

Still, pugilist Keats is ultimately resilient, marking, "This is a mere matter of the moment." Indeed, Keats writes, "In *Endymion*, I leaped headlong into the sea and thereby have become better acquainted with the soundings, the quicksand, and the rocks—than if I had stayed upon the green shore and piped a silly pipe and took tea and comfortable advice."

~CONFESSIONS OF ST. KEATS

"What shocks the virtuous philosopher delights the chameleon poet. It does no harm from its relish of the dark side of things any more than from its taste for the bright one—because they both end in speculation. A poet is the most unpoetical of anything in existence. It is a wretched thing to confess."

SCOTT

As the Shelleys' daughter is dying in Venice, Keats initiates his migrations through Scotland, Ireland, and the Lake District. While the Shelleys are in Naples, Keats meets with Wordsworth and initiates his own rivaling, masterful *annus mirabilis*. Keats composes his supplanting epic *Hyperion*, his Titan preparing his fallen fate to the Olympian god of knowledge, Keats's poetics of Apollo's metamorphosis—his "dying into life"—into the divinity of poetry, music, medicine, and the sun. Contrasting *Endymion*, Keats writes, "the hero of the romance, being mortal, is led on like Napoleon—by circumstance—whereas the Apollo in *Hyperion*, being a foreseeing god, will shape his actions like one." In his fullest bloom for six inspirited months, Keats completes his six *Odes*—the best poems of the English language. In this same miraculous year of poetry, Keats also writes *The Eve of St. Agnes*, "La Belle Dame sans Merci," *Lamia*, and his last epics.

As his own high year closes, he and his fiancé are engaged on Christmas. "My love has made me selfish. I cannot exist without you. I am forgetful of everything but seeing you again. My life seems to stop there. I see no further. You have absorbed me. I have a sensation at the present moment as though I was dissolving. I should be exquisitely miserable without the hope of soon seeing you. Love is my religion. I could die for that. I could die for you." Keats's fiancé adores *Frankenstein*, and that Christmas is the happiest day of her life. As her act of the feast day's magic, Keats's fiancé copies out his love poem to her on the Day of St. Agnes. Keats writes to his love, "I have two luxuries to brood over in my walks, your loveliness and the hour of my death. O that I could have possession of them both in the same minute."

Yet, in two tragic months, Keats contracts advanced tuberculous and breaks off his arduous, cursed engagement. He will die in a year. During Keats's last summer, Percy invites him to move to Pisa and live with his bold family. "Consumption is a disease particularly fond of people who write such good verses as you have done." Expecting Keats's arrival,

Shelley intends to be the physician of his soul. He writes to Keats, "I feel persuaded that you are capable of the greatest things, so you will be. Avoid system and mannerism. Excel me." After revealing the influence of Shelley's *Alastor* in his *Endymion*, Keats responds to Shelley, "Load every rift of your subject with ore. My imagination is a monastery, and I am its monk. The thought of such discipline must fall like cold chains upon you, who *perhaps* never sat with your wings furled for six months together. Therefore, there are four seasons in the mind of man: his lusty Spring, his Summer of dreaming heavenly high, his soul's Autumn of idleness—when his wings furleth close—and his Winter of pale misfeature."

~STICKY P.

"'But he doesn't write any great lines. Tell me one of his verses that stick in your memory like Keats's. See there, you can't do it. And what kind of a poet is a man who can't make lines to stick in your head?'"

SCOTT

Although Keats ultimately declines to live with the Shelleys in Pisa, he *had* intended fruitful visits with them in Italy. Though—during their last scholarly stroll in England—Keats had felt that Shelley's "mind was like a pack of scattered cards," Keats closes his last warm letter to Percy, "in the hope of still seeing you." Notably, Shelley writes to the editor of the vicious review against Keats's *Endymion*. "Surely the poem is a very remarkable production for a man of

Keats's age, and the promise of ultimate excellence is such as has rarely been afforded even by such who have attained high literary imminence. There was no danger that it should become a model to the age of false taste, which, I confess, it has rather replenished. You have embittered his existence." Shelley comforts Keats, writing him, "This people, in general, will not endure, which is the cause of the few copies of yours that have been sold."

During his last autumn, Keats sends Shelley his newly published volume of poetry—*Lamia, Isabella, The Eve of St. Agnes, and Other Poems*. To Shelley, this relished book of Keats's poems is his "dark paradise of happy gloom." Published after Keats had only been writing poetry for five years, it is the height of the Romantics. Keats's eminent book receives flattering reviews, but Keats will not live to bask in them, and Shelley will drown with this book in less than two years. When Keats's blood vessels rupture in his lungs, he recognizes his dark arterial blood as his "death warrant." Before Keats's miserable voyage to Italy, he is passionately restrained from his heartbreaking attempt to kill himself.

~PRESAGER

"The excellence of every Art is its intensity." "When an immortal like Keats makes a mistake, that too is immortal."

"'Isn't this the hour when most people die—between now and morning?'

'Shh! What's that?'

'A bird.'

'Do you suppose he suspects anything?'"

SCOTT

Shelley and other poets defend Keats in their own reviews, countering the foul pair of "slanderous abuses." Shelley appeals to the reviewers' "humanity and justice"—to acknowledge the Latin proverb that "it is right to be taught by one's enemy." Shelley cites promising passages from *Endymion* and exhorts their attention to Keats's second book of poems. Singularly, Shelley solicits their "special attention" to *Hyperion*. Although Shelley lauds that "the great proportion of this piece is surely in the very highest style of poetry," Keats had been anxious to include it in his masterful second volume because of its poetics of "monumentality" and its lack of his method of negative capability.

Responses of other poets are published in the Press. "The very passages which the reviews quote as ridiculous have in them the beauty that sent us to the poem itself." Keats's promoter strikes back with his own *ad hominem* assaults. "The poem that evinces more natural power than any other work of this day is abused and cried down in terms which would ill grace any other pen. No one but a 'government-critic' could, with a false and remorseless pen, have striven to frustrate hopes and aims so youthful and so high as this young poet nurses. Reviewers are creatures that 'stab men in the dark'—and young, enthusiastic spirits are their dearest prey."

"We see glimpses of a high mind in this young man, and surely the feeling is better that urges us to nourish its strength than that which prompts a reviewer to crush it in its youth—and forever. Does the author of such poetry as this deserve to be made the sport of so servile a dolt? Malice is a thing of the scorpion kind—it drives the sting into its own heart. If he could not *feel*, he ought to know better." Subsequently, Shelley's fatal crossing in his *Ariel* had been to return from joining his and Keats's joint-promoter on his arrival to Italy—in order to commence, with Lord Byron, their own rivaling literary journal.

Keats's youth and hopes are desolated during his migration from England to Italy. He arrives in the Gulf of Naples on his tormented twenty-fifth birthday. Keats writes to his last friend. "I wish for death every day and night to deliver me from these pains, and then, I wish death away—for death would destroy even those pains which are better than nothing. Land and sea and weakness and decline are great separators, but death is the great divorcer forever. When the pang of this thought has passed through my mind, I may say the *bitterness* of death is passed. I think without my mentioning it, for my sake, you would be a friend to my love when I am dead. You think she has many faults—but, for my sake, think she has not one. If there is anything you can do for her by word or deed, I know you will do it." Keats will write nothing more. In less than four months, he will die in Rome.

A week before Keats dies, Shelley writes, "If *Hyperion* be not grand poetry, none has been produced by our contemporaries." On the death of Keats, Shelley feels it is the reviewers that had tragically destroyed his genius. "These wretched men know not what they do. Without heed, their poisoned shafts light on hearts made callous by many blows—or those of more penetrable stuff." The year before Percy Bysshe's own outlandish death, he publishes his greatest accomplishment—*Adonais*—his immortalizing masterwork elegy to Keats, his noble pastoral of triumphal, despairing lament. Before acquiring his fateful *Ariel*, Shelley tours Ravenna and writes at Dante's tomb. Although Shelley recognizes—and praises—portions of higher poetics in Byron and in Keats, he contemplates the ultimate superiority of Dante's epic to be more than any of their own.

~PROFOUND PUZZLES

"In the last century, literary reputations took some time to solidify. First, they were esoteric with a group of personal claqueurs. Later, they came into a dim rippling vogue. Their contemporaries 'tried to read one of their books' and were puzzled and suspicious. Finally, some academic critic would learn from his betters that they were 'the thing' and shout the news aloud with a profound air of discovery."

SCOTT

Byron, Shelley, and Keats—all three men leave England for Italy and all three men will die young. During Keats's first year of writing poetry, he composes "To Lord Byron": "O'ershadowing sorrow doth not make thee less / Delightful: thou thy griefs dost dress / With a bright halo, shining beamily; / As when a cloud a golden moon doth veil." A few years later, Byron says, "I'm always battling with the Snake about Keats and wonder what he finds to make a god of in that idol of the Cockneys—and why he does not make himself one," considering Keats "a tadpole" of the Lakers. Byron denounces "Johnny Keats's piss-a-bed poetry" to be "Bedlam visions produced by raw pork and opium."

Godwin, in his *Thoughts on Man*, wrote, "Shakespeare, amongst all his varied characters has not attempted to draw a perfect man—as Pope wrote, 'A perfect man's a thing the world ne'er saw.'" In the Press, concerning the poetry of Alexander Pope, there is a brief controversy between Byron, Keats, and others. Keats had criticized the aristocratic sound of Pope's neoclassical, rhyming, end-stopped couplets "so tame and pleasing to conservative tastemakers"—"musty laws" well-bridled and saddled for a "rocking horse" that critics "misname Pegasus." L. B. had emulated Pope's "heroic couplets" in his own early poetry and defends Pope against attacks on Augustan poetry. Conversely, Byron writes to Shelley, "You know my opinion of that second-hand school of poetry, but I am very sorry to hear what you say of Keats—is it *actually* true? I would rather he had been seated on the highest peak of Parnassus than have perished in such a manner. Poor fellow! I have published a pamphlet on the Pope controversy, which you will not like. Had I known that Keats was dead—or that he was alive and so sensitive—I should have omitted some remarks upon his poetry to which I was provoked by his attack upon Pope and my disapprobation of *his own* style of writing. Yet, man should calculate his powers of resistance before he goes into the arena." Even so, Shelley frequently reminds Albe that *the Lord* Byron never has to experience the artistic frustrations borne from the methodical, targeted neglect of the critics, and, poignantly, Shelley composes *Adonais* in the stanza form that Keats had praised in his first poem.

~TO: TASK / FROM: KEATS

"A man's life of any worth is a continual allegory—and very few eyes can see the mystery of his life. Lord Byron cuts a figure—but he is not figurative. Shakespeare led a life of allegory, and his works are the comments on it. You speak of Lord Byron and me. There is this great difference between us. He describes what he sees, and I describe what I imagine. Mine is the hardest task."

SCOTT

"Both were victims to the envenomed shafts of invidious critics." Defending Keats's epics—and his own—Shelley pens *Adonais*. "The savage review blighted his young bud—sweet dust to the dust.

My solemn and exalted tone, I have dipped my pen in consuming fire to chastise his destroyers." "Thou wert the morning star among the living, / Ere thy fair light had fled; / Now, having died, thou art as Hesperus, giving / New splendor to the dead." Shelley coins his term "Adonais" from both the Greek term concerning the cult of Adonis and from transferring this Greek term into the Hebrew process of becoming deified, conflating "Adonis" with "Adonai," memorializing Keats's focus of metamorphosis from his epics.

~ROSILY

"I think all the reviews I've seen, except two, have been absolutely stupid and lousy. Someday, they'll eat grass, by God! This thing, both the effort and the result, have hardened me, and I think now that I'm much better than any of the young Americans without exception. If it will support me with no more intervals of trash, I'll go on as a novelist. If not, I'm going to quit, come home, and go learn the movie business. I can't reduce our scale of living and I can't stand this financial insecurity. Anyhow, there's no point in trying to be an artist if you can't do your best. I had my chance to start my life on a sensible scale and I lost it, and so, I'll have to pay the penalty. I was growing rather tired of being a popular author. When people go wrong after one tragic book, it is because they never had any real egos or attitudes—but only empty bellies and cross nerves. The bellies full and the nerves soothed with vanity, they see life rosily and would be violently insincere in writing anything but the happy trash that they do."

SCOTT

"In this elegy, it is my intention to subjoin to London a criticism upon the claims of its lamented object to be classed among the writers of the highest genius who have adorned our age." Seven months after the death of Keats, Shelley contends, "*Adonais*, in spite of its mysticism, is the least imperfect of my compositions. It is the image I wish it to be for the regret and honor of poor Keats."

~ALLEGORICAL MASKS

"There never was a good biography of a good novelist. There couldn't be. He is too many people if he's any good."

SCOTT

Shelley writes, "For my part, I little expected when I last saw Keats that I should survive him. In spite of his transcendent genius, Keats never was, nor ever will be, a popular poet. The total neglect and obscurity in which the astonishing remnants of his mind still lie were hardly to be dissipated by a writer who, however he may differ from Keats in more important qualities, at least resembles him in the accidental one—a want of popularity. I have little hope, therefore, that the poem I send you will excite any attention, nor do I feel assured that a critical notice of his writings would find a single reader." As Shelley enters his last year, he writes, "I wish I had something better to do than furnish this jingling food for the hunger of oblivion—called *verse*—but I have not."

~LEFTOVERS

"'Well,' I said, 'have you found it?'

Shutting the book and going to the window, he replied, 'No, I have lost it.' He deeply sighed, 'I have lost a day.'

'What is this?' I asked as I was going out of the room, pointing to one of his bookshelves with a plate containing bread and cold meat on it.

'That—*coloring*—why that must be my dinner. It's very foolish. I thought I'd eaten it. The day is gone, and all its sweets are gone!'"

SCOTT

Although Shelley considers a brief refrain, he goes ahead. "My torpid faculties are shaken to atoms. I can write nothing. If *Adonais* has no success and excites no interests, what incentive can I have to write? The man must be enviably happy whom *reviews* can make miserable. I have neither curiosity, interest, pain, pleasure, nor good, nor evil in what they can say of *me*. I feel only a slight disgust and a sort of wonder that they presume to write *my name*. I value neither the fame they can give nor the fame they can take away—therefore, blessed be the name of the reviews. What motives have I to write? I had motives and I thank the god of my own heart that they were totally different from those of the other apes of humanity who make mouths in the glass of the time. I detest all society. I am glad that my good genius has said, 'refrain.' I see little public virtue. I foresee the contest is between blood and gold."

Still, throughout his last two years, Shelley composes the majority of all of his best short poems, culminating in his mighty longer work, *Triumph of Life*. Here, Shelley recreates the parade of the triumphal chariot that's carved into the Arches of Titus at the Roman Forum. His visionary, variable image of "the Chariot" dominates his last poem as "the triumph" of this Roman ritual—the procession of conquest that *Life* achieves over all people, ideals, and dignities—in a moving, malevolent carnival of masked, historical, and demonical macabre figures. All of its Dantean onlookers and partakers are fruitlessly destroyed by the hallucinatory, protean Chariot—altering and shifting in distortions of misleading, mutable light.

Janus, the leader of *Life*, in his shifting military of four faces returns ever successful from war—from his rolling history of refusing the hopes of imagination to be fulfilled. His *triumphs* are devastations, culminating in the triumph of Time. All the romantic ideals of revolution fail. The wolves and leopards will not lie with the kids and lambs. The oppressors shall not dwell with the oppressed. No matter the prayers, the predators prey on their quarries. "And what a tyrant thou art, / And what slaves these; and what a world we make, / The oppressor and the oppressed."

~NOW SEEMS

"The noble and the proud would feel their stars and honors dwindle into baubles and child's play. *This* we say if he is alive. After a little wonder and a little shuddering, he finds himself *the dead alive*—finding no affinity between himself and the present state of things. He bids once more an eternal farewell to the sun. Followed to his grave by wandering villagers, he sleeps the true death-sleep of his twice-buried remains."

"A year before he had poured into verse all such ideas about death as to give it a glory of its own, he had, as it now seems, almost anticipated his own destiny. There is much in his *Adonais* which seems now more applicable to Shelley himself than to the young and gifted poet whom he mourned. The poetic view he takes of death and the lofty scorn he displays towards his calumniators are as a prophecy on his own destiny when received among immortal names, and the poisonous breath of critics vanishes into emptiness before the fame he inherits."

SCOTT

Keats is buried with a lock of his love's hair in a plot a few yards from the grave of Wilmouse Shelley. Next to their Wilmouse, Mary inters Percy's ashes in the summer cemetery of protestants—as names momentarily "writ in water"—under the pyramidal tomb of ancient, shattered Rome. However, of Keats's headstone, Shelley had consciously repurposed his wary epitaph—not of flowing unto evaporation, but as immortally frozen in ice. "Death, the immortalizing winter, flew / Athwart the stream— and time's printless torrent grew / A scroll of crystal, blazoning the name / Of Adonais!"

In winter—as if not bound to remain the things of Caesar—this desolate graveyard is covered in violets and daisies that *star* the dark earth, spreading like the light of an infant's smile that might make one in love with death. His epitaph—"Heart of Hearts" in Latin—adorns Shelley's headstone above lyrics from "Ariel's Song" in Shakespeare's last play. "Nothing of him that doth fade, / But doth suffer a sea-change / Into something rich and strange."

~IVY ETERNAL

"From his grave, the dome of the Capitol blotted out the setting sun. The flowers wilted, and the children planted jasmine vines and hyacinths. It was peaceful in the old cemetery. Wildflowers grew there, and there were rosebushes so old that the flowers had lost their color with the years. Crape myrtle and Lebanon cedars shed their barbs over the slabs. Rusty Confederate crosses sank into the clematis vines and burned the grass. Tangles of narcissus and white flowers strayed the washed banks, and ivy climbed in the crumbling walls."

SCOTT

"Our loved and lovely Italy appears a tomb, and its

sky appears a pall. His unearthly and elevated nature is a pledge of the continuation of his being, although in an altered form. Rome received his ashes. They are deposited beneath its weed-grown wall, and 'the world's sole monument' is enriched by his remains." Shelley's adventuring friend—who will also be buried here later—memorializes, "At his grave, where the souls of heretics are foredoomed by the Roman priests, I planted eight upright seedling cypresses. I saw them more than twenty years later, and seven remained—about thirty-five feet in height"—seven signaling towers of homage.

~FEAR NOT THINE OWN WELL

"And he is gathered to the kings of thought / Who waged contention with their time's decay, / And of the past are all that cannot pass away." "Here, pause. These graves are all too young as yet / To have outgrown the sorrow which consigned / Its charge to each; and if the seal is set, / Here, on one fountain of a mourning mind, / Break it not thou! Too surely shalt thou find / Thine own well full, if thou returnest home, / Of tears and gall. From the world's bitter wind, / Seek shelter in the shadow of the tomb. / What Adonais *is*, why fear we to become?"

(78.) <u>Sonnet 116</u>

~ENTRENCH

"Solitude is my only help and resource. I can at those moments forget myself until some idea—which I think I would communicate to *him*—occurs. Then, the yawning and dark gulf again displays itself unshaded by the rainbows which the imagination has formed. Despair, energy, love, despondency, and the excessive affliction are like clouds driven across my mind, one by one, until tears blot the scene and weariness of spirit consigns me to temporary repose. Each day adds to the stock of sorrow. Death is the only end. 'Usefulness'—accept as far as regards my child—and 'fame' are all nullities to me.

Yet, I shall be happy if anything I ever produce may exalt and soften sorrow. But how can I aspire to *that*? The world will surely feel one day what it has lost when this bright child of song deserted her. Is not *Adonais* his own elegy? How lovely does he paint death to be. With what heartfelt sorrow does one repeat that line—"But I am chained to time and cannot thence depart." I am now on the eve of completing my five and twentieth year—how drearily young for one so lost as I! The eight years I passed with him was spun out beyond the usual length of a man's life—in what I have suffered since will write years on my brow and entrench them in my heart. Most sure should I be—were it not for my boy. I live to make his early years happy."

SCOTT

Fame is fatal. As Godwin had endured at the death of Wollstonecraft, Mary now suffers abusive detractions in the Press. Like her mother's death, her husband's death is popularized as a form of divine judgment.

Receiving the ruthless news of his *Shiloh*, Byron asserts, "another man is gone about whom the *world* was ill-naturedly, and ignorantly, and brutally *mistaken*. I have seen nothing like him, and never shall again, I am certain." Before Percy dies, the first translation of Mary's novel is published in French—*Frankenstein; ou le Prométhée moderne.*

~GHOSTS OF GHOSTS

"I awoke with a horrible effort from a dream of Italian beggars. I could understand at last why the French loved France. They have seen Italy. We had been to Oxford before—after Italy we went back there arriving gorgeously at twilight when the place was fully peopled for us by the ghosts of ghosts— the characters, romantic, absurd or melancholy. But something was wrong now—something that would never be right again. In how many years would our descendants approach this ruin with supercilious eyes to buy postcards? Money follows the rich lands and the healthy stock, and art follows—begging after money. How soon? Your time will come, New York, fifty years, sixty. Apollo's head is peering crazily in new colors that our generation will never live to know—over the tip of the next century."

SCOTT

"Now my boy is all that is left to me—and a thousand recollections which never sleep." After her tragic losses, Mary commits to being a professional author and single mother, writing of herself, "I think I can maintain myself, and there is something inspiriting in the idea." In the last three years, Mary has written two poetical dramas of myths and two other novels. "Both of them were of the race of artists—pursuing the inner designs that demanded much of them—and married to the writing life as much as to each other." To cement Shelley's notoriety, Mary arranges for his works from Italy to be published, but these efforts are quickly suppressed by his father, leveraging Mary's duties in securing her future prospects for Persino against her duties as a widow.

At Shelley's death, Ianthe resumes her life with Harriett's parents, and Charles is raised by Shelley's parents as their baronet-in-waiting, disallowing any biographical blights to be published against the landed Shelley family—against the Baronetage. Mary *Shelley* is now the same age as Keats was as he had arrived in Italy to die. Although Mary succeeds in preventing the attempts of Shelley's father to assume guardianship of Persino, Mary laments, "It is past. I am returning to England. I have lost my hopes of utility and glory. I have lost."

At Shelley's death, Godwin had written Mary, "This sorrowful event is perhaps calculated to draw us nearer. Perhaps now we shall mutually derive consolation from each other." A year after Percy Bysshe has died, Mary and their son return to London—to her indefatigable father and his social circle. Mary continues to paint, and Godwin is completing his two lengthy meditations on Stoicism—on misery, death, the brevity of human life, and the longevity of true worth. Mary journals. "As we arrive at the wharf, I am reminded of the northern land of infinite light—land now confirmed *darkness*. Father greets us, and Persino plays about the deck in high glee." Godwin is enchanted with Persino's unique mix of fluency—his blend of Italian with English—and Godwin informs Mary that the term "Frankenstein" is becoming a household word.

"Lo and behold," Mary writes, "I found myself famous." This summer—with "Mary W. Shelley" as the author—Godwin himself edits and publishes the second English edition of her famed novel, maintaining that it is the most wonderful work to have ever been written by anyone at nineteen years of age. As Godwin is editing and revising Mary's third novel, her first novel is alluded to in a political speech at Parliament as "the splendid fiction of a recent Romance." Together, Mary and Godwin enjoy the misrepresentative staged version of her admonitory text and its "anonymous androdaemon." Forever adapted in superficial form, the first reproving play is entitled *Presumption, Or the Fate of Frankenstein*. On the stage this same year, there are five other runs from various adaptations of her novel—her novel that has initiated two new genres into fiction. When

Frankenstein was first published anonymously, C. D. Friedrich painted his Romantic masterwork *Wanderer above the Sea of Fog*, and once *Frankenstein* is staged, he paints his greatest work *The Polar Sea*—both of which will become the cover art adorning future republications of Mary's first novel.

~LOST

"As I return, I feel as I am a ruin from where the singing birds are lost. Drearily, the rain splashes on the pavement. I look upward, and the blotted sky tells me only of my changes. I hardly feel pleasure for cultivation, but I will pine for it again. This is life. All is so changed. The new, grating, vulgar voices of English are so displeasing. In this world, it always seems one's duty is to sacrifice one's *own* desires—and this claim ever appears the strongest which claims such sacrifice. Yet, I resolve to not think on such certainties, but to take all as a matter of course—and thus contrive to keep myself out of the gulf—the edge—of melancholy."

SCOTT

From her third novel, Mary's abandoned heroine questions "What is the world except what we feel?" Having written this novel in the Godwinian manner, Mary's lead is an aristocrat similar to St. Leon and Mandeville who sacrifices love for ambition and becomes a tyrant. As Mary is sketching attempts in different genres, Mary offers Godwin her third novel "to make the best of it" and to retain the proceeds from its publication. Although Godwin is impressed with the novel as he modifies it, he humorously complains to Mary of its length. "No hard blow was ever hit with a woolsack!" "The ultimate business of education," Godwin writes, "is to enable us to govern ourselves with steady severity." Mary is contemplating her fourth novel and delivers her working manuscript of a tragedy to Godwin, seeking his advice.

~GEOMETRIC TEARS

"To read your specimens, I should suppose that you had read no tragedies but such as have been written since the date of your birth. Your personages are mere abstractions—the lines and points of a mathematical diagram—and not men and women. If A *crosses* B, and C *falls upon* D, who can weep for that?"

— Godwin to Mary

SCOTT

Mary becomes resolved to live on her own terms and will write her post-Godwinian works. From her own howling creature—in which *I* also confirm dearest Zelda's creatureliness—is labored their mutual assertion, "beware, for I am fearless and therefore powerful." Her fourth novel will illustrate the dangers of egalitarianism—its levelling chaos staged as a plague—that erases "the patrician spirit, the gentle courtesies, the refined pursuits, and the splendid attributes of rank." As Mary is envisioning the rapid devastations of civilization as her new setting, Godwin is writing his eminent volumes on the *History of the Commonwealth.* "Giving work to the industrious," Mary writes, as she pursues her literary labors, "is one of the best ways in the world of doing good." In London, the accent has changed. It is loud, flat, and full of money.

~THE GREAT PICKPOCKET

"And, oh! That quickening of the heart, that beat / How much it costs us! Yet each rising throb / Is in its cause, as its effects, so sweet, / That wisdom is ever on the watch to rob / Joy of its alchemy."

SCOTT

As she is developing the characters for her fourth novel, Lord Byron dies as he is funding insurgents in Greece, and Mary views his body in England before he's buried. "The sword, the flag, the battlefield, / The dead Spartan carried on his shield was not more free than I." Even though he is considered the best poet of his days, L. B. is denied burial in Westminster Abbey. In leaving Italy to join and source Greek rebels for their independence, the best of Byron's mind had been a tribute to Shiloh—the Eagle of Greece—opposing "custom's hydra brood," the "One Power of many shapes," the "One Shape of many names."

~PISTOLS FROM ANIMAL HOUSE

"Death-dealing in a turbaned masquerade . . . and a

nice judge in the age and smack of wine."

SCOTT

Mary now feels like a sole survivor—"the last relic of a beloved race," her "companions extinct." Although Mary's memorial article on Bryon is declined for publication, she is commemorating the competitive collaborations of Shelley and their Albe in the drafts of her upcoming novel. Yet, now clearly understanding the devastation that "biographical sincerity" provides, Mary and Godwin effectively persuade a journalist to avoid printing recently discovered love letters from Wollstonecraft to a famous artist—of "reptile vanity"—whom Wollstonecraft was passionate for in London as she was leaving for Paris.

After Godwin's Juvenile Library closes, Mary's next best novel, *The Last Man*, is published, further originating a third genre for works of fiction. Mary's lead in this story is another double of Shelley—in a better version of his more *arrived* qualities—metamorphosing her first portrait of him as "Victor." The year this book is published, Charles Bysshe Shelley is struck by lightning, and Mary's Persino is made a public person of consequence as heir presumptive of the Shelley baronetcy. On the tombstone of Charles, he is listed not as the son of Shelley, but as the grandson of Sir and Lady Shelley. Questioning the uncertainty of her fate, Mary finds no security in Persino's promotion and is paranoid that their days are numbered by a cruel destiny.

Responding to Mary's glum musings, Godwin writes, "How differently are you and I organized! In my seventy-second year, I am all cheerfulness and never anticipate the evil day with distressing feelings—till to do so is absolutely unavoidable. Would to God you were my daughter in all but my poverty, but I am afraid you are *a* Wollstonecraft."

~THRUST YOUR SWORD INTO HIS HEART, MARGARET

"Let us learn what love is in learning what a poet is. The mind requires more contribution than even our corporeal frame. Ennui is the offspring of plenty and comfort. While we contrive to shut out the evil elements, listlessness and weariness pervade the soul and *pale* every enjoyment. Though *they* waste the time–professions, trades, ambitions, employments of pleasure—even the delightful pursuits of wisdom and the engrossing discoveries of science are inefficient to take the *sting* from life. This miracle is left for the affections. The best form of affection—from the excess of its sympathy—is love. The spirit of love is most powerful in the best and most delicate natures. In its greatest purity and force, is not a poet an incarnation of the very essence of love?

Love restores voids. The beauty of the object resides in *his* eyes—instead of in *her* mind or form. There's something rugged, harsh, and unnatural in a man whose fate is not allied to a female from whatever cause is devested of every poetical attribute. Thus, worthiness of the beloved object must stand as an excuse for inconstancy—or, for the poet, the fervency in the truth of his passion. A woman's love is tenderness—and *may* wed itself to the lost and dead. A man's love is passion—and *must* expend itself on the living. We know no cause—in reason and morality, and hardly in good taste—which should condemn the lovely, bereaved, and ardent heart to perpetual widowhood. When a woman finds one man on whom she may bestow—without sorrow—her tenderness, it is very unlikely that losing him, she will find a second."

SCOTT

As Mary writes Godwin that she is assiduously writing "every morning," she is now the same age as Shelley at his death. She soon writes to her friend, "Alas, my twenties have now passed, I am already old." Researching histories and manners for her fifth novel, Mary visits Paris. Through the Garnett social circle, she meets General Lafayette and later writes him, "the hero of three revolutions," referencing Shelley's efforts for freedom, "the lyrist liberty made life a lyre." In London, before and after Paris, Mary corresponds with the reformer Frances Wright. The year Byron had died, Frances Wright had accompanied General Lafayette to the U. S. and is now inviting Mary to join her in a utopian community that she has started in West Tennessee. The year after Frances was born—and a year before Mary was born—Tennessee was granted statehood, joining the Union. Though, when Frances abandons Lafayette's last tour of the U. S.—as she had endured the constant praises of Lafayette as the "Champion of

Liberty" amongst U. S. slaveholders—she purchases communal land to educate and prepare slaves for emancipation. Founding this new community on the edge of the settled world, Frances envisions her methods to be applied throughout the States. Wanting to recruit Mary as the symbol of the continuance of Godwin and Shelley, Frances founds her community on the tenants of *Political Justice* and publishes the first American version of *Queen Mab*. Although Lafayette is a trustee of Frances's enterprise, Mary declines her kindred invitation to Tennessee.

~FANNY FOR FREEDOM

Named after the native word for the Wolf River—Nashoba—a tributary of the Mississippi, this town is later charted as Germantown, a suburb of Memphis in West Tennessee. During the Great War, the town returned to its name from Frances Wright—Nashoba—in protest against Germany and in tribute to "Fanny" for having personally freed the thirty-one slaves in her woodland test-trial for liberation.

~QUEEN MAB VISITS AMERICA

"He was arraigned, tried, and convicted of heterodoxy, which was enough to justify—in the world's eyes—the murder of his reputation. This is the man against whom much clamor has been raised by poor prejudiced fools and by those who live and lap under their tables. This is the man whom—from one false story about his former wife—I had refused to visit at Pisa! I blush in anguish at my prejudice and injustice. Yet, it is not as a poet that Shelley's character appears in its fairest light. It is as a high-minded reformer, as an unbending lover of truth, as an enthusiastic friend of human improvement. He was one of those pure beings who seem to be born some ages before their time—whose high aspirations after excellence scarcely belong to this generation."

~TENNESSEE UNVISITED

"Of myself, I have little to say. I have added three years to my life since I saw you. As alive as I am, such a fact says *also* that I have enjoyed and suffered many things. My enjoyments show themselves outwardly on the surfaces of things. My son is well—developing talents and excellent qualities enough to satisfy almost my maternal desires. My father is well—enjoying a most green old age. These are the circumstances to gild my life with permanent sunshine. Yet, ah, my Fanny, life is a toil and a cheat. I love it not. If I could live in a more genial climate, it would be something, but here in my island-prison, I sigh for the sun and a thousand delights associated with it—from which I am cut off forever. My youth is wasted, my hopes die, I feel *fail* within me all the incentives to existence, and I cling to my child as my sole tie. Yours is a brighter lot, a nobler career. Heaven bless you in it and reward you. You have chosen the wiser path, and I congratulate you."

SCOTT

As Godwin completes his sixth novel, Mary also

completes her fifth novel for publication. The next year, Mary writes the biographical sketch of her father once his most famous novel—Mary, Percy, and Byron's favorite novel of *any* author—is republished for wider readerships. The antagonist of Godwin's novel will soon be the inspiration for Inspector Javert in *Les Misérables*. "Man only," Mary quotes, "is the common foe of man." "The principal object of his study and contemplation is 'man, the enemy of man.'" Mary continues, praising the aesthetics of her father's art and the self-analyses of his characters.

This same year—as Godwin's republication—Mary revises and then sells her copyright of *Frankenstein* for its third edition in English. In her introductions to both republished novels, Mary credits Godwin as the influential link to the heavy authors who will become known as the British Romantics. Though the basic ideas of both of these novels had been stated in formal treatises of their age, it is the additional imaginative poetics of Shelley that significantly amplify the persuasive art from both of these "novels of purpose" to appeal to "the common reader" in addressing "Things as They Are." More than three thousand copies of *Frankenstein* are ordered at its reissue, and *The Literary Gazette* boosts the novel's popularity with its own influential review of "vigorous interest sustained to the last."

In the success of The Great Reform Bill, there is viable, palpable spreading of Shelley's influences throughout British society, flourishing the "enlightened" concepts that were repressed during the revolutionary wars and their reactionary period. "One by one, the nations take up the echo"—of the Romantics—"and mine will not be the last." As the epigraph to his seventh novel, Godwin quotes a couplet from Pope, "Why that bosom gored? / Why dimly gleans the visionary sword?" Throughout this novel, Godwin offers vigorous reflections on morality, corruption, error, and passion. The daughter of his title character laments, "Oh, why have not human creatures a confidence in the force of truth and justice?" Continuing his voluminous histories and erudite essays, Godwin is soon recognized by the reformed governance of England and given a pensioned post by the Prime Minister. In his office at the Houses of Parliament, Godwin appears "so comfortable" with "a salary, a dwelling, and coals and candle" that he has "evidently no mind to die." During these radical rectifications, Mary is now the same age as Byron in his final heroic year, and Coleridge dies.

In her sixth novel, Mary first memorializes her sister Fanny, their mother, and Fanny's favorite aristocrat, Aaron Burr. In fond harmony, "be reanimated." In her novel, Lord Lodore flees overseas to avoid a British duel, but later dies in an American duel outside New York. Before his death, he raises his daughter in America on the principles of Wollstonecraft and Godwin—by which Burr had raised his daughter. Memorializing her dead sister in this novel—as her heroine's inspiring friend—Mary writes, "Fanny zealously guarded her individuality and would've scorned herself could she have been brought to place the treasures of her soul at the exploitation of any power. She was kind, generous, true, and was guided by the tenderness of her heart." Mary reanimates Wollstonecraft as an estranged, tarnished mother who salvages her bond with her adult daughter.

As Mary is copying out Percy's poems for posterity, she is writing introductions to clusters of his works. Concerning Percy's early dedication to *Queen Mab*, Mary writes, "Poor Harriett to whose sad fate I attribute too many of my own heavy sorrows at the atonement claimed for her death." Penitent, Mary is still effectually haunted nineteen years after Harriett has died by suicide. As an act of reparation, Mary then memorializes her lead heroine's role in this penultimate novel, *Lodore*, as the double of an idealized Harriett, vying for love amidst social constraints and ensuant poverties. In sixty years, American Mark Twain will also write an essay—a legal brief—opposing the silencing and repurposing of Harriett amongst all her enemy idealists and the deceptive, artistic "cakewalk" of the biographer who will be chosen by the future Sir Shelley.

~STRANGE AND TERRIFIC

"'Even so—for my heart whispered to me that *this* was my doing. Who could recall the life that waned in your pulses—who can restore, save the Destroyer? My heart never warmed to your life as then it did to your wasted image, as it lay, in the visions of night, at my feet. A veil fell from my eyes, and a darkness was dispelled from before me. Methought I then knew for the first time what life and what death were. I was bid believe that to make the living happy was not to injure the dead and I felt how wicked and how vain was that false philosophy which placed virtue and good within hatred and unkindness. You should not die. I would loosen your chains and save you, and bid you live for love. I sprung forward, and the death I deprecated for you would, and my presumption, have been mine. Then, I first felt the real value of life—but that your arm was there to save me, your dear voice to bid me. It blest me for evermore.'"

SCOTT

Widowed for twenty-eight years and remaining with their son, Mary advances, authoring many more works. She masters Latin, French, and Italian. Godwin persists in uninspiring her to his reverent stoicism. "Godwin was versatile, he bore combined / A woman's tenderness, a Cato's mind. / Stern to himself, and rigidly severe, / He played the stoic, while he shed the tear." A year after her sixth novel, Godwin is dying in Westminster. Mary, now the same age as Wollstonecraft during her final year, sits at Godwin's bedside for days.

"Sympathy is nothing less," Godwin had written, "than the luminary of the moral world. The end of the commandment is love. The true key of the universe is love." Nursing her father as he dies, Mary laments, scrawling, "tracked by unutterable wretchedness, my heart dies within me." Across "the pond," Aaron Burr dies in obscurity five months after Godwin. Together with Wollstonecraft, Mary inters her father in the tomb under the willows where Mary had declared her love to her Shelley. At his death, Godwin had completed his final work—his twenty-first solid publication. Within the same year as Godwin's death, Mary publishes her seventh and final novel.

~KNOT

"I was brought up in great tenderness and though my mind was proud to independence, I was never led to much independence of feeling. While my mother lived, I always felt to a certain degree as if I had somebody who was my superior and who exercised a mysterious protection over me. I belonged to something. I hung to something. There is nothing that has so much reverence and religion in it as affection to parents. The knot is now severed, and I am, for the first time, at more than fifty years of age, alone."

— Godwin (at the death of his mother)

~WITHOUT

"'I'd thought you'd know why when our bodies ought to bring surcease from our tortured minds, they fail and collapse—and why, when we are tormented in our bodies, does our soul desert us as a refuge? Why do we spend years using up our bodies to nurture our minds with experience and find our minds turning then to our exhausted bodies for solace? Why, Daddy?'

'Ask me something easy,' the old man answered.

'When man is no longer custodian of his vanities and convictions, he's nothing at all,' she thought. 'Nothing! There's nothing lying on that bed—but it is my father, and I loved him. Without his desire, I should never have lived.'"

SCOTT

In bittersweet stings, Mary records the various ways her Persino resembles his father—in his living gestures and glances—throughout his pivotal years. Though, conversely, Mary resists Shelley's wish that "all" should think for themselves. "To think for himself! Oh my God, teach him to think like other people!" Mary resists inspiring any drive in Persino "to reform the world." "When I think how Shelley loved him and the plans we had for him—and his education—my boy's sweet and childish voice strikes me to the heart. Why should he live in this world of pain and anguish? The idea that my circumstances may at all injure him *is the fiercest pang* my mind endures. And, so, here I am? Although I continue to exist—to see one day succeed the other—and to dread night, but more dread morning, and hail another cheerless day. People used to call me lucky in my star. The prophecy is true. I was fearlessly placed by destiny in the hands of a superior being—a bright planetary spirit enshrined in an earthly temple—and would not change my situation as his widow with that of the most prosperous woman in the world."

Persino administrates Godwin's funeral and then attends the same university as Byron—Trinity College, Cambridge. As Byron flashed his eccentric *braggadocio* across Cambridge with his pet bear on a leash—dogs being prohibited—Persino is as tame as Mary has cultivated his temper to be brought together, "blending in" with the other young men. The next summer, Mary begins to publish all of her husband's works. Dedicating their longsuffering work to their son, Mary publishes *Poetical Works of Percy Bysshe Shelley*—as words that love but *live* no more. "The ungrateful world did not feel his loss, and the gap it made seemed to close as quickly over his memory as the murderous sea above his living frame. Although the intolerant—in their blindness—poured down anathemas, the Spirit of Good, who can judge the heart, never rejected him. I lay the first stone of the monument due to Shelley's genius, his sufferings, and his virtues."

Though, once Mary completes the publications of all of Shelley's works, she is frayed. "My strength has failed under the task. Recurrence to the past, full of its own deep and unforgotten joys and sorrows—contrasted with succeeding years of painful and solitary struggle—has shaken my health." She had been prepared to write thorough biographies of Shelley and Godwin, but she writes neither.

~SAVE ME A WALTZ OF LIGHT

Well, here's both, my frayed doll—a bit of unfinished chaos (like Byron in Greece). Chin up, forever. Send me a line if cake is still "a bit of shit"—like here.

SCOTT

The summer before her Persino graduates Cambridge, Mary journals, "There is something strange and dreamlike in returning to Italy. Though so much scenery is so familiar, *youth* has fled, and my baby boy is a man—and still I struggle on, poor and alone." Persino is developing his tastes in the delights of amateur theatre, photography, and the steam yachts that his father envisioned. Three years after Cambridge, all the *vino* of the landed gentry raises to Mary's blue-eyed Persino. Her Percy *Florence* inherits the Shelley estates and title. Just as Mary was revealed to her Bysshe in his adoration of the words of Wollstonecraft and Godwin, Jane St. John is presented to "the issue" of her own pair of literary idols. *Sir* Shelley marries Jane. Mary writes Persino, "Darling, you are very happy. So, with a thousand blessings, I am." Mary writes Jane, "My own dear child, a thousand blessings on you, my darling Jane. I know you will make Percy happy. Please God, you will be happy together." Afterward, for all their remaining years, masterminds Jane and Mary work to fashion and enshrine Shelley's reputation.

~TERMS

Shelley is sometimes lampooned "as a grateful, frail flower or some pantomime Ariel," *but* he had a psychic nature and such a spiritual gaze that are not easy to explain in any other standing—than in supernatural terms."

SCOTT

Lady Shelley and Mary sentimentally recreate Shelley as the tender lyricist rather than the severe revolutionary, canonizing him for the Victorians. Even so, Shelley's progressive efforts further sprout in other European countries in the brief freedoms, hopes, and emigrations of the Forty-Eighters. Karl Marx credits Godwin with developing the theory of exploitation, and Shelley is recognized as the foundational author of the decade of the Chartists. "Things as they are can change." This same year, as Persino, Jane, and Mary plan to move into Shelley's ancestral home, Shelley's mother strips the property bare as she leaves from fifty-seven years at Field Place. There, Mary lives in Shelley's boyhood room for a year as she and Jane arrange a small memorial museum in their last home—their manor where Persino is having a performance theatre installed.

~SCORNFUL SOLIDARITY, OLD SPORT

"In that home he was born, played as a child, dreamed as a boy, and suffered as a man—the mansion of his forefathers—I found deserted. I walked in moody sadness over the neglected shrubberies, paced the paths—weed overgrown and leaf strewn—of the once neatly kept flower gardens where we had so often walked together and talked in the confidentiality of early and unsophisticated friendship. There, too, he had in many in a solitary hour brooded over his first disappointment in love and had had his sensitive spirit *torn* by the coldness of alienation from those dearest to him. There's a flattering inscription that blazons the virtues of his father, but I was shocked to find that no cenotaph has been raised to the memory of *the* Shelley that was a poet. He lives in his works—'art inspires action.'"

~HAPPY P.

"Field Place now stands deserted and bare, / No laughter, no voices, no love lingers there. / In the heart of Field Place, the floorboards did creak / As the tortoise, the dragon, and wizard did speak. / A pact they did form, to protect and to guide / In the quietest places—this world full of magic—where mysteries are pried."

SCOTT

Fifteen years ago, Mary had written, "I was always a dependent thing—wanting fosterage and support. I am left to myself—crushed by fortune." Overlooking the wistful coast of the English Channel, Mary lives with her son and Lady Jane until her death, achieving domestic stability for the first time in her last home. Safe, warm, and contented with Sir Shelley and his wife, Mary finds the time to dry her tears. Her eyes full of strived life, Mary dies twenty-seven years younger than her father had lived. "Change and variety of wrecks and fortunes; / Till, laboring to the havens of our homes, / We struggle for the calm that crowns our ends." The next year—wealthy, yet tragically renounced by her peer activists—Frances Wright dies alone in America.

~"E" IS FOR ENGLAND

What's the difference between the grand British dream and the American? Little—except things like the spellings of grey and whiskey and crepe. Do what you're good at—enough to make a family. The great dream's a ballad, a popular song, for the populace to sing into the night about—over their popular fires—so that they can have something to be happy about when they have to wake to work as their ashes smolder.

SCOTT

Lady Jane Shelley exhumes both Godwin and Wollstonecraft, reinterring them with Mary between her eminent parents in "the Shelley tomb." In a lavish chapel a few miles from this churchyard vault, Lady Jane installs a marble monument with Mary as the Madonna—*love bears all things*—upholding Shelley's broken body. With a passage inscribed from *Adonais*, this sculpture memorializes their births and their deaths, outsoaring "that unrest which men miscall delight."

Five years after Mary dies, Keat's prequel to *Hyperion* is published, recasting his epic to illustrate a quest of moral testing to overcome the desires to avoid suffering—and to be rewarded with elevated understanding from a dream-vision at sunrise. Latterly, after publishing *Relics of Shelley*, its editor later praises Percy Bysshe's productiveness. "The work in the main—of little more than five years—it is one of the greatest marvels in the history of the human mind."

Once widowed herself, Lady Jane also arranges an incarnate reversal of our eternal one-year "Oxford Man." In his own portion of University College—in the living *irony* from his former tyrannical expulsion—Lady Jane arranges the installations of other immortal passages from *Adonais* to amplify the ornate marble sculpture commissioned to depict Shelley's death in a formal memorial cove dedicated to the passions and pains of his aspiring *pursuit*. Portrayed on her broken lyre beneath her Percy—sculpted in dark green bronze—the Muse of the Seas weeps.

A living myth arises a year after dear Mary departs into the unknown hands of her unborn critics. Opening his revered mother's private writing desk, Sir Persino Shelley finds the lovelocks of his deceased brother and sister that were treasured by Mary for thirty years—the lovelocks of his siblings whose deaths had preceded his birth. Looking further in his mother's desk, Persino also discovers a silken vessel that contains the salvaged remains of the heart of his vanished, avant-garde father. Byron had watched as this heart would not take to the boiling yellow flames of frankincense and wine.

~CLAIM

"The corpse fell open, and the heart was laid bare. The heart remained entire. In snatching this relic from the fiery furnace, my hand was severely burnt. Shelley's heart, which would not consume with his ashes, became an amiable dispute compared to that of Ajax and Ulysses for the arms of Achilles. When one of Shelley's friends put a claim on it, Byron had quipped, 'He'll only put in a glass case and make sonnets on it.'"

"I will only say that all except his heart—which was unconsumable—was burnt, and that I went and beheld a small box that contained his earthly dress. I forward the remains of him to Rome—to be buried there beside our darling boy whom we lost years ago, near whom he always desired to be placed. But he is not there—he is with me, about me—life of my life and soul of my soul. If his divine spirit did not penetrate mine, I could not survive to weep thus."

~AND CRASHING BORES

"The world is full of orphans."

SCOTT

Alongside the "Child of Love and Light," these heart vestiges of the great Romantic—in darkness and distance—are later buried with their childless son. Mary has no descendants. The lineages of Wollstonecraft and Godwin are concluded. The

Shelley baronetcy passes to Persino's cousins. Only through his estranged first child—Ianthe, whose life is framed by neglect *from* and drownings *of* her parents—does Shelley's afflicted line prophetically persist.

(79.) *<u>in the becoming</u>*

SCOTT

No personality as strong as Zelda's could go without its criticisms, and as the old pack says—from Bunny to Ernest—she's not above reproach. I've always known that, but I fell in love with her—her courage, her sincerity, and her flaming self-respect. It's these things I'd believe in even if the whole world indulged in wild suspicions. But of course, the *real* reason is that I love her, and that's the beginning and end of everything.

It is eternity that mans all the suffering admirations and longings that will not be fulfilled. It is really a happy thought, and not melancholy that I feel as I always have—closer to Zelda than any other human being—and wouldn't mind if in a few years we snuggle up together in some old graveyard and take fearful courage under the same stone of all our losses and living grief.

Reading the cardiogram tattoos of the moon, I now know that the heart repairs itself after its prices are paid for its loving. Our antics have been an illusional, heady insulation in this dark, tangling crescendo of our dissipation. We will ruin ourselves and then we will ruin each other.

~REEF YOUR SAILS

"First our pleasures die—and then / Our hopes, and then our fears—and when / These are dead, the debt is due, / Dust claims dust—and we die too."

SCOTT

Carrying around broken decalogues that we cannot read, it at least does us no harm when we turn from the neuroses of professors to the psychoses of poets, to their labors to command our language. We learn some about beauty—enough to know that it has nothing to do with truth. We learn this in the eventful death of each literary age when we listen to the lyrical punishment of each romantic craving—each unobtainable ideal, always *in the becoming* until extinguished.

~UP

"He put himself, in all modesty, in the line of greatness. He judged himself in a large way." "To write something that's unbearably beautiful, one must be associated with the losses and failures of life."

SCOTT

The luxuries of our dreams assure us we can ascend our shadows. "The aerial edifices, the crystalline palaces seemed to detach themselves from earth and to float up as though drawn by an invisible force." We promise ourselves with poetry and then we hallucinate for a spell when the ripe promising heir of a fistful of a few more decades—*unpromised*—is drowned and incinerated. Branding with the epitaph "Always the Prince, Never the King," this shadow trance is a nativity for those who feel they must make a life out of ink. *Tap. Tap. Tap.*

Less than two years after Mary died, my father was born. A few years before I was born, the monument of Shelley was installed at Oxford, and both of my siblings had already perished. After I was thoroughly a toddling two-year-old, old Lady Jane Shelley had just died. I was born with the wealth of the knowing aura of the fragility and brevity of all things. From my gilded mother's ledger, the first word that I spoke was "up"—young Francis Scott *up, up, and away*!

Shelley's grandfather had started from New Jersey. In my first year of prep school in New Jersey, I pitched for the second-string baseball team, wrote my comic operas, got into debating, and read *Frankenstein* as it was first published in America. I didn't know until I was fifteen that there was anyone in the world except me—and it cost *me* plenty. My glorious mother wagered the last of her inheritance from my grandfather's enterprise to ensure my tenure in private school—and later at Burr's Princeton—as I will do all I must to ensure Scottie will have her fresh dance with old, menacing American Chance.

Not wanting to appear ill with priggishness, the Admissions Board of Princeton had let me in when

I told them *why* they should—which was "because it's my birthday." Although I keep *up* with the times, time's up. The first movement *is* joy, but it is taken away—"to whose frail frame no second motion brings one mood or modulation like the last." There are no second acts. "France was a land, England was a people, but America, having about it still that quality of 'the idea,' was harder to utter. It was the graves at Shiloh, Tennessee, and the tired, drawn, nervous faces of its great men, and the country boys dying in the Argonne for a phrase that was empty before their bodies withered."

I have lost my splendid mirage, and the conjuror's hat is empty. From the roof of the last and most magnificent of towers, I see that Manhattan is not an endless succession of manmade canyons of achievement. It fades out into the suffering of the country on all sides, into an ancient expanse of green and blue—seeing aware the old island here that flowered once for sailors' eyes as the fresh green breast of the New World. The American Dream is a spirit, and I fill my ears with cotton balls to dampen its enchanting ballad. As the ship we have shared is sinking, I find this spirit as a cloven-footed lover whose false riches dissolve.

Although beauty is a hysteria that must not be renounced, beauty can be taken. Before my eyes, the dream was gone. It had existed. It exists no longer. I wanted to care more than I did, but there was no beauty but the gray battleship beauty of steel that withstands all time.

Like old Eckleburg with eyes dimmed by paintless days under sun and rain, I can now see the desolate valley where ashes take the forms of men who move dimly—already crumbling through the powdery air. I see this blurred vale, bounded by a small foul river, and, when the drawbridge is raised above this haze, the passengers—like now myself—on halted, waiting trains stare at the dismal scene of the ash-gray men swarming up with their leaden spades and hideous vocation.

My own performance in a magician's show when I was nine was the third-best acting I'd seen in theatre. Outside theatre, with tender flowing sentences, I was the magician that could write myself out of misery and out of debt, but the magic has chosen another sorcerer. The willingness of the heart alters, the silver cord is cut, and the golden bowl is broken. Zelda is the only god I have left. I was raised Catholic, yet since Princeton, I close my eyes and I can feel oblivion's extermination nearing. Like wilting humid in winter, a writer not writing is a maniac—jazz without bones.

~FAIR CREATURE OF AN HOUR

"Before my pen has gleaned my teeming brain,
When I behold, upon the night's starred face,
Huge cloudy symbols of a high romance,

And think that I may never live to trace

Their shadows with the magic hand of chance

And never have relish in the faery power

Of unreflecting love—then, on the shore

Of the wide world, I stand alone and think

Till love and fame to nothingness do sink."

SCOTT

Maxwell had first rejected my *Romantic Egoist* because "the hero failed to discover either himself or his ideal mate." Then, I made my mantras. My second declaration was to become the great lover man. That's been edited. Someone else has grabbed that wheel of words. Equally, the last of my heroic duty was sadistically beaten from me after my curiosity had shifted to disgust when studying a pair of savage Cuban gamecocks trying to kill each other. Yet, I remain the great novel-man, avowed. I must muster my utmost into mastery. Write, man! Write through the curves and panic. Keep your hands on the wheel, Scott-boy—every pure hour of every clean day—this typewriter staying me in the lines. Keep naïve—denial and smile like all the sad young men that arrive wistful to this abortive world. Keep typing, typing anthems of nice people that give out waves of interest and laughter—back and forth—across the hearths of their happy fires.

(80.) *the green cistern*

~SCOTT KEATS

"Keats's sayings about poetry keep pretty close to intuition. His Letters are certainly the most notable and the most important ever written by any English poet. Keats's egotism, such as it is, is that of *youth*, which time would've redeemed. His Odes—especially, perhaps, "Ode to Psyche"—are enough for his reputation."

NICK

The most brilliant carrying the darkest shadows, they carried the light—the fluorescent currents of their minds, the luminous voltage of their hearts. Scott believed in the green light. Percy believed that the green light believed in him. Mary wanted to warn us about the green light. To Zelda, it was a light that Scott remembered being green and *orgiastic* when her fairy-eyed originator got trashed and stared into his gold-tasseled banker's lamp. Even though our dreams are mostly wasted on us, you could just hear Zelda quipping to Scott that he could even make the patches on old pants *dreamy*.

~THE READINESS IS ALL

"I confess that today the problem baffles me. All I can think of is to say, in general, to avoid such phrases as 'a picture of New York life' or 'modern society'—though as *that's* exactly what the book *is*, it's hard to avoid them. The trouble is that so much superficial trash has sailed under those banners. It is a love story and it is sensational. I'm sick of the book myself—I wrote it. I've worked it over at least five times and I still feel that what *should be* the strong scene (in the Hotel) is hurried and ineffective. Also, the last chapter, the burial and Gatsby's father, is faulty. It's too bad because the first five chapters and parts of the seventh and eighth are the best things I've ever done. The third chapter bars it from the women's magazines." "Regardless," Scott writes soon after, "My book is wonderful, and I think my novel is about the best American novel ever written."

NICK

Scott's first run of twenty-thousand copies of *The Great Gatsby* sells out—a prestige of critical and personal arrival. T. S. reads right through it three times and writes to Scott that he likes the melody of his dedication and that it is a comfort that beauty and tenderness are its background. The book is immediately translated. In French, it is *Gatsby le Magnifique.* Quickly transferring the stage rights and the silent film rights of *The Great Gatsby* finance Scott to his apex. From his toils, Scott's efforts are finally on Broadway, fulfilling his failed literary ambition from which he felt had forced him to leave the States the year before.

~TAKES A HEEL

"In mid-story, and along comes a wire from

Hollywood from an agent who wants to buy the sound rights to *This Side of Paradise*. Paramount owns the old silent rights for $10,000, but never made it. We got $7,500 for sound rights alone to *Gatsby*, but, that being a play too, had already brought $60,000 for silent rights. Think I'll ask $5,000. *Rats!* I wish I wasn't such a rotten businessman and I wish Ober wasn't a perfect gentleman. It takes a heel to deal with those vermin out there."

NICK

The Keats House, the memorial writing retreat in Hampstead, opens one month after *Gatsby* is published. This same year, Scott—in his literary cares of doubt and loss—also launches the commencement of his remarkable fourth novel, titling it with a memorable line from "Ode to a Nightingale," his favorite poem of his favorite Romantic. It will be the last novel that he will publish. Out west, digging it out of himself "like uranium," Scott will plot his unfinished, great American elegy—as seen through Hollywood defrocked.

~ETC. — ETC. — ETC.

"Advertising notes and suggested line for jacket: 'Show transition from his early exuberant stories of youth, which created a new type of American girl and the later and more serious mood which produced *The Great Gatsby* and marked him as one of the half dozen masters of English prose now writing in America. What other writer has shown such unexpected developments, such versatility, changes of pace?' Etc.—etc.—etc.—I think that, toned down as you see fit, *is* the general line. Though, don't say 'Fitzgerald has done it!' and then in the next sentence that I am 'an artist.' People who are interested in artists aren't interested in people who have 'done it.' Both are okay, but they don't belong in the same ad. This is an author's quibble, and all authors have one quibble. However, you've always done well by me (Except for the memorable excretion in the *Alumni Weekly*. Do you remember—'Make it a Fitzgerald Christmas!'?) and I leave it to you."

NICK

Yet, the sinking rivalry has its sinking prey—the trickling leak of vitality and enthusiasm, expedited. Against all dreams after returning to New York, Scott and Zelda—in darkness and distance—are each more lost than they were in their wounds on the Riviera, or Rome, or Paris. Their cistern has dried. Deadpan, Scott writes to their Scottie that the highs and lows of melodramatics that happen onstage don't happen in real life. *Ain't we got fun?*

Scott does not write to Pie that it is *worse*—that it's terms at inpatient places, and sunrises with nice breakfasts that taste like ashes, and settling for wages that can buy enough isolation to eat a candy bar alone and read the mail. For our Fitzgeralds, it is *worse*— Death standing quizzical in the corner, smoking, pointing at them with her long cigarettes, *ashing.* Increasingly subdued after the publication of *The*

Great Gatsby, Scott dies in fifteen years, and in seven more years, Zelda—in her own deteriorations—is consumed in a tragic, eradicating fire. Becoming a journalist and political activist, Scottie marries her soldier from Princeton and afterward has Scott exhumed and reinterred with Zelda in the graveyard of St. Mary's in Maryland—just outside D.C.—where it is customary to leave a bouquet of peacock feathers and a bottle of gin.

Writing Zelda during his last year, Scott prides in Scottie's collegiate, literary, and social advancements. "It is strange too that she is repeating the phase of *your* life—all her friends about to go off to war and the world again on fire." While the Nazis are bombing London, and the Americans are drilling to soldier all the world, Scott also sends Scribner's new memoir to Zelda and their erudite Scottie. "It's a melancholy book now that France has fallen, but fascinating for all that. It certainly is sad to think that *that's* all over—at least for our lifetime."

~AMERICAN STAMP COLLECTION

"Has *Gatsby* had its chance? Would a popular reissue make it a favorite with classrooms, professors, lovers of English prose—anybody? But to die—so completely and unjustly—after having given so much . . . Even now, there is little published in American fiction that doesn't slightly bear my stamp. In a small way, I was an original."

NICK

Undeployed for the "first" World War, a few years after Scott dies, Scott vicariously participates in the next with France and Germany—in the pocket-editions of *Gatsby* sent to GIs to keep their minds dreamy for their star-spangled returns home. Scott is buried as a veteran, and *Gatsby* will be immortal. "With a great poet, the sense of Beauty overcomes every other consideration, or rather obliterates all consideration." Delayed until after the Second World War, coronating plaques of Shelley and Keats are installed above Shakespeare in the coveted memorial of Westminster Abbey.

~NICK *CARES AWAY,* SCOTCH'S SYMBOLISM

"It's in our thirties that we *want* friends, and in our forties, we *know* they won't save us anymore than love does."

Nick would always stay a few weeks past thirty. He stayed on with me after it was only that warehouse that stocked our story. In all our lunch cups of UK liquor we'd emptied down-the-hatch, Nick had become my brother-in-arms, my Nick-the-Tilde. We'd have an afternoon bender, and his hair on his forehead would always shape into a *tilde*—and I'd never let him fix it when it got that way: a wave right above his eyes~Auntie *Tilde* and all her old asides~her epigrammatic epigraphs. Every skunked time, he'd smile when I'd call him "my Great Aunt Tilde" . . . cause Nicky knew he'd outlive me.

NICK

Shadows and types and firelight, our incapacities this side of paradise are "the allegory of the cave." As the natives of Middle Tennessee were launching attacks to exterminate its settlers the year that Shelley was born, the first celebration of Columbus Day was held in New York City. This same year, the foundation of the federal district—named after Columbus and Washington—was laid, and Washington was reelected. The New York Stock Exchange also began the year Shelley was born, and its Great Depression will instigate its reign four years after *Gatsby*. The past is forever in the present—boats against *the current*.

Three years before *Gatsby*, both Scott and James Joyce publish their second novels in the greatest year of English literature. The next year, Scott, "the prophet and voice of the younger American smart set," lists James Joyce's *Ulysses* as "the great novel of the future." The next greatest year of English literature is the year Scott's *Gatsby* is published.

Three years after *Gatsby*, Zelda and Scott dine with James Joyce as he laments that his current novel is going to take three-to-four years to finalize. In agreeable self-loathing, Scott mumbles "years, years, *years*." Undergoing seventeen drafts, Scott's evolving novel will take six more years, and James Joyce's novel will take eleven more years. Eight years after *Gatsby*, Zelda will begin to spend her ghost-book seasons of "summerlands" at the base of Mont Blanc in Geneva, balancing her mind with ECTs. Keats will become the most anthologized poet in English, and—boats against the current—*Ulysses* and *The Great Gatsby* will be the two greatest English novels of the twentieth century . . . of what's left of it . . .

~OZY P.

"And on the pedestal, these words appear
Of that colossal wreck, boundless and bare:
'Look on my Works, ye Mighty, and despair!'"

~IF IT'S NOT LOVE

In the old three-star Volunteer State, three years before Zelda dies, our American Prometheus—Oppenheimer—fissioning, completes his bomb-grade Franken-Uranium . . . Fat . . . Man . . . the great dream . . .

~THEN IT'S THE BOMB

. . . Fat Man . . . the great dream . . . we destroy . . . what we find . . . what we love . . .

(81.) <u>recipe for Pie</u>

~FREE WILL, ETCETERA

"After the Armistice—our twenty years together—our marriage began jazzy when they were calling it the 'great war,' but it wasn't all just a bunch of 'book talk.' We lived our thematic. So, well, there's *nothing* I care to have done any different if I look back, remembering honest, and watching old Necessity weave its destinies through its fetching little fairytales of 'old us.' There's going to that party of Bunny's at the Algonquin with you riding on the tailboard and with me splayed on the hood—it's one of the eternal gestures that will stay alight. To name something makes it real. So, it's the second "world war," and the suffering of the everyday is enough, digesting into our imaginations the Nazis goose-stepping the European continent and obliterating the good old towns of Jolly Old England.

Nobody knows what day or time it is here—in this dreamy world where days lose themselves in nostalgic dusk, and twilights prowl the alleys lost in melancholic quest. Life itself has become so *imperative* that no individual destiny can stand against its deep insistencies—save Hitler or Mussolini. So, here, we're all doing whatever we can about whatever we're able—and trying to stay out of jail—while the ego is orienting itself in these forceful wiles of less 'free-will' as far as one can fling about the charms of the word in this too mutable world.

Following on, like a boy scout and his girl scout, let's tell it exact to each other, what we've got and where we're at—fingers crossed—and not so much fixed on what we can't know. Yet, I know *nothing* is as obnoxious as other people's luck. Well, they'd all whispered about how my brother went crazy (then about how he killed himself), and, now, they're all whispering about how I'm going crazy—and about how we've spoiled the reputation of our distinguished daddy—which is much sexier than what the truth is. So, Hubby, what a pair we are when we rendezvous— you with your bad heart, and me with my bad head. Certainly, we're all little birds of god singing little songs to god—etcetera. Anathema, anathema, anathema—etcetera, I love you, etcetera."

— Zelda to Scott

SCOTT

From Wollstonecraft and the belles and suffrage and the flappers, and revving up war-bond-drives with "Rosie the Riveter," the world was ready for Pie—oh yeah! Since Scottie's early lavish birthday in Rome, I've geared her up with riveting letters I've sent each season. We'd left Rome for the atrocious magic of Capri after the *meatball* Italian police brutally beat all the stars and Shelley out of me at the station because I hadn't bothered to learn their language—or French, or their alien cultures—because I preferred Cockney and all I'd bothered to learn how to say was *"Tres bien*, you son-of-a-bitch!" Hence—since Scottie was mastering French—postcards and letters became my preferred method for furthering the philological art of *English*.

~RHINO KNOWS

"Dear Pie-physiognomy: Large rhinoceroses often eat little rhinoceroses—and I'm afraid that's the case with me. I love you.

—P. S. Washington is the Capital of England. 2x2=5. Venus is the God of War. 3+7=12. K-A-T-T spells cat."

— Sincerely yours, A. Rhinocerose

~TO: YOUR CHRISTENING
FROM: YOUR PAPPY

"'Egg Fitzgerald.' How would you like *that*—to go through life with 'Eggie Fitzgerald' or 'Bad Egg Fitzgerald' or any form that might occur to fertile minds? Why borrow trouble? Just try calling me 'Pappy' once more, and I'll christen you by the word 'Egg.'"

— Scott to Scottina

SCOTT

Scottie, enter into *their* lives—instead of insisting they enter into yours. Realize that you're a young member of the human race who has not proved herself in any but the superficial manner—a *head-start* with prettiness and the 'gift of gab.' Write me a one-act play about other people—what they say and how they behave. Unleash yourself in your letters to your mother. Summer's only summer—and I know you're brave and able to adjust to changing conditions. Above all, you have to have your own fences to jump. It pleases me when you can make a connection between the Louisiana Purchase and why Fred Astaire lifts up his foot for the world's pleasure.

"No one felt like this before"—says the young—"but I feel like this. I have a pride akin to a soldier going into battle—without knowing whether there will be anybody there, or anybody to distribute medals, or even anybody to record it." "But remember"—says the *not*-young—"you are not the first person who has felt this—like this—not the first person who has ever been alone and alone." Pie, I need to *feel* that you are "going somewhere." When I see life and intention in you, there is no other company in the world I prefer.

~DADDY-DADDY-DADS

"Cause her daddy is a living-fortress, that girl thinks she can get away with whatever she wants."

SCOTT

The mind of a little child is fascinating, for it looks on old things with new eyes—but the adolescent offers nothing, can do nothing, can say nothing that the adult cannot do better. I have lacked prudence—that blind instinct of self-protection, which the writer needs in double measure. When I was your age, I lived with a great dream. The dream growing, I learned how to speak of it and how to make people listen to it.

~STARRY BURDEN

"The dream had been realized early, and the realization carried with it a certain bonus and a certain burden. Premature success gives one an almost mystical conception of destiny—as opposed to will power—and at its worst is the Napoleonic delusion. The man who arrives young believes that he exercises his will because his star is shining. The man who only asserts himself at thirty has a balanced idea of what will-power and fate have each contributed."

SCOTT

The dream divided when I decided to marry your mother—even though I knew she was spoiled and meant no good to me. Being patient in those days, I made the best of it and got to love her in another way. You came along, and for a long time, we made quite a lot of happiness out of our lives. Yet, I was a man divided—working too much *for* her and not enough to the dream. She realized too late that work was dignity—and the only dignity. She tried to atone for it by working, but it was too late—and she broke and is broken, forever.

~SCOTTINA DIAMANTE

"I want you to be among the best of your race and

not waste yourself on trivial aims—to be useful and proud. You've got to say 'I'm dedicated to a scholastic life for the moment,' *or* 'I'm going to play around.' So, likewise, I would like you to be a defiant little *point* at the end of a diamond—and if you have fools to be with, make them a setting. Without dulling your enthusiasm, learn to accept sadness with a certain *esprit*—It'll take one more 'big kick,' but I want it to be mild. So, there, you've one good *crack* coming, but you'll survive—just like Milton—oh yeah!"

(82.) *American Pie*

SCOTT

Scottie Pie—of my eye—your pride is all you have. If you let it be tampered with by another who has a dozen prides to tamper with before lunch, then you are promising yourself a lot of disappointments. As you're not going to be a professional scholar, don't try for "*As*"—don't take the things in which you can get an "*A*," for you can learn them yourself. Try something hard and new. Try it hard and take what marks you can get.

What little I've accomplished has been by the most laborious and uphill work. I wish now I'd *never* relaxed or looked back—but said at the end of *Gatsby*—that I've found my line, that from now on, this comes first, that this is my immediate duty, and that without *this* I am nothing—those nine months of the honesty of imagination and conscience . . . the great dream.

Scottie Girl, I've stopped worrying if you're most like me or your mother—and about what traits have most combined in you. I've become protective in a different way, knowing that you and your parents have *the* eternally valuable element—that we can be strict on ourselves, even in the lavish times. Yet, my Old Pie, there is an electric current of agony that surges through me, challenging myself when I feel too exultant—when I shift my strictness and senselessly begin to abuse another's love. Before you *"daddy-daddy-dads"* me, I want you to plan more of your vistas and futures for *work* than for too much blind tenderness—so that you don't later turn against love, or life, in times when nice thoughts are nothing to having a robust firmness.

You'll know the big party's over when everybody seems so old lately while you don't feel a bit old. You'll have affections and confidence for your work that will steady you when things don't go according to any rules—when there's splits in the skin, or the spirit, that won't heal in hiding when no one's looking. You will be able to transition—and not be alone. The best way to pay for things is through work. Don't let them make you pay with *regret* or anything else that's not work, or they'll make you pay forever.

Though I want to spoil you—like your mother—I don't want you to spoil yourself. There's good magic to resisting being *infallible*—and suffering *some*. I'm glad you're happy—but I've never believed much in happiness. Worry about courage. Don't worry about popular opinion. Don't worry about growing up. Don't worry about anybody getting ahead of you. Don't worry about insects. Don't worry about preachers, or shadows, or the empty eyes of birds. Understand *people* and get along with them.

~CHIC PERFECTION

"Oh God! She had almost forgotten about her daughter's mind going on and on, growing. She was proud of her parents the same way Alabama had been proud of her own as a child, imagining into them whatever perfections she wanted to believe in.

'You and Daddy are very "chic." You should have a car. I suppose I shall be very rich.'

'My God, no! You must get things like that out of your head. You will have to go to work to get what you want.'

. . . Alabama reproached herself *bitterly*, 'she must be awfully hungry for something pretty and stylized in her life—for some sense of a scheme to fit into. Other children's parents were something to them besides the distant *chic*.'"

SCOTT

In strong mystery—with the force that it was given—our first love is taken. It's in its absence—spellbound and sick—that we seek the trail of the hair of the elusive dog that bit us. We yield when our loves cannibalize our passions—and have us live backward.

~WHEN THE DOG STAR BITES

"Certain bodies, called 'solar phosphori,' after having been exposed to light, exhibit a luminous appearance in the dark; and this appearance is rendered more vivid by the increase of their temperature. By a high degree of heat, indeed, it is at length destroyed; but it is capable of being restored by a second exposure to light."

SCOTT

After the flipped images have merged in our brains from the shutter of each blue eye—as always—we see backward the light that moves both ways. Yet, now I know it's the other way—like it was before. We destroy what we find. If *Trouble* is to have its second bloom, our stems must be youthful enough—reverent green expectant enough—to house its incarnation before we say goodbye to all our fathers.

~SHELLEY AND SCOTTIE SITTING IN A TREE

On a clear day when we *see*, / Two diurnal lights immix in disharmony. / The Sun, first, of Necessity shines, / Good's constant, unwavering lines. / Yet, also beams then the light of Venus, / Simultaneous, mutable, shifting / —Rays whisper criminal in the bright day / Change and chaos into the fray. / Shafts of both lights blend in the azure heights, / And in the fixed from the fleeting ever-meeting, / Truth and illusion—illuminations—vie / And mingle, strained, on gray as well as the clearest skies."

NICK

The year before Scott dies—on a belated birthday of Keats—he writes to Scottie. "Anyhow, I'm alive again. Getting by this month did something—with all its strains and necessities and humiliations and struggles. Although I don't drink, I'm not a great man, but sometimes I think the impersonal and objective quality of my talent—and the sacrifices of it, in pieces, to preserve its essential value—has some sort of epic grandeur. Anyhow, afterhours, I nurse myself with delusions of that sort." Afterward, a few weeks before his erratic death, he insists to Scottie, "the wise and tragic sense is that life is essentially a cheat, and its conditions are those of defeat—and that the redeeming things are not brief 'happiness and pleasure' but are the deeper, enduring things that come out of veteran struggle."

SCOTT

From the best shelf to *my* best—my Mag-Pie—these two well-worn works of the Romantics are yours. "These fragments I have shored against my ruins."

In the back cover of the novel, here's more of Daddy-o's old teenage *scratch*—his resolves:

~study electricity;
~*work*;
~practice elocution and poise;
~study needed inventions;
~no wasting time;
~no more smoking;
~read improving books;
~save money;
~be better to parents.

~BORNE BACK

"Now, the business is over—'*Wolf!*' has been cried too often. The public, wary of being fooled, has gone back to its Englishmen, its memoirs, and its prophets."

SCOTT

Though, *Pied* daughter, start with the poetry. It's been my chestnut and my touchstone. Words are only as alive as their audience. Enthusiasm must meet enthusiasm. If either are a bore—both are. On your second read of the other one—the novel—though, ask yourself, "is the exultant young man absorbed in his task at Ingolstadt not also *the great dream*?" Why not? Come around answering again, questing—on your own full terms—the first time that your great heart is greatly broken.

I'm in your heart and I'll know. I will bring the beer. I will bring the fire and the music. You will bring the slow *spell* that will expunge your heartache. The fire and the music might help, but you will have to bring language, your own signs that must first travel their own darkness. You will have to write, and it will be good practice at living—if unprofitable otherwise. Write to the patient rivers that run dirty—tell the embers and flames of the firelights—and, trusting, write to the patient rivers that run clean.

(83.) *Orpheus*

~SUCH COLOR

"Language is the perpetual Orphic song, / Which rules with Daedal harmony a throng / Of thoughts and forms, which else senseless and shapeless were."

"With regard to 'the great question,' the system of the universe, I have no curiosity on the subject. I am content to see no further into futurity than Plato and Bacon. My mind is tranquil. I have no fears and some hopes. In our present, gross, material state, our faculties are clouded. When death removes our clay covering, the mystery will be solved."

SCOTT

Shing. All in time. *Tap. Tap. Tap.* All in time, boyo.

Banker's lamp needs a new bulb. *Flicker.*

Tassel's loose. *Click.*

Tap. Tap. Tap. Match light, red light, moon light, green light, / But the dark eats the light, beer lite, there is no light. *Flick. Flicker. Clink.*

~SPIKED PUNCH

"Death—mysterious, ill-visaged friend of weak humanity—why of all mortals have you cast me from your sheltering fold? O, for the peace of the grave!

That thought would cease work in my brain, and in my last heartbeat, end emotions varied only by new forms of sadness! Am I immortal? I returned to my first question.

In the first place, is it not more probable that the beverage of the alchemist was fraught rather with *longevity* than eternal life? Such is my hope. Then, be it remembered that I only drank half of the potion prepared by him. Was not 'the whole' *necessary* to complete the charm? To have drained half the elixir of immortality is but to be half immortal—my 'forever' is thus truncated and null. Still, who shall number a half of the years of eternity?"

SCOTT

I did understand then and I do understand now. *Tap. Tap. Tap.* All at once, I knew it, and it knew me—*the dream*—the sand of a new beach, claiming a new shore. Yet, like Orpheus, I looked back. I, this year, feel too old—the whole burden of this novel—the loss of those illusions that give such color to the world that you don't care whether things are true or false as long as they partake of the magical glory . . . once again . . .

~SUCH AS ONE

"The thoughts it would extinguish—'twas forlorn, / Yet pleasing, such as *one*, so poets tell, / The devils held within the dales of Hell / Concerning God, freewill, and destiny: / Of all that earth has been or yet may be, / All that vain men imagine or believe, / Or hope can paint, or suffering may achieve."

SCOTT

Savage, ashing slave of desperate men . . . *tap tap tap* . . . and patience who dwells with sickness—and in letters from mailboxes and in the firelight mirth of tobacco smoke—Death, in the smolder of her curiosity and long cigarettes, she will find my sounds pleasing. *Tap. Tap. Tap.* Penniless, I will tell Death a rich story, and she will be kind to me. *Click.*

~VERY PRETTY

"'I remember my father. He brought me toys from Louisville, and thought that girls should marry young.'

'Yes, Grandma.'

'Except I didn't want to. I was having too good a time.'

'Didn't you have a good time when you were married?'

'Oh, yes dear, but different.'

'I suppose it can't be always the same.'

'No.'

The old lady laughed. She was very proud of her grandchildren. They were smart, good children. It was very pretty to see them together, both of them pretending great wisdom about things, both of them eternally pretending.

'We shall be gone soon,' the little girl sighed.

'Yes,' sighed her grandmother."

DEATH

But I want to hear "The Poor Boy Story" again.

SCOTT

It will be the same math and tobacco ashes as to the riddle of the "Fox, Goose, and Bag of Beans" *again*.

DEATH

But what is light?

SCOTT

Light is . . . a rich story . . . light's the great *promise* . . . that things are going to *happen*.

"Does he still sing? / Methought he rashly cast away his harp / When he had lost Eurydice" . . . "That Light whose smile kindles the Universe, / That Beauty in which all things work and move, / That Benediction which the eclipsing Curse / Of birth can quench not, that sustaining *Love* / Which through the web of being blindly wove" . . . The vying, mingled lights, winter weeds, and Nick emptying the ashtrays, and "another Orpheus dies" and "a new Ulysses rises."

. . . "Far from the trembling throng—as a star beacons from the abode where the eternal are—I am borne darkly, fearfully, afar" . . . drink our sighs . . . the rose-garden . . . behold our tears . . . "The One remains, the *many* change and pass. / Heaven's light forever shines, Earth's shadows fly. / Life, like a dome of many-colored glass / —Until death-trampled to fragments— / Stains the white radiance of Eternity."

DEATH

—I see. Got *a* light?

SCOTT

Scott Fitz got to have Zelda. *Flick. Flick.* Got to have her eyes . . . her ghost green eyes in the ghost green mist . . .

DEATH

See why I smoke? . . . Lot's *wife* . . . *Flick. Flick.* Sometimes, the invisible smiles at me through the mist of a cherry's flickering light—consummating us enmeshed like a small, heroic pyre at its curling tip.

SCOTT

"The villagers" wanted to know if hazel eyes see the same as grey and blue . . .

Old eyes and young too . . . the evident energy of the unseen . . . jellybeaning . . .

And the clairvoyant poet ended his *sermon* to them, "Love's not *Time's* fool."

DEATH

Time. Time. *Flick. Flick.* Time, *Goofo,* do as we wish.

SCOTT

With his spiked cold beverage, Time watches.

Time . . . drinking, measuring . . . Time hums the deathless song . . . writing, typing . . . Time enlarges—when it sees what the heart is . . .

TIME

Tap. Tap. Tap. Love—they wished—was light. *Click. Clink.*

AUTHORS

a.riordan@riordanwalton.com

h.walton@riordanwalton.com

speaklowpoetry.com

Nashville & Chattanooga, TN